A SUDDEN EXPLOSION
OF PASSION

The last glimmer of the day's light fell across the beauteous maid. She had risen partially from the water, her wet tangle of ebony hair not concealing her as wholly as she believed. One full breast eluded the mass of hair completely, while a silken hip curved seductively from the small waist and disappeared beneath the dark waters. The sight of her was his undoing.

Brienne's heart turned over as Rurik's hungering passion burst through the thick walls of restraint. He swept her into his arms, his mouth crushing down on hers. He was like a man starved, and she the feast . . .

D0369807

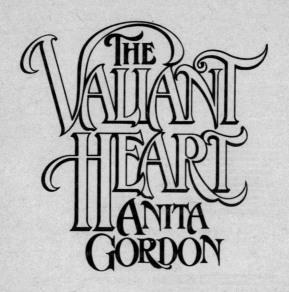

THE VALIANT HEART

ANITA GORDON

JOVE BOOKS, NEW YORK

THE VALIANT HEART

A Jove Book / published by arrangement with
the author

PRINTING HISTORY
Jove edition / August 1991

ISBN: 0-515-10642-9

Jove Books are published by The Berkley Publishing Group,
200 Madison Avenue, New York, New York 10016.
The name "JOVE" and the "J" logo
are trademarks belonging to Jove Publications, Inc.

PRINTED IN THE UNITED STATES OF AMERICA

10 9 8 7 6 5 4 3 2 1

For my husband Mark.
Your unwavering support and unbounded
patience enabled me to reach for the stars
and fulfill my dreams. "Through The Years,"
I'm still loving you.

Author's Note

The language of the ninth century Norsemen is preserved and spoken today in Iceland. "Old Norse" *(Íslensk)* has changed so little through the millennium that school children can read the *Eddas* and sagas in their original form. Though *Íslensk* was handed down from mainly Norwegian colonizers, at the time of the settlements Scandinavians spoke easily among themselves, their dialects being a variation of an original tongue. For these reasons and with few exceptions, I have used Icelandic *(Íslensk)* throughout the book, feeling it to be a more authentic usage for my Danish-born Norsemen than modern Danish. The term *viking*, a relatively recent word, is avoided altogether. My special thanks go to Mr. Jón Sigurdsson who assisted me in translating the various dialogues.

Note on pronunciation: the character "ð" is pronounced like the *th*-sound in "the"; "Þ" is pronounced like the *th*-sound in "thin"; and "æ" is pronounced "i" as in "like."

Prologue ❖ ❖ ❖ ❖ ❖ ❖ ❖ ❖ ❖ ❖ ❖ ❖ ❖

Valsemé, France, 912 A.D.

THE TALL BLOND Norseman did not move as the Frankish emissaries quit the hall. Not until the great oaken door groaned shut behind them. Then, in two long strides, he mounted the dais and slammed his hands down full force on the table in front of him. His steel-blue eyes locked with a second pair that perfectly matched his own.

"Surely you do not intend to accept their offer."

"Calm yourself, Rurik." The older man settled back in the carved chair and emptied his drinking horn. "There are advantages to be gained with such a match."

"I tell you it reeks fair full of devilry."

Gruel Atli wiped his mouth with the back of his hand, then squinted up from beneath a sagging lid. "Does it trouble you that I would take a wife so soon after your mother's death?"

"Nei." Rurik released a long breath as he straightened to his full height. "But the king was quick enough to unearth this heiress and foist her upon you. Why, she is probably a dragon of a woman, ancient and diseased. Why else would they shut her away for nearly a decade?"

Atli threw back his head and roared with laughter. " 'Tis a Christian holy house, Rurik. Beaumanoir's daughter dwells in cloister at the Abbey of Levroux." He wiped tears of mirth from his eyes. "Ah, my son, you have been too long at sea."

Rurik grunted and crossed his arms over his broad chest. "Mayhaps. But I know much of dealings, fair and foul. The king's terms are as transparent as they are unpalatable. What is to be gained by wedding Valsemé's displaced heiress? The barony is yours now."

Atli rose at that and beckoned Rurik to the narrow window of the keep.

" 'Tis a year past that I stood with Rollo at the river St.-Clair-sur-Epte when King Charles bestowed on him this fiefdom." He cast an eye upon his son. "Of course, we already controlled these lands through conquest, but Charles is shrewd. In exchange for our fealty, he granted us a homeland, buying himself a watchdog in the bargain to guard against those who would ravage his kingdom." Atli cracked a smile. "Especially our own kind.

"Behold. Valsemé." He gestured toward the gently rolling contours of his domain. "Her good rich soil lies beneath our hands like a ready woman, waiting for man to plow her tender loins and plant his seed deep within." He brought his fist down against the stone sash. "But we be too few to do the deed. Charles drains me for his endless campaigns whilst time grows short. The land must be cultivated, and soon, if our storehouses are to stand full next winter. Most of the villeins fled at our coming, and I sorely need them back." He vented his frustration against the ledge once more, then pushed himself away and crossed to the dais.

"Do you know what these Franks call us? *Normanni.* Spring we of Danmark, Norge, Sverige, Zealand . . . it matters not. To them we are one and the same—Northmen—and they tremble before us. While that is to our advantage upon the battlefield, here 'tis an accursed burden."

Snatching up a cup and flagon of wine, he filled the vessel to its rim. "This heiress may prove the key," Atli rumbled, then tossed the contents down his throat. "Valsemé's villeins were fiercely loyal to Richard Beaumanoir whilst he lived. His daughter is perfect bait to lure them home."

Rurik frowned. "Still, why would she agree to such a union? Surely 'tis bitter gall that her titles and holdings are forfeit. Perchance she desires only to slip a bit of cold steel betwixt your ribs as she warms your bed."

Atli shrugged broadly, unconcerned. "Evidently, the woman is eager to recover her lands and position."

"Too eager and for her own gain, I'll wager." Rurik cocked a golden brow. " 'Twould take little time to journey by longship to Levroux and observe this bride firsthand. I could be back in a trice."

Atli held Rurik's gaze for several moments before he yielded. "Very well, but send your *broðir* in your stead. I have another task in mind for you." Refilling the cup, he offered it to his son. "And do not worry overlong on these terms the king has set. The Franks are not so clever as they think."

Atli barked laughter at some unspoken thought and pressed the flagon to his lips.

Chapter One

✖ ✖ ✖ ✖ ✖ ✖ ✖ ✖ ✖ ✖ ✖ ✖

Levroux, France

" 'TIS A WEED," Brienne protested as she considered the spindly plant dangling from her friend's hand.

"Nay, mugwort," Aleth insisted good-naturedly, "and a prize for Sister Ursuline's collection. 'Tis a powerful medicant, you know."

Brienne sighed and smiled indulgently. "Are all the good sister's lessons for naught? Mugwort does not grow here in the forest, dear Aleth. 'Tis but a weed."

"We shall see. Sister will know the truth of it."

"Aye, she will. And if you're ever to be a healer, you must learn to identify these herbs properly."

Aleth laughed. "I have. 'Tis mugwort!" she proclaimed with finality and deposited the wilting greens in the basket.

Brienne rolled her eyes heavenward. "May the Good Lord in all His mercy grant that I never need tending by your hands"—she flashed a devilish smile—"or your precious weeds!"

A small shriek escaped Aleth as she caught up a handful of tender shoots and tossed them into Brienne's midnight hair. The two girls dissolved into a fit of uncontrollable giggling, laughing till tears filled their eyes and they collapsed breathless upon the forest floor.

Brienne clutched the stitch in her side and blinked the moisture from her dark lashes. Laughter was sweet salve to the soul and a blessed release, for when its merriment overtook her as now, all thought and shadow fled. Then, for a sliver of time, she could forget. . . .

"Enough, enough," she pleaded as she struggled to her feet and shook out her long tresses. "We've been over-long at this. I know of a little clearing ahead. Are you hungry yet?"

Aleth nodded heartily and stretched forth her hands.

Carefully, Brienne braced herself and pulled the small form upward, allowing Aleth to favor the thin rail of her right leg. A glimmer of pity chased across her eyes and she quickly dropped her gaze to shield the look from Aleth.

Life was often unfair. There were many reasons for families to send their daughters to nunneries aside from love—or fear—of God, as well she knew. Aleth was a gentle maiden with pleasant features, honey-brown hair, and a sprinkling of freckles across a small, abbreviated nose. No doubt it was her infirmity that brought her to the doors of Levroux's Abbey. A husband would be difficult to find for a disabled girl, and spinsters were a burden not to be had. Convents were a useful answer to so many problems.

Brienne pushed away her thoughts and caught up her basket. Offering an arm to Aleth, she guided them cautiously along a crooked path back toward the forest's edge, then abruptly veered left to follow a faint trail. In a short time the woodland opened onto a small sunlit glade, carpeted in the vibrant green of spring and bejeweled with violets and primroses.

Aleth's face brightened like that of a small child presented with a splendid gift. At times, Brienne wondered if the girl had ventured much beyond her solar before leaving her family's estates. Life was ever fresh and fascinating to Aleth; as though she were seeing it for the first time.

Brienne unfastened her mantle and spread it over the soft new grass. After settling Aleth down, she joined her on the makeshift blanket and set the basket between them. Dipping under herbs, bandages, and little pots of curatives, she produced a small bundle wrapped in linen.

"Bless you, Sister Clothilde," she murmured, setting out a prize wedge of tangy cheese, crusty bread, and dried apples from last autumn's bounty. A small skin of wine completed the repast. The young women bowed reverently

over their little feast, giving humble thanks, then eagerly
attacked the fare.

Brienne sampled the pleasant wine and stretched out contentedly to study the lacy canopy of leaves unfurling above
her. It had been a pleasant day that began with prayer and
chores at the abbey. Then they had tended the sick of the
village and visited a favorite little patient who nursed a
broken leg. Brienne cheered him with the gift of a nice
fat frog that she had captured along the way. The girls had
been allowed to go by themselves today, the freedom rare and
much appreciated. Before returning, they sought out herbs in
the fringes of the forest, being careful not to venture too far.
Sister Ursuline would be so pleased!

Brienne rose from her grassy bed and moved about the
glade, gathering delicate flowers for weaving into chains.

Aleth could only admire Brienne's effortless beauty. Her
glossy black hair spilled down over her shoulders, framing a
nearly perfect oval face except for its slightly pointed chin.
Her startling violet eyes were set under long dark lashes, and
her slim nose tilted pertly.

Aleth thought it odd that Brienne's father had not sought a
wealthy match for her rather than cloistering her away, but
Brienne seldom spoke of it. She was a private person, even
more so after the deaths of her parents and only brother. The
young women had known one another for nigh on to eight
years. Still, Aleth knew little about her closest friend.

Brienne settled down again near Aleth and shared out the
fragrant blossoms. For a moment Aleth fumbled with a few
stems, then, against better judgment, decided to broach the
subject that plagued her.

"How is it you came to the Abbey of Levroux?"

Surprise touched Brienne's violet eyes, then quickly her
expression died, becoming unreadable. She looked away and
focused upon the fluttering dance of a small white butterfly.

"I mean, 'tis not common for a family to cloister their
eldest daughter," Aleth added hesitantly, then broke into a
wide grin. "Tell me, did you do something terrible? Did you
refuse to marry some rich, hideous toad your father desired
for you?"

"Oh, nay, Aleth! Nothing like that," Brienne declared. She drew her knees under her chin and considered the odd shape of a billowing cloud. "Though I've often thought, had my sister been sent in my stead, *I* would now be the wife of Robert Coustance, the Seigneur d'Esternay." She grimaced slightly. "He is a brutal man, though Lisette loves him well."

"Then why?" Aleth pressed.

Brienne stared pensively into a thicket of trees and a frown traced across her delicate brow. "I was the pure and holy offering," she said enigmatically, then fell silent.

Aleth was taken aback by the unexpected comment, but her curiosity sternly drove her on. "I don't understand."

Brienne broke away her gaze from the woodland and tossed Aleth a small, thoughtful smile. " 'Tis all right, Aleth. God is good. Life is much better here, away from men and their lust for battle and blood."

"You do not like men?" Aleth blinked, misunderstanding her.

A glint of pain touched Brienne's darkening eyes, then was gone. "It matters not," she sighed softly. " 'Tis my intent to take the veil."

Aleth dropped the flowers she had been carelessly weaving into a circlet, her eyes widening. "But you cannot! Not now," she blurted out, daring to say what Brienne would not admit. "You have rightful claim to the barony of Valsemé. And what of your mother's lands at Chaudrey? You are an heiress, Brienne, and ward of the king. Surely he will call you forth from Levroux and arrange a good marriage."

"Oh, dear, sweet Aleth." Brienne shook her head sadly. "You do not know the way of it. I am heiress to a Norseman's acre." She could not suppress the tear that sprang to the corner of her eye. "Valsemé is no more." Her voice faltered. "And Chaudrey is entailed to Lord Robert. 'Twas part of my sister's dower."

Brienne turned away as tears blurred her vision. Valsemé. Her heart cried out through a mist of time and pain. But that was a world ago, shattered by the marauding Northmen.

Out of their icy lairs they came, sweeping boldly up the rivers in their *drakken,* the dreaded dragon boats. As if from nowhere they appeared, plundering and killing for booty, raping for pleasure, kidnapping those they would sell as slaves, then vanishing back from whence they came. They were vaporous devils at best, and the barons were hard pressed to deal with them.

In time, the Seine and Loire became favored among their watery highways, and it was at the mouths of these two mighty rivers that the Norsemen wintered and entrenched themselves. No longer did they lust for booty and flesh alone, but now for the land itself. Aye, they rooted themselves in Frankish soil and the death bell knelled for Valsemé.

Brienne shut her eyes tight against the keen edge of memory. The barony lay along the river Toques, which flowed to the great Channel, *La Manche*, nearby, as did the Seine. So close, so close to the pirates' den.

Coming back to the moment, Brienne found herself gazing into Aleth's small, distressed face.

"He tried so hard, but to no avail," she explained achingly, as though she had been sharing her thoughts all the while. "Valsemé lay too close to the Norsemen's lair."

"Who tried?" Aleth prodded.

"Father . . ." Her thoughts slipped away on a river of memory.

Richard Beaumanoir defended his lands tirelessly for many years until he, as other neighboring lords, was forced to abandon them. He withdrew with his family and retainers to his wife's dower lands at Chaudrey. The shame of failing to protect the barony festered in his soul like a rotting pustule.

He soon became a king's man, allying himself with the powerful, and pursuing the Northmen relentlessly in a private war of revenge to regain his forsaken lands. Then in his obsession he sought to win God's favor—and Brienne was his offering. A younger daughter would not suffice, only the firstborn, the beautiful unblemished lamb, a sacrifice pure and holy. Overnight, Brienne was dispatched from the heart of her family into cloister at Levroux.

Lisette's marriage was subsequently arranged to gain the might and power of Esternay, that self-made knight, the king's own champion.

For a time, God smiled on Beaumanoir. He triumphed in the meanest of battles till his fame swelled throughout the realm.

Despite his success, Beaumanoir was bitterly disappointed that Brienne refused the veil, as though she would invite God's displeasure. She argued that many noble ladies lived in cloister without benefit of vows, and she was not yet prepared to make her profession. Angrily, he warned that such stubbornness would bring misfortune upon their house, and when the wheel of fate turned round, it was she that he blamed.

Brienne's mother soon succumbed to a mysterious ailment. Shortly after her death, Brienne's elder brother, Thomas, was cut down at their father's side by a Norse blade. Not a year had passed when Beaumanoir himself was felled before the walls of Poitiers in a daring ruse against the heathens.

"Brienne, Brienne," Aleth broke through her ruminations. "What do you mean, 'a Norseman's acre'? What of Valsemé?"

"Do you not know, Aleth?" She looked hard at her companion. Truly, the girl *had* never left her solar. "King Charles seeks to control the Norse menace. This year past he conceded lands to their chieftain, Rollo, in return for his homage and created him duke. My father's lands are part of the new duchy. They belong to the foreigner now."

Rollo, she thought bitterly, and his hated duchy of Normandy.

"I'm so sorry." Aleth groped for a comforting word.

"I am happy here at Levroux," Brienne reassured her, "and I feel safe, if that is possible. 'Tis a man's world, Aleth, and they threaten to tear it apart.

"The abbey seems set apart from our enemies, and I have not known such peace since I was a small child. Here, I am an equal with my sisters, not a man's piece of property. I have learnt reading and ciphering, and have been taught the gift of healing." Brienne sighed and managed a small smile. "The Lord is a gentle and loving master. 'Tis to Him I shall pledge my troth."

Aleth abandoned the subject, grieved at the fresh pain she had caused her friend.

*   *   *

The soft pealing of bells, sounding distantly across the vale, roused Brienne from her drowsy state.

She suddenly became aware of the lengthening shadows of the trees and the low angle of the sun.

With a sharp gasp she scrambled to her feet and swiftly gathered up the remains of the half-eaten meal.

"Aleth, wake up! We've overstayed and I was to help Sister Margaret in the scullery this eve," she groaned.

Aleth stirred and rubbed her eyes. "No doubt you volunteered for that honor," she said through a yawn.

"Nay, not so. I do it for Lutigard. 'Tis spring and she suffers the rheum."

" 'Tis naught but her delicate hands that suffer from scrubbing pots! Ever she slips out of her duties, that one!" Aleth retorted.

"Come along or I'll have a sharper tongue wagging at me."

Their eyes locked in merriment. "Sister Margaret!" they chorused.

Progress toward the abbey was slowed by Aleth's frail leg. By the time they reached its high brooding walls, the light was falling rapidly. Brienne did not look forward to the scolding and lecture Mother Annice would surely deliver for their tardiness. Worse, she feared losing the privilege of ministering in the village. Perhaps if she revealed her intentions to take her vows, Mother's heart would soften.

Even as the girls approached the stony portal with its heavy iron gate, Brienne sensed something out of the ordinary. She detected movements and sounds uncommon to the hour. Her breath caught as the soft nickering of horses and low rumble of male voices drifted clearly above the courtyard beyond.

"Soldiers!" Brienne exclaimed in hushed tones.

It was not unusual for the abbey to offer its hospitality, as it was a place of rest and healing. That men had been permitted past the outer wall pricked her curiosity mildly, but such was allowed when the escorts were small and composed of kindred to the noble ladies who resided within.

Levroux was an unusual abbey in that it had been built upon the site of a Roman fortress overrun by invading Franks

centuries before. The ruins were incorporated into the present
monastery and offered the advantage of two enclosure walls.
The inner partition embraced the tight cluster of buildings and
church comprising the heart of the abbey, while the outer wall
encompassed a sizable tract of land boasting orchards, a fish
pond, storage sheds, stables, livestock shelters, and quarters
for the servants that attended the abbey's needs. It was here
that the travelers would be lodged, though several cells were
reserved near the abbess's chambers for the more important
guests.

Normally, Brienne would have eagerly looked forward to
the worldly news the visitors brought with them, yet after her
disturbing reminiscences of the afternoon, her stomach knotted painfully at the prospect of encountering men-at-arms.

"Perhaps we should use the side entrance, Aleth. I shouldn't
like to walk through a courtyard of destriers." She shuddered
at the thought of the enormous war horses.

The girls slipped around the corner of the abbey as quickly
as they could manage and proceeded to a small gate toward
the far end, where they set off a jangling of bells.

A plump little figure garbed in black bustled across the
grounds. "My lambs! Where have you been?" Sister Ursuline
puffed excitedly, thrusting a massive key into the heavy lock.
"Nothing is amiss? Come along. Come along," she jabbered.
"Brienne, your hair! 'Tis sown with grass. Saints be with us!
Hurry now. Mother Annice has been seeking you for ever so
long. No, not you, Aleth, only Brienne."

"Yes, sister." Brienne held forth the basket, barely suppressing her amusement. "We brought herbs for your
medicants."

Sister Ursuline peeked into the basket delightedly, then her
eyebrows flew up in astonishment. Snatching up a bedraggled
green, she exclaimed, "Good gracious! Wherever did you
find this!"

" 'Tis mugwort," Aleth proclaimed, tossing a little look
of triumph at Brienne.

Sister struggled to compose herself. "My ladies, 'tis an
aphrodisiac!"

Brienne and Aleth choked on the pronouncement as Sister
Ursuline scuttled off toward the garderobe. An instant later

she reappeared, rubbing her palms vigorously against the rough wool of her gown.

"We are well rid of *that*! Now, be off with you, my lady. Aleth, you may help me in the scullery. Lutigard fell victim to her rheum."

"I know," pouted Aleth. "Ever I pray for her deliverance!"

Brienne quickly plaited her hair as she darted across the cobbled pathway, past small stone buildings, and through a heavy archway. She hurried down the length of the refectory, rounded the corner, then halted abruptly, barely catching herself as she pitched forward.

At least twenty pairs of eyes greeted her own, now wide with surprise. The courtyard before her was filled with a colorful assemblage of grooms, pages, men-at-arms, and their magnificent destriers, all seemingly frozen at their tasks as they studied her with undisguised interest.

Quickly, Brienne drew her mantle over her head, clutching it to her throat protectively as color flamed her cheeks. She thought at first to retreat from the scene before her, then realized that this was the quickest way round to Reverend Mother's quarters.

Swallowing hard, she stepped forward and gingerly began skirting the assemblage of men as their eyes raked her admiringly. At a few overly loud and suggestive remarks, she broke into a run and dashed across the remainder of the courtyard. Husky laughter followed her to the shelter of the portico.

Men! How dare they, Brienne raged silently. *This is a convent, not a brothel!* They would respect her more when she wore the habit. She moved rapidly along the covered porchway, hoping for no further encounters, and at length stopped before Mother Annice's chambers.

With a last straightening of her tunic and mantle, drawing in a deep breath, Brienne rapped softly upon the door. Noiselessly, it drew open and a small nun motioned her inside.

The room was dimly lit and smelled of musty parchment and burning tallow. A simple table served as a desk, flanked by hard wooden chairs and a basket of scrolls. In the corner, a precious psalter lay open atop a waist-high stand adorned with a richly embroidered cloth.

Mother Annice stood silently before a crude crucifix affixed to the wall. She was a tall, lean woman of uncertain age. As she turned toward her visitor, Brienne noted how unusually drawn and weary the abbess looked tonight, her face a pale testament to the burdens of her office.

"Sister Catherine, please leave us." Mother Annice nodded to the diminutive nun.

When the door swept closed, Brienne could no longer contain herself. "Reverend Mother, please forgive my belatedness. I am remiss beyond doubt. After ministering to our sick, I stayed awhile in the forest, seeking herbs and meditating . . . and the Lord has blessed that time, truly He has, for I have come to a most important decision. I desire to take the veil, Reverend Mother. I wish to profess my vows." She caught her breath and smiled hesitantly, awaiting the abbess's response.

Mother Annice closed her eyes for a few moments, and when she opened them again they glistened with unshed tears. "Come, child. Let us pray for our Lord's guidance."

The aging nun gripped Brienne's hands and pulled her down to the hard stone floor before the crucifix, her touch chill and dry.

With eyes fixed upon the broken body of Christ, Mother Annice intoned the ancient prayer, *"Pater Noster qui es in caelis, santificetur nomen tuuam. . . ."* At length she pronounced, "Amen. So be it."

She pulled her gaze from the crucifix and looked deeply into the girl's lovely eyes. Brienne's breath caught at the abbess's pain-filled expression.

"Are you familiar with the Book of Isaiah, child? Look to the second chapter and remember it well: 'He will teach us what He wants us to do; we will walk in the paths He has chosen.' "

Silence fell like a pall over the room. Tears brimmed the old nun's eyes. She rose in a slow, fluid motion. Taking Brienne's hands once again in her own, she drew the girl up and gently kissed her forehead.

"Come," Mother Annice barely whispered, and ushered her from the room.

A certain dread crept into Brienne's soul as she and the Reverend Mother walked silently down the covered passageway and traversed the courtyard. She did not really notice how it had emptied of horses and grooms, or that only a few men now milled about in the dusk. She sensed only that something was amiss. Tendrils of apprehension spiraled through her.

A few moments later, Mother Annice swung wide the heavy oaken door to the refectory. Brienne paused cautiously upon the threshold.

The hall was filled with Frankish knights and men-at-arms. Some sat at table, devouring savory meat pastries and drinking heartily of cold cider that the good nuns proffered, while others stood about in small groups deep in their arguments and banter.

As the two women entered the hall, a hush rippled over the room. All eyes seemingly turned as one and settled upon the beautiful maid. She trembled slightly under their intense regard. There was something in those looks to which she could not put a name.

A tall dark figure broke away from a small cluster of men at the far end of the hall and strode confidently toward them. A moment passed before Brienne recognized the commanding frame of the Seigneur d'Esternay, Robert Coustance.

"My Lord." She dropped into a deep curtsy, overcome with surprise. "How good it is to see you again. I pray all fares well with you, sire."

Esternay paused a moment, drinking in her intoxicating beauty. Damn Beaumanoir, anyway. The girl's existence had been hidden from him until his betrothal was sealed with her sister, and then, only on the wedding day itself, was the elder daughter brought forth from cloister to celebrate the festivities.

Lisette was a comely enough wench and agreeable in all matters that concerned him, but she lacked the vividness and the spirit he witnessed in this beauty. Such a match they could have made. And now this cursed business that brought him to Levroux. Damn Beaumanoir again!

Brienne felt uneasy under Seigneur Robert's bold stare.
"Is all well with my sister, my lord?"

He rubbed at the scar above his heavy brows. "*Oui, oui.*
She is abed with child again. We fervently hope she will
carry this babe to term." A trace of bitterness steeled his
voice. Undoubtedly he could have sired several sons by
now upon the healthy young woman before him, but her
frail sister had miscarried all she had conceived thus far.

Uneasiness gnawed at Brienne as she beheld Lord Robert's
persistent gaze. He was not really a handsome man, with
a long, slightly crooked nose, and heavily lidded eyes, yet
his bearing was impressive and imposing. His thick black
hair was worn tapered to the shoulder and his beard was
cropped close along the jaw, lending him a sinister air.
Lisette confided once that the beard hid a most hideous scar
acquired in his youth.

Brienne felt oddly entrapped, much like a fragile butterfly
entangled in a spider's web. "If you think me not too bold,
how is it that you come to our fair abbey, my lord?"

Esternay's look darkened. "I come on the king's business,
Lady Brienne, concerning your barony."

"Valsemé?" Her brows lifted in surprise. "Does our good
king regret his generous gift to the Norse vermin so soon?"

"Nay, my lady. Rollo has thus far honored his oath of
fealty to Charles, and proves his mettle by repulsing his own
kind from despoiling the kingdom. He even joins us against
Flanders."

"Ah, the noble pagan!" she snorted.

Esternay smiled at her unbridled fire. "The *noble pagan*
received baptism at the hand of Archbishop Franco himself,
as have his men. Already he begins a cathedral at Rouen."

"Do you defend this glorified cur of Normandy, who has
stripped me of my father's lands?" she spat, her temper
flaring.

" 'Twas the king's gift, not mine," he retorted. Indeed they
would have been his to claim had Brienne been his bride. But
Beaumanoir played him false, giving him the second-born
daughter. When Beaumanoir fell in battle, Charles moved
swiftly to place himself as protector over both Brienne and
her lands of Valsemé. By the Rood, he himself would wrest

the lands free of the Nordic claws given half the chance.

"The king would harness these Norsemen and use them to our own benefit." He echoed Brienne's thoughts from earlier that day. "My mission here will further bind them to our side."

"How so, my lord? What has it to do with Levroux?"

"Not with Levroux, my dear. With you."

Brienne swayed momentarily under the weight of his words.

The dark knight turned abruptly and began to pace, choosing his next words carefully.

"Rollo has proven to be quite astute in matters of state and fashions his duchy in the true Frankish manner. Whilst he retains sole power as its duke, he has appointed his most loyal men and relatives to hold his lands in obeisance to him."

Esternay measured the maid with a penetrating gaze before delivering his next tidings. "Valsemé has been awarded to his sister's husband, a man named Gruel Atli."

The words settled like a chilling mist upon Brienne and she stiffened perceptibly.

"Atli sought to bring forth his wife from the northern climes to join him," he continued, his eyes never leaving hers, "but she fell ill and died before the journey commenced."

"And how does this news concern me, now that my lands are forfeit?" she asked tightly.

Esternay swept the soft curves of her body with a sharp eye, and began to pace anew, circling his quarry.

"As I said, the king seeks ways to influence the affairs of the duchy as much as he dare without directly interfering."

His towering nearness was suffocating as he drew behind her, his warm breath falling on her neck. Her heart hammered furiously.

"The Normans brought few of their own women. In truth, they appear to prefer our own Frankish beauties." He lifted the heavy ebony plait from her shoulder and inhaled its fresh scent. Brienne bristled at his familiarity. "Their blood already begins to mingle with our own. In time, it will be so diluted they will be more Frank than Norse." He replaced the lustrous braid, allowing his fingers to brush the curve of her neck.

"But, of course, that will require several generations." He strode across the room.

"Our king would hasten the process by returning our own villeins to the land. Most fled in the wake of the Norsemen. They are understandably afraid. But Charles is ardent in this matter and would grant them, shall we say, a *noble* example."

"You speak in riddles, Lord Robert," she said testily as icy fingers gripped her heart. "Be out with it! I would have an end to this and think no more upon the Norse pox that infests our fair lands."

The Seigneur d'Esternay smiled grimly. The girl was strong-willed and unpredictable like her father. It did not bode well. With a heavy sigh, he withdrew a parchment from his vest and held it forth, displaying the king's great seal.

"As your sovereign king and lord protector, His Highness Charles III decrees that you are to set henceforth for Valsemé, the land of your father, and thereupon pledge your troth in marriage to the new lord baron of that holding, Gruel Atli, that your blood may mix with his in the future heir of Valsemé, and that in your presence you may intercede in behalf of your people."

"Nay!" she shrieked wildly, and whirled to clutch frantically at the nun's sleeves. "What madness is this! Reverend Mother, tell him!" she pleaded urgently, her voice breaking. "Tell him I am to take the veil! I am pledged to God!"

"Is this true?" Esternay turned blackly on the nun. A chit of a girl must not be allowed to thwart these tenuous politics, however distasteful.

Mother Annice smoothed Brienne's hair. "She revealed these intentions to me only moments ago."

"You did not tell her of this?" He waved the parchment menacingly.

"Nay, 'twas God's own inspiration."

Esternay paced angrily like a great caged panther, then wheeled abruptly. "No matter. Charles was not advised of his ward's wishes, nor has he given consent to such. This is the course he has deigned and so it shall stand."

With a murderous look, Brienne hurtled her lithe figure against the black knight, furiously pummeling his chest, pure venom in her heart.

"What manner of man are you, to deliver your kin to the bed of the heathens that slayed my father and brother and stole my lands? You have no honor!"

Esternay's hand struck without warning, and Brienne reeled, the light shattering before her eyes as she fell against the wall. Blood trickled from the corner of her bruised mouth.

Esternay retreated a few steps. He had not wanted to harm the girl, but she pricked him sorely. He would tolerate no slur upon that which he held above all else, his honor.

"Prepare yourself, my lady, for in two days hence we depart for Valsemé."

Brienne crumpled at the feet of Reverend Mother and sobbed uncontrollably. There must be a way. By all that was holy, she would find an escape. She sought solace then in the labyrinth of her mind and did not know when the kind hands of Mother Annice guided her from the room.

Chapter Two
❖ ❖ ❖ ❖ ❖ ❖ ❖ ❖ ❖ ❖ ❖ ❖

THE ABBEY BELLS tolled in the crisp early morn, signaling Prime and the call to devotions.

Brienne rose stiffly from her pallet and quickly began her ablutions. She flinched as her fingertips grazed her tender mouth, and the memory of the night before flooded back.

Brienne flung open a small wooden trunk and slid her hands deftly among the folds of clothing until they closed about a prize disk of polished steel.

She examined the ugly discoloration spread along her jaw. No doubt it would turn a sickly purplish-yellow in several days' time, and she wondered briefly how the Normans would receive a battered bride. Perhaps she should goad Lord Robert into beating her till her entire face was swollen and misshapen. Then, with luck, Gruel Atli would reject her.

Brienne sighed at her foolishness and stood to pull on a chemise of soft ivory linen. Nothing deterred men such as he, or Lord Robert, or even the king. Power was what they were born to, suckled upon, and bred to wield ruthlessly in attaining their precious ambitions. What match a mere maid? Somehow she must elude their mad schemes.

Donning a shorter, rose-colored tunic, she folded back the wide sleeves to reveal the creamy undergarment. A simple belt of metal links girdled the gown, its clasp embossed with a falcon, her father's personal emblem. Her emblem now.

Coiling her hair loosely at the nape of her neck and catching up her woolen mantle, Brienne stepped forth from the small cell into the fresh morning air and set off to join the community for first devotions. Her footsteps froze as she realized that a soldier kept pace with her a short distance away.

She studied him through narrowed eyes. This was no escort granted as courtesy due a lady. Did Lord Robert fear she would slip from his grasp? Had he the gall to set a guard to her heels, here, within the abbey walls? In truth, she had found little time to formulate an escape, and it nettled her all the more that he could so easily hold her prisoner. Squaring her shoulders, Brienne walked briskly toward the church, heaping curses upon Robert Coustance through gritted teeth.

The Seigneur d'Esternay awaited her, leaning casually against the side of the steep, aged steps. Brienne met him with what she hoped was a chilling silence and unparalleled aloofness. How she longed to wipe the smugness from his face.

Throughout the service the dark knight held close to her, keeping her separate from the other women. When they broke their fast in the refectory a short while later, she became thoroughly vexed, for Lord Robert was never more than an arm's length away.

She tasted her wine in small, agitated sips, her amethyst eyes flashing above the goblet's rim.

"How impressive that so noble a lord rises early to join our humble community in prayer," she taunted. "Perhaps 'tis repentance you seek for some foul deed."

Esternay observed her dispassionately.

"Of course, 'tis more surprising still that I am granted this day of grace to pack my meager possessions before being sacrificed to the Nordic gods."

Esternay lifted a dark brow and wiped his hands on the folds of cloth that hung from the table.

"In truth, we wait upon two monks, missionaries to the Northmen. They will serve as my interpreters and remain in the duchy to tend its 'flock.' One is reportedly a Dane." He smiled, taking in Brienne's surprise. "'Tis said that he atones for the sins of his wayward brothers by zealously evangelizing them." Esternay drained his cup and rose. "Attend to yourself, my lady. We leave once the churchmen arrive and are suitably refreshed."

The crust Brienne nibbled caught in her throat. The man was insufferable! Doubtless, had the monks accompanied him and his party to Levroux, he would not have granted her time to use even the garderobe before departing.

Brienne was shadowed with fervor throughout the day. If she ventured near the abbey's gates or stables, she instantly found unbidden company at her elbow. When she thought to pray in the chapel and plead her case before God, she discovered herself surrounded by questionably devout soldiers.

Sanctuary might well be her only hope, but if Lord Robert and his men feared she would gain it, Brienne only despaired of having the chance to try. A sense of hopelessness began to poison her resolve. Naught would assuage the dull ache that now spread from temple to crown, born of the day's tensions.

At length she sought refuge in the privacy of her room, but here, too, she found no peace. A coffer of elegant clothing awaited her, a wedding gift and peace offering from the king. It contained a rich array of gaily colored gowns, transparent veils, fur-trimmed mantles, and jeweled girdles.

The beautiful clothes served only to inflame Brienne's ire and mounting frustration. How typically male! She would not be bought with finery to kindle the passions of a Norman. In a furor she flung the garments about the tiny cell until they covered the floor and hung askew from the solitary chair that graced the room.

Angrily, she stripped off her tunic and chemise, then donned her meanest garb, a worn and faded gown of a dull greenish-brown.

Flinging open the cell door, she stalked past the two startled soldiers hovering nearby and headed for the stables. There she found a length of rope and tied it about her narrow hips, creating a coarse girdle of sorts.

Good, she thought. *'Tis fitting raiment for one condemned.*

Pivoting sharply on her heels, she marched stiffly toward the scullery, determined to engross herself in the most noxious task available till she awoke from this nightmare.

A shrouded figure moved across the stable rushes and paused in the shadows of the door. His icy blue eyes followed her with keen interest.

"The maid was to be willing, yet she bears the mark of a heavy hand."

An older man emerged from the stall where he had just quartered an undersized palfry, and frowned from beneath a thatch of bushy brows after Brienne.

"Patience, my son. We will soon know the truth of it."

Brienne's ever-present escorts followed hurriedly behind her clipped steps. Much to her relief, they remained outside the small stone building as she whisked inside.

Brienne halted abruptly on the threshold. A dozen women worked furiously sanding pots and implements, all seemingly driven by the same madness.

Red-rimmed eyes lifted to greet her. As she spied Aleth, Lutigard, Sisters Ursuline, Clothilde, and Margaret, she realized that these women ached for her.

Suddenly, the crushing reality of the king's directive overwhelmed her, and she slumped against the wall, burying her face in her hands. What had she done to merit this misbegotten lot? She bitterly regretted not having taken the veil when her father had pressed her to do so. She would be safely tucked away from the world and forgotten now. As a nun, she would be considered dead to it.

Aleth limped forward with a stricken look, tenderly stretching out her arms. Brienne clung to her dearest friend and the floodgates opened anew. No words could express the depths of her grief.

As Aleth's own tears spilled unchecked, she stroked Brienne's hair. "Shhh. Do not cry, *chère amie*. I will help you. Somehow, I swear it, I will help you."

"What goes here!" A deep voice thundered across the room as Esternay's dark frame filled the doorway.

Brienne whirled, fearing that he had overheard Aleth, but then she realized his gaze was fixed upon her shabby gown.

"Why do you dress yourself as a beggar and waste your time at these chores?" he demanded.

Brienne raised her chin a notch and looked at him evenly. "I do penance, my lord, for surely my sins are great to have warranted such a fate as the one set before me."

Esternay growled and quickly surveyed the room. "You are to cease these petty tasks and ready yourself for our departure on the morrow. 'Tis the will of the king."

"The king? And what is your will, my lord?"

"I am sworn to Charles. My will must need comply with that of my overlord . . . for honor's sake," he challenged.

"Then what is your gain? Land? Gold? Thirty pieces of silver?"

Esternay winced at the reference to the traitorous apostle. "Nay, my lady, I take no bribe. Charles is set on this course and deems me the proper escort as your closest kinsman."

He could not admit to the sovereign's persuasiveness, or to his own private ambitions. Indeed, if all progressed well, the king thought to offer his daughter, Gisla, to Rollo himself.

"You may think upon it as your family's restoration to Valsemé."

"*Certes*, to Esternay's advantage! Is that it?" she snapped, stepping closer. "You tie the swine's loyalty to your shield through the bonds of my marriage. Then will he keep his Norse brethren from your door, and join you upon the battlefield? Is that it? You would use the heathens' bloodlust to strengthen the ranks and power of Esternay?"

His eyes glittered and she knew she had struck the mark. Yet there was something more guarded within the depths of those impenetrable eyes. Something dark and deadly. She sucked in her breath sharply and fell back a pace.

"What else? What plans have you laid that not even Charles foresees?" she hissed, ice splintering her eyes.

"You are distraught, my dear, no doubt from the shock of your impending nuptials," he replied evenly, outwardly unfazed. "Do not allow your fears to twist your reasoning."

"Do they? And does Lisette quite agree with your *mission* here, my lord?"

"She will not be told till the child is born. 'Twould be unwise to distress her overmuch at this time."

Brienne threw her head back and laughed derisively. "Oh, a most noble lord indeed! And I thought my enemies all lay without, yet I find a viper hiding in my sister's bed!"

Esternay drew back his hand to strike her, then slowly lowered it. She would not get the better of him again. Damn, but the wench didn't know when to hold her tongue. She deserved a thorough thrashing, but he would not oblige her in front of so many, particularly not those of the cloth.

Grabbing her roughly by the arm, he dragged her from the building and back across the courtyard toward her cell. Throwing open the door, he quickly surveyed the room's disarray, then brutally drove his fingers into her flesh and yanked her to him, holding her a breath away.

"I suggest you accept your fate and prepare yourself, for we face a most arduous journey."

"Never," she breathed between clenched teeth.

Esternay shoved her roughly through the door and she stumbled to the floor, the stone biting her hip.

"Heed me well, vixen. Willingly or not, we leave on the morrow. You may ride of your own accord or trussed in hemp, but ride you will."

Esternay's stiff back retreated across the courtyard as his men assumed their posts. Brienne was left to sob upon the satins and furs that littered her chamber.

The awakening skies were threaded with lavender and rose, and an assortment of birds trebled noisily from their lofty perches, unconcerned with the affairs of humankind.

Brienne paused mutely upon the portal of her cell, still dressed in the drab brown dress of the day before. The sleepless night had been spent in prayer with an unexpected visitor, Mother Annice. Now she waited numbly, exhaustion threatening to overtake her, the mean garb her last silent protest.

She stared vacantly about the familiar surroundings that had served as her home for eight years and could not fathom that she was to be so callously torn away and given over to her enemy. There was naught to hope for. Her royal protector had betrayed her as had her sister's own husband. She was but a pawn in a game of power betwixt men.

Brienne turned back into her chamber. The rich clothes had been returned to their coffer and her own simpler garments added to it. All was in readiness, save her own person, but ready, willing, or accepting she would never be. Though subjected physically to the ordeal, her hatred for the Normans was the armor of her heart.

Gathering her mantle about her slim shoulders, she returned to the doorway and spied Esternay moving across the courtyard, his long strides rapidly eating up the distance between them. She straightened her shoulders and braced herself to be rebuffed for her mean attire.

He halted before her and, after measuring her appearance for a brief moment, grunted and offered his arm. Brienne lifted her cool gaze and, with a faint smile, brushed past it.

In silence they proceeded to the abbey church where a mass was to be celebrated and a final blessing bestowed before the retinue departed.

Aleth waited by the stone staircase looking pale and drawn. She limped forward and grasped her friend's hands. In a familiar gesture, Brienne braced Aleth's arm and they mounted the stairs in slow, measured steps.

The bleakness inside the church matched Brienne's dismal mood. Faint shafts of light filtered through small windows arched high above as candles sputtered in their sockets after the night's long vigil. She hugged herself against the perpetual cold that plagued the stony house of the Lord.

Brienne felt, more than saw, the eyes that embraced her. Lifting her gaze, she found crystal-blue eyes and a pale halo of hair glinting from deep within a monk's hood.

She dropped her lashes and nervously bit her lower lip. The Dane! A Norseman, and so near. She fought to control her watery knees. But he was a holy man now, a Christian, if such a thing be possible. Stealing a small glance, she found him bent to prayer, a silhouette of coarse brown robes.

A second monk entered the sanctuary and ascended the altar steps. Sturdy in stature, with an undisciplined swath of iron gray hair beneath his tonsured crown, Brienne knew him at once to be Brother Bernard. Reverend Mother spoke of him earlier in rather shocked tones. The other she named as Brother Lyting, and confided only that he kept the Rule of Silence to atone for the crimes of his pagan kindred.

As the service progressed and the celebrant droned on in sonorous Latin, Brienne wondered if she supported Aleth or if, in truth, 'twas the other way round.

After the words of consecration were pronounced, Brother Bernard descended the altar stairs, his chalice clasped chest high, and passed through the gates that separated the sanctuary from the faithful. He assumed his station and began dispensing the Host to the communicants.

Aleth hobbled forward painfully, clutching tightly to Brienne's arm. Brienne first took the Host, closing her eyes and tilting her head back as she received the wafer upon her tongue. She then braced Aleth as her friend repeated the ritual, and the two moved aside, allowing Lord Robert forward.

From the corner of her eye, Brienne glimpsed Esternay lowering his lids and tilting back his large head. Suddenly, Aleth shoved Brienne hard toward the gates of the sanctuary with a desperate look that told all. Brienne quickened her pace as a shout exploded from behind, followed by a squeal, then the sound of bodies thudding on the floor.

She glanced back to see that Aleth had thrown herself in Esternay's path and the huge knight now lay sprawled over the slight form, cursing vividly.

Brienne darted forward, the thunder of footsteps on stone closing in on her. A hand shot out and grasped her mantle, but the garment broke free of its clasp and in the next instant she slipped through the gate and gained the altar. She sank upon the marble steps, her sides heaving.

Esternay rose in pursuit, intent on dragging her from the altar.

Brother Bernard fumbled in the folds of his robes and a moment later blocked the knight's way, brandishing a small sword in one hand while still gripping the chalice in the other.

"By all that is holy, you shall not violate sanctuary!" the monk bellowed in his deep, gravelly voice.

Esternay's face contorted with rage and three of his men sought to restrain him.

"Give heed!" the monk warned. "Such sacrilege is committed on pain of excommunication!"

Esternay struggled for composure. A few seconds later, he barked out orders posting several of his men within the church to guard the girl and seize her should she leave the altar area, then angrily quit the building.

Brother Bernard hastily concluded services. Not trusting Esternay, he vowed that he and his companion would alternately keep vigil and assure no offense was committed in the house of God.

Mother Annice, in turn, instructed several of her nuns to remain at their devotions and keep watch over the others, most especially Brienne.

Brienne groaned now at the furor she had created and fell to silent prayer upon the altar steps.

Throughout the day, Esternay returned glowering and seething as he paced about, inspecting the building over and over, noting carefully all exits and passageways, particularly those in the rear of the church where a small maze of chambers lay. At times he strode boldly to the gate to hurl threats at Brienne, one time vowing he would bring the Norsemen themselves to lay waste to the abbey if she did not relent.

It was early evening when Brother Bernard entered the sanctuary with a small parcel of food and settled himself on a step next to Brienne. She stared curiously at the sword that had been resheathed in its rich and unusual scabbard.

Brother Bernard chuckled at her inspection. "We put on quite a show for them, didst we not?"

" 'Twas you who were the spectacle, I think, good brother," she replied with a wan smile.

He patted his weapon. "Aye, my lady. But if you have not heard, I've spent considerable time amongst the heathenous Northmen. It gives me good comfort to keep my friend at my hip whilst I wield the Word of God upon my tongue!"

Brienne's laughter tinkled brightly in the gloomy church, dispelling the melancholy that had shrouded her moments before.

" 'Tis a most unusual friend, and foreign born, methinks, yet quite handsome."

It was the monk's turn to smile as he proudly shifted the scabbard onto his lap to display its fine workmanship. Brienne's eyes widened at the delicate ribbons of silver and gold, inlaid in intricate, interlocking patterns, convoluting gracefully and sprouting into stylized heads of fearsome animals.

"Rollo's gift," Brother Bernard said simply.

Brienne lifted her gaze hesitantly. "You know the man?"

"Aye, indeed, since his early days as *sœkungur*, 'sea king' in their language. I return to labor in his duchy. There is much work to be done in Normandy, and the harvest is promising."

Brienne frowned. "Have you come, then, to persuade me to leave sanctuary?"

"Nay, child. Only to see if you have set the matter before God."

Brienne nodded as sea-green eyes regarded her. "Ever since I learned I was to be given over to Gruel Atli, I have beseeched our Lord for deliverance and He has seen fit to do so."

"Has He, my lady?"

Panic, confusion, and frustration registered all at once in her violet eyes. "What do you mean?"

"Only that you have told God what *you* want, but have not sought out His will for your life."

"This *is* His will. It must be!"

"You want it to be."

Brienne fell silent and brooded.

"Listen to me, my child. Whether it be God's will or not, I cannot say. But do not deny that He may call you forth from cloister to serve Him in a greater way."

"In a Norman's bed? I cannot believe it," she protested.

"Is that all you see? Think, Brienne. The Normans swore fealty to Charles and embraced our faith, though that needs careful nurturing, to be sure. They bring few of their own women. Not even a half dozen have I witnessed. 'Tis our Frankish maids they take to wife. Do you not understand what sway our women hold, first with their husbands and then over their children, the next generation of Normans? They may not realize their own power.

"Our peoples must meld, Brienne," he continued. "Together, they must become one. Men can do so only through words, alliances, and loyalties, but women bring it about through their very flesh. I know 'tis not an easy task, nor is mine, to change the heart and mind of a heathen, but we are all God's children. *All*. As the Baronne de Valsemé, you can wield exceptional influence for the sake of our people and the future of their offspring."

He looked directly into her eyes. "Before you say nay, set
the matter before God and most earnestly seek His direction.
Will you do that, my child?"

Brienne lowered her gaze, and with her heart sinking
somewhat, she nodded in agreement.

The hours to come were fraught with anxiety and fear.
Most desperately, Brienne would have it that her destiny
lay in the arms of the Church, not those of her enemy.
But then she fretted at the prospect of spending years in
sanctuary. Such was known to happen. What future there?
More, she feared the wrath of Esternay should she dare leave
its protection. What matter the day or hour? He would be
waiting to appease his bruised pride and she had no champion
to aid her cause. And what of the king's own anger, or that
of Gruel Atli? Father in Heaven, what had she done?

If her resolve wavered throughout the night, it was quickly
restored at the mere thought of the despicable Normans.
They were Danes, mostly, or so she was told, though no
one seemed certain of Rollo's origins. She had seen such
men once from the tower in the bailey when they laid siege
to Valsemé. She shuddered as she recalled the ferocity with
which those heathens fought. That day was nearly lost, and
it was shortly thereafter that her family was removed to
Chaudrey.

Brienne hugged herself against the chill of night. Once
again she felt the scrutiny of the shrouded monk, Brother
Lyting. Feigning prayer, she glanced at him surreptitiously
from beneath thick lashes.

He studied her intently, of that she was sure, though his
features remained heavily concealed within the folds of his
cowl. He would prove tall should he unfold himself from
his cramped posture. The startling breadth of his shoulders
strained the limits of his robes, suggesting a physique hardened
more by the rigorous training of sword and shield than by cross
and gospel.

Brienne knew she should hate this man for the very blood
that flowed through his veins. Yet he was a man of God.
Could she condemn where the Father forgave?

As the night deepened and melted into early morn, Brienne
lay exhausted upon the cold stone floor, prostrate in prayer

before the altar. Divine guidance had shed no light on the path she should choose, and now she fell into a light, restless sleep.

She was a child of twelve summers once again, standing tiptoe upon an uneven stool and peering out the narrow slit of a window in the tower wall. Below, her father's army was retreating inside the defense works. She anxiously scanned the fields beyond where the enemy pursued a few straggling Franks, racing for the protection of the motte and bailey.

They were huge men, red and golden of hair, wearing conical helmets with noseguards that concealed their features. Her eyes fixed upon a black-haired heathen, the only one of his kind, as he closed in upon a fleeing soldier. Whirling his battle-ax round in a mighty arc, he cleaved the Frank in two from head to shoulder. Brienne emitted a bloodcurdling scream. As though the Norseman had heard her, he lifted his battle-fevered gaze to the high window above and smiled eerily, chilling Brienne to her immortal soul. He hefted his bloodied ax upon his broad shoulder and continued in his pursuit.

Brienne bolted upright, fully awake. Sheer terror washed over her and she began shaking violently. Never could she be a bride to a bloodthirsty spawn of the Devil!

Throwing herself down again, she frantically beseeched the Almighty, fear strangling every fiber of her being.

"Lord, set aside this bitter cup, I beg of thee."

Drink. The word was instantly impressed in her mind.

Brienne's head jerked upward. Had someone spoken? She lifted herself and surveyed the small gathering in the church. Sisters Basiria and Lioba knelt in silent prayer, as did Brother Lyting. Two of Esternay's soldiers whispered quietly together at the rear of the church, while a third appeared to doze near a side door.

Brienne turned back to her prayers, sure that the anxieties of the past days were fast overcoming her.

"Grant, O Lord, that this cup may pass."

Drink. The word was strongly impressed once more. *Live the love that is within you.*

"Nay!" Brienne gasped, pressing her cheek to the cold floor. "Merciful Father, do not ask it of me, I beg Thee."

Hot tears seared her eyes. "I am so afraid."

Scripture poured into her mind. *Perfect love casts out all fear.*

Pressing both hands to her temples, she fought to still the flow of thoughts. "Nay, I am but one, only one"—her breath came in shallow gulps—"and I am all alone."

In that moment, she was flooded with a presence, suffusing her with warmth and wrapping her in a tender, loving embrace.

I am with you always.

The presence lingered awhile, casting away all doubt and objection, and soothing her heart's distress.

As the first golden threads of dawn spun through the lofty windows and spilled down over the altar, Brienne rose to her feet. Smoothing away the tears that stained her face, she bowed reverently toward the altar.

"Thy will be mine."

Turning, she did not notice the wide-eyed stares or gaping mouths of her companions, but descended the altar steps and walked purposely through the gate and out of the sanctuary.

In short order, the Seigneur d'Esternay was apprised of the turn of events, and a flurry of activity swept through the abbey as the escort prepared its departure.

Brienne's "experience" was recounted by the witnesses in glowing terms, recalling how she had pleaded and cried out upon the altar, then, uttering a few words, quit the sanctuary.

Esternay would have liked to throttle the girl outright for the embarrassment she caused him, but he quickly discovered that the soldiers who held vigil with her now zealously watched over her like three clucking hens.

It was rumored about that the Heavenly Father had called the maid forth from sanctuary. Esternay scoffed at this but fought down his yearning to punish the girl. It would be unwise to harm one so obviously sheltered under the "Divine Wing."

Instead, he dispersed Brienne's new champions, sending two, Blanchard and Leveque, ahead to coordinate their rendezvous with the Norman escort. Brother Lyting, though strangely reluctant to leave, agreed to accompany them and interpret the mediations. The men were strictly instructed to make no mention of the girl's initial aversion to the marriage or of her flight into sanctuary. Mortain, the third bemused soldier, remained to attend to the girl's needs.

Esternay kicked back his chair as he envisioned the chit in the Norman's arms. Had he not witnessed her raw fear of their kind? If God protected her, then He also provided a fitting chastisement for the troublesome wench. Aye, the Norseman would tame her with his brand. The image should have placated his craving for vengeance, but it cheered him not at all.

Brienne carefully selected an ensemble for her initial encounter with the Norman host and folded it neatly into her coffer. Knowing it would take several days to reach the borders of Normandy, she chose a gown more suitable to traveling on horseback, nutmeg in hue and devoid of elaborate trimmings.

She wove her luxurious locks into two plaits and coiled them into a crown atop her head. Then she covered her hair with a *couvre-chef,* a long, flowing scarf. She arranged the ends modestly across her throat rather than allowing them to fall freely as she was usually wont to do.

For so many years she had lived in community with other women, equal in all things. Now, in one short hour, she would return to the world of men, surrounded first by Frankish soldiers, then delivered to a cortege of Norman warriors. A small tremor passed through her and she adjusted her *couvre-chef* once more.

A soft rapping sounded at the door and Aleth peeked in. The two girls clasped each other warmly.

Aleth stammered momentarily and stared hard at the floor. "I want to come with you, Brienne."

"Aleth! Do you know what you say?"

"*Oui.* I've thought on it long and well, and would not have you face this alone. You will need a friend."

"Oh, Aleth, your companionship would be most welcome, but I fear for your safety amongst these foreigners."

Aleth studied the toe of her leather shoe. "Surely they will have no cause to harm a cripple . . . or the personal maid of the Baronne de Valsemé."

Brienne smiled brilliantly at this last bit of reasoning and realized for the first time that her position did yield some power. She embraced her friend heartily. "Come, then, Aleth. I shall need a friend such as you."

It was midday before the entourage was finally assembled in the courtyard. Brienne was astonished to be gifted with a magnificent white palfry outfitted in rich Frankish trappings, yet another of Charles's bridal offerings. The sovereign seemed most desirous of this union.

The nuns sent exquisitely embroidered altar linens and vestments for the long-inactive church of Valsemé. To Brienne, they presented the precious gift of a small mongrel puppy which rode in a wicker basket attached to her palfry's saddle.

A tearful moment passed as the women exchanged their last farewells. Sister Ursuline sniffed noisily while many of the ladies dabbed at their eyes, chins aquiver. Mother Annice pressed a smooth hollow reed into Brienne's hand, containing a small, tightly rolled parchment.

"Isaiah. Remember, child." Reverend Mother smiled through her own tears, then clutched Brienne to her with surprising strength. "Godspeed."

The gates swung open, and the column of soldiers, attendants, and carts moved slowly out of the abbey. Brienne and Aleth assumed their positions in the center of the escort, with Brother Bernard trailing behind on his stout little mare.

No one was prepared for the greeting they received as they emerged from the age-old enclosure walls. It appeared that every villager for miles around was assembled there waving bright cloths, throwing flower petals, and uttering their blessings as they hailed the maid that God called forth from Levroux. Surely, Heaven was at long last attentive to their prayers.

Esternay scowled at the delirious scene, wondering how word of Brienne's "holy encounter" had spread so rapidly, then dismissed it. The abbey employed many workers from the village. Since the escort would be traveling the old Roman roads afar of the villages, there was little chance that the spectacle would be repeated. With that consoling thought he commanded the troops forward.

Brienne strained to look back as the gathering faded into specks of color and the silhouette of the abbey melted into the horizon. The last visual tie severed, she turned forward in her saddle to face the uncertain future that awaited her.

Chapter Three

THE FURRY LITTLE puppy licked the last droplets of water from Brienne's cupped palm. She took up the skin from her saddle again, soaking a small scarf, and wiped at her face and neck. She contemplated the soiled cloth with disgust, feeling utterly incrusted with the grime of four days' travel.

The pup whimpered to be out of his basket, and Brienne scratched his ears comfortingly. "Patience, little one."

The pup cocked its head sideways.

"What shall I call you?" She stole a glance at Aleth riding several arm lengths away on a small brown palfry. "Mugwort! Now, there's a fine name."

"You wouldn't!" Aleth exclaimed.

"Nay. He's not so forlorn-looking as that." She laughed at Aleth's withering look.

Brienne studied the uneven splotches that adorned the little fellow's coat and decided upon "Patch." The puppy yapped excitedly as though he approved.

She shifted her attention to the beautiful white palfry beneath her. "You are more difficult." She stroked the shimmering coat. "*Etoile,* perhaps. Star."

"That would be *asta* in Greek," Brother Bernard said, reining in his horse next to Brienne's, "or *stella* in Latin. Of course, there be *candra*, also Latin. It means 'shining.' "

"Candra. *Mais oui!*" She tousled the white mane playfully. "It suits her well, do you not agree?"

Brother Bernard smiled, nodding, then watched Brienne's gaiety fade as she squinted into the distance.

"How much longer?"

"On the morrow, my lady. Blanchard and Leveque returned last even with the details. Brother Lyting awaits us at Valsemé. Did you not know?"

She shook her head.

"Esternay," he said flatly, not expanding on the comment. He had developed an acute distaste for the man from the first when he and his companion were pressed to depart the abbey no sooner than they had arrived. Absurd. He was not a young man anymore, to be jostled about the realm on a broken-down palfrey at the whim of some overbearing knight. He said as much. Years amongst the heathens had given him pluck, by God!

"We meet late morn inside the boundaries of the duchy, my lady, at the site of a Roman ruin. The precise location is marked by an ancient oak. These Norse believe spirits dwell in trees and mounds and such. Hold them sacred. Yet 'tis an odd place to meet a bride. Mayhaps they think it home to some fertility goddess," he mused with a shrug. "Sorry, my dear. Ah, well, Blanchard and Leveque will direct us."

"I vow, you are a most irregular churchman with your sword and colorful jests," she chided.

"I have a colorful past." His eyes twinkled.

"Pray tell me what to expect when we meet these Normans. Will Lord Robert leave us to them?"

"Nay, child. Both escorts will accompany us to Valsemé. As the king's representative, the Seigneur d'Esternay must see you safely there and wed before he returns to court."

Brienne fidgeted a moment with Candra's reins, lacing them between her fingers.

"Having second thoughts, my child? Regrets?"

"I am only apprehensive, and in truth, a little nervous now that I shall come face to face with my . . ."

"Enemy?" the monk supplied. "You must try not to think of them as such. They are men, the same flesh and blood as you and I—"

"But not the same heart," she interjected.

"That is why we are here." He reached over and patted her hands.

"What are they like?" Color faintly tinged her cheeks. "I would know how they treat their women."

"Do not worry overlong on it. Generally, they are good to their families, though I would warn you of one thing: the *More Danico*."

He rubbed a bristly chin. "You see, in their homeland, a man may take as many wives as he can afford. They are a rather polygamous lot by nature. Even when they embrace our Christian faith, they are reluctant to lay aside this custom, and simply keep handfast wives alongside their legal ones."

"Paramours?"

"In essence. But fear not. Any issue of your union with Atli will be his legitimate heir to Valsemé. You must face the possibility, however, that he may keep other women as well."

"Do not concern yourself for my sake. I almost welcome it. Perhaps he will desire their favors over mine and not bother me overmuch."

Brother Bernard knew that any full-blooded male could not soon forget the exquisite creature that rode next to him. He diverted the conversation into a lighter vein.

"Would it amuse you to learn a few words in the Norse tongue, perhaps a simple greeting that you can share on the morrow?"

The ensuing hours slipped pleasantly by as Brienne contorted her tongue around an impossible combination of sounds, laughing at her ineptitude.

Later, with the camp settled for the night and the coarse provisions eaten, Brienne made her only request of the journey: water for a bath.

She had to content herself with a scrubbing from a large basin set inside her tent. Aleth worked long soaping and rinsing Brienne's hair till it squeaked clean. It took several more hours to dry the silken mass before the campfire.

Esternay watched intently from a distance. Thus far, he had avoided Brienne altogether during the journey, lest she stir his wrath anew. Now he found that it was not his ire that she kindled, but his naked desire.

The simple gown she had donned after bathing clung to her damp, lush contours, and her delicately boned features were pleasantly flushed by the warmth of the fire. As she combed out her glorious black mane, he craved to wrap it about his arm and trap her softness beneath the length of him. His blood was infected with her.

He growled deep in his throat, damning Richard Beaumanoir in his grave once again. The girl should have been his. His! And despite her troublesome nature, he meant to have her.

He stroked his beard thoughtfully, reassessing his carefully laid plans, plans that would one day assure him control of Valsemé itself, right in the midst of the Normans. Brienne was the centerpiece to those designs.

A feral gleam lit in the dark eyes as he decided upon his course and how best to press his advantage. Most likely, the maid would be as desirous of the liaison as he. His offer, of course, was irresistible. Freedom from the Norman yoke, and rule of the barony.

He smiled, skimming over her inviting curves once again. Of course, there was a price, but he held no doubt that she would prefer his touch to those of a Norse jackal. *Oui*, her terror of the Norsemen would serve him well. Esternay measured Brienne closely, confidently, as she chatted with the little cripple, her laughter a soft melody against the night. She was a delectable morsel, and one he intended to savor for many years to come.

At length, Brienne returned to her tent, unaware of the passions she had inflamed. She collapsed on her pallet, refreshed and tingling to the tips of her toes, and quickly nodded off.

As the night skies lifted their heavy veils, Brienne nudged Aleth awake to begin preparations for the new day.

Dashing her face with cool water, she wondered briefly of Gruel Atli and whether he would be present among his men. No mention of it had been made. Still, she must leave nothing to chance.

In a few short hours, the escort would pass into Normandy and her life would be forever changed. Brienne knew if she was to succeed in influencing these people, she must establish herself at the outset. Today, she represented her kingdom as Frank met Norman, but even more, she embodied the very essence of Valsemé. She was part of a yesterday that once was, a part that would triumph again in that joining.

God grant her strength. Despite the nobility of the cause, the reality truly repulsed her.

Time slipped swiftly away and the call to mount their steeds sounded. Esternay strode boldly to the women's tent smiling inwardly to himself as he envisioned Brienne recoiling before her new masters when he presented her to them later that day. He would seize the moment and salve her fears, offering her fresh hope, and more, oh, so much more.

Moments later he swallowed that smugness as Brienne stepped forth from her tent.

She was stunningly gowned in a rich tunic, deeply cut and the color of a fine crimson wine. Unlike the voluminous garments currently favored, the gown molded her contours snugly then fell gracefully to her knees over an ivory chemise. Both were lavishly embroidered about the neck, sleeves, and hem with wide borders of purest gold thread. An exquisite girdle, studded with garnets and pearls, lay atop her hips, accentuating her tiny waist.

Brienne's ebony tresses cascaded luxuriantly past her shoulders like a midnight waterfall, crowned with a circlet of gold. The band was set with a single gemstone, a large ruby, centered above her brows. To the back, the circlet secured a sheer golden veil that fell in misty layers nearly to the ground.

Esternay stared greedily at the vision before him. *Soon, my dove, soon.*

The aging Roman road, which the entourage had followed for nearly a week, was abandoned for a much narrower route that wound through lush meadowland and open orchards.

Brother Bernard joined the women, who were still ensconced in the center of the escort, offering his encouragement and briefly reviewing the greeting Brienne had prepared in the Norse tongue.

A short while later, the retinue entered a little valley whose steeply sloping sides cradled the ruins of a once palatial Roman villa.

As the horses and carts cautiously descended the narrow rutted road, Brienne spied a great gnarled tree near the ruins, incredible in size, impossibly massive in its girth.

"Yggdrasil," she marveled softly.

Brother Bernard had taught her a smattering of the Norse religious beliefs to break the monotony of their journey. This mammoth oak recalled his tales of the great World Ash of Asgard, Yggdrasil, a gigantic tree bearing up the universe. Among its numerous fascinations were two wells located beneath its roots.

Mimir watched over the Well of Wisdom, and it was to him that Odin sacrificed an eye for a draught of the magical pool. The Norns dwelt by the Well of Fate and tended men's destinies. Urd, Verdandi, and Skuld by name, they personified the Past, Present, and Future.

How appropriate, Brienne reflected, for undoubtedly this was the rendezvous. What mischief were the Fates weaving for her?

She quickly scanned the grounds below and caught sight of a large host of men mounting their steeds near the crumbling walls and reassembling beneath the mighty oak, Normans to be sure; red and golden of hair. An icy finger of memory traced down her spine.

As the Frankish column neared the bottom of the valley, the road straightened and Brienne could no longer see ahead past the hulking soldiers. Shortly, the retinue came to a standstill and waited patiently to be signaled forward. She surmised that Esternay was now advancing with his select retainers to meet the Norman complement in the open field.

Brienne bit her lower lip. The moment was at hand and she did not know if she could still her pounding heart.

Time weighed heavily upon their idleness. The men's saddles creaked as they strained to see, and they mumbled among themselves. Ghostly images of a smiling, black-haired heathen floated before her, and she fought down her rising panic as the aromas of grasses, horses, and leather bombarded her senses.

Leveque suddenly appeared at her side, his pride and concern for her reflected clearly in his hazel eyes.

"We have spoken with the Normans, my lady. You are bid forward to make your presence known."

Brienne froze momentarily, unable to move. She watched dazedly as the troops parted on command to either side of the road, creating a pathway before her. Aleth squeezed her hand, then extracted the whining pup from its basket. Leveque nodded solemnly for her to begin.

Swallowing hard, she pressed Candra forward, feeling much like a lamb approaching a den of hungry wolves. *For the love of God, for the love of my people,* she chanted silently, over and over. *Dear God, don't abandon me.*

As she approached the front of the Frankish lines, Brienne gained her first close look at the men of the North. Larger than the Franks and powerful in build, they were not wholly unpleasant to look upon. They were a fair-haired lot for the most part, and not a few favored scarlet mantles.

Brienne continued toward Esternay and Brother Bernard who sat astride a roan and a gray, conversing with the Norse leader, entirely blocking her view of the man. She wondered wildly if this was Gruel Atli.

Her pulse quickened and her mind raced, barely capable of coherent thought. She dropped her gaze, feeling stripped bare under the curious stares and open assessment of the Norman host.

With a start, she realized that Esternay and Brother Bernard had reined their mounts aside. She was left face-to-face . . . with whom?

Slowly, Brienne lifted her eyes but for a moment could go no further than the powerful stallion, as satiny black as Candra was silken white. Then, inhaling deeply, she willed her eyes upward over the expansive chest and astonishingly wide shoulders to look fully upon the Norseman's countenance.

She could not breathe for several seconds, only stare dumbly. Never had she seen a man so devastatingly handsome. Like some glorified hero acclaimed in the legends of old, he was a magnificent golden warrior. Dear God, why did he have to be a Norman!

His steel-blue eyes locked with her wide violet orbs and an energy passed between them, igniting ripples of warmth through her trembling limbs. She wondered breathlessly if this was the man who held her future.

He released his gaze then swept appreciatively over her every curve, down to her slender feet and back again, like a gentle caress. She flushed warmly as he paused at her full, ripe breasts. Shockingly, they grew taut under his intimate appraisal, the firm buds clearly outlined against the soft cloth of her gown. His eyes widened a fraction, and for a moment Brienne wondered if it were possible to die of acute embarrassment.

How dare he examine her like some prize bauble! Did males never see more to a woman than a passive plaything to warm their beds? Well, passive she was not. She was fully capable of returning like for like. When his eyes captured hers again, she smiled winsomely and initiated her own bold perusal of his splendid frame.

Briefly, she traced over the finely hewn features and square set of his jaw, lingering at the enticing cleft of his chin. She moistened her lips as though she would taste it, unaware of the provocativeness of the gesture. Her gaze slipped lower, skimming over the sleeveless suede jerkin of dove-gray to explore thickly muscled arms wrapped in the spiral embrace of silver arm bracelets.

As her eyes roamed across the flat abdomen, Esternay cleared his throat sharply. Her eyes flew upward and were claimed at once by the Norman's captivating smile and a quizzically arched brow. Brienne bestowed a dazzling smile upon the golden man, missing the heightened color and ominous scowl that darkened Esternay's mien.

"*Velkominn.*" The voice was beautifully rich.

Brother Bernard hastened to make the introductions. "My lady, may I present to you Rurik, eldest son of Gruel Atli. He bids you welcome."

A crushing disappointment flickered across her eyes but she tried not to betray her feelings otherwise. How could she have been so childish to hope for even an instant that this man was her betrothed? She puzzled over the strong force of the feelings in her body that he evoked, causing her to forget that he was a Northman and deserving of all her hatred. Yet he was a man all the same. Flesh and blood, was that not what the good monk said?

"My lady, he bids you welcome," Brother Bernard prompted, sending up a small prayer that she would commence with her speech.

A thousand thoughts swirled through Brienne's mind. Her lips parted then closed, the strands of memories demanding a new course.

"I am Brienne Beaumanoir, by birthright Baronne de Valsemé. 'Tis I who bid you welcome to my ancestral homeland and to those lands your people now claim. May the Norman rule prove wise and worthy of my forefathers."

Brother Bernard's eyes rounded. "My lady, we dare not provoke—"

"Tell him exactly." Her tone brooked no argument.

Brother Bernard grumbled to himself, then began conveying her message in the odd tongue. A gleam lit in Rurik's eyes, and his reply set the monk to sputtering.

"My lady, Rurik thanks you for your generous greeting. He asks that you would settle a question that plagues him overmuch."

Brienne nodded.

"Forgive me, my lady, these Normans are rather blunt—"

Brienne frowned impatiently.

"He wonders why a woman so beautiful and . . . ahem . . . obviously desirable as yourself was locked away in a house of virgins."

Brienne's mouth dropped open, but she quickly recovered herself as a surge of mischievousness bubbled up. "My father sought to save me from the Northmen."

As the reply was translated, Rurik smiled broadly, showing even white teeth, then issued a rejoinder. Brother Bernard blustered incoherently for a moment.

"My lady, he says, to the contrary; 'twould seem your father saved you *for* the Northmen."

Esternay sliced through the repartee, barely suppressing the fury that consumed him. The chit slavered over the heathen like a bitch in heat!

"Enough of your bantering, Lady Brienne. You are dismissed. Return to your position in the column at once."

Brienne was stunned. "My lord, if I have offended any—"

"Offended?" Esternay snapped. "You are either amazingly naive or appallingly wanton. If you continue to encourage the man, you'll next find him between your thighs!"

Brienne recoiled at his crudity, astounded. Had the man gone utterly mad?

Brother Bernard gasped, his eyes darting nervously over the towering Normans. "My lord, 'tis unwise—"

"Silence!" Esternay hissed, emboldened since the foreigners could not understand his Frankish tongue. He glowered at Brienne. "We shall finish this matter later. Your years in cloister have left you surprisingly lacking in the finer points of decorum." He signaled brusquely for one of his men-at-arms to remove her.

Rurik suddenly spurred his destrier forward between the maid and menacing knight, catching up Candra's reins and swiftly drawing Brienne aside.

Esternay's hand flew to his sword hilt, but the monk stayed him.

Rurik glared coldly at the Frank, the blue tinge of his eyes draining to a flinty gray. When next he spoke, Brienne detected a dangerous undercurrent to his incomprehensible words.

"Sire, we are to depart at once." Brother Bernard mopped his brow. "The Lady Brienne is to ride with Rurik and an escort equal in number of Normans and Franks. He bids you choose ten."

Esternay snarled at the conceit of the man. "Tell this arrogant bastard that I represent the king. The lady is my charge and shall remain under my protection until she is wed. I'll share her with no cockscomb of a Northman till then."

Rurik's eyes glinted like polished steel. Before another word could be uttered, he bellowed out a string of commands.

Two dozen of his men quickly surrounded the small group of Franks that stood in the open field, hands poised, ready to unsheath their blades.

Brienne paled and quickly searched Rurik's stony face.

The monk hastily signed himself. "Seigneur, 'twas no request. We are in Normandy now."

Chapter Four
❖ ❖ ❖ ❖ ❖ ❖ ❖ ❖ ❖ ❖ ❖

BRIENNE SPENT THE next hour reconstructing the tense scene that had erupted at the ruins, wondering what she had done to provoke Lord Robert's reckless display of temper. In a corner of her heart, she marveled at Rurik's keen perception and rapid command of the situation, claiming her from Esternay's side in a daring gesture that was as startling as it was perplexing.

Of course it was her fault. She was much too bold. The troublesome trait had caused her countless embarrassments and had inspired many a lengthy sermon on the modest virtues befitting gentlewomen.

After years in cloister, Brienne tended to view everyone as her peer. She was unaccustomed to dealing with men, let alone this fearsome breed. How should one react to such as they, long-standing enemy to the kingdom, now the crown's ally? Brienne sighed. How should she behave toward a man who could steal her breath away and set her heart to racing with a single look? She glanced ahead at Rurik's powerful back and gilded mane as he rode easily astride his mount. How indeed.

Rurik kept his silence after departing the ruins, never quite allowing the Seigneur d'Esternay beyond his field of sight. The day held many surprises thus far, the most pleasurable being the mysterious lady from the Frankish holy house.

He did not fathom this custom of shutting away maidens and half expected the bride to suffer some odious malady. Atli's lack of concern did little to ease his apprehensions, but

then his father was more familiar with these Christian practices, even accepting their religion alongside the old gods. .

He, on the other hand, had spent the years past chasing
adventure and trading amongst different peoples in the far
reaches of the known world. He was *prímsigned*, of course,
so that he might deal with the Christian merchants. But
beyond this quasi form of baptism, which involved no more
than a cross being signed upon the brow, he knew little of
their curious rites.

Rurik invoked Brienne's sweet image and her innocent
response to him. Loki must be laughing that this beautiful
girl was to become his stepmother. Were she destined for
anyone save his father, he would not think twice on sweeping
her away in his *drakkar* to some hidden nest.

Brienne was absorbed in her thoughts as the retinue passed
through the undulating hillsides and broad green valleys of
the Perche. Horses grazed idly in rolling pastures, and the
fragrance of peach and apple blossoms from nearby orchards
delicately scented the air.

A distant rumbling intruded upon Brienne's musings, growing steadily louder. Her head snapped up as the sounds clarified
into the muddled shoutings of human voices. Shielding her
eyes from the brilliant sunlight, she traced the thatched roofs of
a small village nestled snugly in the neighboring vale. Patches
of color moved hurriedly across the open fields toward the
escort.

The troops grew agitated as the forms assumed recogniz-
able shapes, brandishing objects in their upheld hands. Rurik
halted the retinue, quickly assessing the unruly crowd.

Brienne distinguished her name upon the lips of the
approaching villeins as a sword sang out among the guard.
Dozens of soldiers followed the edgy knight, unsheathing
their blades in a deafening clamor.

"Nay!" Brienne cried as she dug her heels sharply into
Candra's sides and bolted from the line. The ground blurred
beneath her as she drove the palfrey across the sloping
meadowland. Moments later, she reined in before the
crowd, shielding them protectively with her white steed.
Rurik appeared instantly beside her, the Norman and Frankish
guard trailing short of his pace.

The villagers cowered before the flashing metal, but Brienne glared at the soldiers defiantly, like a mother lion fearlessly guarding her young. Norsemen required little provocation to shed blood. Forsooth, 'twas their favored pastime. If these simple villeins were deemed a threat, they would be hewn down where they stood. Such was the way of this barbarous race. Well, she would be the first to taste their metal, she vowed, tossing her ebony mane. Her eyes fell, then, to the sword at Rurik's hip, still buried deep within its scabbard.

Rurik pinned her with a penetrating look, silently probing the corners of her mind, then, at the flick of his wrist, the Norman swords were resheathed. Esternay likewise signaled his men after heaping choice curses upon one particular soldier for his hasty actions.

Brienne sickened. One of her own was responsible for the near calamity. 'Twas the astuteness of a silvery eyed Norman that saved her people. And they were silvery, she noted as Rurik continued to hold her gaze. The man had the most changeable eyes. Didst their grayness herald his anger or his displeasure now? she wondered. Had he guessed her condemning thoughts?

Cautiously, a few villagers ventured forward, regaining their shattered confidence. As their fervor returned, they showered their blessings upon Brienne, crowding round and thrusting gifts of food and flowers into her hands. Some lifted their children to be cradled and kissed, while others clutched at her garments, babbling out a mixture of praise and woe-filled tales. Still more kept a small distance apart, reed crosses clasped to their breasts, tears marring their features as they quietly observed the young noblewoman, resplendent in crimson and gold, perched upon her snowy palfrey, Beaumanoir's daughter, God's chosen vessel.

Brother Bernard reined in alongside Rurik, chuckling. " 'Twould seem Lord Robert's messengers could not keep their tongues in their head."

"What say you, monk?" Rurik furrowed his brow.

"Do not be alarmed, my son. These people believe that the maid is a sign from Heaven, plucked from her cloister expressly to intervene in their behalves." He cocked a bushy brow at the Norman. "She is their hope for the future.

I would venture that many of these villeins are displaced from the soil they once tilled, perhaps even the soil of Valsemé."

Rurik watched Brienne as she leaned down just then to clasp the hand of an elderly, snowy-haired Frank, surprise and joy reflected clearly in her face.

He grunted his agreement as the monk moved off to minister his blessings. Still, Rurik failed to comprehend the furor that Brienne's presence created.

He studied the perfection of her profile, allowing his gaze to wander over the elegant curve of her neck and rest upon the swell of her breasts where they flirted above her gown. She spoke animatedly with the old man, unaware of the arousing image she created.

What was the king's purpose in offering so tantalizing a prize? Why did the sovereign insist that the offspring of this marriage inherit the titles and lands to the barony, disregarding Atli's grown sons, nephews to Rollo himself? He pondered that a moment, shifting his attention to the white-haired Frank who suddenly fell silent and stared at the ground. Brienne continued speaking as the man considered her words.

Of course, there would be no heir. 'Twas a point the Frankish envoy neglected to question and his father did not offer. Atli was no longer capable of siring children, not that the girl would remain a virgin. Atli boasted that he could rut as well as any stag after the scent. Better, by thunder! But for a man once known to easily swell a woman's belly with his seed, there had been no issue in over a decade. Not since a Saxon lance spitted him through the groin. His father was well pleased that he could foil the game yet gain the prize.

Rurik returned his attention to the white-haired man who nodded slowly, then bowed over Brienne's hand and brushed it with his lips. Straightening, he trudged away in the direction of the village.

Rurik settled back in his saddle, watching the old man's retreat. The Frank's bearing was proud and straight, not bent like that of a field laborer, his manner almost courtly. There was no hint that he had ever strengthened his body for the skills of war or wielded an instrument heavier than his eating knife. It spurred Rurik's curiosity. Rurik looked about him. He would have a name to this place and the Norman lord who ruled here. Odin's eye! Where be the liege's men? 'Twas unlikely they would remain at their tasks while the inhabitants emptied the village. The absence of his Norse kindred settled ill with him. He thought to follow the villein and question him.

As he pressed his heels to the stallion's flanks, he felt a tugging at his boot. The war horse pranced sideways as Rurik spied a small, disheveled girl clinging to his toe and tendering up a fistful of wilting wildflowers.

"Easy, Sleipnir," he soothed, fearing the steed would trample the sprite. He swept the child up in a well-muscled arm and set her before him.

Gasps punctuated the air at the sight of the Northman snatching up the little girl. The crowd fell silent, distrusting the man's purpose.

"Elsie!" A round little woman, obviously stricken, rushed forward but stopped short of the great black.

Brienne was instantly alert to the fear-laden mood and guided Candra alongside the destrier. Leaning across her saddle, she smoothed the child's mass of brown curls, then casually laid her delicate hand on Rurik's arm and embraced the two with a warm smile. The contrast of the huge warrior and the small child pulled at her heartstrings; she could not say why.

As though a new dawning broke, the villagers came back to themselves, now chattering and smiling, nodding their approval of the striking couple. Brienne was oblivious of their excited speculations as she tilted her face upward and lost herself in the blue sea of Rurik's eyes.

Elsie squirmed in Rurik's arms, snuggling against his broad chest. "Can I come to your wedding?" she asked, her eyes sparkling with innocent hope. Without waiting for an answer, she chattered on. "When you make your babies, I will come sing them to sleep. I'm very good with babies," she proclaimed, confident of her talent. "Mama says so."

Warmth flushed through Brienne at the thought of being intimate with this man, but she had not the heart to crush the child's fantasies and reveal that Rurik was not her husband-to-be. Looking out over the smiling faces, she realized with a start that most of these people shared Elsie's impression, obviously mistaking Rurik for his father. She drew her eyes back to his handsome face, wondering for the first time of his age. Mayhaps he had seen twenty-nine or thirty years. A frown twinged her brow. How old, then, was Atli? She had never considered that the bridegroom would prove long of tooth, and resolved to question Lord Robert more thoroughly on the matter.

Brother Bernard appeared at Rurik's side and promptly set to conveying the small girl's requests. Rurik smiled gently at the tousle-haired mite and, cupping her chin, whispered in her ear.

"Elsie, come down," called the sturdy little woman, shifting the babe at her hip.

Rurik carefully lowered the child to her mother's arms, then secured Elsie's flowers in his belt with some flourish.

"Don't forget!" she trilled gleefully.

A short while later the escort took up its travels, wending its way through the picturesque countryside, steadily conquering weed-choked roads and deeply rutted byways. Brienne found herself flanked between Rurik and Brother Bernard who engaged in light banter. She interrupted what she suspected to be a ribald jest and prodded the monk to discover what Rurik had whispered to Elsie, not that the child could have understood a word of his peculiar tongue.

At first it seemed that Rurik would not answer, but when she stared overlong at his fine profile, he turned his eyes on her. Blue. That was a good sign, Brienne mused, smiling expectantly.

"Ho!" Brother Bernard smacked his thigh when the Norman finally spoke. "My lady, Rurik would barter with you one morsel of information for another." He leaned toward her in jovial conspiracy. "Be warned, my lady, he is skilled at his trade. He has bargained his way from Hedeby to Constantinople, only to double his profit along the Volga and return a wealthy man to the envy of every merchant from Birka to Kaupang. Hold for the better deal and guard well your valuables."

Brienne tossed a challenging look at the Norman and joined in the badinage. "Fear not, noble monk, I can haggle over a crumb like a fishwife. And my treasures are hidden safe within my heart where I alone hold the key."

"Ah, then secure the key against the day, for he will surely test your skills. And if you be not firm of purpose, he will wrest that prize in a twinkling and claim the riches therein." Brother Bernard chuckled at his cleverness, missing Brienne's startled expression.

"*Certes*," she agreed softly, touching her hand to her breast. She settled her violet eyes on the golden man and took up the waggery once again. "But warn yon Northman that I am no simple maid, nor easy prey to honeyed words and silken tongues. Bid him name his price."

After a brief exchange, Brother Bernard sat back in his saddle with an exaggerated sigh. "You are spared this day, my lady. He seeks but to know of the old man with whom you spoke earlier."

"Bolsgar?" She hesitated to disclose the man's identity but yielded under Rurik's penetrating look.

"He was Valsemé's seneschal, steward to my father's estates. I have not seen him since . . ." She quashed the dark memories and struggled to still the tremor in her hands. "He did not accompany my family to Chaudrey, but sought out his sister and her children. We feared his end was sealed with a Norse ax." She smiled slightly, her eyes moist. "But he lives, good brother. For now, he dwells with his family at Ivry. I was amazed to discover him there."

" 'Tis strange that the Norman presence was so lacking."

"Bolsgar said that there are several *pagi* that have yet to feel the duke's hand."

"*Oui*, Rouen and the king eat up his energies. He has not yet fully extended his authority to all corners of Normandy. Go on, my child."

"Rumors abound that the lands which include Ivry are to be granted as a benefice to one of the duke's kin. He is said to be a man of fearsome reputation." Brienne moistened her lips. "I confess, I may have overstepped myself. The people would pledge themselves to a Norman lord if he be fair, but they fear this new master. I assured Bolsgar that Valsemé's arms are always open to those who seek her doors."

"Did he put a name to the man?"

"*Oui*. The name be Hastein."

Rurik's eyes hardened to brittle shards.

"Mayhaps Rurik has knowledge of him."

"No need to ask." The monk ran a hand through his coarse hair. "Hastein is his half brother, and a devil if there ever be one."

Brother Bernard turned to Rurik and they engaged in a discussion of such length that Brienne thought her original question forgotten. Just as she sought to interrupt their exchange, the monk cleared his throat and smiled over at her.

"Rurik confesses he promised the child that she may nursemaid all his children when they come."

"Oh," was all Brienne could manage. It was an agreeable answer, yet the image of Rurik siring babes with some faceless woman pricked her not a little.

The man was indeed magnificent. Women must fall at his feet. She denied that it discomfited her and, instead, pondered his words, *when they come*. Evidently, he had fathered no children thus far—at least none beknownst to him.

As his rich voice mingled with Brother Bernard's gravelly tones, she slid her eyes over Rurik unobserved, and for a fleeting moment envisioned those powerful arms enveloping her. She shook the thoughts free and berated herself for such folly. 'Twas sheer madness! This man was the offspring of her betrothed. Would she bed the father and lust after the son? And if her heart be read, what fate would befall her people? Nay, she would guard well the portals of her heart and bury deep its key.

The entourage continued on for several hours until the light began to wane. As the camp was laid out, a controversy erupted between Rurik and Esternay over the location of the bridal tent. They argued heatedly, each in his own tongue, while Brother Bernard hopped about trying to interject his fatherly guidance. Brienne slipped away from the uncomfortable scene to seek Aleth, while the two mighty bucks thundered over the tender doe. At length, the tent was erected in the center of the small settlement, with a Norman guard to one side and a Frankish to the other.

Brienne and Aleth paid scant attention to the evening's simple fare. They were enormously happy to be off their mounts and wished only to stretch their limbs and move about the campfires. Leveque soon joined their aimless wandering, and the trio fell to sharing lighthearted complaints of life in the saddle. The knight pined for a well-laden table, and Aleth longed only for a soft cushion to ease her sorely abused posterior.

Seeming all innocence, Brienne guided her companions into the camp's Norman sector, regaling them with a rather spirited episode from her childhood. Her outward calm and grace of movement were won through sheer determination. Soon she would be baronne to these fierce warriors and, as such, would be entitled to the same loyalty they pledged to her husband. But 'twas their respect she would gain, and, yea, even a measure of affection. 'Twas essential if she was to be influential in her new role and not merely an ornament for her husband's arm. She dare not betray her deep-rooted terror.

Brienne smiled and nodded, observant to the smallest detail, as she and her companions made their way among the Normans. She marveled at the color of their hair, pale golds and vivid reds. They were a tall race, clean and well groomed, though the sight of a braided beard gave her pause. Their clothes were carefully tended, and she noted again the penchant for scarlet mantles. She had heard of the Norsemen's fondness for dress, and recalled tales of their taking the Christian baptism on repeated occasions only to procure the white baptismal garments.

She stopped to examine a bubbling kettle and watched as a flaxen-haired cook added chunks of dried fish, vegetables, and a smattering of herbs to the steaming broth. Small game quickly appeared on spits over the fires, while planks were assembled into makeshift tables and set with a variety of cheeses, butter, nuts, berries, and rounds of flatbread. Whatever their shortcomings, the Normans appreciated good provender and were far less Spartan in their travels than Lord Robert. The man offered Brienne a sampling of the festive board and, before she parted, supplied a handful of slender carrots for Candra.

Aleth and Leveque stood a short distance apart, captivated by a game of draughts. Brienne studied the intent faces of the players and onlookers, and thought better of disturbing their concentration. Quietly, she withdrew and headed toward the horses with her sweet offering.

As Brienne approached the animals, she heard a beautifully deep voice humming an unfamiliar tune. Rurik, stripped bare to the waist, stepped from behind the great black stallion, totally engrossed in the care of his steed.

Brienne watched in unabashed fascination as his muscles flexed and rippled with each movement. Never had she seen the like.

Rurik stopped abruptly and whirled round. He released his breath at the sight of her and smiled disarmingly.

"Gott kvöld."

Brienne swallowed hard, her cheeks flaming. "I . . . I was just . . . going . . . Candra. . . ." She gestured toward the white, dismayed momentarily that she could not make herself understood. "My horse . . . I have carrots . . . see?" She held them forth. Then, embarrassed as much by his nakedness as by her stammering, she stepped quickly away and hastened to Candra's side.

Several moments passed before she could breathe evenly again. What magic did Rurik work to affect her so? Candra nudged her, greedy for the promised delicacies. Brienne started to rub the palfrey's muzzle and coo soothingly when she felt a presence towering over her and warm breath caressing her shoulder. She straightened, tingling, and turned somewhat unsteadily.

"My lord, I—"

She gave a small cry as she lifted her soft violet gaze and was entrapped in the black depths of Esternay's eyes. A passion raged there, intense and hungering.

"Brienne," he whispered huskily, "so brave . . . so pure . . . so very beautiful." He brushed aside a tendril of hair and stroked her cheek. "I will not abandon you to a life with these heathens. Trust me."

His fingers traced down the smooth column of her neck and paused at the silken swell of her breast. She froze under his touch but he took no notice and bent to her ear. "There is a way." His breath fell hot and heavy as he pressed his lips beneath her delicate jaw.

Brienne heard the harsh sound of stone scraping on metal and caught sight of Rurik sharpening his sword. A cold, bitter smile curled his lips. Esternay drew himself up, scowling blackly, while Brienne seized the moment to extricate herself from her embarrassing position. Catching up her skirts, she darted past Lord Robert and rushed for the safety of her tent.

The knight sneered. "She'll never succumb to your kind, Norman. She belongs in a Frankish bed." He gave a small, derisive snort and strode away.

Rurik watched after him, sharpening his sword with long even strokes. He had expected treachery, though his counsel went unheeded. The Seigneur d'Esternay's duplicity was predictable. The knight held a personal interest, after all, as the heiress's brother-by-marriage. But it was the implication of Brienne's actions that troubled Rurik most. He had not anticipated that the bride would share in that deception and castigated himself for being so beguiled by the woman.

Uppermost in his mind was the nature of Esternay's and Brienne's alliance. He could not quite grasp their game. During the marriage negotiations, the Frankish envoy disclosed that Beaumanoir's eldest daughter resided in a religious community at Levroux, having been there for nearly a decade. Lyting witnessed her there and assured Atli that she was an acceptable bride. He made no remark upon her person, nor did he praise her as being fair of face. Oddly, with a sparkle in his eye that was not lost on Rurik, he urged that coin be spared to gown the new baronne, stating that she had been reduced to the meanest of attire, unbefitting her new station.

But Brienne was uncommonly beautiful and exquisitely robed, more like a *lagskona,* a lover, than a cloistered maid. *Lagskona!* The word jolted him. Rurik's mind flew back to earlier that day when first they met. Was she not forward, boldly appraising him till Esternay exploded in a fit of jealousy? Then there was the knight's undisguised appetite for the woman. Was it possible that Brienne, in truth, was not Beaumanoir's daughter but the Frank's paramour?

White-hot anger blazed through him, and he stabbed his blade into the ground with a mighty thrust. His chest heaved as he fought down foul images of lovers entwined. Yet in his mind's eye, Brienne's form refused to clarify itself and play the scarlet vixen.

Rurik pulled loose the sword, reconsidering. Brienne had valiantly defended the villagers without regard to herself. Then, too, there was Bolsgar. The man undoubtedly recognized the maid and bore her genuine respect. If Brienne *was* the heiress, would she bed her sister's husband?

Rurik frowned and resheathed his sword. His arguments were running full circle, devouring one another till they scarce made sense at all. He vowed to lay bare the truth this night and be done with it. There was one who could be trusted.

Brother Bernard quaffed down a liberal measure of amber liquid, then sighed contentedly as the last effects of the dusty, travel-worn day were cleansed away. The heady brew was undoubtedly one of the more commendable achievements of the Nordic brethrens. An unsuppressed belch gave credence to his thoughts.

"I see you have a taste for Norman beer." Rurik's shadow fell across the stout monk, a wide grin splitting his face. "But, tell me, have you sampled this fair beauty?" He held aloft an unusual flask of azure glass fitted with an ornate silver closure. "A temptress from the courts of Byzantium."

"Ah, my son, have you not heard? I am a celibate man." His sea-green eyes danced beneath unkempt brows.

"Then we must remedy your sad condition at once." Rurik crouched down and produced two carved cups. "But be warned—she is a potent wench."

"A devil-woman, eh? Females are a deceptive lot, are they not."

"Precisely my concern."

Chapter Five

❖ ❖ ❖ ❖ ❖ ❖ ❖ ❖ ❖ ❖ ❖ ❖

RURIK WINCED AT the light of day and cupped his tender head in two large, sun-bronzed hands. Spying a bucket of water in the corner of the tent, he moved gingerly from his pallet and doused his head. The startling iciness brought him instantly to his feet, gasping sharply and groping blindly about for a cloth.

Throaty laughter erupted nearby.

Rurik opened one eye and peered through his dripping locks at the bemused face of Ketil Blunt-nose, thrust through the flap of his tent.

"You're a wretched sight." A toothy grin spread beneath the man's decidedly flat nose, obviously resculpted numerous times since birth. "Wasn't sure what mischief you were about when I found you outside the bridal tent last night, smiling like a besotted pup. Brought you here before you could disgrace yourself."

Rurik ignored the jovial giant and grunted. "Feels like Thor has taken his hammer, Mjollnir, to my skull."

Ketil clapped him soundly on the back, chuckling as the younger man groaned in misery. " 'Tis good that you can feel at all. I've heard sorrowful tales of those who abuse that cursed brew you were swilling. And with a holy man, no less! Have you not heard? We've taken the Christian baptism whilst you were away."

"Don't be fooled by his cross, friend. The monk's capacity rivals your own."

"Indeed?" Ketil stroked the flaming red hair fringing his battle-scarred face. "A man worth the acquaintance."

"Later. First, I would have that bundle I entrusted to you."

"The brooches? But I have not yet put the runes to them. Are they not for Katla?"

"She has many baubles already and I have others. Atli bid me choose a welcoming gift for his bride, and the brooches will suit her well."

Ketil nodded thoughtfully. "They are a fitting ornament for one so fair. Does she find favor with you, then?"

Rurik smiled to himself, recalling the evening's exchange with Brother Bernard.

After several rounds of the fiery drink, Rurik had inquired of the heiress's journey from Levroux, then discreetly questioned her reception of the marriage offer. Refilling their vessels, he probed more pointedly, seeking to verify Brienne's true identity and unveil her motives for accepting wedlock with his father.

When he dared suggest that there was something unseemly, perhaps even intimate about her relationship with Esternay, the monk came out of his cups, hurling a score of slurred oaths and waving his little sword about in feeble defense of the lady's besmirched virtue. Rurik had to sacrifice the remainder of the flask to calm the outraged man, who had then proceeded to relate a most remarkable, albeit somewhat incoherent tale of the beautiful maid.

Rurik's smile broadened as he envisioned Brienne boldly defying the Frankish Knight. "A Beaumanoir to the last," the churchman had proclaimed, "full of spit and fire. No fainthearted damsel, that one. Nay, she spurned the king's champion and bore his wrath upon that tender frame. . . ." The clouded reference was lost in a trail of mutterings as the monk drained his cup.

It pleased Rurik enormously that he had so misjudged Brienne. He shifted his attention back to Ketil, who eyed him speculatively.

"Let us say that the night's revelations are well worth my present discomfort. Now, if you will stop gawking and bring me the parcel, Brother Bernard undoubtedly requires assistance this morn." Rurik pulled on a fawn-colored jerkin. "And I have need of his skilled tongue."

*   *   *

"Hurry, Brienne! The Norman approaches."

Brienne stepped quickly past Aleth and slipped a glance through the tent flap. Rurik stood several paces away, his broad back facing her as he gestured to someone in the distance.

"Quickly, Aleth." She motioned to the coffer that stood open against the tent's thin wall. "Sister's medicant."

Aleth snatched up a small earthen pot and deftly smoothed its contents over the discolored bruise that marred Brienne's jawline. " 'Tis nearly gone. None will notice."

Brienne emitted a small sigh. 'Twould do no good to draw attention to the matter, she thought. 'Twas her sharp tongue that won the knight's token. Sister Ursuline cleverly concocted a curative, a cream tinted with flesh-colored pigment, to conceal the telltale marks and hasten the healing.

" 'Tis a shame we are unable to apply this balm to your arms, but the stain it bears would ruin your gowns," Aleth remarked, completing her ministrations.

Brienne nodded, remembering Lord Robert's viselike grip as he dragged her from the scullery and hurled her to the floor of her cell. Ugly discolorations had appeared, creating perfect imprints of his powerful fingers. In truth, those were far more unsightly than the blemish she suffered upon her face, but at least her arms were easily covered.

Brienne adjusted her deep blue tunic and secured the falcon-crested girdle about her slim hips.

"Wait!" Aleth draped the *couvre-chef* over Brienne's crown of braids. "There be no horses betwixt the two of you now, and you may find yon Northman but a hair's breadth apart. The scarf will help hide our handiwork."

Aleth made a slight adjustment to the drape of the scarf, bobbed her head in approval, then swept open the tent's portal. Before Brienne could move, Aleth stumbled backward, trampling Brienne's toes.

"Sweet Jesu!" she gasped, crossing herself swiftly.

Brienne followed Aleth's gaze to a giant of a man with flaming red hair. He dwarfed his companion, Brother Bernard, whose eyes surprisingly matched the giant's fiery mane.

Brienne swallowed and, tugging along the gaping Aleth, willed her leaden feet forward.

A movement caught the corner of her eye, and she turned to see Rurik. The bitter smile of yestereve was banished to some distant plane. Now his eyes crinkled in amusement at her anxious regard of his rugged friend. Rurik's high spirits amazed Brienne, her curiosity mounting as he retrieved a small bundle from the giant and slipped away the wrappings.

"By your leave, my lady," said the monk, his voice more gritty than usual. "Atli honors your forthcoming marriage to him with this small offering."

Resting in Rurik's hands were two golden brooches, large convex ovals covered with lavish decoration.

"They are exquisite," she breathed, lifting one brooch and examining its extraordinary craftsmanship. Finely wrought threads of gold swirled vivaciously over the surface, twisting and knotting and coiling in the vigorous patterns so beloved by the Norse. Brienne fingered the pearllike grains of gold encrusting the design. Truly, the work was without equal. A pin was cleverly hidden beneath the shell of the brooch, and Brienne thought, as she reversed the ornament and cradled it in her hand, that it resembled a small, elegant bowl.

Brienne smiled her pleasure. The brooches were chosen with great care and cost. In truth, they seemed more a gift of Rurik than the faceless Atli, for the few personal adornments he wore rivaled the brooches by their own magnificence.

The large buckle at his waist was embellished with a riot of gold filigree and granulation, and was further enhanced with five sizable garnets. His spiral arm rings were fashioned from ropes of silver twisted over themselves. Closer inspection revealed them to be serpents entwined, their heads gleaming with small emerald-chip eyes. Even his sword was unsurpassed, its pommel bearing beak-headed creatures and the silver hilt chased with ribbons of black niello.

Perhaps a woman's logic hath no reason, but in her heart of hearts she knew: 'twas Rurik who selected her gift and none other.

Violet eyes met blue steel and the day seemed a little brighter, the sun shone a little warmer, and the world was

yet more beautiful. Suddenly, she wished to please him in
some small way.

"Aleth, search my coffer for the scarlet mantle." Her
eyes sparkled. "I would show the brooches to their best
advantage."

Hours later, the entourage picked its way over the rolling countryside. Rurik was ever near, and Brienne's only
encounter with Lord Robert was when she received a scath-
ing glance for displaying the Nordic finery so prominently
upon her person. She counted it a small triumph that her
gesture goaded the knight, for she remained sorely pricked
by the liberties he had taken with her the night before.

Brienne slid her fingers over the golden brooch securing
her cloak. A Norsewoman's attire required two brooches,
explained Brother Bernard, thus she was gifted with a
matching pair. 'Twas disappointing that her Frankish dress
could utilize only one of the splendid ornaments at a time.

As a village appeared in the distance, Rurik drew Brienne
to the front of the column, setting her at his side. Again, the
villagers clamored to greet Valsemé's heiress. This time, no
swords were drawn and the soldiers kept their distance as the
crowd thronged around Brienne.

Outwardly, the Frankish lands seemed unchanged by
their new Norman masters. But it was here, among
the people, that the transformation was most apparent.
Flaxen-haired babes clung to their mothers' gowns, while
strong Frankish youths were strangely absent, having sought
their fortunes apart from Normandy. Along the fringes of
the crowd stood the newest inhabitants of the village, tall
fair-haired Northmen, silently observing the unaccountable
scene before them.

The villeins engaged Brienne with their praises and peti-
tions. As she leaned down to receive a small garland, her
hand was gripped painfully.

"Save yourself, my lady! Flee to the winds!" a woman
cried out, her eyes red and swollen. "No maid is safe from
these rutting boars."

The woman's face crumpled then, and she began to sob
in earnest.

"My daughter . . . my only child. Ravished she was, and her father cut down when he sought to protect her." The woman shook her head mournfully. "The swine carried her away and now my husband lies dying from the bite of a Norse blade." With renewed vigor she grabbed Brienne's arm once more. "Save yourself if you can!"

Brienne cast the distraught woman a sharp look. "Where lies your husband?"

The woman pointed toward a mean hut. "God have mercy, I aided him best I could, but his leg be gashed clear to the bone and filled with infection. He rages with fever and knows me not at all."

Without hesitation, Brienne dismounted and pressed through the crowd.

As she paused on the portal of the one-room dwelling, a foul stench assailed her nostrils. Determinedly, she caught up her mantle to her face and crossed to the thrashing form on the pallet.

The man clutched blankets about him as though he were whipped by an icy wind, yet his flesh was ablaze with fever. He tossed wildly from side to side and fought imaginary creatures in his delirium.

Brienne struggled to free the covers from his grasp, ducking a fraction too late as he lashed out at an unseen specter and next found herself sprawled on the dirt floor.

Strong hands lifted her from behind and set her to her feet.

She turned and swayed into Rurik's expansive chest. He steadied her, concern etching his face, and she thought she would swoon again as his powerful arms tightened protectively about her.

It seemed an eternity before he released her, though scarcely a moment had passed. Rurik moved quickly to the pallet and held down the bedeviled man, allowing Brienne to draw back the blankets. If her fingers trembled, it came not from the grim sight that greeted her.

A viscous yellowish substance oozed through the man's leg wrappings, its putrid odor near choking her. By contrast, the bandages binding his side appeared clean and unsullied.

Brienne regained her concentration and wheeled round to the woman who stood wringing her hands and bemoaning her misfortune.

"Build the fire and set water to boiling, then get my woman, Aleth," Brienne ordered briskly.

Unclasping the brooch, she shrugged off her mantle, folded it and set it aside. She pulled away the head scarf, freed her girdle, and slipped the fine tunic over her head.

Rurik's gaze followed her comely form about the room as she busied herself gathering clean cloths and inspecting the contents of various pots and jars sitting near the hearth.

He was momentarily transfixed as Brienne stepped before the fire, unaware that her slender limbs were plainly silhouetted through the thin fabric of her chemise. He was further taxed when she bent to set her eating knife in the flames, her full round breasts shifting perilously above the bodice and threatening to overflow their confines.

His grip tightened on the feverish man as he fought down the urge to lay the maid on her backside and sample the feast she so unwittingly set before him. Thor, but she tested him sorely! Brienne raised her violet eyes just then and smiled her thanks for his help. Rurik nearly groaned aloud.

Aleth's appearance was a welcome distraction, and Rurik hoped his torture was at an end. Ketil followed closely on her heels, bearing several small pouches. It was an odd sight, the massive Norseman hovering about the frail, limping girl. There seemed no need for words as Ketil did Aleth's bidding and laid the little bags on a small trestle near the hearth.

The two women quickly set about mixing their poultices, while Ketil moved to relieve Rurik. Cloths were added to the steaming kettle and Brienne selected herbs from the pouches and crumbled them into goose grease. She tested several knives that she discovered among the kitchen implements, but found them dull and unusable. Before she could brood further over the matter, Rurik offered his own sharp blade.

Settling down at the foot of the pallet, Brienne motioned Rurik to hold the man's leg. Carefully, she cut away the bandages and laid open the festering wound. They were assaulted anew with the sickening stench of fouled flesh.

The leg was swollen to thrice its usual size, the mottled skin drawn so taut it appeared it would split open. The laceration ran long and deep, disgorging a vile fluid, while angry red streaks snaked outward. Gently, Brienne probed the gash. Rurik marveled at her calm and sense of purpose. Where another maiden might swoon or cry out at the repulsive sight, Brienne flinched not at all but bent silently to the task.

A moment later, Brienne sat back on her heels, uncertainty clouding her features as she addressed the woman. "I can save your husband, but I am not so certain of his leg."

The hours passed slowly. The soldiers had long since been ordered to dismount, while inside the hut steaming cloths were applied again and again to draw the poisons from the corrupted limb. When Brienne was satisfied, the wound was painstakingly cleansed with herbal waters. All the while, she relied on Rurik's and Ketil's strength to keep the man immobile. At last she called for needle and thread, and meticulously stitched the tissue closed.

The maid was like no other, Rurik decided as he watched Brienne labor. She rivaled the beauties from the Northern fjords to the court of Byzantium. Yet for all her loveliness and aristocratic blood, she did not turn from the unsavory, but plied her skills with care and compassion for the simplest of men. He knew many elegant and high-flown women, yet none demonstrated such selfless generosity or courage of heart.

Brienne packed the leg with a hot poultice and wrapped it in fresh linens. The side wound proved less troublesome but required a quick searing to safeguard it from infection.

After a seemingly interminable length of time, she rose unsteadily, her legs threatening to cramp. She left Aleth spooning broth into the man and instructed the woman at length in the proper ministration of the wound. With careful attendance and the grace of time, the leg would be whole again.

"But . . . my daughter—" the woman pleaded as Brienne turned to gather up her medicants. The girl's sorrowful plight was retold and a name placed to her abductor. "May the pox take him!" the woman spat.

Exhaustion swept over Brienne, but she drew herself up.
"I will do what I can."

Stepping to the doorway, she beckoned Brother Bernard
inside the dwelling.

"The Northman Thord Thorolfsson has carried off this couple's only daughter. Her father sought to save her but. . . ."
She gestured to the man on the pallet. "Tell Rurik that if our
people are to meld, justice must begin here, today. Tell him,
nay, ask him," she sighed heavily, "to set this affair aright."

The monk consulted with him briefly, then gave Brienne
a half smile.

"Rurik would know if you intend to mend all the ills of
Normandy."

She lifted her delicate chin and met Rurik's assessing gaze.
"Where I can."

His features softened then, and to her amazement he slipped
off one of the precious silver arm rings and presented it to the
woman. The words that followed were firm and filled with
authority. She looked to Brother Bernard for their meaning.

"Rurik vows that the man Thord will be found and compelled to either marry the girl or return her to her family.
He offers the ring as a bride-price should the two wed, and
a *wergild* should they not, to compensate for the girl's lost
virginity."

The woman found the judgment more than fair, and having
never possessed such wealth at any one time, she deemed
the armlet a rich restitution indeed. She thanked Rurik and
Brienne profusely for their many kindnesses.

Finding the heat of the room unbearable, Brienne left
Aleth and Ketil to gather up the unused medicants and her
discarded clothing. As she passed through the door, she
caught up a clean linen and began wiping away the fine
film of moisture that covered her face.

Rurik joined Brienne as she stepped into the fresh air and
sunlight. She was well pleased with his sense of justice and
turned to him, intending to bestow a most dazzling smile.
But as she looked up, withdrawing the cloth from her face,
his features went rigid.

Her heart pounded wildly. What had she done? How had
she displeased him? His gaze dropped to the cloth, and their

eyes locked over the flesh-colored stain.

Her hand flew to her face but Rurik was upon her, intent on examining the bruise spread across her jaw. He grasped her by the arms, but she cried out in pain and tried desperately to wrench away. A muscle flexed in his jaw as he rapidly debated her ailment. His knife appeared in his hands, and in the next instant he slit her sleeve wide from wrist to shoulder.

Anger coiled within him as the fabric fell away. Multiple bruises marred her creamy skin. He swung her round, set on baring her other arm.

"Nay!" Brienne struggled with him. "Wouldst you shred all my garments to satisfy yourself? It matters not. 'Tis done."

Rurik stared at the discolorations, striving to recall the monk's ramblings of the night past. Soberly, he lifted steely eyes and sought the offender.

Esternay, who was standing at a distance, straightened his stance and shifted his hand to his sword hilt, the unspoken gesture giving testimony to the deed.

Rurik's voice boomed loudly for all to hear, and Brienne did not miss the harshness of his clipped words. When Brother Bernard conveyed the message, he seemed more than a little pleased, echoing each word as it was given as though he were delivering his own personal admonishment.

"There are those who ill use their positions and abuse their duties of wardship. I am not so careless. Any amongst you who would bring harm to Valsemé's lady will know a Norseman's justice."

With that, Rurik drew Brienne along with him. He saw to it that one of the village matrons put needle to thread and mended Brienne's sleeve. The task complete, he called for their mounts and lifted her easily to Candra's back.

Rurik paused for a moment, his hands lingering about her small waist. For the first time in many years, Brienne felt completely safe.

With the day half spent, the escort pressed on as long as they dared, for it promised to be a moonless night. As the sun began its descent, camp was pitched near a favorable river that bent wide and deep around a wooded finger of land. Rurik anticipated refreshing himself in the cool, inviting waters and was well pleased with the site. Brother Bernard, however, argued against the location, warning that Frank and Norman had clashed here in living memory. He feared it to be an ill portent indeed.

A pace of time later, Brienne and Aleth settled beneath a leafy elm, each with a small piece of handwork. Rurik sat nearby, propped against an outcropping of rock, and carved a block of wood.

Patch reveled in his freedom, romping to and fro betwixt the women and the man. Spying the bright threads spread on the ground by Aleth, he snatched at the skeins and dragged them into a tangle before she could retrieve them. Aleth scolded him roundly, and he scurried away to nuzzle Rurik. The Norman chuckled at the pup's antics and engaged him in a game of fetch.

Brienne was struck with wonder. Since departing the village, Rurik had never left her unattended. Either he or Ketil was ever present. A small smile curved her lips, and Brienne warmed herself in the knowledge that somehow she pleased him.

Patch scampered off after the scent of something that, no doubt, would prove larger than himself. Brienne watched as Rurik took up his carving again and began shaping the wood with his knife, the same knife he had put to her sleeve earlier.

She took several tiny stitches in the kerchief she worked, and attempted to follow Aleth's small talk, but her attention repeatedly strayed to Rurik. All at once, she stabbed her forefinger with the sharp needle. Muttering, she dropped her threads and fabric and thrust the injured member into her mouth.

"He is a fine stallion of a man, is he not?" Aleth grinned. Brienne blinked at such boldness from her friend.

"Why, you cannot keep your eyes from him!" Aleth laughed gaily, then leaned forward. "Does he fill your dreams as oft as he fills your waking thoughts?" she teased mercilessly.

"Aleth, hush! He will hear."

She gave a light shrug. "He does not understand our tongue,

lest you make it so plainly obvious by your concern. Now, confess. Is not the man most wondrously made?"

"Oui, oui," Brienne conceded. "He is most attractive."

"Attractive?"

"Very well, magnificent. If I tell you true, will you cease this badgering?"

Aleth nodded expectantly and wriggled closer.

Brienne thought to tease Aleth in kind, but when she glimpsed Rurik's marvelous profile and bright mane, her heart swelled.

"He is the most glorious specimen of manhood I have ere laid eyes upon," she avowed, "even in my dreams. There, are you satisfied?"

But Aleth did not hear, her attention being engaged elsewhere. "Would it be so wrong to love a Northman?" she wondered aloud.

"What an incredible question. Long have I thought you overstayed your time in your solar. Now I am certain of it."

" 'Tis true." Aleth gave a small shrug but did not look away from what intrigued her so. "Before coming to Levroux I knew nothing of the world save my tower room."

"Aleth, what *are* you saying?"

"My father could not abide the sight of me. 'Twas more than my twisted leg. My birthing took my sweet mother's life, and that he could not forgive. He set me away from him."

"Dear Aleth." Brienne grasped her hand. "How cruel."

Her tears spent long ago, Aleth smiled dry-eyed. "But I was allowed companions, and one cousin, Blanche, came often. She was of a similar age and cheery disposition. As we grew older, she fell in love," Aleth recalled wistfully. "And when she didst speak of him, her face glowed and she would smile to her very soul. He was born to a station beneath her, but she did not seem to count it. One evening she visited with me quite late. Never had I seen her more radiant. The next morning, Blanche was not to be found, for she had flown with her lover."

Aleth's smile widened. "My father thought I aided her escape, and in his anger he removed me to the abbey. He did not know what a great kindness he dealt me. Ah, but can you imagine such a love"—she sighed and clasped her arms about her—"to cross all boundaries and mount all obstacles to gain one's heart's desire?"

Brienne nodded silently, remembering her own fantasies, long exiled.

"Should birthright and position matter so very much," Aleth argued, "or age, or bearing, or from what land one springs? Does not love transcend all?" She turned to Brienne, her face very serious. "If you could have your heart's desire, what manner of man would gain your devotion?"

Brienne pondered the question, her eyes shining softly as they alighted upon the golden man. "If his heart be true . . . if he be honest, loyal, and caring . . . then I would grant that man more love than he could possibly conceive." Rurik raised intense blue eyes to her velvet gaze. "And I would love that man until the end of time."

Brienne and Rurik held each other's eyes till, at length, Brienne shook herself from her reverie and dropped her lashes. "But my dreams are ashes upon the hearth. My fate is sealed. I cannot allow such passions to tempt me from my purpose, for above all else, there is duty."

She clenched her lower lip between her teeth and did not see Rurik move away.

The fading light glinted off the water as it rippled and ruffled and coursed merrily on its way. Rurik skittered a pebble across the flowing current and watched it disappear beneath the surface.

Brienne's nearness disarmed him, and he feared there would come a time when he could no longer hold rein on himself. For if truth be known, he burned for her. Somberly, he acknowledged that once his father and Brienne were joined in wedlock, he must remove himself from Valsemé.

He bent to loose his boot, and forced his thoughts to center on the soft rushing tones of the river, playing against the night.

"Come, Aleth. Let us refresh ourselves." Brienne gathered her sewing and rose. "I am told that we are free to use the left bend of the river. The Normans confine themselves to

the right, beyond the peninsula, and it is all well wooded."
She stretched lightly. "The day has left me sorely in need of
pampering." She smiled and helped Aleth to her feet.

Brienne was not surprised that Ketil followed, or that
several of Lord Robert's men were already posted along the
"Frankish" side of the river. She and Aleth pushed through
the concealing brush that lined the shore, leaving the men
eyeing one another warily.

Brienne set aside her tunic and loosened her hair. She
grimaced at the sight of her soiled chemise. Debating how
best to deal with the stains, she simply stepped into the water,
gown and all.

" 'Tis easier this way, methinks," she called with a laugh
before Aleth could reprimand her.

She scrubbed the hem against itself and, pleased with the
results, stepped deeper into the river and began working at
the side of the gown. Suddenly she lost her footing, falling
with a splash upon her backside.

Thoroughly soaked, she struggled to stand but found the
garment impossibly heavy and encumbering. She worked at
the lacings and at last freed herself from its imprisoning
folds, stripping herself bare to the skin. She heaved the
sopping mess at the shore, then sank back into the river.

The water was deliciously brisk and invigorating. She
swam out a small distance, delighting in her newfound freedom. It had been ages since she had frolicked with such
abandon. At Valsemé there was a small hidden lake where
she, Lisette, and Thomas would steal away for countless
hours of untold joy. Her brother taught her how to keep
herself afloat and stroke the water. 'Twas a shame that the
sport was so ill favored, but most considered it unhealthful.
Nonetheless, she would not be dissuaded. She relished the
pastime too greatly to deny herself the pleasure.

Brienne flipped over, allowing the water to buoy her up.
The light had grown quite dim now, and she did not fear
any would see. She rested, floating peacefully, her long hair
spreading out and swirling about her.

"Brienne, not too far!" Aleth called out.

"Aleth, you worry like an old woman!" she tossed back.
"We are heavily guarded." She kicked away, still floating on

her back, and moved steadily toward the projection of land.
"I have a mind to look for roots and herbs."

"Brienne!" Aleth called again. "Have a care!"

Brienne smiled at Aleth's concern, hoping she would not
fret herself overmuch on her account. As Brienne neared the
finger of land, she closed her eyes and drifted contentedly.
Indeed, she thought, this was a little corner of heaven.

Brienne floated languidly, listening to the sounds of the river.
Suddenly, she collided with something quite solid and was
swept beneath the water, at once becoming entangled with
she knew not what. She pushed against the mass. Alarmingly, it moved and slid around her hips. Her blood ran cold, for
she had been warned of river serpents but always dismissed
the possibility of their existence.

It moved again, and she thrashed wildly to free herself of
the creature. Abruptly, it fell away. She fought to regain the
surface, but the thing set upon her once more. She kicked
out desperately, but it ensnared her leg. Panic shot through
her as something clamped firmly about each arm and dragged
her upward.

Water sluiced off her body as she broke through the surface. A figure loomed above her, silhouetted against the faint
light. She attempted to scream but managed only a croak
before a hand descended over her mouth, then, shockingly,
her soft naked form was molded against hardened muscle.

"Shhh. Do not be afraid. I will not harm you," the rich
voice warned with the barest hint of an accent.

Liquid fire raced through Brienne as she recognized her
captor.

Rurik scanned the shore, then drew his beautiful captive
along with him to where the land was swallowed by shadows.
Brienne offered no resistance, so stunned was she to hear him
speak her Frankish tongue.

" 'Twould be dangerous to be found together like this,
ástin mín. Did no one warn you that my men are bathing
in this part of the river?"

With a start, Brienne realized how far off course she had
drifted, and that the Normans were much closer than she
imagined.

"I would not have blood shed for this mistake," Rurik continued, "but I fear if we are found like this, your men would surely defend your honor, and mine would protect me . . . and"—he smiled wryly—"I doubt my father would ever understand."

Brienne glanced downward to where her breasts pressed against his furred chest. She was mortified to discover his bare hip beneath her hand, and her leg entwined with his. She squirmed against him, then gasped as she inadvertently brushed his manhood. He chuckled and released her.

Brienne sank into the river, her cheeks burning, and drew her long hair protectively about her.

"You speak our language," she accused. "Why did you deceive us?"

" 'Twas not my intent to mislead you," he assured her. "Most of my men do not speak your tongue, and I prefer they know all that passes. I use only Norse in their presence, though I know many tongues."

Brienne's eyes seemed enormous in the dark. Rurik reached out to gently trace the lines of her face.

"Did you mean what you said?"

Brienne stiffened, realizing for the first time that Rurik had understood every word of her conversation with Aleth. They had behaved outrageously, admiring him so blatantly. She scoured her mind, seeking her precise words.

"Earlier, at the village, you said our people must meld," Rurik reminded her.

"*O-Oui*," she near sighed in relief. "Brother Bernard has much to say on it."

He seemed to consider this carefully.

"And the rest . . . did you mean the rest of what you said?"

"I scarcely recall what I . . ." She prayed that he understood little of what he overheard.

"That if a man's heart be true, if he be honest. . . ."

She flushed. "That was a private conversation."

"Did you mean it?" He drew her gently against him, and as the warmth of their bodies met, she lost the thread of her thoughts. "Could you grant such a love, Brienne, whoever be the man?"

She nodded breathlessly, thrilling to his masculine touch and the sound of her name on his lips.

"Until the end of time?"

"Until the end of time," she repeated in a whisper, heart pounding. Her eyes fastened on his lower lip.

She thought he would kiss her then, but his fingers tightened and something flickered across his eyes. He released his breath sharply at some unknown frustration and, almost regretfully, set her apart.

"I wish you well with my father," he said determinedly, then turned and began to move away.

Brienne ached with the emptiness she suddenly felt and, shamelessly, could not bear to have him leave.

"If he be anything like the son, I shall be well pleased."

Rurik stilled at her words, and it seemed that he strained at some great thing, his every muscle taut. He lifted his face heavenward and clenched his hands.

Filial honor warred with fierce primitive desire. He willed himself to leave her, but his traitorous body turned back, demanding one last glance to fill his dreams.

The last glimmer of the day's light fell across the beauteous maid. She had risen partially from the water, her wet tangle of ebony hair not concealing her as wholly as she believed. One full breast eluded the mass of hair completely, while a silken hip curved seductively from the small waist and disappeared beneath the dark waters. The sight of her was his undoing.

Brienne's heart turned over as Rurik's hungering passion burst through the thick walls of restraint. He swept her into his arms, his mouth crushing down on hers. He was like a man starved and she the feast.

Brienne's lips parted under the assault, and his tongue plunged into that honeyed chamber, seeking its sweet nectar, teasing her to dizzying heights, setting her aflame in a swirling vortex of emotions.

He deepened his kiss and, God forgive her, she leaned into him and, wrapping her arms about him, she answered that fevered quest.

Suddenly her world fell away and time ceased its passage. There was neither Norman nor Frank. Nor kings with their decrees, nor knights with their honor, nor lands, titles, nor duties. There was only Rurik . . . forever Rurik . . . now and for all time . . . her magnificent golden warrior.

He splayed his hands over her hips and pressed her to him. She felt the fiery brand of his passion against her thigh, but there was no thought to object, for she was lost.

His mouth left hers and trailed fiery kisses down her neck and trapped the rosy crest of one soft breast. She moaned in her throat as he swirled his tongue over the taut nipple in exquisite torture. Hot shivers of pleasure coursed through her to some hidden place between her thighs.

He captured her lips once again as his hand slipped lower, seeking the sweet nest of her desire.

"Brienne!" Aleth's voice rang out in the gathering darkness. "Brienne, where are you?"

Rurik groaned and painfully pulled away, keeping Brienne firmly in the circle of his arms.

"Here, Aleth." Her voice sounded strange to her ears. "Just a moment longer."

Rurik's warm breath fell against her cheek, and when she looked up, his eyes were shut tightly as he struggled to master himself. Laying her head against his chest, she listened to the rapid rhythm of his heart and knew it kept pace with her own.

Rurik lifted Brienne's face to his and looked at her longingly, dragging his thumb across her kiss-swollen lips.

"Þu ert unaðsfögur. You are so very beautiful."

He released her then and moved deeper into the river. This time he did not look back, but dove neatly under the water and disappeared.

Brienne held her breath till he resurfaced at a distance and stroked for shore.

"Brienne, have you taken leave of yourself?" Aleth called. "Come away, or I shall call out the entire guard!"

"No need," Brienne called absently, as Rurik disappeared into the night.

Come what may, she would long remember the touch of his flesh on hers.

Chapter Six
✖ ✖ ✖ ✖ ✖ ✖ ✖ ✖ ✖ ✖ ✖ ✖ ✖

BRIENNE ROSE IN the dimness of her tent, abandoning a fitful sleep, and pulled on her chemise. Carefully, she stepped around Aleth's sleeping form and recovered her mantle and brooch from the small chest that sat in the corner. She paused over the golden ornament, fingering its rich filigree, then pressed it to her cheek.

"Sweet Jesu," she whispered, "why have you awakened my heart to this man? So much happier was I to know nothing of the beauty and power of love than to taste its sweet promise and be forever denied."

Slowly, Brienne wrapped herself in her mantle and, holding the brooch to her heart, stepped from the tent and into the early-morning light.

Rurik kept his bridewatch a short distance apart and was in the midst of breaking his fast with Brother Bernard when Brienne emerged from her shelter. He rose at once.

They stood looking at one another for several moments, and Brienne ached for all that must remain unsaid. She crossed the space between them and stood before Rurik, oblivious of the stirrings in the camp.

Rurik slipped the brooch from her hands and fastened her cloak over her breast. "You rise early, my lady," he said quietly.

"Sleep would not come."

He nodded his understanding.

Brother Bernard cleared his throat purposefully, uneasy about the scene playing out before him and keenly aware of Rurik's use of the Frankish tongue. " 'Tis only natural, my child, for a bride to be restless on the day she will meet her future husband."

Pain glinted deep within Brienne's violet eyes. There it was, she reflected simply. Atli lay forever between them, she honor bound by her word and Rurik by his blood. Neither would she imperil her people nor he cuckold his father to appease their unsated passions.

Silence stretched out amongst them till Brother Bernard raked it with his gravelly voice, directing several comments in Norse to Rurik. Brienne smiled at last and thought to lighten the moment.

"There be no need to speak thusly, good brother. This great Norman understands our humble tongue perfectly well."

"That I know, but he indulges me the practice that I might sharpen my own skills."

"You know?"

"Aye." He glanced curiously from Rurik to Brienne. "But how didst you learn of his talents?"

Brienne's color rose at his choice of words, and she silently upbraided herself for not holding her tongue.

"I revealed myself," Rurik submitted chivalrously. "Lady Brienne became disoriented last evening and risked discovering my men bathing in the river."

Brienne gazed up, wide-eyed. Rurik spoke truly yet revealed nothing untoward or improper.

"Indeed?" Brother Bernard studied the two, sensing there was more to this tale, then decided to let the matter lie. "How fortunate for us all that you intercepted Lady Brienne. It could have proved a most indelicate situation."

"Most indelicate."

Ignoring the slight smile that accompanied Rurik's words and the quaver in Brienne's hands as she smoothed the edge of her mantle, Brother Bernard returned to his plate by the fire.

"Pray join us, my dear. Have you ever tasted *flatbrauð*? 'Tis a rye bread, tasty with cheese and herring."

Brienne declined with a shake of her head, grateful for an opportunity to excuse herself. "My herbs are sorely depleted, as I left a good sum with the village wife. I would replenish them whilst the morning is yet fresh, but please, finish break-

ing your fast. I shan't be far." Reassuringly, she gestured
with an upheld hand that they stay, then slipped away.

Rurik gazed thoughtfully after Brienne's retreating figure.
When he turned back, his companion was frowning into
his cup.

"Does something disturb you, churchman?"

The morning dew clung to the hem of Brienne's gown as
she brushed through the tender spring grasses and proceeded
toward the wooded finger of land projecting boldly into the
river. A smile played briefly over her lips as she surveyed
the shoreline where, but a few hours earlier, she reveled in
the magic of Rurik's touch. Aleth had the right of it more
than she knew. Rurik was indeed most wondrously made.

She drank in the sweet morning air and entered the grove
of trees rising majestically from the peninsula. The earth
proved soft beneath her feet as the grasses gave way to
denser growth.

With luck, the moist land would yield a few prized herbs,
mayhaps angelica, or eyebright. Brienne would count her
venture a great success if she could harvest fresh divisions
of comfrey to transfer to Valsemé. These could only be taken
in spring and autumn, and would form the mainstay of her
physic garden. No healer dare be long without the powerful
herb, for comfrey remedied a host of afflictions from fresh
cuts and wounds to ruptures, boils, and abscesses, and even
aided in the welding of broken bones.

Just then, Brienne spied delicate yellow flowers winking
from beneath a thicket of brambles. Celandine! Triumphant-
ly, she stooped down and separated the tangled growth.

Rurik quickened his pace, then fell into a light trot as Brienne
disappeared into the woods. The monk was right. He should
not have allowed her to wander so freely, much less unattended. Thor! What ailed him? If he did not trust himself
with her alone in a secluded glade, he should have sent Ketil
to watch over her in his stead.

Brienne's scream shattered the early-morning silence.

Unsheathing his sword, Rurik bolted into the woodland and
crashed through the thick undergrowth. In the next moment

he was upon her frozen figure. She stood rigid, her hands clasped over her mouth as she stared in horror at the ground before her.

Swiftly, Rurik placed himself between Brienne and the unseen menace, his weapon braced. He scanned the glade, but the object of Brienne's distress still eluded him. Throwing a glance back at her, he followed her panicked gaze to a tangled mass of vines and shrubbery.

Rurik crouched down and cautiously eased back the brush. Beneath lay a skeleton partially encased in the sodden earth, its bones blackened and moldy from the ravages of time. The tattered remnants of clothing proved the remains to be those of a Frankish soldier. The skull lay to one side, split wide into two gaping halves, proclaiming the handiwork of a Norse battle-ax.

Rurik probed the shredded garments, seeking something by which to identify the man, but all ornament and weapon had been scavenged long ago. Rising to Brienne's side, he sought to shelter her in the comfort of his arms, but she shrank back, her face as pale as moonstone.

Her fear gave way to shock as dark specters rose from the past. Once again the grim blade whirred before her eyes in a great and mighty arc. Then there was blood. Oh, so much blood. . . . And the devil smiled up at her, relishing the gruesome victory as though he drew life from death itself.

"Norseman," she hissed, her eyes wild as though seeing Rurik for the first time.

Frantically, she swung round and began to run from the scene, but her steps died at the sight of soldiers moving into the glade. She did not grasp that the men were hurrying to her aid, nor did she discern that there were Franks amongst them. Brienne fastened instead upon the barbarous fair-haired Northmen and knew terror.

A scream rose in her throat but found no voice. As one violent tremor after another racked through her, she managed to back away. Step by tormented step she retreated, her senses reeling. Then, with a startling burst of energy, she pivoted and flung herself forward. At once, she slammed against Rurik's chest, and he grasped her by the shoulders as her knees gave way.

"Brienne? Brienne!" He shook her gently, trying to bring her back to herself.

Esternay emerged in the wood just then. Witnessing the peculiar tableau, he snatched at the dagger in his belt, but a hand firmly stayed him from releasing the blade. Angrily, he scowled down into Brother Bernard's green eyes.

As the world came spinning to a halt, Brienne ceased her struggles and focused unsteadily on Rurik's handsome face. Anguish wrenched her heart anew.

"There is much blood between us," she whispered painfully, tears filling her eyes.

Aleth appeared in the grove, her hair streaming about her as she clutched a blanket over her thin chemise and limped hurriedly to Brienne's side. Reluctantly, Rurik gave Brienne over to the girl's care, conceding that his presence only added to her misery.

Perceiving her friend's distress, Aleth gathered Brienne close and silently led her away.

Esternay broke free of his unwanted guardian and strode forward to inspect the macabre relic in the underbrush. He drew himself up, glaring darkly at Rurik, then turned back to the monk. The sneering challenge in his voice was unmistakable.

"Churchman, a proper burial is in order for this unfortunate soldier. Tell this *heathen* that since Northmen took this man's life, 'tis only fitting that Northmen dig his grave."

"This *heathen*," Rurik bit out in the Frankish language, "will dig the grave himself." He snapped a curt order for his men to bring him a digging implement and left the knight gaping slack-jawed at his back.

Brother Bernard officiated brief rites over the grave, wisely forgoing any personal comment or form of eulogy. Brienne placed a small bouquet of yellow celandine on the fresh earth, and Ketil, to the surprise of all, marked the grave with a small cross he had quickly fashioned of linden wood.

The gesture did much to bridge the heightened tensions among the soldiers. Norman and Frank stood in silent homage, discrepant allies, joined in an uncertain brotherhood by the bonds of their oaths to sovereign, land, and faith. With the task complete, the troops departed without delay.

The day proved long and wearisome. Brienne rode shrouded in silence, drawn into herself, seemingly unconscious of her companions and surroundings. Rurik grew unsettled by her gravity and paleness. Would that he could break through the stony barrier of her quietude and storm the fortress imprisoning her heart. Esternay's recurring presence, however, forestalled his efforts time and again. The knight was like an accursed affliction.

The steep hills of the Perche gave way to the dense woodland, deep valleys, and brilliant green meadows of the Auge. As the cortege passed through small scattered villages, there were fewer and fewer villeins to greet Valsemé's heiress. Yet to those who came forth, she reached out from the depths of her pain, acknowledging their kindness and listening to all manner of complaint. Rurik watched her strained efforts, wishing earnestly that he could blot out her grief and restore some measure of happiness.

Late in the day, the entourage penetrated the baronial lands of Valsemé, pressing on till the light began to fade and the evening dew glistened upon the grasses.

Valsemé's keep suddenly loomed in the distance, rising from the motte and bailey like a lone sentinel. A thrill shot through Brienne as she beheld the staunch old friend from long past. Faint torchlight flickered from the slitted eyes of its windows as it kept vigilance over the countryside and, to Brienne's mind, welcomed her home.

Beyond, straw-thatched dwellings of wattle and daub sprouted across the landscape, while the church's silent bell tower lay silhouetted against the deepening skies. Brienne strained to make out the manor house, but it remained hidden in the shadows of nightfall. She prayed it stood whole.

Commanding the retinue to a halt, Rurik granted a brief respite, then dispatched messengers to announce their approach. He flicked a glance toward Esternay, then motioned to Ketil. Time was of the utmost. There were words that need be spoken before giving Brienne over to his father. Ketil would ensure their privacy.

"My lady," Rurik said as he appeared before her.

Somehow, Brienne knew he would seek her out, and when

he offered his arm, she did not resist but rested her hand atop
his own and allowed him to lead her away.

They proceeded to a small promontory overlooking the
vale and stood for a moment absorbed in silence. Brienne
held her back to Rurik, focusing on the slivers of firelight that
escaped beneath doors and through cracks of the windowless
cottages that lay beyond. But even her raw, tangled emotions
did nothing to quench the heat that swept through her or
the headiness wrought by his nearness. She trembled as he
brushed away a tendril of hair that had escaped the heavy
plait and curled against her neck.

"Brienne." His voice was rich velvet. "I cannot change
the past . . . or give you back that which is lost."

She bowed her head, pressing her lashes shut against the
painful memories gnawing at the edges of her heart.

"Brienne, Brienne, listen to me." He turned her gently
to him. "You have said it well yourself. Valsemé's future
is sown today. In time, the blood of our people will flow
as one."

She looked away, not wishing to think on duty or valor
or all the dismal tomorrows that stretched out hopelessly
before her.

Rurik stroked her cheek thoughtfully. "My father will be
pleased with you, of that I am sure. He is an impatient man
and ofttimes stubborn, but if you do not play him false, he
will treat you well and give heed to your wishes." Tilting
her face up to his, Rurik drew his thumb lightly across her
lips, sending fiery memories shivering through her.

"How often women are used to bind the divisions of
men," he observed quietly. "You, *ástin mín,* are the
friðarmóðir. The peace weaver."

Brienne lifted her large violet eyes as a tear slid over her
cheek and fell on Rurik's hand. His chest constricted. The
maid had slipped into his heart, and he had not felt such
stirrings in that well-guarded bastion for many a year. The
face of another dark-haired beauty flashed through his mind
and along with it the accustomed pain. But he could no more
traverse the netherworld to regain that which was lost to him
than alter Brienne's destiny as his father's bride. Silently, he
cursed the gods for their indifference.

*   *   *

Brienne's mind was in turmoil as the retinue clattered over the bridge, through the thick defense walls, and into the bailey.

This was not right. Why did Rurik lead them here and not through the village and on to the manor house? The keep was a refuge in time of siege, not a residence. It served as watchtower, arsenal, and storehouse, capable of sustaining Valsemé's inhabitants through emergencies. But 'twas unthinkable that anyone would wish to dwell in its cramped quarters when the comfort of the manor house lay beyond.

Of course, to men of the North, the imposing fortress would represent power, wealth, and indisputable authority. It had been an extravagant and stubborn gesture on her father's part, to build of lime, sand, and freestone when the forests were more easily exploited. Most castles were constructed of timber and earthworks. But Richard Beaumanoir, ever determined to prevail over his enemies, placed his faith and wealth in the enduring virtues of stone.

A full dozen Norman soldiers greeted them in the courtyard. Others quickly emerged from the various buildings that lined the fortress walls. Tension coiled in the pit of Brienne's stomach and she forced her attention to the great tower dominating the far end of the bailey. It rose majestically atop the massive, sloping mound of earth that was the motte.

Rurik dismounted swiftly and reached Brienne before Esternay could move from his saddle. Their eyes met and held as she braced her hands on his broad shoulders and he lifted her ever so gently from Candra's back. Her weight shifted against him, and for a moment he held her there aloft, the heat of their bodies branding one another in exquisite torment. He lowered Brienne slowly, her body sliding down the rock-hard length of him till her toes touched the earth.

The sound of Rurik's name being shouted across the courtyard broke the spell that entwined them. A young man bounded forward and, in the next moment, grasped Rurik by the arms, greeting him in rapid Norse. Nearly matching

Rurik for height, his body was lean but well muscled and his hair as pale as snow. He turned sparkling blue eyes on Brienne.

"My lady. Valsemé is graced by your presence. Welcome home." His lightly accented tones were filled with genuine warmth. Turning back to Rurik, he reverted to Norse.

"Did I not tell you, *broðir,* that she is the fairest maid under the heavens?"

"*Nei.* You neglected that piece of information, and well you know it," Rurik retorted lightly. "Did you wish to make sport of me for having sent you to a house filled with women you could not touch?"

The man laughed, his white smile slashing his bronzed face. "A cruel task to set for one bearing so passionate a nature. But, *nei.* You were so mulishly insistent that Frankish devilment was afoot—"

"Brother Lyting?" Brienne knit her brows, staring at the man intently.

The two men exchanged glances, then the younger man bowed gallantly. "By your leave, my lady."

Brienne looked from him to Rurik and back again. The facial resemblance was unmistakable. "You are kindred?"

"Lyting is my brother," Rurik confessed.

"But where are your robes?" Brienne still could not grasp the whole of it.

"Indeed. Where *are* you robes, *brother?*" Esternay challenged as he stepped forward, halting beside Brienne. "Pray enlighten us. Are Norse monks absolved from wearing the tonsure as well?"

Lyting continued to smile easily as he shifted his stance and toyed with the hilt of his dagger. "Life is seldom as it appears, my lord."

"Is this how Norsemen honor their alliances, with trickery and deceit?"

Lyting did not meet the barb and avoided his brother's cautioning glance as well. "My father is pleased to return you to your barony." He smiled down at Brienne. "In the North, 'tis our custom that women are free to accept or reject offers of marriage. My father was assured that you would enjoy that same choice in considering wedlock with

him. I was sent to assure that you did." He cast a brittle look
back to the knight.

Brienne glanced uncomfortably from one man to the other.
She drew the tip of her tongue slowly over her lips. "I come
of my own will. You honor me with your concern."

Something moved in Lyting's eyes, and he withdrew his
wintry gaze from Esternay. "More than that, fair lady." His
sword flashed momentarily as he swept it free of its scabbard.
Dropping to one knee, he lay the blade across his upturned
palms. "My sword and my arm are yours. By the Cross!"

Even Rurik was startled by his brother's impassioned oath.
Several minutes later, as he led Brienne and the Frankish
contingent toward the keep, he still pondered the significance
of Lyting's actions.

The climb up the steep timbered staircase, rising high from
the courtyard to the second story of the tower, left Brienne
thoroughly winded. She took some small pleasure in the
knowledge that the Norsemen were forced to rebuild these
steps to gain entrance to the keep. One of her father's final
acts before departing Valsemé was to burn the stairway, a
defiant gesture that bespoke of a man who never acknowledged defeat.

Once inside the keep, the troop mounted a second set
of stairs, flanking the stone wall and spiraling to the great
chamber above.

As they entered the lower end of the hall, Brienne glanced
quickly about. It was much as she remembered, and she shuddered. The memories were not fond ones. Torches crackled
and blazed in iron brackets, casting eerie shadows about
the room and lacing the air with a thin haze of smoke.
Its acrid odor mingled with that of the stale rushes strewn
over the floor and the ancient collection of debris concealed
beneath them. An assortment of weaponry and animal skins
decorated the walls that Brienne's mother had once adorned
with tapestry panels. Spiked shields, double-headed axes,
spears, and halberds declared the fierceness of the Norman
warlords.

At last, Brienne dared to look toward the upper end of
the hall and seek her bridegroom amongst the men gathered

there. Her heart fell to her toes at the sight of a scarred
and grizzled warrior occupying her father's high seat upon
the dais.

A buxom wench brushed boldly against him as she filled
his drinking horn. But Atli waved the woman away, never
taking his eyes from Brienne. A smile broke over his craggy
features as he slowly rose to his full height.

Gruel Atli stood as tall as Rurik. The resemblance ended
there, except for the steel-blue of his eyes. An unruly mass
of hair fell to his shoulders, a fading copper hue streaked
liberally with gray. His beard was tamed into two braids
reaching to his chest and a jagged scar cut across his left
cheek, tugging the eyelid and face into a fearsome mien. His
thickset torso attested to a solid strength that caused Brienne
to swallow deeply. She held little hope that she could ever
escape the demands, or the desires, of this formidable man
of the North.

Atli's smile broadened as he stepped down from the dais
and crossed the room toward her. Rurik joined him following
a pace behind, while Esternay and Brother Bernard moved to
Brienne's side.

Beneath the folds of her mantle, Brienne clutched the sides
of her gown and mercilessly drove her nails into its fabric.
Everything inside her cried out that she break free and run
till every last breath was spent. Faith! Where was God now?
Had He abandoned her altogether?

As Gruel Atli stood before her, Brienne held her lashes
lowered, finding it difficult to gaze on him without betraying
her feelings. She hoped he would think her properly modest
and shy, not repulsed, as truly she was. But Atli, delighting
in his good fortune, lifted Brienne's chin with a roughened
hand and stroked her cheek. He voiced his pleasure in Norse,
commenting over his shoulder to Rurik, then greeted her in
thick, halting Frankish. Brother Bernard clarified the sentiments, to which Atli rumbled his approval, then confined
himself to Norse once again.

Withdrawing a parchment from his vest, Esternay insisted
upon a more ceremonious presentation of Valsemé's heiress. Atli chafed under the formalities but held his peace as
the knight delivered the king's tidings and blessings over

the union, followed by a subtle yet pointed reminder of
their agreement. Brother Bernard communicated the royal
message in Norse and, finally, the sheaf was folded and
tucked away.

At that, Atli called for refreshment and led his bride to her
rightful place upon the dais. Brienne ran her hand over the
smaller of two carved chairs and thought fleetingly of her
mother as she assumed the traditional seat of the baronne.

Ewers of water and lavers quickly appeared for cleansing.
No sooner were these carried away than an array of breads,
cheeses, and cold meats covered the table. Brienne had little
appetite but accepted a goblet of wine to soothe her frayed
nerves.

Conversation flowed awkwardly at first as Brother Bernard
bridged the barriers of language to convey the requisite cour-
tesies and trivialities. Soon the men eased into more comfortable banter amongst themselves, though Gruel Atli's appreciative gaze returned to Brienne again and again.

To her relief, Esternay engaged Atli in a spirited exchange
on the preferred modes of travel, he himself favoring a smooth-
gaited steed. Atli groused that longships offered swiftness
and ease, but admitted he admired the Frankish practice of
mounting its soldiery. From there, they deliberated over the
merits of various breeds and the most effective methods for
training the great destriers for war.

Brienne's thoughts drifted to Rurik. She missed his presence at the high table. Lifting her goblet to her lips, she discreetly scanned the room over its rim. Rurik leaned against
the wall, idly studying the contents of his cup. Could she
ever bear to be near him yet belong to another?

Atli suddenly laughed and said something in her ear. She
straightened, fearing he would divine her thoughts, but he
only gestured toward the lower end of the hall.

Brienne looked up to see a woman enter. Obviously Norse,
she was tall and regal with jutting breasts and narrow waist.
Her fiery red hair was caught atop her head in an exotic knot,
the wealth of it tumbling freely down her back. She swung
her slim, nubile hips rhythmically as she crossed the room
and molded herself to Rurik's side. Long, milky fingers slid
over his chest and upward to capture his jaw. Moving against

him seductively, she drew his head down and seized his lips fiercely with her own.

A hearty, knowing laughter broke out in the room and the name "Katla" filled the air.

Brienne felt as though a hand closed around her throat while she witnessed the eager display. Heat flooded her cheeks and she looked away, missing the sight of Rurik setting the Norse beauty firmly aside.

Thoroughly amused, Atli drained his cup, then looked down with warm anticipation at his bride. Her dark head was bent and her shoulders sagged with weariness. Atli grunted. When would the Franks learn? Longships were the easiest way to travel. Horseback was accursedly slow and tiresome. His eyes softened. The maid would need all her energies for the days to come. He motioned over a servant and arranged for Brienne to be escorted to one of the garret rooms above.

Numbness enveloped Brienne as she rose from her chair and stepped from the dais. As she turned to leave the room, she cast a parting glance toward Rurik. Katla stood proudly at his side, her hand possessively resting at his waist. With a pang, Brienne noted the exquisite jewelry the Norsewoman wore, so like Rurik's in its lavishness. A lover's gift? The thought stabbed at her. Katla was Rurik's woman. His *kona*. But the word, she knew, had a dual meaning in Norse. *Kona* meant "woman" as well as "wife." Why had he not mentioned this before?

Brienne passed through the arched portal and mounted the cold stone stairs, her desolation complete.

Chapter Seven

❖ ❖ ❖ ❖ ❖ ❖ ❖ ❖ ❖ ❖ ❖ ❖

BRIENNE WATCHED THE bailey stir to life from her vantage in the keep as the early-morning darkness dissolved into a new day. Smoke quickly rose from the kitchens, and the stables and storehouses bustled with activity.

Listlessly, Brienne lay her cheek against the cool stone of the window, her gaze following the diminutive figures below as they shuffled about their duties. Beneath the folds of her garments, she stroked the smooth reed with its hidden parchment till it lay warm beneath her fingers.

"Isaiah, child." Mother Annice's softly lined features came unbidden to her mind. *"Remember it well. 'He will teach us what He wants us to do. We will walk in the paths He has chosen.'"*

A sob broke from Brienne's throat and she nearly snapped the reed in two. Aleth moved instantly to her side, encircling her with her arms, and soothed her gently till the flood of tears ceased.

Composing herself, Brienne straightened and patted her friend's hand, yet the sadness remained in her eyes. "Faith but I am weak, Aleth. I know not how to bear this portion."

For all the world, Aleth longed to ease her plight and give lie to Brienne's fears, but words seemed naught but hollow clamorings. "Mayhaps some wine to hearten you," she offered softly, then crossed the room with her quick, limping gait to fill a goblet.

Dismally, Brienne turned back to the window and looked over the collection of buildings lining the bailey. She had paid scant attention at evenfall when first she arrived, but now, striving to forget the leaden ache within her breast, she quietly surveyed their condition.

Many were of new construction. The kitchens evidenced fresh wattle and daub. No doubt they had burned any number of times since her departure, as kitchens were wont to do. For that very reason the cookhouses were prudently built apart from the keep. The smithy and stables stood in good repair, she noted, and the garrison appeared to have been enlarged since her father's day.

Her violet gaze paused over an unexpected structure occupying one corner of the bailey against the curtain wall. Surprisingly, it was fashioned of stone and of considerable size. Though only partially complete, its walls stood higher than six men, one atop another.

Brienne frowned, uncertain of the structure's purpose. A prickling feeling began at the nape of her neck and inched down her spine as she appraised the stonework more carefully. All at once a chill swept through her as she recognized the pearly gray sandstone of her father's manor house.

Brienne bolted from the window, spinning Aleth round and spilling the wine as she raced from the room.

"But you've been back barely a pace of time," Atli protested, thoroughly displeased that Rurik was intent on returning to his life of trading. True, the lure of the sea flowed strong in a Norseman's veins; he understood that all too well. But Valsemé was Rurik's future. Whatever notions of adventure and distant lands the young buck entertained could wait. He needed Rurik here, now. He counted on it. Atli swore into his beard as he continued walking round the base of the motte beside his golden-haired son.

Rurik avoided his father's disapproving gaze and looked up toward the keep as Brienne emerged from its arched doorway. His lips curved into a smile then froze as she hefted her skirts and dashed down the endless flight of stairs, her legs a blur of white. Making no effort to mask his alarm, he ran forward, fearful she would fall the full length of the stairway and break her beautiful neck.

Abruptly, Brienne stopped midway, her feet slipping beneath her a whit. Grasping for the rail's support, she peered anxiously across the bailey, then resumed her rapid descent. The skirts slid from her hold as she hurried on. Stubbornly, she fought their encumbrance without slowing her pace, but as she neared the last of the stairs, she stepped into the gown's hem. Brienne squealed as she plunged forward and toppled unceremoniously into Rurik's arms. Before he could stand her aright, she scrambled away and darted across the courtyard.

Halting before the stone edifice she'd seen from the keep, Brienne gasped for breath. She paced beside it, incredulous, then placed a hand to the stone, willing it to vanish beneath her touch and prove this all some distasteful dream. Stubbornly, it did not.

As Rurik and Atli caught up to her, she whirled on them, anger and frustration glittering in her eyes.

"My . . . my father's hall. You've despoiled my father's hall!"

Rurik stood speechless at her outburst.

"Why?" she cried out, dashing away a tear. "Why have you destroyed my—" She choked with emotion, unable to finish.

Rurik knew not how to answer, for it was on his own suggestion that the hall had been moved, and that action clearly distressed her.

"*Nei*, Brienne, not destroyed, only . . . transported." He settled on the word uncomfortably.

"But how? To what purpose?" Brienne threw up her hands in bewilderment. " 'Twas solidly built, finer even than Charles's halls."

Rurik looked soberly upon the construction. "We dismantled it stone by stone and moved it to the safety of the bailey. Look, 'tis half restored already. All will be as it was before."

"But the lord needs be amongst his people," Brienne argued.

It discomfited Rurik to defend his actions, sound ones that his kinsmen embraced as brilliant and innovative. But now, as he watched Brienne struggle with her confusion, he longed to enfold her in his arms and explain it all. He wished to open her mind to his vision of what castlery could achieve, of the heights it could attain. He had seen so much in the East. Desire flooded him once more, yet he knew he dare not reach out to her in his father's presence, nor at any other moment that might present itself. His weakness for Brienne necessitated his departure from Valsemé for many years to come.

"The manor house was fine and well built," he granted, clearing the sudden dryness from his throat. "But it sat far distant of the keep. In time of need, should the barony suffer attack and be caught unawares, 'twould offer little protection to the lord or his family and be difficult to defend. By moving it inside the bailey, their safety is ensured." Rurik held her with his steel-blue eyes. "The defense of the keep rests upon the skill of the lord and his men. Without him to command, all suffer."

To her dismay, Brienne could not argue the logic of his words. "But you move it . . . stone by stone?"

Rurik nodded, astonishing her with the Norsemen's energy.

Atli shifted impatiently, irritated that he could not follow the course of their words, yet thoroughly captivated by the spirited beauty as she argued with his son. He liked fire in a woman. 'Twould be a good match! He smiled as his loins warmed with that thought.

Atli rubbed at the numbness that bedeviled the left side of his neck as Rurik conveyed Brienne's concern for her father's house. It did not displease him that she would find issue with his command. Rather, he likened her to a lioness, fiercely protective of her own, and that pleased him well. Now, he would please her.

A shiver of fear passed through Brienne as Gruel Atli stepped forward. The light of day did nothing to soften the coarseness of the man she would call husband. He addressed her in Norse, his heavy voice fairly booming in the quiet of early morn.

Rurik carefully masked his own feelings as he aided his father's cause and translated for him. "Today, the men do not build. The barony prepares to celebrate your marriage on the morrow. Atli invites you to join him in the wedding hunt."

Brienne's knees threatened to crumble beneath her. She had not thought the vows would be exchanged so soon. Why was she not advised?

As she opened her mouth to speak, Rurik continued, allowing her no chance to object and unwittingly affront his father.

"Rollo was to attend the ceremony several days hence, but his courier arrived during the night. Poppa has begun her lying in. The duke will remain in Rouen till the child is born." Rurik avoided her gaze, fixing his own on a distant point beyond Brienne's shoulder as he added softly, "Rollo wishes that your own pleasure be not delayed and will journey to Valsemé forthwith after the baby arrives."

Rurik withheld Atli's mirthful comment that it would be best to wed her and bed her before Rollo arrived, lest the duke be tempted to take her for himself. After all, he had captured Poppa from her father, the Count of Bayeux, and kept her as his mistress.

Brienne swallowed her rising panic and wished desperately to speak with Lord Robert or Brother Bernard. Surely the nuptials could be delayed, if even for a day. Sweet Mary, she wouldst have more time!

"My lady," Rurik said gently, breaking through her thoughts. "The hunt. Atli waits upon your answer."

Brienne braved a tremulous smile as she turned to Gruel Atli and declined as graciously as she could manage. "I fear I am a poor horsewoman at best, having spent so many years in cloister. And I confess that I am greatly relieved to be free of the saddle." She dropped her lashes demurely. "There is much to attend to before our vows are spoken."

Atli accepted her response with nods of understanding and instructed Rurik to ask after her needs.

Encouraged by his good mood, Brienne requested that she be free to leave the confines of the keep to deliver the sisters' altar linens to the church. This drew a frown from Atli, and Brienne felt her hopes wither within her breast. If only she could persuade Brother Bernard to prevail upon the Norsemen to delay the ceremonies.

"Atli prefers that you not be seen by the villagers till you pledge your troth before the church doors and he may present you as his baronne. Lyting will deliver the cloths." A smile tugged at Rurik's lips. "Though I can tell you that it does not gladden my father to send him. He believes Lyting spends overmuch time with the churchman as it is, and fears that one day my brother will return branded with the tonsure."

Despite her heavy mood, a small bubble of laughter escaped Brienne's lips, and she smiled warmly up at Rurik. It was the first time she had done so that day. He returned the smile, wondering how he would bear to leave her on the morrow's eve.

Atli massaged the side of his neck, then worked the tingling from his hand, thoughtfully observing his son and his bride.

Hours later, having changed her attire and dressed her hair, Brienne left Aleth freshening her gowns and descended the tower stairs.

She fastened the golden brooch to her mantle as she went, telling herself firmly that the piece served solely as a reminder of duty—duty to her people for whom she had returned, and duty to her betrothed whose gift it was. Yet even as she schooled her thoughts, 'twas Rurik her heart held fast.

Patch scampered ahead through the hall, on out and down the bailey steps. He awaited Brienne at the bottom, then scurried away, tail awag, following the aroma of fresh-baked bread.

Brienne laughed and stepped quickly after him, her humor much improved since morn. The tantalizing odors tickled at her nose, beckoning her as much as the mongrel to seek their source.

The kitchens were beehives of activity as the servants dashed in and about, preparing for the elaborate wedding feast to come. At Brienne's approach, they paused in their labors, but before she could acknowledge them, a woman's strident voice drew her attention to the side of one of the cookhouses. The Norsewoman, Katla, stood alongside a rectangular pit, raining terse commands on a handful of youths.

" 'Tis for the boiling of broken meats. A Norse custom, my lady." A Frankish maidservant ventured forward hesitantly and gestured toward the open pit.

In truth, Brienne's interest lay more with Katla than with whatever purpose the hole served. She turned to regard the maid and was surprised to find a young woman at an age with herself, her waist thickening with child. Brienne wondered briefly if the girl had been ill used by the Normans, or if a name could even be put to the father. She dismissed the thought as unworthy. The maid stood tired and drawn, yet obviously warmed by the hope that she could assist her lady. Brienne would not abuse such kindness and listened attentively as the girl explained the curious practice of cooking in the earth.

"The cavity is first lined with wood, my lady, then filled with water and heated with scorching-hot stones. The meats and herbs will next be added, and the stones replaced as needed. 'Tis a lengthy process, but renders a tasty dish. Other pits will be used for the roasting of whole animals. 'Tis much the same. The meat and hot stones are covered over in the ground to cook the night long. 'Tis far superior to our stewed meats, most succulent and tender, the best I have tasted."

The girl flushed, realizing her mistake in admitting that she had eaten of the lord's meat.

The slip of tongue was not lost on Brienne. Had the girl simply taken a portion for herself, she wondered, or was it a lover who offered the delicacy, tempting her to his bed? Perchance the maid already knew more of love and tender entreaties than she herself would ever experience. Atli seemed not a man given to gentleness, and Brienne doubted that she could ever find more than tolerance for him. Certainly not love.

Brienne shook the thoughts away and looked over to where several youngsters stacked clean, flat stones next to the cooking fire. A small lad, no more than five, struggled with one particularly heavy stone before it dropped from his grasp, bounced several feet, and smashed against Katla's ankle.

Katla shrieked in outrage and viciously cuffed the child. He stumbled to the ground, then, as if by reflex, curled into a tight ball and covered his head, waiting for the assault to continue.

Brienne bristled as Katla raised her hand to deliver a second blow. "Hold!" she cried out as she swept before the Norsewoman.

The youths attending the pit ceased their activity and bowed in deference to Valsemé's lady, fueling Katla's temper to an explosive level.

"What goes here?" Brienne demanded, unable to conceal her own anger and having no wish to do so.

Katla assessed the Frankish heiress with a cool measure of disdain, arching an elegant eyebrow. "We prepare for the celebration of your marriage." She spoke in heavily accented Frankish. "Does it distress you?"

" 'Tis the mistreatment of babes that distresses me."

"The child is worthless."

"No child is worthless. The task you set is unsuitable for one so small."

Katla stabbed Brienne with a venomous look. *How dare the Frankish bitch reprimand her before inferiors!* This affront would not go unrepaid.

Too late, Brienne caught the flash of fury in Katla's eyes and realized her error in confronting the Norsewoman so openly. She did not regret her words, but feared Katla would wreak a greater vengeance upon the child if he be left to her care. Best to bear the brunt of Katla's wrath herself, Brienne decided.

She turned back to the boy, now enfolded in his mother's skirts. Surprisingly, she was the same Frankish maidservant with whom Brienne spoke moments earlier.

"How are you called?" Brienne coaxed, and was rewarded when the child peeked out from the folds of cloth.

"Waite."

"Well, Waite, I have need of a houndsman. Think you can tame yon beast?" She pointed toward Patch sniffing at something of interest in a woodstack.

The child's eyes brightened with excitement. "Oh, yes, m'lady."

"He needs be fed twice daily, groomed free of spurs, and trained up properly. Patch is a most ungovernable fellow," she confided. "See you that he does not tangle my threads or steal off with my broidery. How say you, Waite?"

The boy nodded eagerly.

"So be it! Henceforth you shall answer to me, and to any who ask, you are the 'baronne's houndsman.' Now be off with you." Brienne watched the boy scramble after Patch and waited expectantly for Katla to challenge her authority.

Katla bit her tongue down upon her anger. For the time, she would endure the bitch's presence. 'Twould be unwise to do aught else. Gruel Atli favored this spawn of Beaumanoir, and took her to wife upon the morrow. But he could not live forever. One day she, Katla, would sit proudly at Rurik's side and oversee Valsemé as its mistress. By the gods of her ancestors, *she* would be baronne!

The two women regarded one another warily. To her chagrin, Brienne found that it was not their argument that plagued her thoughts but the vision of Katla filling Rurik's arms. The Norsewoman was striking with her blazing hair and flawless features. She wore the traditional dress of the North, a pleated linen chemise that fell to the ankles, covered front and back by two long rectangles of fine cloth. These were fitted at the top corners with loops, enabling the two sections to be joined over the shoulders with large oval brooches, much like her own but not nearly so grand. Katla's only other jewelry consisted of an elaborate necklace of amber and jet fitted with gold coins.

Katla's eyes moved insultingly over Brienne, then widened as they fastened on the elegant brooch. Only the famed goldsmiths of Gotland were capable of such extraordinary craftsmanship. The piece was easily worth a small ransom.

Her eyes narrowed dangerously. Only one man had recently arrived at Valsemé from distant shores, only one who was wealthy enough to afford so fine a treasure. Rurik Atlison.

It rankled Katla that he had not seen fit to present the brooch to her upon his homecoming. It rankled her all the more that Rurik made excuses last even when she welcomed him to her bed. Now she suspected his reluctance had something to do with this Frankish sow.

"The brooch is magnificent," Katla forced out.

" 'Twas Atli's gift," Brienne returned a bit too quickly.

Katla scoffed at this. The only finery Atli was expert in selecting was his sword. *Nei*, Rurik chose the gift, even if he did so for his father. Still, it irked her that he had neglected to procure something for herself of like value. Katla tossed her hair. She would draw a little blood. The bitch deserved it.

"For so fine a treasure you must reward Atli well on your wedding night," she taunted, and was pleased to see Brienne shudder.

"Now, Rurik—" Brienne's eyes flew to her face. Katla well knew Rurik's effect upon women and, ironically, it pleased her that Brienne was not immune. She gloated inwardly as she decided how best to toy with her prey.

"Rurik is above all men in gifting a woman. I assure you my coffers are filled with many fine pieces, for I pleasure him in so many ways," Katla purred, sliding a hand over the side of her bosom, down to her small waist, and over a hip. "He knows well how to ride a woman. May you find such joy beneath Atli."

Brienne colored fiercely and would hear no more. Katla's laughter followed her as Brienne stalked away and headed toward the manor house.

Moments later, Brienne ducked inside the walls of the building, passing through a small arched door, her cheeks still flamed by the encounter. She closed her eyes and leaned against the wall, heart pounding. Brienne slowed her breaths and inhaled deeply of the rich, earthy scents.

She stood, she knew, in the ground-level storage area of the house. The hall would occupy the second level, and above it the bedchambers, save the lord's, which would be partitioned off directly behind the dais in the hall.

Brienne opened her eyes to the clear blue sky stretched high above. The wood floors had yet to be sprung or the building roofed over. 'Twas little more than a great stone shell.

She traced the square holes that marked the walls where the floor beams would be secured and planks laid over, then dropped her gaze to the rows of sturdy stone pillars standing like soldiers before her. These would further reinforce the floor and its overhead structure.

A smile played over her lips. She crossed the room to run her hand over first one, then another of the pillars. Ofttimes she, Thomas, and Lisette had amused themselves in this place, playing hide-and-go-find amongst the great boxes and casks, the pillars and crates.

Mayhaps that was what she found so disturbing about the manor being moved. Oh, 'twas a bold idea on Rurik's part, inspired even. But these stones held the shadows of her past, precious memories of days spent long ago. If only she could somehow squeeze them out, bring them to life again. How she longed to hear her brother's and sister's laughter ringing out in the hall, or see her lovely mother dressed in velvets at Christmastide. Her father would lavish his wife with compliments then, in his rich, deep tones . . . not unlike Rurik's.

She laid her head against the pillar, pondering how her life had been fragmented, just as the manor house, stone by stone, piece by piece, had been dismantled. It could never be put back quite the same. She closed her eyes against the dreary thought and rested quietly.

A chill feathered down Brienne's spine as she heard the faintest of footfalls. Again, she detected movement and the soft rustle of cloth. Her stomach clenched into a cold knot. She was not alone. Slowly, Brienne turned, pulse racing.

Her blood turned to ice as she beheld the black-haired heathen who tormented her dreams.

The devil impaled her with strange, colorless eyes. His lips twisted into a smile. "What have we here? You're a lusty bit I have not laid eyes to afore."

The heathen advanced, and she fell back against the pillar, a cry strangling in her throat. There was a cruelty about his face, the harsh planes etched with scars and the sharp jaw shadowed by a day's growth of bristles. Dark brows slashed over eyes so pale they seemed devoid of all color, yet they glowed from within with a menacing light.

It was all Brienne could do to inch round the stone pillar as she fought the sudden paralysis in her limbs. That the heathen spoke her tongue did not occur to her, so desperate was she to put something solid betwixt them.

He peeled off his gloves with a maddening slowness as he continued toward her. Backing away with small steps, Brienne swung herself toward the safety of an adjacent pillar, but the heathen sprang forward and shackled her arm.

"Not so fast, my lovely vixen. You promise a more tender sport than I have enjoyed these past days astride my dun."

He eyed her concealing mantle and reached to draw it back, envisioning the delectable fruits hidden within. But he stopped when his hand brushed against the ornate brooch. He scowled darkly.

"So, the *Barnakarl* has bought himself a pretty piece to warm his pallet with his fancy trinkets. Where did my *broðir* chance on you, my sweet-breasted dove?"

Brienne trembled as the devil drew a finger down the column of her neck.

" 'Tis not my practice to take my *broðir*'s leavings, but you . . . you are exceptional."

Brienne's cheeks brightened as his meaning came clear. The man thought her a whore! Anger momentarily overcame fear. Would he be so confident if he knew she was plighted to the lord of the keep?

Clenching her teeth so they would not rattle, she raised her chin. " 'Twas a gift of Gruel Atli." Brienne could not bring herself to call Atli "baron," but she hoped her words carried their weight.

"My *faðir*?" The man halted in his attack. Brienne thought her cause won as surprise flickered across the heathen's face. But then his smile broadened.

"Gratefully, my father is generous with his women. Surely he will not keep you to himself."

"Atli is your father?" she stammered, revolted by his presumption and shocked by what he implied.

"*Ja*. I am his *sonir*, Hastein."

Icy fear twisted around her heart as she recalled the name and all that was said of him. He was a dangerous man, even by Norse standards, and not to be trusted.

Brienne tried to snatch her arm free of his grasp, but he tightened his hold, chuckling deep in his throat. Then he fell silent, raw desire smoldering in his eyes. Slowly, he pushed back her mantle.

"Now, let us see what treasures you have hidden there."

Brienne brought her hand soundly across his face with a resounding slap. Lightning swift, Hastein caught her wrists

and jerked them behind her back, crushing her breasts hard
against his chest.

"Do not think you can thwart me. I'll taste of you when
and where I want." He seized her hair viciously, yanking
back her head to expose her silken neck. His ardor blazed
as he drank in her beauty. "And I find I'm near to starving
now."

He ravaged her lips with a bruising kiss, then thrust his
tongue boldly into her mouth. Gripping both her wrists in
one hand, he freed the other to roughly explore the full
swell of breast. She struggled futilely against his superi-
or strength, her protests muffled under the assault. In the
next moment, he pinned her against the pillar, shoving a
knee between her legs. Brienne sickened as he slid her
gown upward. His callused hand traveled the smooth length
of leg to caress her bare thigh, then moved over her buttocks. She bit into her lip, steeling herself for what was to
come.

Abruptly, space opened between them as Hastein hurtled
backward. He scarcely glimpsed Rurik's distorted features
before his head exploded in a splintering light. The force
of the blow sent Hastein sprawling to the dirt floor. Before
he could recover, Rurik stayed him with solid strength and
pressed a knife firmly against his throat.

"Do you defile our *faðir*'s bride?" Rurik raged with a
scalding fury.

"Upon the runes, I didst not know," Hastein swore, clearly
stunned.

Rurik's iron grip did not lessen, his anger so great that
his arm fairly trembled. "See that you remember it well,
broðir,"—he spat the last word with contempt—"or next
time I will not spare my blade."

Slowly, Rurik released Hastein and rose to his feet, but
he made no move to resheathe his weapon.

Hastein drew himself up, wiping blood from his lip. He
slid a glance over Brienne then looked back to Rurik. "Does
the *Barnakarl* safeguard the woman for Atli, or for himself?"
he sneered, brushing the dust from his garments, then dropped
his voice. "We will see this to an end another day, eh, *broðir*?"
He turned on his heel and strode from the building.

Scarcely had Rurik secured his blade, when Brienne threw herself against him with great racking sobs. This surprised him, for he feared she would recoil from him as she had after happening upon the skeleton. But now she instinctively sought comfort and safety in his arms, and he pleasured greatly in that. Rurik gathered Brienne close, his heart racing. In truth, he did not know if 'twas wrought more from the encounter with Hastein or by her nearness.

He stroked Brienne's hair, whispering softly in Norse against the midnight tresses. She trembled in his arms and he pressed her closer, brushing his lips against her temple, her brow, her eyelids. Brienne lifted her lips to his, and he grazed them gently at first, then kissed them slowly, tenderly. Her lips parted, inviting him further, and needing little encouragement, he covered her mouth. Brienne met him fully, pouring herself into him, releasing her fears and pent-up emotions into the strength of him. Their kisses caught fire, becoming quick and feverish, urgent and hungering. Consumed with desire, they clung to one another.

Rurik battled against himself and nearly lost that struggle before he broke the kiss. His breathing came heavy, tortured. "*Nei*, Brienne. *Nei*, *ástin mín*. I am pledged."

He chastised himself for behaving little better than Hastein. How he ached to lose himself in the sweet depths of her, to strive as one with her, couple with her, meld with her in passion's fiery inferno. Rurik shuddered with repressed desire. He would not forswear his father for the lust he harbored in his loins.

Rurik's words jolted Brienne from her reverie. In her need she had forgotten Katla. Rurik was pledged to the torrid Norsewoman and, honorably, would not betray his wife. She could not ask it of him. His unyielding sense of honor should please her, yet it left her empty, bereft, unfulfilled.

Rurik stroked the back of Brienne's slim hands with his thumb, debating how to best tell her of his resolution to leave Valsemé. Now, more than ever, he knew he must depart, for if he stayed, surely as the sun rose and the rains fell, he would have her. Deciding on straightforwardness, he looked at her evenly and took a formal tone.

"My lady, I am away at morrow's eve, after the wedding celebration is . . . complete."

Verily, he would see Atli unto his marriage bed. He owed him that. But he held no desire to remain till morning to view the bridal sheets displayed with her virgin blood, witnessing the gift of herself to his father. He pushed down the thought and gripped her hands firmly in his.

"Your protection lies henceforth with your husband. Look to him in your need. No harm shall befall you from my brother Hastein or from any other."

His heart wrenched as he looked into her pain-filled eyes, and he wished to ease her sorrow in some small way.

"If I were not so certain, I assure you I could not leave."

Brienne withdrew her hands from Rurik's as the last fragments of her world crumbled at her feet. She was truly alone amidst a barbarous race. Why had she thought 'twould be otherwise? She drew her mantle tight about her, retreating into its folds. A helpless shield for a helpless maiden.

Brienne near missed Rurik's offer to escort her to the keep. She shook her head, then glanced about the room.

"What has passed within these walls is best left to rest." To rest, she thought, yea, but ne'er to be forgotten.

Dispirited, Brienne preceded Rurik out of the building.

Katla satisfied herself that the slack-witted cook had not ruined her latest batch of *skyr* before setting herself to her next task. The thick curds would normally be whipped smooth with milk and mixed with porridge for a fortifying meal. Tomorrow, however, it would be sweetened with honey and served as a pleasant dessert.

Now she gave herself over to making the festive bread that Rurik favored, studded with currants and spiced with the precious cardamom that he had procured from the East. This could not be trusted to doltish Frankish hands.

Katla took up her station outside the kitchen at a long wooden dough trough that stood hip high. Carefully, she measured together the ingredients, working wet into dry as the sticky mass took shape. She then set to kneading the bulk vigorously, folding and pushing and turning till it became elastic and smooth.

Her hands stilled as Brienne emerged from the manor house, followed by Rurik brief moments later. Atli's bride appeared distraught as she traversed the courtyard with leaden steps, clutching her mantle fast about her. Suddenly, she sobbed and hurried up the stairs.

Katla flicked her eyes back over Rurik. He stood watching grimly after Brienne, the intensity of his gaze hidden to none.

Katla slapped the dough harder, then gave it her fist.

Chapter Eight
❖ ❖ ❖ ❖ ❖ ❖ ❖ ❖ ❖ ❖ ❖ ❖

RESTLESSLY, BRIENNE PACED the confines of her chamber as she awaited Aleth's return with Brother Bernard. She felt ill and weary and ready to retch.

Supper had proved an unnerving and stressful affair. Rurik remained absent throughout the course of the meal, but Hastein joined the high table and brashly claimed the place beside her, displacing Lyting. Lyting's sentiments toward his half brother were as apparent as his displeasure in having to share a trencher with Katla.

Brienne massaged her throbbing temples.

Katla. The woman had taunted her throughout the evening, making a grand display of the lavish jewelry she wore while laughing loudly and uttering clever, double-edged jests. But for every barb hurled, Lyting intervened with ready wit, deftly deflecting the intended blows, and often as not, 'twas at the Norsewoman's expense. Katla had seethed with indignation, clawing Lyting with cat-green eyes.

As the evening grated on, Brienne had grown increasingly unnerved by Hastein's presence. 'Twas more than his contemptible behavior that afternoon. She was tortured by the thought that Hastein was the same murderous heathen she had spied from her tower window so long ago.

She could not say with any certainty. Helmet and noseguard had obscured the man's features. Yet the smile . . . the smile she would never forget. 'Twas cold as death.

Brienne had tried to cast the image from her mind but found herself, instead, drawn to the assemblage before her. Any of the Northmen there could have partaken in that day's carnage. Twin kernels of fear and loathing blossomed deep within her breast. She scrutinized them more closely, searching out every nick and scar—badges of warfare, warfare wrought against her people. Never had the distinctions between Norse and Frank seemed more manifest or foreboding than in that moment. Their hair, their dress, their mannerisms, their countenance and bearing—such a rugged lot they were, carved from the severity of the ice-bound North.

Brienne had then shifted her gaze to watch Atli slice a choice piece of meat upon the trencher they shared and sickened inwardly to think of those coarse hands moving over her body. Suddenly she felt light of head and was forced to brace herself against the table's edge as the room swam before her eyes.

Unable to bear more, she made her excuses and retired from the hall, leaving the men in high spirits. Their hunt had been good, and the feasting was well under way as they toasted the bride and drank merrily to Atli's final hours as an unfettered man. Even now, snatches of bawdy song and echoes of bellowing laughter drifted from below.

Brienne tried to rub warmth into her arms as she continued her pacing. Aleth had left with her message what seemed like hours ago. She strived to fill the time with prayer but could not hold rein on her thoughts and was much too restive to remain on her knees. Now, despite her constant movement, she felt chilled to the core, as though, in her distress, the warmth of life refused to flow.

A solid rapping sounded upon the door. Brienne fairly flew across the room to drag it open. Her face fell as the darkly clad figure of the Seigneur d'Esternay swept through the portal.

"Lord Robert."

"My lady." He bowed curtly. "Brother Bernard is detained at the church. I understand there is a matter of some urgency." The words stilled on his lips as his eyes passed over her waxen features.

"Lady Brienne, are you ill? You are trembling." He caught up her hands, but she quickly reclaimed them and stepped away.

Brienne held no wish to confide in Esternay, or parry words. Nor did she wholly trust him. She breathed deeply, trying to clear her mind.

Still, he was Frankish and he was kin. If the churchman would not heed her desperate summons, 'twould seem her last shred of hope lay in Lord Robert's keeping.

She bit nervously at her lip, struggling to form the words. When at last she opened her mouth to speak, a loathsome fear gripped her heart and her face crumpled. She turned away, overcome by a fresh onslaught of tears.

"Forgive me, my lord, but God has chosen a frail vessel to champion His people."

Moving behind her, Esternay reached out to touch her, then dropped his hand. At last. He had been waiting for her confidence and high purposes to crack under the weight of reality. Now his patience would be richly rewarded. She would be malleable to his will. For that, he could gird his patience a pace longer.

"My lady, is there aught I can do?"

Brienne whirled on him, her eyes huge and pleading. "Return me to Levroux, I pray thee, Lord Robert. I cannot face life with . . . I cannot marry this man. Do not leave me here." She clutched at his tunic.

Esternay grasped her firmly by the arms. "You know not what you speak. Atli favors you and will not be denied. 'Twould mean death to do so." His words held not a mullet of truth, but he suspected she would believe them easily enough.

Brienne shook her head. "Better dead than . . ."

"What, then, of your people? Wouldst you have them suffer as well? Surely they will bear the Norseman's wrath should you dare depart."

Her head sagged forward in utter defeat.

A smile crept into Esternay's eyes, his triumph near. "Faith, my lady. Didst I not tell you that I would not abandon you to these heathens?"

Slowly, Brienne lifted her face to his.

"There is a way." His eyes held her in their black depths.

Neither heard the door ease open nor glimpsed the shadowy figure of the woman who stood without.

"What if I were to tell you 'tis possible to regain your title and lands yet rule them free of the Norse dogs?"

Brienne blinked, uncertain whether her ears deceived her. Esternay read the look with encouragement.

"There is naught I can do to forestall the nuptials. But I will aid your plight, my lady, and free you of your Norman husband. Your father's lands will once again rest in your keeping."

"Impossible," she breathed at last.

"Nay, not so, but 'twill require courage and forbearance, Brienne . . . and a son." He had her full attention now. He plunged on, unmasking his plans.

"By the terms of the marriage contract, any male child born of this union will be recognized as heir to the barony. Your marriage to Atli need not be long, only fruitful."

Brienne blanched at the remark, increasing the knight's confidence.

"Once the child is born, I will see you widowed upon the battlefield." His lips slid into a smile. "The matter of a small accident. You will retain your place as baronne, ruling Valsemé through your son. The Normans will pay him obeisance and I will abet you as well."

Anger blistered deep within her breast. "And the price? Surely you expect recompense for the deed?"

"Everything has its cost, my dear, but not all is met with coin." He stroked the creamy smoothness of her cheek. "My requirements are few. In sum, only three."

Brienne fought the urge to recoil beneath his touch and carefully schooled her features. "Pray, name them, Lord Robert. What be the terms of my deliverance?"

He relaxed his hold of her, confident the maid was playing easily into his schemes. "Once you are widowed, I will assume guardianship as the child's closest male relative, lending you my strength of arms and men, as well as the benefit of my governance. I will provide for you in every way."

"Continue." Her temper flamed to new heights. In his arrogance had he forgotten Atli's sons, or didst he intend to arrange "accidents" for them as well?

"Your father played me false, Brienne. You should have

been mine," he said bitterly, drawing her against him. "I would have you still."

"Must I remind you? You are wed to my sister."

"I speak not of marriage, but of an arrangement that will profit us both." He gazed at her with hooded eyes. "When I am in residence, you will attend to me, and care for me, as you would a husband true. And—"

"And?" Brienne choked fiercely at this outrage.

"Your heir. I desire the chance to sire the child myself."

Brienne's legs nearly folded beneath her, but she refused to succumb. Esternay pressed on with his suit, not heeding the storm gathering in her violet eyes.

"Your sister is ill with this pregnancy. Shortly after you are wed, I will send a missive as to the gravity of her condition. You will plead with Atli to allow you to journey to her sickbed. There are many private rooms at Castle Roubaix. . . ." He shrugged, leaving the statement suspended betwixt them but the meaning clear. His fingers closed tight about her arm. "But once widowed, you are mine, Brienne. None other." His grip loosened just as quickly, and he toyed with a lock of her hair. "But you will suffer no complaint, for I will keep you *very* well."

Brienne's blood fired to boiling. Still, she bit back her fury. "Perchance Atli's seed will already grow within me."

"Perchance," he returned coolly. "But I would have the opportunity to see that the child's veins flow with pure Frankish blood. *My* blood."

Esternay caught the rebellion simmering in her eyes.

"Would you prefer to spend your days in the embrace of that hoary bear of a Norseman down below who even now must be savoring the sweet promise of your body? Let me give you a taste of what is to be ours, my sweet." He drew her against him in one swift move and covered her lips.

Brienne was only vaguely aware of the faint clinking of metal bracelets and of the soft creaking of the door as it eased closed.

She held herself rigid beneath Lord Robert's ardent kiss, outwardly as cold and unyielding as a block of marble. But inside she seethed with rage.

Deep from within, a new strength welled, pulsing solidly

to life. She pushed free of the knight's embrace, catching him
by surprise. Eyes flashing and filled with revulsion, she drew
herself up with the air of true nobility.

"You dishonor the house of Beaumanoir and disgrace it
with your treachery. By the blood of my father, I *am* the
Baronne de Valsemé. I'll whore for no man."

Blackest anger flashed across Esternay's features, and he
instinctively drew back his hand to strike her.

"Do your worst," she dared boldly, "that you may know a
'Norseman's justice.' " By the flicker of his eyes, she knew
he remembered Rurik's warning.

Esternay clenched his hand, then slowly dropped it. His
lip curled into a sneer. "Do not covet your virtue overmuch,
my sweet. You may yet find my bed more desirable than
that of a Norse jackal." Brushing past her, he stormed from
the room.

Swelled with her momentary triumph, Brienne moved to
the window and drew a shaky breath. Below, an elderly Frankish servant hobbled across the courtyard carrying
buckets of water. Spying his lady in the window above, he
set them down and snatched the soft cap from his head. He
smiled as he bobbed a small bow, then picked up his burden
and continued on his way.

Brienne lay her cheek against the coolness of the stone.
Somehow, the encounter with the knight renewed her purpose and buttressed her for the morrow. She closed her eyes
as a gentle breeze played over her.

A cheer greeted Brienne as she emerged from the arched
portal of the keep and paused at the top of the staircase.
Self-consciously, she smoothed her finely woven gown, a
deep forest-green edged with marten and cinctured with a
narrow belt of gold. A small gust of air lifted her hair from
her shoulder where it fell unbound in luxurious waves.

Below, the bridal procession awaited, a mixture of Norman
warriors, Frankish servants, and the king's escort that had
seen her here. They seemed eager for the festivities to begin,
or continue, as was more likely the case. She imagined that
many a man had not found his pallet the night before.

A groom walked Candra to the foot of the stairs, and

Brienne smiled to see that flowers had been added to her trappings. But the smile vanished from her lips as Esternay strode forward and took the reins. Even at this distance, she could feel the challenge in his dark, steady gaze.

Oh, that God would smite his insolence! she railed silently, then set her jaw. *Bones of the saints, he would find such audacity well met indeed!* Plucking up her courage, she looked out over the gathering and graced them with a wide and beautiful smile. Then, with head held high and steel in her spine, she descended the timbered steps.

Horns trumpeted as the gates creaked open. The bride alone rode mounted, while the well-wishers walked alongside, crowding merrily around. Esternay led Candra by the reins as was his privilege as her kinsman. There was naught she could do to forestall him. At least, this way, he could taunt her no further.

The villeins who had been assembling at the gates since early morn now joined in the procession, hailing their new mistress joyfully as they strewed fragrant flower petals on the ground before her. Valsemé's villeins were so few, Brienne reflected sadly, and not a one did she recognize.

As they approached the church, Brienne could see Gruel Atli standing with Brother Bernard before the church doors, resplendent in his Nordic finery. Rurik, Lyting, and Hastein held to one side below the steps, and with them, Katla.

Once again, the Norsewoman appeared weighted down with her wealth of gold and jewels. They shone at her ears, in her hair, around her neck, and again at her waist. An abundance of bracelets crowded her arms, and each finger boasted a heavy ring. The woman could not move without jangling and clinking, Brienne mused. At least she would know where the cat roamed.

As Lord Robert lifted Brienne from her horse, he whispered in her ear, "My offer remains, should you find life unbearable in your husband's arms."

Finding the ground, Brienne trod purposely on his instep and gave it her full weight.

"If for no better reason than to escape *your* arms, I will find it bearable. Now, release me and bedevil me no more with your vile purposes. I'll have none of it."

"As you wish, my dear." He gave her a mocking smile and offered his arm. "Your bridegroom awaits and appears eager to rut."

Gruel Atli smiled his pleasure as his exquisite bride mounted the steps. As Brienne was formally presented, Atli clasped her hand warmly in his much larger, thicker one and lifted it to his lips.

Brother Bernard began to protest, for the vows had yet to be exchanged and such display should be constrained for the moment. But seeing Atli's enchantment with his bride, he reconsidered. Why risk the man's ire when the matter was easily solved? He cleared his throat and prayerfully joined his hands.

Only once did Brienne allow her gaze to meet Rurik's. The single look did more to fracture her resolve than all of Esternay's effrontery. A deep, searing pain pierced her heart through. She forced her attention to Brother Bernard as he began the ceremony.

The oaths were exchanged outside the church for all to witness. Atli spoke in clear tones, first in Norse, then in Frankish, carefully pronouncing each word as the monk bade him. Brienne repeated her vows softly, her voice barely audible.

Atli smiled wide, utterly charmed by her beauty and sweet innocence. Absently, he flexed his left hand as Rurik came forth with the ring. The accursed tingling had persisted since yestereve, a damnable nuisance since he favored that hand except when wielding a sword. Determined not to let the affliction best him, he reached out to take the small gold band, but the partial numbness caused him to fumble and drop it.

Gasps were heard round. Atli scowled at the ill omen as Rurik quickly retrieved the ring and offered it up once more. Brienne, too, was affected by the mishap, paling somewhat. Hastily, Brother Bernard continued, twice blessing the ring before he concluded the ceremony.

As the small circle of gold slid into place, Brienne felt its weight many times over. Hot tears threatened, but she fought them back. 'Twas done. Her fate was sealed. A ring for her finger, a manacle for her heart.

Atli turned toward the crowd and, lifting up her hand, proudly presented his wife. A hearty shout went up, hailing the Baronne de Valsemé.

The wedding party moved inside the church and did not emerge till much later after the marriage was blessed with a lengthy mass. Atli and Brienne were met with a shower of grains, then were accompanied amidst much song and jollity back to the keep where the wedding feast and games would begin in earnest.

Atli and Brienne presided over the festivities from the high table upon the dais. There, sharing a trencher, they partook of their first meal as husband and wife. Each place gleamed with silver—knives, spoons, goblets, and *mazers,* shallow wooden bowls rimmed with the precious metal. Those not so fortunate to sit at the high table contented themselves with steel implements and soapstone bowls, a Norse commodity.

Atli selected choice meats for his bride, attentively cutting them into small portions and setting them to her side of the trencher, or *manchet,* made from a thick slice of day-old bread.

Brienne found the array of food mind-boggling. An unending line of servants bore platters of pit-roasted suckling pig, braised boar, plovers and quail, fish tarts with sauces, venison pasties, mullets and eels. There were thick soups, creamy cheeses, custards, and a selection of fruits. The Norsemen supplied the table with exotic fare including sugar made with roses and violets, figs, dates, almonds, and pomegranates. *Flatbrauð* appeared alongside crusty Frankish loaves, as did other Nordic favorites such as smoked herring and salmon, served with mustards, and a curious dish called *skyr,* a sweet, puddinglike affair topped with cream.

Brienne sampled many of the foods but tasted little of what passed her lips. Her nerves constricted her appetite as she thought fleetingly ahead to where the night would end— in Atli's bed.

Once well sated, the celebrants moved outside for the wedding games to commence. Atli paused momentarily before leaving the hall and pounded at the burning in his chest. He grunted into his beard to be plagued thusly and motioned to a servant to refill his drinking horn with mead. Seeing

Brienne's concern, he smiled reassuringly. A Norseman's feast was enough to roil any man's stomach. If only he could tell her that. On the morrow, he would begin learning the Frankish tongue. He was grateful that the barrier of language would not impede the evening's pleasures.

Satisfying himself that his bride's goblet brimmed with spiced wine, he escorted her below.

When they arrived outside the bailey walls, men were pairing off for the first event, wrestling. Brienne noted that only the Normans participated in the sport. Apparently, Lord Robert barred his men from joining the games. There had been much drinking already and, no doubt, he did not wish to risk some hapless incident that could lead to bloodshed. At least he was prudent where his men were concerned.

Lyting caught Brienne's eye as he stripped away all but his snug-fitting breeches and, grinning widely, walked over and clamped a hand soundly on Rurik's shoulder. Rurik turned, then laughed genially.

"So, you think to best me this year, little brother?"

"I wager you grew soft on your last voyage, coddled in the laps of the Eastern beauties. I am obliged to see that you do not decline in your advanced years."

Unable to resist, Rurik bared his powerfully muscled chest and arms.

"I'll go easy on you, little brother." He flashed a smile, but the air whooshed out of him in the next instant as Lyting tackled him about the waist. Swiftly hooking a leg behind Rurik's, the younger man drove him off-balance and took him to the ground.

Twisting his body, Rurik managed to take the fall on his side. Quickly, he rolled to his stomach and pressed up onto his palms and knees. But before he could gain an advantage, Lyting seized one arm from beneath him and plowed his head into Rurik's side, beneath the arm, propelling him forward, hard against the earth.

Rurik grimaced as his shoulder took the impact, grinding into the dirt. Lyting was no more the stripling youth he preferred to remember, but a man full-grown, and a worthy opponent at that.

Agilely, Lyting shifted round in a quarter circle and moved

overtop Rurik. In one rapid movement, he slipped his arms over neck and between leg, then locked both hands together beneath Rurik's belly. With Rurik thusly "cradled," Lyting rolled with him onto his own back in a maneuver designed to encumber one's rival.

But Rurik would not be dispensed with so easily. He kicked out vigorously with one leg, breaking the hold, then rolled away and sprang to his feet.

Lyting charged again, but this time Rurik caught him, snaring one arm under and around Lyting's and locking onto the side of his neck. With the other arm, Rurik seized Lyting around the waist and hoisted him off his feet. Quickly, Rurik dropped to the ground, covering Lyting with his own body while never breaking his hold on Lyting's head.

Try though he might, Lyting could not move. Forced to yield, he laughed with good humor.

"Next year, brother, I won't let you off so easily."

Before Rurik could rise, another hand clamped him on the shoulder and he looked up into the grinning face of Ketil Blunt-nose.

"Now that you children have had your play and done little to impress the ladies, 'tis time to take on a real man."

Rurik groaned as Ketil lifted him from behind in a bone-crushing bear hug. It took considerable strength to pry Ketil's hands apart and force one of the arms down and away from his waist. But Rurik broke free and reversed their positions. Slipping in back of Ketil, he grabbed the giant from behind. Ketil, however, gave out a great guffaw and, giving way his weight, sat back on Rurik. The two thudded gracelessly to the ground with Rurik pinned flat on his back, the air knocked out of him. Ketil sat atop, an immovable, laughing mountain.

"Oaf! Is this how you bedazzle the maidens?" Rurik smote Ketil's back, then groaned.

Several men hurried forward with buckets of water and doused the two. While Ketil rose, shaking his woolly head till water sprayed everyone near, Lyting stood to one side laughing heartily.

"Better you than me, *broðir*!" He offered Rurik a hand up. "Let's go soothe our aches with a bladder of wine."

The crowds cheered and clapped as the two brothers strode from the field.

Brienne, too, cheered enthusiastically, now that she could be assured no necks or bones would be broken, and she could breathe easily once again. Forgetting herself, she watched after Rurik and Lyting as they walked side by side, two splendid stallions, their muscles rippling and bunching with every movement. It did not gladden her when Katla sallied forth across the field to join Rurik. She looked away rather than bear the sight of the two embracing.

Brienne's enthusiasm for the games pleased Atli. The men's play obviously impressed her and livened her blood. Well, he was not so ancient or so in his dotage that he couldn't participate as well! When the horn sounded, announcing the start of the next game, Atli swallowed the last of his mead and stepped forward.

Angling a glance to where Aleth stood in the crowd, Ketil joined Atli and a dozen others for the traditional sport of boulder lifting. Numerous rocks, varying in size and weight, rested in the prescribed area, waiting to test the brute strength of the challengers.

"Shouldn't you be saving your energies for your bride?" Ketil chided as Atli doffed his tunic.

"Just warming up, lad. But are you sure you wish to embarrass yourself here? These are a might heavier than that young pup of mine you just tossed about. 'Twill take more than the muscles in your backside."

Ketil threw back his head and laughed heartily. "We'll see what you can lift this day," he said meaningfully, then stooped over one of the larger rocks and hefted it easily to his chest, then up above his head.

Atli chose another, slightly greater, and lifted it the same way, forcing the other contestants to choose rocks of equal size. The men continued for what seemed an interminable length of time, lifting progressively larger and weightier boulders. Their bodies glistened with sweat as they grunted and heaved the rocks over their heads and into the air.

At last only Ketil and Atli remained, the others having exhausted the limits of their brawn and endurance. But it seemed to Ketil that Atli strained his own bounds. When not lifting, he rubbed at his chest, and his face had long remained flushed a ruddy hue. Ketil preferred to end the game yet would not embarrass Atli before his men.

As Ketil lifted a final boulder, he gave an exaggerated groan under its weight, laboring as he hefted it chest high. Pressing it above his shoulders, he allowed it to slip from his hold, then cursed soundly as the rock thudded to the ground.

Whether Atli suspected the mishap, he accepted his triumph without question, parting with a few mirthful barbs. In truth, he was glad to be done with it. Now he desired but two things, a long cool draught of mead and the sight of his bride's beautiful face.

Just as the crowd began to disperse and return to their feasting in the keep, Hastein thundered forward on his great dun.

"A challenge, brother!" he shouted out to Rurik. "Surt against Sleipnir. Let them fight!"

Brienne stiffened at the smile that poisoned Hastein's lips. She quickly turned to Brother Bernard who stood scowling at her side.

"What is his intent? What does he wish?"

"To stallion fight. 'Tis a wicked sport. The beasts will tear at each other—unto death if not restrained. Hastein would favor that."

He patted Brienne's hand, then voiced his concerns to Atli. Atli looked down at Brienne then back at his sons as he contemplated the monk's words.

"I advised him that such a display would upset and affront you, my dear. Let us pray that he will put an end to this savagery before it begins."

"But why does Hastein do this?"

"Hastein is a jealous man. He has specially bred his horse for meanness, just for such a fight. He wouldst like nothing better than to deprive Rurik of the black."

"But to what purpose?"

"Atli gifted Rurik with Sleipnir when first he returned from the sea. Hastein felt the horse should have been his."

Before the monk could say more, their attention was drawn back by the sound of Rurik's voice.

"I will not risk such fine horseflesh for your amusement, *broðir*."

"Does the *Barnakarl* cower before my challenge?" Hastein ridiculed.

"*Stoðva!* Cease!" Atli bellowed angrily. His next words were lost on Brienne. She looked to the monk as he sighed his relief.

"Atli has commanded that there be a race instead. You will find this more enjoyable, my dear."

"But why does Hastein call Rurik the *Barna*—" Horns blared nearby, preventing her from finishing the question.

Brother Bernard pointed to where the starting line was marked and the course set. Men hurried to deposit objects in small piles at different intervals. Some laid down their goblets, while others donated valuable rings and bracelets, even the silver brooches securing their garments. The richest prizes were placed at the greatest distance from the starting point. The farthest mound of treasures included a small ivory casket carved with figures and trimmed with gold.

"You see, my dear," Brother Bernard explained, "each man must determine which prize he will seek, depending on the swiftness and sturdiness of his mount. To ill choose means no gain at all."

"Wouldst you care to add your own prize, my lady?" Lyting appeared before her, smiling down from his dapple-gray courser.

Brienne returned the smile, then creased her brow. "I have nothing of value . . . except my girdle."

"*Nei*, 'tis too fine a gift for the bride to offer. But something small. A slipper, perchance?"

Brienne laughed gaily, removing one of her leather shoes and handing it up to Lyting. Atli seemed to approve, addressing his own suggestion to his son.

Lyting turned his mount and sprinted down the full length of the course till he had well passed the last small pile of riches. Swiftly dismounting, he held the shoe up for all to see, then he set it on the ground by itself. The bride's slipper would be considered the most valued prize of all.

As nearly three dozen contestants jostled and vied for better positions behind the starting line, Hastein cast a secretive

smile in Rurik's direction. No one noticed when he slipped
a small metal spike into the back of his heel.

At the blast of trumpets, wild whoops filled the air and
the riders bolted forward.

Sleipnir stretched out easily, taking the lead as Rurik
leaned into him and became one with the steed. Hastein
closed behind but failed to overtake the great black.

Rurik passed one pile of goods after another, pressing on
till at last he approached the slipper. Slowing his mount and
holding fast to Sleipnir's mane, he slid partway down the
side of the stallion and scooped up the small shoe. The black
continued in an easy gait as Rurik reseated himself and gave
a yell of triumph, holding his booty high overhead. A shout
went up from the crowd, approving the capture.

Just then, Hastein loosened his hold on the dun and kicked
his spiked heel into its flank. Screaming his protest, Surt
reared. To the onlookers, it appeared that the beast rebelled,
breaking from Hastein's control and issuing challenge to the
black.

Surt lunged forward on the low whistle of his master's
command. With ears pinned back and teeth bared, he rapidly
closed the distance between himself and Sleipnir. Impatient
to gain the vantage as he converged on his opponent, the
dun bit at the black's hindquarter, tearing away a piece
of flesh.

But Sleipnir, trained for war, reacted instinctively. He
sprang upward, and upon coming back to earth, kicked
straight out and caught the dun solidly in the face.

Nearly unseated by Sleipnir's reprisal, Rurik wrapped the
reins around his wrist and gripped the stallion's mane. Pressing his legs tightly against the horse's sides, he braced himself as Sleipnir pivoted sharply on one hind foot and reared
to deliver his next strike.

Surt, too dazed to evade the assault, stumbled under
Sleipnir's crushing blow to his shoulder.

Forced to retreat before the black could inflict further
damage, Hastein lost his moment. Still, he smiled with a
measure of satisfaction as he called back lamely, "Sorry,
broðir. He broke from my grasp."

Rurik would have called Hastein out, but the horns sounded

urgently, demanding an end to the fray. Bridling his fury, he turned Sleipnir and galloped toward the crowd.

Brienne stood trembling, her heart beating wildly as Rurik approached. She had feared desperately for his life during the clash. Now, a frantic and delirious joy swept over her as he dismounted, whole and unscathed. She battled an overwhelming desire to fling herself into his arms and forget aught else.

Holding his gaze from Brienne, Rurik proffered the slipper on outstretched palm and waited for his father to place it on her foot. But Atli, feeling that his son had well earned the right, gestured for Rurik to perform the deed.

As Rurik's eyes met Brienne's, their cool gray warmed to blue. She smiled gently to behold this small window to his heart.

His gaze traveled over her face, impressing each beautiful and delicate feature to memory. These he would carry with him and cherish all the days of their parting.

Brienne raised her gown, revealing a trim, well-turned ankle. As Rurik knelt down, she placed her hand on his broad shoulder, steadying herself as she offered her foot.

Rurik could swear that Brienne's touch burned clear through his leather jerkin. He swallowed deeply as his fingers slid around her slender ankle and he lifted her leg. Carefully, almost reverently, he replaced the slipper.

Color stroked Brienne's cheeks but did not betray the fire coursing through her veins or the thundering of her heart against her ribs. She moistened her lips and looked away as Rurik rose to his full height. Her gaze strayed to the stallion's bloodied coat.

"Sleipnir needs be tended. I will bring medicants to the stables—"

"*Nei*, my lady." A mixture of sadness and resignation tinged Rurik's words though his eyes spoke of desire and longing. " 'Twould be unwise for us to meet thusly. Have Aleth collect what is necessary and send them with Ketil. I will see to Sleipnir." He, too, shifted his gaze to the black. "Your presence is required in the hall this night."

The reminder of her duty at Atli's side quenched her spirit, and she knew only a hollow ache within her breast.

"Will we see you before you take leave of Valsemé?"

"Verily, my lady." *Verily, unto your wedding chamber,* he added silently, then led the stallion away.

The feasting continued well past dark as the men consumed enormous quantities of food and drink. Golden beer and spiced wine flowed freely, though the more stalwart preferred a heady mead, as did Atli. Musicians strolled about, gladding the hall with viele and harp, while jugglers amused with their deft skills and comical distractions.

At one point a strange device was brought forth, dubbed a "halter cup," that proved a challenge for even the hardiest of men. Both a drinking vessel and an elaborate harness combined, the contrivance was carved from a single block of wood. The Norsemen took turns sitting in a chair, with hands clasped behind them. Slipping their heads through the halter's opening, they leaned back in one motion and downed the entire contents of the cup.

Again, Esternay forbade his men to participate in the sport, and kept them to watered wine as well. Reputedly, a Northman's feast could be as hazardous as the battlefield.

But Atli was not about to have the evening ruined with drunken misbehavior. When his men had enjoyed their play long enough, he ordered the cup taken away and called for the skald, Evyind.

The hall hushed as the skald plucked at his harp, recalling the exploits of heroes, kings, and warrior gods. He sang of terrifying serpents in oceans deep, of flaming swords and misty realms where the frost giants dwelt.

Averse to being outshone by their counterparts, and disgruntled for having been excluded from so many of the day's diversions, the Franks called on one of their own to rival the skald.

Surprisingly, Leveque came forward and, taking up the lute, proved himself a respectable trouvère. To everyone's delight, he reminisced of the glorious age and heroic achievements of Charlemagne.

As Leveque wove glittering tales of far-flung conquests, Rurik rejoined the festivities and took his place next to his father at the high table. Lyting was present there too, sitting to one side of Brienne, but Hastein remained conspicuously absent. Rurik observed him a moment later, moving about the hall.

Katla slid into a seat next to Rurik and pressed her bosom against his arm. Purring throatily, she dragged a fingernail down his arm and into his lap. He caught her hand and thrust it back, disgusted by her whorish ways. Thoroughly piqued, Katla rose, tossing her head, and stalked from the dais.

Rurik returned his attention to Leveque, who now recounted the celebrated legend of Roland and of Ganelon's betrayal at Roncesvalles. When the tale ended, even Evyind clapped enthusiastically for the Frank.

Atli rubbed at his neck and beckoned for more mead. His breathing came short and labored. He despised weakness, especially in himself, and refused to pay heed to the pains now shooting through his left arm.

Evyind appeared before the high table and, caressing the strings of his instrument, sang tribute to the bride's beauty.

Brienne warmed under the attention. Although she held the regard of every male in the hall, she felt only the heat of Rurik's gaze, drawing her eyes to his. She lifted her lashes to seek that steely blue sea, but Atli broke the enchantment as he stroked the back of her hand and then pressed it with a wet kiss.

The men cheered and, being well into their cups, clamored impatiently that the bedding ceremony begin.

Brienne paled. No longer could she close her mind to the reality of her wedding vows. She must summon her courage, for there was no escape. A wife must give freely of her flesh to the man she called husband. She shuddered, knowing full well that somewhere in the hall Esternay was silently laughing.

Aleth and two maidservants appeared to escort Brienne to Atli's chamber and prepare her to receive him. Brienne's possessions had been transferred there earlier and added to her husband's. All was in readiness. The final adornment the room required was the bride, herself, to grace the marriage bed.

The Normans grew boisterous, eager to begin. With much merriment and jesting, they would carry off the groom, stripping him right down to his pink buttocks, and present him to his bride. If luck be theirs, they would glimpse her silken contours when they drew back the covers and heaved him into bed.

Atli smiled down on his young wife, anticipating the pleasure her body would yield him this night. She trembled and his heart softened as he reminded himself that she had been shut away for these many years. 'Twas never easy for a maid the first time. He would use her well. But, for now, she needed fortification.

Rising from his chair, Atli called loudly for mead. An elderly Frankish servant hobbled forward with a flagon of the strong spirits. Atli unburdened the man and filled Brienne's goblet to the rim. He then emptied the remainder of the container into his drinking horn. Gesturing for her to take up her cup, he lifted his horn and toasted Brienne's health and loveliness.

Atli paused for a moment, tilting her chin up with a curled finger, then brushed his knuckles along her delicate jawline. Pleased beyond measure, he saluted her with his drink and drained the horn.

Atli suddenly sputtered, eyes bulging. Pain crushed his chest and overwhelmed him. Clutching at his heart, he collapsed to the floor.

Brienne and Rurik were first to his side. Rurik quickly loosened Atli's tunic where it constricted his neck while Brienne felt his face and hands. Atli had broken into a cold, clammy sweat. Obviously in pain, he fought to breathe, managing only short, quick gasps.

"Can you speak?" Rurik asked urgently. "What smites you?"

"Feels . . . like . . . Sleipnir . . . sitting on . . . chest."

Atli's eyes darkened as an impending sense of doom engulfed him. He snatched at the ceremonial arm ring that encircled his forearm.

"Help . . . me."

Rurik eased the ring from his father's arm, but when he placed it in his hand, Atli pressed it back into Rurik's palm.

"Hold . . . all that is . . . mine." He looked over to

Brienne, then squeezed his eyes shut in pain. "All!" he rasped.

A low murmur passed among those gathered round the dais as Atli made his pronouncement.

The pain subsided for a brief moment and Atli rolled his head back, gulping the air.

"My sword . . . must . . . have *Bíta*."

Several moments later, Lyting appeared with "Bite" and placed it in his father's hands.

Atli suddenly grabbed at Rurik's jerkin. "Do not let . . . these Christians . . . commit my body . . . unto the earth." His breathing came labored and rapid. "Promise . . . my spirit . . . will fly . . . straight to the heavens. . . . Promise!"

Rurik vowed, easing Atli's anxiety over the matter.

Atli seemed to relax at that. A gleam touched his eye as he fingered the cold steel of his sword.

" 'Twas not the blade . . . I sought to wield . . . this night!" He smiled faintly.

Pain flooded him anew. He groaned out the full length of his breath, then slumped to the floor in death.

Brienne bowed her head and whispered a prayer. Several moments later Rurik raised her gently to her feet, as Brother Bernard and Lyting knelt beside Atli's lifeless form.

A commotion erupted in the hall, fracturing the sepulchral silence. When Brienne cast about for the source of the disturbance, she found Katla standing alongside Hastein, her lips curled in triumph.

Hastein drew on his dagger as he shouted out commands that the Franks be surrounded.

"God's wounds!" blustered the monk. "They believe Atli has been poisoned at the hands of our people. Hastein means to kill every Frank, if needs be, one by one till a confession is wrought."

"Nay!" Brienne shrieked, seeing the elderly servant who had borne the mead forced to his knees and a knife put to his throat.

Rurik started forward, but before he could intervene, Brienne sprang to action, sweeping past him to the dais's edge.

"Not poison!" she screamed in protest. "Atli died of a malady. 'Twas no foul deed!"

Hastein snorted in reply, unconvinced.

"Since first I arrived, Gruel Atli suffered an affliction. He sought to conceal it but didst not wholly succeed—especially this day. Were you blind to it?"

" 'Tis true." Ketil came forth. "Atli was bedeviled even as we competed with the rocks."

"Lies!" Hastein growled fiercely, pressing his knife deeper into the Frank's flesh.

Frantically, Brienne searched for Atli's drinking horn, but it lay empty upon the floor. Grabbing up her own goblet, she held it high in the air.

"Behold!" she shouted above the din. "You all witnessed Atli fill my vessel before his own, both from the same flagon." A rumble of acknowledgment passed through the Northmen. "If Gruel Atli's drink was tainted, then so is mine."

Fearing her intent, Rurik leaped to knock the cup from her hands, but Brienne whirled away from him and rapidly downed its contents.

She gasped as fire seared a trail down her throat and through her chest, scorching its way to the pit of her stomach. Doubling over sharply, she groped for the table and pushed herself up again.

Rurik moved to assist her, but she waved him back. Brienne knew she must see this moment through alone and prove her people's innocence. She dare not collapse or faint, lest she awake to find that every Frank had been put to the sword.

Wiping the back of her hand across her mouth, Brienne rallied. Angrily, she snatched up her goblet and hurled it at Hastein's feet.

"Not poison!" she proclaimed defiantly.

"Enough!" Rurik bellowed. "Release the Franks!"

Reluctantly, Hastein drew away his blade but grazed a the servant's neck as he did, so that a thin trickle of blood followed his knife's point.

"As you wish, *broðir*." His lips twisted with a cold smile.

Ketil stood before the assemblage and quieted the hall with

upheld arms. "Before he drew his last breath, Atli recognized Rurik as his heir."

At that Ketil turned and dropped to one knee. Closing his hand into a fist, he struck his chest once, over the heart. "I am your liege man by life and by limb. Accept this my oath." His shout went up and was joined by a chorus of male voices. "Hail, Rurik, son of Atli, Baron de Valsemé!"

Hastein snarled as his kinsmen paid homage to his despised brother. Angrily, he stalked from the hall.

Esternay watched Hastein's departure with interest. Atli's death complicated matters, for a certainty, but there were always alternatives. A new plan began to form in the crevices of his mind.

After Rurik entrusted his father's body to Ketil and Lyting, he escorted Brienne from the hall. She insisted on crossing the room unaided, even if somewhat unsteadily. Once they passed through the portal and reached the bottom of the stairs, she swayed, hiccuping loudly. Unable to restrain himself any longer, Rurik swept her up in his strong arms and carried her above, two steps at a time.

Languidly, Brienne laced her arms around his neck, the drink taking its effect, and rolled her head against his shoulder. She breathed deeply of his clean male scent and snuggled into his chest.

Heat shot through Rurik's vitals. He shifted her in his arms as he grappled with his rising desire. 'Twas a time of mourning, not passion, he chastised himself. Still, his heart remained at variance with his head.

Halfway up to the garret rooms, Rurik stopped and reconsidered. Making his decision, he retraced his steps and headed for his father's chamber.

Somehow, he suspected the room had once belonged to Brienne's parents, for it was larger than the rest. Atli had appropriated the quarter when first he arrived at Valsemé. This night it was meant to serve as the bridal chamber as well. The room could yet serve a purpose.

Booting open the door, Rurik crossed to the bed and gently laid Brienne down. She sighed drowsily and burrowed into its soft comfort as she drifted into a deep slumber.

Rurik smiled down at her, proud of her courageous spirit.

"Rest, *ástin mín*." He kissed her tenderly upon the forehead. "Rest, my love."

Chapter Nine

✥ ✥ ✥ ✥ ✥ ✥ ✥ ✥ ✥ ✥ ✥ ✥ ✥

BRIENNE CRACKED OPEN one eye then squeezed it shut against the stream of sunlight invading her chamber. Her limbs felt strangely numb. She wiggled her fingers successfully, but her toes were another matter. She would have to risk a glance to assure herself they were still attached. And then there was her mouth. It felt as though it were stuffed with a sturdy woolen stocking.

Again, she peered from beneath sleep-heavy lids and surveyed her surroundings. The room was familiar yet different. Her parents' bedchamber? she wondered dimly. Skins were scattered everywhere—across the floor, over chests, and onto the spacious bed. She felt lost amongst their furry presence. More pelts stretched over the walls, crowded by a host of weaponry. Her gaze traveled over the unfamiliar chests and chairs, deeply carved with a rich tangle of design.

Panic gripped her. No! 'Twas a Norseman's chamber and a Norseman's bed. Atli's bed! She bolted upright, instantly regretting the action as a sharp pain ripped through her brain. Groaning loudly, she caught her head in her hands and eased herself back down onto the pillows.

Yestereve's calamitous events came back in a rush, sweeping away the foggy haze that first encumbered her. Soberly, she lifted her hand and studied the small gold band encircling the third finger of her left hand.

"Ah, you wake at last," Aleth called softly as she entered the room bearing a platter of broken meats, cheese, and bread. Setting the tray on a small table before the fire, she filled a goblet and crossed to the bed.

"Here now, a bit of wine to stir the circulation. 'Tis nigh on to noon. The first courses have already been served in the hall, not that any could attend to their meal amidst all the argument there. The men are in a terrible humor."

Brienne found it difficult to follow Aleth's stream of chatter. She cocked a questioning brow as she took a tiny sip of the wine.

"They have quarreled the morning long over the funeral preparations, bickering to no end as to what shall be done with Atli's—" Aleth clamped her hands over her mouth, mortified by her thoughtlessness. "Oh, I am sorry, Brienne. My tongue outpaces my poor mind, I fear."

Brienne gave Aleth a small, reassuring smile. "Do not fret yourself. Pray, go on." She gestured for Aleth to continue as she attempted a second small sip, her stomach not yet objecting to the first.

"Brother Bernard insists Atli be buried according to the prescribed rites of Holy Mother Church, but Rurik has set himself to honor his father's dying wish."

Aleth's eyes rounded wide and she leaned forward. "Why, some of the Norsemen think to place Gruel Atli in his long-ship, together with his belongings, and set the entire thing afire as it drifts out to the open seas. You can well imagine what Brother Bernard had to say about that!"

Indeed, Brienne could all too well envision the monk haranguing the hall with a spate of vivid remarks and punctuating each one with his trusty little sword. She suppressed a smile. "And Rurik?"

"Rurik favors the torch." Aleth shook her head. "He wouldst forgo the ship for a pyre and minimum of grave goods."

A cold chill passed through Brienne. Rarely had she regarded Rurik as the Norseman he truly was. Had she childishly thought to deny that part of him? She preferred to ignore his fierce Nordic heritage, setting him apart—nay, above—his own kindred.

Aleth interrupted Brienne's thoughts as she settled on the bed, her brows knit over troubled brown eyes. "What will become of us now?"

To her dismay, Brienne could offer no answer.

*   *   *

With a sharp little needle, Aleth picked out the stitches from her broidery for a third time, then angled a glance sideways to where Brienne stood staring out the chamber window.

Aleth opened her mouth to admonish her friend for neglecting the platter of meats and cheese but thought better of it.

Brienne was absorbed deep in her thoughts, virtually motionless except for the quiet movement of her hands. Slowly, she turned the smooth band of gold round and round her finger. Aleth shook her head with a tiny sigh. Thus her friend had stood for a seeming eternity, sorting through the many burdens of her heart as she lingered over the beloved contours of Valsemé.

Just then, Brienne turned, apparently having come at last to some decision. To Aleth's surprise, she slipped the ring from her finger then lifted somber violet eyes.

Aleth rose as Brienne crossed the room. Next she knew, Brienne was placing the ring in her palm and folding her fingers around it.

"Add this to my coffer, Aleth. Bundle it along with the brooches."

Brienne forestalled Aleth's unspoken questions with a gentle squeeze of her hands. " 'Tis all right, Aleth. But there are matters to be settled. I need find Brother Bernard."

Aleth hesitated, searching the strained lines of Brienne's face, then allowed that the good brother could best comfort her.

But was there need for comfort? she wondered unabashedly. Brienne had feared her lot with Atli but, providentially, she had been spared. Not that Brienne wished the man dead, Aleth quickly amended, and mentally crossed herself. Now Rurik would be baron, and she suspected Brienne cared more for the golden man than her friend dared admit.

Of course, Katla's presence posed an awkward dilemma. There could be but one baronne. Aleth doubted that Brienne could easily step aside while the Norsewoman directed the affairs of the keep . . . or warmed Rurik's bed. A small nagging voice pricked at that last thought in the back of her mind, but Brienne snagged her with an expectant look before Aleth could examine it further. Well, if not comfort, then certainly the churchman could offer guidance and advice.

"The men abandoned their arguments in the hall a short while past," Aleth said simply. "Mayhaps Brother Bernard has sought some respite at the church."

Brienne nodded gratefully. Drawing on her mantle, she moved toward the door.

Aleth took a quick limping step after her, unsaid words poised on her lips. Brienne read the concern in Aleth's eyes and regretted that she could not yet disclose the course she felt bound to take. Perchance Aleth would choose differently for herself, though more likely not. How uncertain their futures had suddenly become. Brienne's eyes darkened.

"Who can know the mind of the Lord?" she said with a quiet sadness. "But we must ever seek His way, even when we would rather follow the whisperings of our hearts."

Katla's snappish tones assailed Brienne's ears as she approached the hall. She made a moue. Oh, what she would give for a hidden passage to secret her leave-taking! It had long been a childhood fantasy, one that she could well put to use at the moment. She sighed. Alas, to gain the stone staircase leading down to the entrance of the keep, she must pass first through the hall.

Brienne slowed her steps as she verged on the portal. If luck was hers, Katla would be so engrossed in ordering the servants about and putting the great chamber to rights that she would not mark her progress there. But luck was not to be found.

Katla stood grandly in the center of the room directing the dismantling and stacking of the tables against the far wall. She ceased her dictates as Brienne entered, and turned fully to confront her rival. Deliberately allowing her arm to drop, she caused the large ring of keys that she now wore prominently at her hip to jangle noisily.

Brienne's brows winged upward. Katla had lost little time claiming her place, Brienne thought as she noted the symbol of authority that signified her position as mistress of the keep. She was surprised and somewhat hurt that Rurik would allow Katla to so boldly displace her while her own status was uncertain and he himself had yet to be confirmed as baron. It struck her curious as well that, until now, Katla had never worn the keys. As Atli's daughter-by-marriage and the only Norsewoman present, she certainly held the right. Brienne could only wonder at Atli's reasons in denying her that privilege.

"Is there aught you seek here, Lady Brienne?" Katla's sharp voice cut through her thoughts.

Brienne bristled at Katla's overbearing manner. "Nay," she responded stiffly, thinking of several scabrous remarks she would like to level at the woman. "I need speak with Brother Bernard."

Katla laughed harshly. "You wish to seek *his* counsel? The man is a fool."

The bald charge took Brienne aback. Apparently, Katla had been privy to the morning's deliberations, and the monk, being his verbal self, had managed to thoroughly estrange the Norsewoman.

"You Christians are *all* fools," Katla hissed contemptuously, taking a small step forward. "You take those you honor and shut them away in the moldering depths of the earth."

"Atli accepted Holy Baptism and embraced the Faith," Brienne countered defensively. "He merits a Christian burial."

Katla scoffed. "He simply took no chances. What is one more god?"

Brienne felt her hackles rise, but before she could bite out a retort, Katla turned and fixed her gaze on a crackling torch braced against the wall. Even at this distance her green eyes captured the flickering light. They glowed oddly as Katla smiled into the flames.

"Fools," she muttered. "We Norse set their spirits free in an instant so they might escape to the heavens undelayed."

A chill spread down Brienne's spine as Katla continued to stare into the licking flames, entranced. Silently, she withdrew and slipped from the hall.

Brienne briskly traversed the courtyard, eager to place the greatest distance between herself and the Norsewoman. A frown puckered her brow and she mumbled beneath her breath as she stalked toward the gate. She stood ready to defy any who would thwart her in departing the confines of the bailey. To her amazement, the tall young Norman who guarded the gate bestowed a warm smile and a slight bow as she crossed the bridge. His words seemed pleasantly given though she could grasp but one word—baronne.

Brienne increased her pace, pleasuring in the exertion as she stretched her limbs and inhaled deeply of Valsemé's sweet fragrance. Brother Bernard would not be pleased with her decision, but she saw no other course.

Esternay smiled as his dark eyes followed Brienne's purposeful strides toward the gate.

"A rare beauty to warm a man's bed, is she not?" he asked, baiting his companion.

Hastein scanned Brienne's elegant profile as she passed over the bridge, his hands aching with the memory of the full swell of breast and silken thighs.

" 'Twas the king's desire to award her to Valsemé's Norman lord," Esternay continued casually, "regardless the man who claimed that title."

Hastein cast a glassy eye back over the knight. "What do you want, Frank?" Not awaiting an answer, he crouched down and flung his small dagger into the dirt.

"Rumor has it," Esternay began, propping a foot on a small boulder, "that Rurik is not the eldest of Atli's sons."

"Didst you tumble one of the village whores for that worthy piece of gossip?" Hastein sneered. He bent to retrieve his knife, flinging it into the dirt a second time. " 'Tis no secret, Frank. Atli captured my mother in a raid upon the Celtic kingdom. She was his slave."

"And his lover?" Esternay pressed.

" 'Twas his right." Hastein shrugged dispassionately but twisted the knife free of the ground with more force than was necessary. "Atli favored her above the others. He would have set her free and taken her to wife had it not been for the high-strutting Ranneveig."

"Rollo's sister?"

"Rollo's sister," Hastein repeated sourly, digging at the ground with his blade. "He was bedazzled by her golden beauty and quickly forgot my mother."

Esternay gave a slight nod of understanding. "And so you served your father in his hall, no more than a slave yourself?"

Hastein cut the knight with a sharp look. "We are not uncivilized, Frank. A Norseman's bastards do not suffer for the accident of their birth as do yours. My mother may have remained a slave but I was raised as an equal alongside Ranneveig's sons."

"Equal?" A challenge laced the word. "Yet 'tis Rurik who shall rule Valsemé."

Hastein gripped the knife, his eyes hardening, and slowly straightened. He fixed the king's man with an icy glare as he stroked the keen edge of his dagger with a callused thumb. "Whose cause do you serve, Frank?"

The Seigneur d'Esternay likewise straightened his stance. He met Hastein with an even look. One corner of his mouth curved upward. "My own."

Hastein suddenly flipped the weapon end over end. Catching it by the tip of the blade, he hurled it at a log in the woodstack. The knife thudded solidly into its newfound home. "As do I."

Esternay contemplated the quivering piece of steel. Hastein was a dangerous man but would be manageable enough till his usefulness was past and he could be eliminated.

The knight smiled inwardly. Hastein's hatreds blinded him where Rurik was concerned, and his lusts played to advantage. Of all the Norsemen they had encountered thus far, Brienne clearly feared this man the most. She would yet be pliable to his terms.

Hastein worked the dagger free of the wood then, turning slowly, allowed a rare half smile to cross his face. "Now, Frank, what is it you want?"

It took several moments for Brienne's eyes to adjust to the dimness inside the church. Yestermorn the nave was brightened by dozens of candles while her marriage vows were blessed. She curled her fingers into her palm, all too conscious of the golden weight missing from her left hand.

In part, the past week seemed some ghastly dream. There were moments when she feared she would awake and find herself, still, Gruel Atli's betrothed. Charles would not use her to his ends again!

Muffled voices drew her attention to the rear of the church, where a small door stood ajar in the back wall, behind and to one side of the altar. This, she knew, led into the sacristy, a robing room where clergy vested for mass.

Brienne called the monk by name as she started down the long, narrow interior of the church, genuflecting once as she passed before the tabernacle. Brother Bernard poked his head out the door, obviously taken by surprise.

"My lady!" he gasped. "One moment, please."

Hastily, he turned back to his companion. So many sheep to tend this day! 'Twas unforgivable that he should have forgotten the Lady Brienne.

"My son, you need not bother yourself with these simple repairs."

Lyting glanced toward the nave where Brienne waited, then looked back to the sacristy's side door, which opened to the outside. "*Nei*," he said, testing the planks of the door for a second time. " 'Tis good that I use my hands and rest my mind apace. See here, the wood is rotted round the lock and the latch is rusted. 'Twill scarce secure the church."

"Very well. There be tools in the coffer, there by the wall."

Lyting marked the monk's retreat into the church proper, then crouched down to rummage through the chest.

"My lady, forgive me. That you must seek me out in such an hour, alas—" Brother Bernard gestured with open hands. " 'Twas a morning given to much confusion and cross purposes. I fear I have sorely neglected your own needs. Does all fare well with you, Lady Brienne?"

Brienne managed a small smile. "I am fine, truly, but I would avail myself of your wisdom."

"Of course, my child. How might I aid you?"

"I need clarify a matter of some import." She caught her lower lip between her teeth for a moment before adding, "Concerning my position here."

"Your position here? At Valsemé?" The monk puzzled, uncomprehending. "You are the baronne."

"I think not, good brother." Brienne stepped away to stand before the altar, giving him her back, and gazed up at the crucifix.

Brother Bernard looked at her blankly. He had not yet threshed out the ramifications of Gruel Atli's death. His energies had been consumed, thus far, in preventing the Norsemen from sending Atli off in a blaze down the river Toques.

"Is it not so," Brienne began carefully, "that even though vows be spoken, if one of the spouses dies before the marriage can be consummated or the *Morgengabe,* the morning gift, be endowed, that the marriage is invalid?"

Brother Bernard's bushy brows flew up. At the same time, the shuffling noises in the rear of the church ceased.

"Aye," he forced out at length, settling a ponderous look upon the maid. " 'Tis so."

"Is there aught required, papers from Rome's legate or the archbishop, perchance?"

"Nay, my lady. 'Tis as though the vows were never spoken. Nothing further is required. I myself am witness."

"All is as it was before?"

"Aye, I have said as much."

"Then it follows that I am still the ward of the king."

"Aye," the monk granted cautiously. He could not fault her logic but neither could he perceive where her vein of thought led.

Brienne brought her eyes from the crucifix and faced Brother Bernard with solemn countenance. "I have fulfilled our king's commands and faithfully so. Those bindings are dissolved. There be no place for me here now. I wish to return to the Abbey of Levroux."

The clattering of wood and implements sounded in the rear chamber.

"Leave Valsemé?" the monk blustered. "My lady, 'tis unseemly. How can you say there is no place for you? You are the baronne."

"By your own admission, I am not." The words choked in her throat. She turned quickly to the altar before he could see the tears glitter to life in her eyes. "All is as it was before," Brienne whispered, her heart silently breaking. How could anything ever be the same again?

Curse Charles for his interference! She shook with anger and despair. Curse him for reopening old wounds still raw beneath their scars. Better that he had left her buried in cloister and not tampered with her heart. Now, for the second time in her life, she must forsake the lands that nurtured her and once and for all set aside her rightful place as baronne . . . for her people's sake . . . and for him whom she loved so desperately and wouldst ever be denied.

Brienne pressed her lashes shut to keep the hot tears from spilling. Rurik would be Baron de Valsemé and Katla his baronne. Where would be her place? Beneath the Norsewoman in her own home? And if she stayed atime, how long before the sovereign would seek to use her noble blood to tie alliances to his throne? Who this time? A Magyar henchman to quiet the East, she wondered outrageously, or a Muslim brigand to avert the raids on the southern coast?

But even should she remain and suffer Katla's domination and the misery of knowing the woman filled Rurik's bed each night, her own presence could cause naught but division. Her people would never accept the Norsewoman whilst a Beaumanoir dwelt on Valsemé's soil. No doubt they would look first to her and create greater problems for Rurik as he established his authority. 'Twould be direful indeed if he be forced to chasten them for their loyalties to herself should they openly reject his wife. Nay. She would leave whilst she may to live out her days in cloister beneath the veil, haunted by the memories of her golden warrior.

"And what of our Frankish villeins, my lady?" Brother Bernard asked gravely, his heavy brows butted together. "Didst you not return to intervene in their behalf?"

Brienne brushed a tear from the corner of her eye and sternly composed herself. "Rurik is a fair and just man. I do not fear for our people under his hand. Those who choose to come to Valsemé and those who remain will do so because of his goodness, not because of my presence."

Brother Bernard pursed his lips, thoroughly perplexed. Why was the maid so decided on leaving, especially now

that Rurik would assume lordship over her lands? There were
times in recent days when he worried over their heated looks
and stolen glances. Could he have so misread . . . ?

The low wail of a distant trumpet signaled approaching
troops.

" 'Twould seem we shall soon have guests." He gave a
mental shudder, wondering whether the visitors would beset
him with yet another crisis. "Best we see you to the keep,
my lady." He led her toward the entrance. "We shall speak
of this anon."

Brienne declined his offer of escort, more in need of
the time to herself, and promised to return to the bailey
forthwith.

When Brother Bernard turned back into the church, Lyting
stood framed in the portal of the sacristy, his mouth set in
grim lines.

Brienne made haste to the bailey but did not go straightaway
into the keep. She took refuge, instead, in the confines
of the manor house. Once she was certain that none were
about, she secluded herself in a far corner and gave in to
her tears.

A short time later, she willed herself to climb the endless
flight of wooden stairs and entered the keep. Wearily, she
garnered the last of her strength to mount the inner steps that
confronted her.

Where the entries of most keeps opened directly into the
hall, 'twas her father's design to incorporate a second staircase. His mind was ever bent on defense. Should the tower
itself fall under siege and be overrun, the enemy would be
forced to scale the curving, open stairs with their sword
arm against the wall. The keep's garrison, descending from
above, would fight to the advantage, their arms being free.

Waite suddenly appeared, charging like a little bull down
the stone staircase with Patch at his heels.

"Oh, m'lady! You must come, m'lady!"

"Waite, you gave me a terrible fright," Brienne scolded,
clutching the boy and pulling him away from the edge and
over to the wall. "These steps are fair uneven and clear
open to below. You must have care, child, or you will be

splitting your fine skull, and that I cannot mend so easily."

"Sorry, m'lady," Waite mumbled, instantly contrite, then remembered his urgency. "But, m'lady, Katla is quarreling with the limp-legged girl in your chamber."

"Aleth?"

"Aye, m'lady, and she is fierce mad, too."

"Katla?"

"Nay, m'lady, Aleth."

Brienne gathered her skirts and hurried up the steps. The squabbling reached her ears before she gained sight of the chamber. In the next moment, she found Aleth blocking the portal with her small frame, feet and arms braced wide, as servants tried to pass out of the room with Brienne's clothing chest in hand.

"Stand aside, you useless cripple," Katla shrilled, "or I will see your other leg—"

"Not if you value your life!" Brienne exploded, pushing between Aleth and Katla. Her nerves were frayed beyond measure, but no one, ever, dare speak in such a manner to sweet Aleth and think to come away unscathed.

Katla's eyes narrowed, then she suddenly threw back her head and laughed. "You think I would truly harm your woman? What honor is there in damaging that which is already impaired?"

Brienne started forward, but Aleth grabbed at her sleeve. "Nay, Brienne, please—" Her voice broke in an anguished plea.

Katla smiled with satisfaction as the pathetic chit clung to her mistress. How easily words cut at the heart. 'Twas a talent of hers and one that amused. But these were such mewling creatures. It robbed the pleasure from her play.

Katla shrugged at Brienne. "I but sought to return your possessions to your former room and ready the lord's chamber for Rurik. *We* have need of it now." She clawed with precision.

"But, Brienne," Aleth wailed, "I found her sniffing through your coffers. Methinks she—"

"Do not fear, Aleth. We shall account for the king's gifts later," Brienne reassured, cutting the Norsewoman with a hard look. "For I intend to return them, each and every ell of cloth and every fine trinket. If there be a shortage, I am sure Rurik will right the matter directly."

Brienne was satisfied to see Katla's smile thin, though it did not fade altogether. There would be little use for such luxuries in cloister, but, by the milk of the Virgin, Katla would not lay claim to the least of them.

"Till then, we are best in our garret room."

"How gratifying." Katla uttered a small, throaty laugh laced with derision. "A scrap of Frankish sense is yet found this day." She clapped her hands sharply at the servants. "Remove the chest."

The two men hefted the long, narrow chest to their shoulders and bore it from the room. Not a moment lapsed before they backed into the chamber and set the chest down once more.

"Dullards!" shrieked Katla. "Do you wish the lash? I command you to remove—" She swallowed her words as Rurik filled the doorway.

Brienne's heart skipped a beat at the sight of him and a smile spread through her being.

"Explain yourself, woman," he growled, cold eyes boring into Katla.

"I have been readying our . . . your chamber," she sputtered.

"On whose authority?"

"Why . . . I assumed—"

"You assume much, Katla." Rurik's voice was low and taut with anger.

Katla gasped softly. Mastering her wits an instant later, she crossed to him. The jangling of her keys drew his eye but she quickly pressed against him and trailed her long fingers over his broad chest.

"My only wish is to please you, Rurik," she cajoled, toying with the edge of his jerkin.

Rurik's look was inscrutable as he gripped Katla firmly by the wrists.

"You may begin by restoring all that you have seen fit to remove."

"But 'tis your right—"

"My father is barely cold, yet you eagerly cast his widow from his chamber. I shall not have it!" Rurik blazed, his patience finding its end.

Katla's cheeks flamed. She conceded with a curt nod, chafing smartly under his reproach.

"My lord—" Brienne hesitated to correct him. The words slipped from her tongue, yet it seemed most natural to call him "lord." "I am no widow."

Rurik's eyes snapped to her face.

"I shall gladly render up the room for your ease."

"*Nei*, my lady. You *are* my father's bride and you shall remain."

Brienne tensed. "No longer his bride," she amended firmly, "and most certainly not his widow." She was loath to broach the subject in Katla's presence, but she could not allow Rurik to misconceive her position.

"The marriage was not consummated and is therefore invalid. All is as it was. I am still the ward of the crown." She drew in a deep breath and pressed on. "I have little need for the room, as I shall be returning to the Abbey of Levroux."

"*Nei!*" Rurik's heart lurched out of place, then came jolting back to slam against his ribs. Confusion, frustration, hurt, and anger collided within him. Brusquely, he motioned the others from the room. "Leave us!" he ordered, his eyes remaining fixed on Brienne.

Astonished nearly as much as Rurik by the exchange, Aleth gathered Waite from where he hovered outside the portal. Katla obligingly drew the door shut behind her, the corners of her mouth turning upward.

Rurik stood motionless for a prolonged moment, holding Brienne bound by his steely gaze. He could not fathom her reasons for wishing to depart Valsemé. Had aught befallen of which he was not advised? He released a long, bewildered sigh, suddenly drained by the day's exactions.

Long into the night, he had sat in counsel with his father's men. Before dawn shed its light, he was on his feet again after a few hours of fitful rest, attending to the needs of the keep. The day grew into an unwieldy affair, often of high temper, as he debated over the funeral provisions and dealt with the burdens of his new authority.

Rurik raked a hand through his bright hair. He sought to escape for a time and seek comfort in Brienne's warmth. How he ached simply to hold her in his arms and allow the day's frustrations to seep from him and ease the pang of his loss.

True to his Norse heritage, he detested displays of weakness, though he had found long ago that 'twas not so easy a matter when death claimed one near to the heart. Tears he would deny. Still, he desired Brienne's healing presence to salve the pain he carried within.

"Surely you cannot mean to leave." Rurik reached for her.

"Nay, we must not." Brienne tried to pull away as he held her against his chest. "Oh, Rurik, can you not see? All is changed." Her violet eyes pleaded for understanding. "I cannot remain here. Not now," she said miserably, all too aware of his heart beating beneath her palm. "There is no place for me. I must leave. I must."

He strained to follow her reasoning but grasped not one shred of logic in the appeal. An ugly suspicion reared to life in the depths of his confusion. Could it be his Nordic blood, his and his kindred's, from which she sought to flee? He rejected the thought though it remained obstinately lodged in a corner of his heart.

"I know not of what you speak but I will hear none of it," he avowed, his mood grim. "Your Christian laws may not recognize your vows, but you forget: I hold to the ways of my ancestors. By Norse custom you are my father's widow and my responsibility now."

Unconsciously, Rurik increased the pressure on her arms as he held her to him, his temper rising more from the thought of losing her than from any real anger. "You will go nowhere! You will remain here, at Valsemé, where you belong."

Brienne's next words were lost as horns trumpeted in the bailey. Rurik drew her along with him to the window.

Brienne's eyes rounded wide and her jaw dropped open. Into the bailey strode the most tremendous man she had ever seen in her life.

Rurik smiled down on the giant with golden hair much like his own. "Hrolf," he identified the man. Seeing the amazed expression that captured Brienne's face, he laughed softly.

"In my land he is called Ganga-Hrolf, the Walker. In the halls 'tis sung that no horse can uphold his massive frame, so he must walk into battle. Your people have christened him with a new name. Rollo, Duke of Normandy."

Chapter Ten

❖ ❖ ❖ ❖ ❖ ❖ ❖ ❖ ❖ ❖ ❖ ❖

"HOLD STILL, BRIENNE!" Aleth tugged at the gown's laces.
Barely had she finished the ties but Brienne pulled away and
rushed to the window.

Below, soldiers crowded the bailey. To her eyes, Valsemé's
Norse garrison was indistinguishable from the duke's retainers
except that they held to a formal posture around the perimeters
of the assemblage. The latter continued to pass afoot into
the courtyard, exchanging smiles and nods of recognition. It
skirted Brienne's mind that these men were acquainted from
their days of ravening the land. Frankish land. Her land. She
clenched her jaw.

From their lighthearted bearing, Brienne realized that the
men of Rouen arrived anticipating Atli's wedding feast, not
his funeral. The grave tidings scarce had time to reach them
even by longship, if indeed any had thought to dispatch a
missive. Debate and argument had gripped the keep since
early morn, not to mention the altercation wrought the night
before.

Even now, the day was barely half spent. Brienne surmised that the duke and his soldiers had journeyed by water
these past hours. No horse accompanied them and the men
appeared fresh, neither damp with sweat nor caked with dust.
They moved with energy, many bearing small chests and
cloaked objects in their hands. Wedding gifts? she wondered with a start. Others braced carved wooden planks of
varying lengths upon their shoulders, possibly disassembled
furniture.

The tightness in her mouth relaxed into the beginnings of

a smile as it occurred to her that the duke traveled about with his great bed. 'Twas fortunate if true, she mused, for the keep housed no construction that could easily hold the Norse Goliath.

At that moment, Brienne caught several of the measured looks and wary glances that the Normans cast to where the Seigneur d'Esternay and his Frankish contingent stood near the motte's swelling mound of earth. Her smile spread to see her countrymen gauging the newly arrived Northmen with an equal intensity and portion of mistrust.

Scanning the crowded courtyard, Brienne easily located Rurik and his brothers by their uncle's mighty frame. Rollo stood rock-still, intent on Rurik's words. A frown creased the duke's heavy brow as he suddenly turned and lifted his gaze toward the keep.

Brienne shied away from the window, fearing he would glimpse her there. But curiosity spurred her to ease back and peer from the opening once more. She found Rurik's and Rollo's bright heads bowed in solemn conversation. No doubt Rurik was recounting the details of his father's death. The duke expelled a long breath, then broke from the exchange as Brother Bernard approached with the Seigneur d'Esternay.

"Quickly, Aleth." Brienne motioned toward the coffer. "My blue slippers and a girdle that becomes the gown."

Swinging her dark mass of hair over her shoulder and splitting it thrice, she wove it into a thick plait. Swiftly, she threw a glance from the narrow window to ensure that the men remained in conversation.

"Will you present the wine, then?" Aleth held forth the slippers and a fashionable belt of silken cord twisted with thread of gold.

Remembering the prick of Rurik's parting words, Brienne compressed her lips and, taking the slippers, shoved a foot into each shoe.

"Does 'my lord' afford me a choice?"

A smile stole over Aleth's features, and Brienne rendered her a patient arch of the brow for such unmasked approval.

Rurik had insisted that Brienne greet the duke in the hall with the first goblet of wine, a gesture both befitting and expected of the lady of the keep. She had argued the point but was met only with his iron resolve to have it so. He had dismissed her remark that Katla should rightfully bear the cup. Instead, his time and patience spent, he had hurled a well-aimed barb.

"Was it not my uncle who drove your father from his lands?" he had asked. "Yet Richard returned time and again to devil the Ganga like a she-wolf intent on recapturing prized game for her cubs."

Brienne had known her cause lost as he towered above her, steely-blue eyes penetrating her very soul as he added, "Does Beaumanoir's daughter give sway so easily before the victor?" Then he was gone, the challenge issued, the glove cast down.

Brienne lifted her chin, knowing that as long as she still drew breath in her father's hall, she must stand firm and proud, as did her sire, before the Norsemen. A Beaumanoir to the last.

The faintest of consolations rose in her breast. 'Twas no more than a slender straw but she grasped at it, thankful all the same, for it tempered the bitterness that ached deep in her heart.

Though 'twas true that Rollo had warred on Valsemé, her father and brother were not felled by his hand. 'Twas the Norsemen of the Loire who had claimed their lives. Odd, that fate should see Rollo the champion of that which he once despoiled. He set his sword against his own kinsmen— including the pirates of the Loire—and any who would prey upon his duchy or ravage Charles's heartland.

She ran her fingers thoughtfully along the girdle's silken cord then handed it back to Aleth. "This will not suffice if I am to greet the 'Duke of Normandy.' I wouldst have the one that bears the Beaumanoir falcon."

Aleth grinned and hurried to fetch the favored belt while Brienne returned to the window. When she looked out, the men were advancing toward the wooden staircase with Rurik, the duke at the fore. Without a moment's pause, Brienne ran to Aleth to secure the girdle in place, then dashed from the room.

Mentally, Brienne braced herself as she entered the great

chamber, expecting to match wills with Katla over the privilege of offering the first cup. To her surprise, Katla was absent from the hall. Rurik, she reasoned, most likely had arranged for the Norsewoman to expend her energies—and temper—elsewhere.

Brienne constrained a sudden laugh that begged to be given voice as she imagined Katla relegated to airing the duke's bedchamber. Just as quickly her amusement evaporated. Somehow, a bedchamber seemed a fit setting for Katla's wild beauty. Did she satisfy Rurik's desires as fully and lustily as she claimed? Brienne could not doubt it. Katla seemed possessed with an excessive appetite.

Brienne shook away Katla's taunting image and hastened to locate a cup and flagon of wine. Servants scuttled about laying cloths over the tables, stacking trenchers at the ends, and readying ewers and lavers for washing. They paused in their tasks as Brienne approached, radiating their affection by eye and lip as they awaited her command.

When Brienne made her needs known, an elderly manservant, smiling gap-toothed from his furrowed face, disappeared behind the screens passage and into the service area. Several moments later he proudly returned with a lavish goblet chased with silver and gold and brimming with a clear ruby wine. As exquisite as the vessel was, Brienne couldn't help but think how pitiful it would seem, lost in the duke's great hands.

The rumble of male voices and scraping of boots against stone brought Brienne round. In the same instant, Katla entered the upper end of the hall behind the dais.

Brienne tightened her hold on the goblet and set her mouth at the Norsewoman's contemptuous look. Stiffening her spine, Brienne whirled away but not before noticing that the ring of keys was missing from Katla's hip.

Brienne had no time to ponder what significance might lie in that, but felt for a surety that it stemmed from Rurik's stubborn will to hold her there. But to deprive his wife—? She could not grasp his purpose.

Brienne gained the lower end of the hall just as the men mounted the last of the stairs. Her eyes widened in amazement and she could not stop herself from taking several steps backward as Rollo, Duke of Normandy, Count of Rouen, strode through the portal. Craning her neck, she gazed up. 'Twas impossible to take him in all at once. The man was colossal!

The duke's lips spread into a generous smile as his crystal-blue eyes fastened on Brienne. They were so like Lyting's in their brilliance, and yet his thick curling hair was the same fine gold as Rurik's. He wore it combed away from his face, tapering to the back of his neck but stopping short of the shoulders. Neither greatly handsome nor ill favored, his features were strong and regular, the solid, square jaw being clean-shaven though he possessed an exceptional mustache that draped well past the chin.

A tremor quaked through her under his sharp appraisal, but she held strong, reminding herself of her noble lineage. Boldly, Brienne met his assessing eyes. After a prolonged and calculated moment, knowing she had stretched the bounds of courtesy but had not been so foolish as to be disrespectful, Brienne began to dip gracefully into a curtsy as propriety required.

Appallingly, she could not manage it. Her knees seemed locked and refused to bend. A shiver of panic ran through her, solidifying her limbs' paralysis. Though her eyes remained anchored on Rollo, she caught Rurik's rigid stance in the corner of her vision. Her pulse jumped as it fluttered through her mind that her actions, or lack thereof, were being interpreted as an intentional slight upon Normandy's duke.

Rurik fumed silently as he stood beside his uncle, his own anxieties coiling through him. What was Brienne about? Did she goad Rollo apurpose? Then, too, he did not welcome the gleam that had crept into his uncle's eye. True, Rollo greatly favored his highborn mistress, but Rurik knew 'twas a dry season for any man when his woman was filled with child or first delivered. Of course the duke eased himself where he would, but Rurik would allow no quarter to any notions his uncle might entertain about Brienne.

Time spun out as tension wreathed the room like a heavy mist on a chill morn. The ordeal fast grew into a test of purpose and honor. Brienne realized unhappily that even if she could now execute the maneuver, it would appear she had acquiesced before the "victor" and thus disgraced her father's memory. What was a curtsy if not a gesture of obeisance, a token of submission? She could not award such deference to Valsemé's usurper, especially not here, in her own hall.

Her hall? The mental slip spiraled sweetly through her, but she quickly disclaimed the thought. She stood firmly rooted to the small patch of floor, locking eyes with the massive Norseman and awaiting his displeasure. Surely she had earned his wrath and would taste of it. A single blow from his powerful hand could break many bones.

Rollo suddenly burst into laughter. " 'Od's blood! But you are Beaumanoir's daughter!" Laughter reverberated around them, slicing through the curtain of tension. He spoke something jauntily to his men in Norse and more laughter erupted.

Rurik, Brienne noted, barely broke a smile but cast her a cautioning glance instead. She trembled slightly as she continued to clutch the goblet, watching his brows pull together, and wondered where this would end.

"Well, my lady?" Rollo asked heartily. "Wilt you offer me the cup or must I capture it from you?"

Heat suffused her face and spread down her throat as she extended her arms and yielded up the goblet. As predicted, the cup proved a paltry thing in the duke's enormous hands.

Rurik stepped forward then, resting his palm possessively on the small of Brienne's back and turning her toward the dais as he motioned for the men to proceed into the hall.

Rollo made note of his nephew's familiar gesture. It surprised him somewhat, not because the lady had been wed and widowed of Rurik's father the day afore, but because of what Atli had once shared in confidence.

Rollo's brow furrowed into a frown as he cast about for Atli's exact words, but they escaped him. There was something about a woman, an Eastern beauty whom Rurik loved to distraction. When she died, Rurik took to his ship, journeying restlessly along the trade routes, sowing no roots and 'twould seem—if his father had the right of it—little masculine seed as well.

Atli had troubled over that, contending 'twas neither a natural nor healthy state for a young, virile man such as his son. But Rurik seemed immune to the fawnings of even the comeliest of maids. As far as Rollo knew, Rurik still committed himself to no deep or lasting attachments. It had been so since the Byzantine girl . . . Helena, the name sprang to mind . . . since Helena had died.

Rollo glanced down on Rurik and Brienne as they walked by his side, which was no slight upon his nephew's stature as he viewed everyone as though from a perch. He recalled once questioning whether Rurik preserved Helena's memory or guarded his heart or both. Now he was curious as to whether the Lady Brienne had penetrated those defenses and knew he would be confounded all the more if she had, for she was Atli's bride, or at least she had been.

Rollo smoothed his flowing mustache as he determined to measure the depth of his nephew's interest in this daughter of his old adversary.

"Lord Richard, your father," the duke began, claiming Brienne's attention from Rurik and offering his arm, "was an admirable man and exceptionally skilled in the arts of soldiery."

Brienne found no choice but to accept the proffered arm and allow the duke to guide her the remaining distance to the dais. Rurik dropped his hand from her waist but continued to stride alongside, a muscle flexing in his jaw.

Upon gaining the platform, Rollo directed that the high chairs of the baron and baronne be separated, each to one side, then beckoned for his man to assemble his portable traveling chair and set it betwixt the other two. It proved a sturdy piece, attractive in its simplicity, designed to comfortably bear the great bulk of its owner.

This accomplished, he called for his personal tankard and bid the assemblage find their place at table, gesturing for Brienne and Rurik to assume the baronial high seats flanking his own.

" 'Tis more a pitcher than cup, is it not?" jested Brother Bernard, eyeing the Duke's tankard as he settled to the right of Brienne.

Rollo leaned forward grinning, his hand closing around the carved vessel. "Grant pardon, my lady, if the size of my cup gives offense, but this churchman wouldst have me sipping daintily from these little bowls he passes for goblets."

Brother Bernard snorted at that, but the duke settled into his stride. "I suspect he secretly covets it for himself." Rollo winked and gave an exaggerated sigh. "I shall be forced to save his immortal soul from the burden of sin by commanding a like one fashioned. I wouldst gift him at Christmastide but I fear he cannot bide the wait."

"Careful, Uncle," Lyting cautioned with mock seriousness, "or you'll have Ketil fair green with envy."

Laughter rippled down the table and in the hall amongst those who gave ear to the repartee. Rurik tipped back in his chair, amusement flickering in his eyes as his mouth eased into a wide smile at the monk's expense.

Brienne laughed as well as her gaze settled on Rurik's strikingly handsome face. A shudder of desire flashed through her and her heart rose in her breast. Her fingers suddenly ached to trace the firm curve of his lips and explore the deep cleft in his chin.

Brienne arrested the course of her thoughts with a sound mental shake and averted her gaze to Lyting who sat chuckling, well pleased with himself.

An unexpected chill skimmed over Brienne as she felt the pull of another pair of eyes. Tensing, she glanced past Lyting and met with Hastein's silent regard. The corners of his mouth curled with the satisfaction of his thoughts as his gaze lowered and slowly roamed over her.

Brienne recoiled, remembering the assault of his hands on her body. Anger flashed in her eyes but it served only to amuse him. He taunted her with smirking self-confidence, then leveled his gaze past her shoulder. Brienne turned to find the object of his interest. Only two held seats to the right of her—Brother Bernard and Robert Coustance.

Her stomach knotted as Esternay inclined his head. A faint smile tipped his lips yet failed to reach his dark eyes. Contentedly, he lifted his goblet and savored a long draught.

Suppressing a wave of panic, Brienne fought to concentrate on the progress in the hall as the first courses were presented. Rollo kept his conversation light, yet she sensed his mind was turned in on itself, dissecting some weighty

matter. He avoided discussing Atli, diverting the tables'
parley into other paths instead.

Brienne grew restive under his attentions. That he desired
to share her trencher was obvious when he separated her
from Rurik and placed her to his right. She had no qualms
over usurping Katla from her mother's chair and expected
the fiery Norsewoman would take a position with Rurik. To
her surprise, Katla was relegated to the far end of the table
aside Hastein.

The vaguest of impressions settled over Brienne. It bore
no sense, but it seemed that Rollo's attentiveness was aimed
to an end other than gaining her smile or blandishments. In
truth, it appeared that Rollo sported with Rurik, the little
considerations but a guise to nettle his nephew. Had he
read their hearts so easily? Brienne attempted to channel
the conversation into a safer harbor, asking of Poppa.

The glowing pride of fatherhood charged the duke's features as he settled back into his chair. "The birthing was
swift. Young William now has a sister, Gerloc. And such a
tiny mite. She fits in one hand, but her lungs are fit and hale."
He laughed, recalling the child's squalling protest when he
held her overlong, keeping her from her mother's breast.
"Poppa," he added, his eyes shining softly, "has promised
many other sons and daughters."

Brienne did not trouble over the duke's attentions after
that, perceiving the lay of this great Norseman's heart. He
grew pensive at times and spoke quietly with Rurik in Norse.

Brienne was lost to her own thoughts when Katla's voice
scraped away the calm. The Northwoman rose, hurling a terse
remark in her direction. Brienne felt the hairs on the back
of her neck rise. A heartbeat later, Brother Bernard leaned
forward and retorted in the Nordic tongue. She hooked onto
Atli's name and was flooded with relief to know that she
was not the mark of Katla's attack.

Ketil quickly joined in the verbal fray, drawing in Rurik
and Lyting who seemed at odds in their opinions. Rollo
next entered the dispute, and when it spilled into Frankish,
Esternay added his own unsolicited comments. Additional
sentiments echoed in the hall as the argument reverted to
Norse once again.

Rollo's patience suddenly gave way. He brought his tankard down so hard upon the table that Brienne thought it would crack. Slowly, he rose from his chair and fixed the hall with a quelling look.

"Gruel Atli was a man of *heiður og sæmd,* honor and respect. Fearless in battle, steadfast in friendship, and true to a trust. More than once he saved my life and stood in my place, unflinching before the jaws of death."

Rollo's gaze swung over the assemblage, then to Brother Bernard. "Verily, Atli took the Christian waters at my side this year past. But he was raised to manhood amongst the Vendel, and *bálför* is their practice." His voice rumbled in his throat as he thumped his massive chest. "The roots of youth tap deep into a man's soul."

Turning back to the hall, his words carried strong and clear. "My friend . . . *minn 'broðir'* . . . shall have his last wish. Build the funeral pyre high at the river's edge. In deference to the Christ, the deathship and goods shall be forsworn save for personal weapons. Let the preparations begin! We send Atli to his reward at sunset."

Brienne drew away from the chamber window and chafed her arms. The great keep stored the winter's cold in its stony marrow and remained a chilly fortress against the warmer airs of spring.

"The sun is nearly set," Aleth observed, moving to stir the embers in the small hearth. The flames leapt to life as she added bits of wood, brightening the darkened room and exaggerating the shadows to eerie dimensions against the walls.

"Are we to await Rurik?" Aleth inquired as she huddled near the fire.

Brienne shook her head, lifting her hands to warm them. "He departed the bailey a short time ago, but he promised an escort. Another will come."

Aleth's lashes fluttered to her cheek. She turned back to the fire but could not hide the anticipation washing over her. Brienne smiled, wondering if her friend silently hoped for a particular escort, one possessed with flaming red hair.

Her smile slipped a degree as she gazed back into the

flickering light. She must leave Valsemé. Aleth, too. And though it lay like a stone in her heart, 'twas foolery to consider otherwise. First, she must bear through the coming hours. But on the morrow, she would reassert her will to leave.

She fingered the small cross that lay at her throat, her thoughts churning with frustration. Rurik intended that she participate in the funeral ceremonies, precisely how, she didst not know, but he was adamant that she stand with him and his brothers as a member of Gruel Atli's family.

She released a weary breath. Did he think to strengthen his claim over her by insisting she play the widow before all? Mayhap Rollo would aid her return to Levroux. She dismissed the thought. Blood ran thick amongst these Norsemen. Rollo would heed the wishes of his nephew. Nay, she must argue the issue with Rurik. Could he not see how it tore at her?

The discordant creaking of the oaken door pulled Brienne's and Aleth's eyes to the portal. A figure was poised there, silhouetted against the glimmering torchlight of the passageway.

Brienne felt a cool whisper of air curl through the room and brush over her. Instinctively, she moved to Aleth's side as a thousand pinpoints seemed to prickle over her scalp and down her spine.

The form moved, accompanied by the soft rustle of cloth and faint clinking of metal as it stepped from the shadows into the golden glow of the hearth.

Brienne released her breath as Katla emerged from the darkness, splendidly robed and bearing a small tray with an object hidden beneath a linen.

"I am instructed to see that you are prepared," Katla announced as she crossed to the small table.

"Prepared? How so?" Brienne's pulse quickened, her senses sharpening.

Katla paused and regarded Brienne. The play of firelight and shadow distorted the contours of her face. "For the rites, of course. Surely you realize why Rurik keeps you here." Her lips spread into a thin smile. "He has need of you."

She set the tray down, turning it a quarter, her gestures smooth, ceremonious.

"You *are* his father's widow. And Rurik is a loyal son

who will see his father's requests . . . and necessities . . . fulfilled *completely*."

Katla withdrew the linen, revealing a heavy silver goblet incised with mysterious angular markings about its base.

"Atli must not go unattended to the nether regions." Her voice carried a strange, distant note as she stared into the cup's dark contents. "You must join him."

Stark fear shot through Brienne as Katla lifted the vessel and faced her. The woman was mad! She breathed with difficulty as Katla moved toward her, proffering the cup. From the corner of her eye, Brienne glimpsed Aleth reaching for a stick of kindling, but Katla's dulcet tones netted her attention.

"Do not be frightened," Katla continued in a lulling tone. "The *nabid* will take away your fears. It will soothe you. When the moment of passage comes, you will know naught but tranquility."

Katla stopped before Brienne, her green eyes dark, hypnotic pools. "Drink the *nabid*," she chanted, holding out the cup. "Drink the *nabid*."

Without thinking, Brienne knocked the cup away. Crimson liquid swashed wide of the goblet, catching Katla against the side of the face and spattering her dress. The Norsewoman shrieked her fury. Curling her fingers like talons, she lashed out at Brienne. But Brienne pitched to one side as the nails raked through air and barely missed her head.

"Leave, Frankish bitch!" Katla hissed. "Either attend Atli in the realms beyond or run back to your tight-legged sisters and hide behind your cloister walls. This keep will not hold the two of us, nor do I share Rurik!"

Katla lunged forward, but suddenly her feet left the floor and she was jerked backward. An arm seized her from behind, lifting her high in a swirl of gown and hair, and flung her to the rush-covered floor.

Lyting loomed above her, filled with rage, his vivid blue eyes slashing into her. He spat into the rushes then thundered furiously at Katla in rapid Norse. Yanking her to her feet, he shoved her toward the door.

Katla hurriedly snatched up the goblet from the rushes and clasped it to her bosom. Hastening through the portal,

she halted abruptly and spun round, knifing Brienne with a
poisonous look. Her mouth held an ugly slant and her eyes
flashed pure hatred.

"Be gone, *hóra!*" Lyting stormed.

Brienne swayed, her legs dissolving beneath her. Aleth
caught her by the side and at the same moment Brienne felt
Lyting's hands close around her, encompassing her more
fully.

"Brienne! My lady!" Lyting's voice seemed distant above
her.

Brienne clung to him till the rushing in her ears receded
and the room righted itself. Looking up, she found his eyes,
usually a brilliant blue, now clouded with worry and anxiously questing her face. Carefully, Lyting helped her into
a chair while Aleth brought wine and a damp cloth to cool
her brow.

Suddenly conscious that he still clasped Brienne's hand,
Lyting released it and straightened. Even in the poor light,
Brienne could see that his features had deepened with col-
or.

"My lady, I am sorry. This should not have happened."

Brienne was unsure if he spoke of Katla's bizarre behavior
or of his holding her in so familiar a manner, though in verity
she knew he sought but to aid her. She cleared her throat and
decided to keep to the safer course.

"What nature of drink didst the goblet hold?"

Lyting pressed his lips into a line. "*Nabid*. 'Tis an
intoxicating potion used in our funeral ceremonies and
imbibed during the many feasting days that accompany
them."

"Given, I presume, to the unfortunate souls who are sacrificed upon the pyre?" She could not keep the small thread
of hysteria from rising in her voice. "To the luckless wife
who survives her husband and finds she must now perish
with him?"

" 'Tis not as it seems." A look of pain lanced his eyes.
"Customs vary greatly amongst my people. *Bálför*, burning
the dead, is practiced chiefly amongst the worshipers of
Odin, most notably the peoples of Sverige, such as the Vendel and the Valsgärde, and the Rus along the Volga. If

any accompany the deceased, whether upon the pyre or into a bog, they are thralls who volunteer." Lyting gave her a considering look. "This may be difficult for you to accept or even conceive of, my lady, but 'tis considered a privilege to follow one's master and serve him in the afterlife."

"And wives?" Brienne asked warily.

"Wives are not sacrificed," he reassured her gently, shaking his head. The corner of his lips tugged upward. "Though, if she wished. . . ."

Brienne stiffened at his attempt at levity, and found fresh strength flooding her limbs. "She does not!"

Lyting's smile broadened. "May I assume by your words that you acknowledge you are my father's widow and shall therefore remain at Valsemé?"

"I cannot," Brienne sputtered, then her eyes widened as she realized 'twas Lyting who had tarried in the church's sacristy when she spoke with Brother Bernard. "You overheard and still you ask?" She quickly rose to pace on unsteady legs. "There is no place for me now. Rurik shall be baron and Katla—" An involuntary tremor shuddered through her.

"Katla has naught to do with this."

"Katla has everything to do with it!"

"Katla is a warped, self-seeking creature who nourishes her hatreds and jealousies and clings implacably to the old ways," Lyting argued. "She can be dealt with or sent away if need be."

Brienne was aghast at his suggestion, disbelieving Rurik would discard a wife so casually for her sake. And to what purpose? Could she remain at Valsemé and prevail as what? Rurik's lover? She knew with a certainty that if she dare stay, her days would inescapably find their beginnings and endings in Rurik's bed.

Brienne squeezed her lashes shut and expelled a breath. "I *must* leave, surely you understand that."

Lyting's voice hardened with exasperation. "That, my lady, is what I understand least of all."

Rurik stroked Sleipnir's glossy coat, then he rechecked the steering traces that ran from the leather harness to the wagon's front axles.

Each of the thick ropes was capped with a *rangel,* a long, conical iron mount. One end was connected to the harness by means of an iron ring from which hung a collection of smaller rings, rattles to ward off evil spirits. The other end hooked onto a larger eye-mount that encircled the wheel's fixed wooden axle. It was a simple but effective device by which to guide the cart. The reins passed separately through a richly decorated harness bow of gilded bronze that rested on the horse's back and, in turn, supported the traces.

His mother had loved this wagon, Rurik remembered as he smoothed his hand over the swirling tangle of menacing creatures that embellished its surface. She had delighted in how easily it disassembled. With little effort, the body could be removed and fitted to runners, converting it into a sledge for winter's passage over ice and snow. It could also be packed tightly with goods for a voyage and driven down to the sea. The troughlike body would then be unlashed from the undercarriage and hoisted directly onto the ship. How often had he done just that for his mother when he took her with him on trading excursions to Hedeby? Not often enough, came the answer as his hand stilled over the carvings. A scant four months past, he bore Ranneveig to her burial chamber in this wagon. Today it would bear his father.

Rurik guided Sleipnir and the elegant wagon to the motte near the stairs. Once inside the keep he seized one of the torches from its bracket and descended into the bowels of the tower. Ketil and two of Atli's loyal soldiers, Eirik and Gyrr, awaited him by the stone well that supplied the keep. Casks of wine and grain were stacked shoulder high around the wall save where a door stood slightly ajar, revealing a small storage room.

"The women have prepared him and clothed him as you bade," Ketil offered somberly, and started toward the door.

Rurik stayed his old friend: "I would have a moment."

Ketil grunted and stepped aside, allowing Rurik to enter the chamber unattended.

The crates of glassware, silver, and plate that normally cramped the room had been banked against the walls and a table assembled in the clearing. It claimed a goodly portion of the cell's mean dimensions and supported Atli's bier.

Rurik inhaled deeply then released the breath with measured slowness as he contemplated his father's lifeless form. Slipping his hand inside his jerkin, he withdrew a small glass reliquary containing a lock of his mother's golden hair.

Atli had been sorely aggrieved when he learned of Ranneveig's passing. Despite the infrequency of his visits to their home at Limfjord and their many years apart, Atli ever desired to bring Ranneveig to his Frankish holding and set her by his side. But when Rurik sailed to fetch her, he found her suffering a terrible wasting disease. He could not even touch her flesh for the pain she suffered. This he did not tell his father, only that she died in his arms.

Though Atli was not a man to display his heart, Rurik discovered him brooding over the reliquary more than once. Ranneveig herself had provided the keepsake when Atli first went *i viking* in Francia. Rurik slid the small gilt-trimmed box inside his father's tunic and drew the robe of fine brocade over him.

"I know not if your men shall follow me, Father, but I shall honor my promise and safeguard that which is yours by my life's blood. Be assured that Brienne is protected under my shield. King be damned, I'll not forfeit her to his grasp." A muscle flexed in his jaw. "Together we will hold Valsemé, I for you and she for her sire, Richard. 'Tis a time for healing in these lands, as well you understood."

Rurik's gaze moved over Atli. The lines in his brow deepened.

"No man can predict the hour of his death. Yet even in that moment you contrived to have your will of me and moor me here with Brienne as my anchor. You knew I would set aside my wanderings to see her well." His eyes widened with comprehension. "You knew."

Brienne and Aleth stood to the fore of the Norman garrison alongside Rollo, Lyting, and Hastein. The crowded bailey flickered with scores of torches as Atli was borne with great solemnity from the keep and laid upon a bed of furs in the ornate wagon.

Rurik caught and held Brienne's eyes with his. She felt the

warmth of his approval flow through her and wrap around her heart. Flushed with pleasure, she was gladdened by the comfort her presence obviously gave him. 'Twould have been unforgivable—feckless and weak—to cower in her chamber as impulse pleaded after the turbulent episode with Katla. Nay, 'twas not a time for spineless indulgences. She wouldst bring solace where she may. There was so little time left to them.

She watched with a faint ache in her heart as Rurik stepped to the great black. Gripping Sleipnir's reins, he led the procession out of the courtyard. As the cart lumbered across the bridge and down the road toward the church, the Norsemen intoned a dirge and beat their shields with sticks.

Brother Bernard awaited the mourners outside the church as did the Seigneur d'Esternay and his men-at-arms. With sacramentary in hand, the monk offered up his prayers, then sprinkled horse, cart, and its occupant with holy water. He trod ahead of the procession as the journey progressed to the river's edge, sprinkling the ground as he went, striving to hallow the pagan ritual.

Lyting escorted Brienne and Aleth to a position short of and to the right of the pyre. Leaving them in Rollo's care, he and Hastein joined Rurik and together the brothers set to loosing the ropes that secured the wagon. For a moment they paused as Lyting appeared to question Rurik on some point. When Hastein shrugged at Rurik's reply, Lyting conceded with a nod and the three finished their task.

To Brienne's amazement, they lifted the entire body of the wagon off its wheels and carried it to the pyre. Cautiously, they climbed the small ramp onto the platform and set the beautifully wrought coffer down amidst the dry tinder. As Brienne studied the complex carvings of snarling monsters and clutching beasts, she realized their intent was to burn the piece along with Atli and deemed it a sad waste of fine craftsmanship. But Rurik must own good reason, she decided, for his brothers obviously approved the gesture as well.

Several moments later, Lyting rejoined Brienne and Aleth. Brienne's eyes rounded as he stepped behind her, muttering to Rollo, "Let us hope Rurik has the good sense to keep on his loincloth."

The remark struck her as exceedingly odd and certainly in poor taste if purposed as a jest. But when she looked over, Rurik already stood bare-chested and was removing his boots.

Heat climbed to her cheeks as he stripped away his tight-fitting breeches to reveal long, hard-sinewed legs. Her throat parched as her eyes riveted on his hands and followed them to the top of his loincloth. His fingers worked the fastenings and parted the material. Her breathing grew quick, shallow, then ceased altogether as his hands stilled. A mixture of relief and disappointment flooded through her when Rurik secured the cloth back in place.

Brienne's face burned with the wantonness of her thoughts and the startling desire that jolted through her. She drew into her mantle, grateful for the concealing darkness.

Ketil came forth weighted with Gruel Atli's prized sword, shield, and spear. Rurik first accepted the spear. Raising it high with outstretched arms for all to see, he addressed the crowd with gravity in his Norse tongue before bringing it down and snapping the shaft over his knee. With marked formality, he placed the fragments upon the furs in the cart, next to his father.

Rurik next relieved Ketil of both sword and shield. Again he raised the weapons, extolling Atli in somber tones, this time evoking a rejoinder from the Norsemen. Some cried out and waved their torches, others beat against their bucklers. Setting the shield upon the platform, Rurik smote it with a heavy, sweeping blow and sundered it in two. As before, he placed the fractured weapon alongside Atli.

Sword in hand, Rurik leaped from the pyre and bore it to a burly-looking man tending a coal fire in a brazier. Brienne judged him to be a smith by trade, for tongs and hammers of varying sizes were laid out next to a small anvil, this sunk into a stumplike block of wood. Rurik thrust the blade into the brazier and waited as the smith packed it with glowing charcoal and pumped the flames with his bellows.

When the metal tested to the smith's satisfaction, Rurik clamped on to the sword with heavy tongs, withdrew it, and laid the steel across the anvil. With powerful blows, he hammered the blade till it bent. Brienne stood awed by his beautifully corded muscles as they rippled and bulged with each jarring stroke.

The sword hissed angrily as Rurik thrust it into a waiting tub of water. Drawing it out, he mounted the pyre for a last time and placed the misshapen blade atop Gruel Atli.

Before Rurik could move, Brother Bernard hastened forward and, taking the cross from his neck, handed it up to Rurik with instructions to fold it into his father's hands. This done, Rurik abandoned the platform and took up a torch.

He waited as additional kindling was heaped beneath and around the sides of the pyre. Holding the torch high as he faced the crowd, Rurik backed ceremoniously toward the pyre. Then he turned and set it aflame.

Wordlessly, Lyting conducted Brienne forward along with Rollo and Hastein. Quick, disturbing thoughts stabbed at Brienne, and she shook the haunting image of Katla from her mind. She was safe, she reassured herself, but her eyes briefly searched for the Norsewoman before settling on Lyting. He supplied her with a fiery brand, and following his lead, she tossed it into the tinder. The garrison now crushed forward, each soldier hurling torches and kindled sticks onto the pyre.

Brienne watched the flames feed hungrily on the tinder, devouring it greedily, the licking tongues battling amongst themselves. Her thoughts drifted to Rurik. Then he was suddenly standing beside her. Their eyes met and she perceived the strain and exhaustion buried within. She wished to take him to her breast and ease him there as she would a child. A child? Her eyes slipped over the hard planes of his chest and shoulders, sculpted in firelight and shadow. When she looked up, he smiled softly and turned her back toward the pyre, his hand lightly at her waist.

Together they gazed silently on the crackling fire. In that moment it seemed to Brienne that they stood on the brink of time—of their past and their future. A crossroads of sorts. Rurik took up his future at Valsemé and she was satisfied that her people were safe under his hand. But her days would be lined with cloth of black and high brooding walls. A lump constricted her throat. Valsemé her heart could relinquish to his care, but Rurik it held fast. She chastised herself. Rurik had never been hers to have.

A breeze stirred about them, rousing the flames to billowing heights. Brienne caught sight of Katla then, and a deathlike chill passed through her. The Norsewoman stood enraptured by the brilliance and splendor of the fire, oblivious of all.

A great cracking noise brought Brienne round. She watched the coffer disappear as the blaze engulfed the pyre and climbed to the dark skies, releasing Atli to the heavens.

Chapter Eleven
❖ ❖ ❖ ❖ ❖ ❖ ❖ ❖ ❖ ❖ ❖ ❖

RURIK BRACED A stiff arm against the sandstone pillar and massaged the back of his neck. The day had racked him, mind and body. He forswore the hall a short while past, greatly in need of a breath of time to himself.

The manor house drew him. Or was it the memory of sweet torment and desperate yearning that lured him here? Of Brienne, soft and yielding beneath his touch?

Brienne. How could she think to leave? He squeezed his eyes shut and rubbed the bridge of his nose. Her stubborn insistence 'twas but one of the spiny concerns that afflicted his ease.

The scuffing of boots brought Rurik round to see Lyting duck through the entrance. Mildly surprised, he smiled, then chided, "Have you done with feasting so soon, *broðir*, or has the ale run dry?"

"We need talk, Rurik." Lyting was all seriousness, his mouth set in firm lines.

"Is aught amiss?" Rurik straightened, puzzled. "Has some unpleasantness disrupted the hall?"

Points of light shimmered in Lyting's crystal eyes as he stepped forward. "I wouldst know your intentions toward the Lady Brienne."

"My intentions?" Rurik stared at Lyting.

"Wilt you return her to Levroux or . . . ?"

"*Nei!* Not to Levroux."

"You cannot hold her here without proper position."

"She has position enough as Gruel Atli's widow."

" 'Tis no position at all and well you know it," Lyting bit out tersely. "She is simply a captive of wardship. Brienne Beaumanoir returned to Valsemé to assume her place as baronne. Can she claim that right by blood or marriage now? *Nei.* Yet you wouldst force her to remain without station and suffer the insults of that *hóra!*"

Stunned by his brother's outburst, Rurik opened his mouth to counter, but Lyting thundered on without heed.

"How long do you think to keep her? Your oath this night shall bind you to duke and king alike. Charles has proved his artfulness in using the lady to benefit his crown. He'll seek another match. And what of our celebrated uncle who sups with her even now in the hall? Think you he is immune to her beauty?"

"Enough!" bellowed Rurik, his forbearance snapping.

"*Nei!* Hear me in this, *broðir.* Let her go or place her at your side, but decide. And if you canst, then release her to me. I wouldst pledge her more than my sword arm. I will take her to wife and pledge her my love as well."

A searing bolt of jealousy ripped through Rurik. He struggled with it for a moment, clenching his hands so he could not wrap them around his brother's neck. It had long been evident that Lyting honored Brienne, that he was bemused of her. But that he loved her as well . . . ?

Rurik stood wholly speechless, astounded as much by Lyting's challenge as by his own violent reaction. He strove to shake off the green-eyed serpent that gnawed at him and form some reply, but Ketil's ill-timed appearance forestalled him.

"Rurik, 'tis time!" Ketil squeezed his hulking frame through the small arched portal. Taking in the two somber faces, he gave each a critical eye yet resisted comment. "Rollo awaits. He would receive your oath and confirm you in your father's stead as the Baron de Valsemé."

Rurik pulled his eyes from Lyting, holding mental rein on their disquieting exchange. Gravely, he regarded his massive friend and weighed an earlier concern. "My father's men, wilt they follow me?"

Ketil cocked his fiery head as though he had misheard, then laughed greatly to shed the perturbing remark. "Has a maggot infected your brain? What manner of question is that?"

Rurik's jaw locked, in no fettle to bandy wit for wit, but Ketil held up a hand. "What troubles you, Rurik? Do you doubt yourself?"

"*Nei,* but I was never part to Rollo's campaigns in Francia. I am an *utlenður maður* here, an outsider, and unproved."

"*Utlenður maður?*" Ketil spluttered incredulously. "You, a member of the Varangian guard, the Byzantine emperor's crack troops, unproved?" He disgorged a few raw remarks into his beard. "Why, Atli boasted of your feats. He even instructed the skald to set the tales to verse and recite them in the hall."

"How didst he know of my—"

"He had his ways," Ketil returned at once, taking in Rurik's surprise. "I assure you, the garrison holds you in highest esteem."

"What of Hastein? Has he not poisoned their minds?"

"A man is judged by his deed, Rurik, and by the way he conducts his life. Those who serve in the garrison are not blind to Hastein. They know him for the man he is."

Ketil pulled a bundle from beneath his mantle. "I thought you might be in need of this," he said as he withdrew Atli's golden arm ring from the wrappings, "unless you have considered otherwise."

Rurik sighed, bone weary, then looked to Lyting who stood more at ease now. "I shall weigh your words, *broðir.* We shall speak anon."

Lyting acceded with a nod and Rurik turned back to Ketil. Slipping the ring onto his arm, he led the two men from the manor house and headed for the keep.

Brienne's heart swelled as Rurik entered the hall. His stride was filled with a leonine strength and sense of purpose as he moved toward her. The long, powerful legs stretched out in front of him, easily bridging the distance, while the golden hair flared from his handsome face.

His eyes sought and held hers briefly, and she knew in that single moment that she would love him always. Fiercely and unrepentantly would she love this shining man of the North. Beyond the frail boundaries of mortal existence. Until the very ends of time.

Rurik halted before the dais, his bearing taut and expectant yet nothing less than lordly. As the duke rumbled out a Norse salutation, Brienne spared a glance down the length of table and met with Esternay's tethered expression. The nebulous apprehensions that had abraded her throughout the evening now returned, mixing with solid alarm, and tingled over her flesh.

Brother Bernard shifted forward just then, blocking her view of the knight. Brienne withdrew her gaze and, after a moment's hesitation, cast it past Rollo's imposing dimensions to the opposite end of the table. Her pulse stilled as she watched Hastein pass viperish eyes over Rurik then down a bracing mouthful of ale.

Alarm raced through her. She swung hard round to warn Rurik through a look, a gesture, that something was afoot. But Hastein chose that precise moment to fling himself from his chair and hammer his voice throughout the hall.

A challenge! Her heart clogged her throat. No one need tell her what venom he spewed. 'Twas all too plain.

"Speak your grievance, Hastein." A chill clung to the edge of Rollo's words, these in Frankish.

At that, Hastein vaulted over the table and leaped from the dais. He took up his stance an arm's length from Rurik and appealed to the gathering with a sweeping gesture.

"I, Hastein, am Gruel Atli's first male child and I claim those rights due me as his eldest son." He spoke in Norse but repeated himself in Frankish so that all might grasp his protest.

Turning to Rollo, Hastein pressed his suit. "Didst not Atli set me upon his knee before the Assembly and acknowledge me publicly as free and equal to all his other spawnings? 'Tis I, not Rurik, who should receive my father's mantle. Do you less for young William, come the day you bind yourself with wife?"

The barb found its home and Rollo shifted uncomfortably at the thought of his fine son. "Have out with it," Rollo groused.

" 'Twas I who fought at your side these many years past,

securing our foothold along the Seine. 'Twas I, along with those here present, who accompanied you to St.-Clair-sur-Epte. And all the while, Rurik played the merchant, filling his coffers with riches and easing himself in luxuries untold. Now he returns like a prince of the East to partake of our weal.

"I have earned Valsemé. Give the barony to me. And if you feel bound to confer benefice on Rurik, grant him Ivry instead. 'Tis fitting, is it not?" Hastein sneered, flickering colorless eyes over Rurik. "Ivry is a *ville* of old men and suckling babes. Who else wouldst follow the *Barnakarl*?"

Argument erupted throughout the soldiery and quickly convulsed the hall. Brienne could not tell if they championed or decried Hastein's claim, or if 'twas the slur upon Rurik's shield of valor that inflamed them. She inclined her head toward Brother Bernard.

"*Barnakarl*, what means it?" she asked urgently.

"The 'Children's Man,' my lady." He took a brisk sip of wine. "Years ago, when Rurik had barely attained his manhood, he joined Hastein on a raid. 'Twas his first and last, for he had no stomach for his brother's 'entertainments.' Pillage and rape alone ne'er satisfied Hastein. He sated his bloodlust in unspeakable ways. But Rurik fouled his play that day and saved the . . . A moment, my lady." The monk gestured hastily. "Rurik doth speak."

Brienne's eyes flew to Rurik but encountered his back as he turned to address the hall.

"I find no sport in catching helpless babes midair upon my sword," Rurik ground out.

Brienne gasped in horror and buried her face in her hands.

"*Barnakarl* is a title I bear with honor." His steady gaze swept slowly over each member of his father's garrison, silently challenging them to take issue with him. " 'Tis not cowardice that a man prefers to put a cause behind his blade—a cause nobler than another's perversities."

Brienne sucked in her breath, anticipating Hastein's reprisal, but he made no move.

"True, my sword was not hardened in Frankish blood," Rurik conceded, his rich tones filling the chamber. "But 'twas hardened all the same. Emperor Leo Sophos found it served him well, well enough to trust his life to it. If any doubt my willingness or ability to wield this length of steel"—his hand went to his scabbard—"*Svíða*, 'Sting,' awaits."

The words struck Brienne to her very core, that he should lay himself open to any and every blade in the keep.

An uneasy silence hung over the large room.

"I do not doubt you, Rurik," Rollo declared firmly, signaling his own position and the attitude he expected his Normans to espouse. The matter was closed. Closed to all save Hastein.

"Do not be swayed by the ties of kinship, Ganga-Hrolf. Your sister's blood may run through his veins and her image stamp his face, but I am the better choice."

A flash of anger grazed Rollo's eyes. He settled back in his great chair, steepling his fingers, and carefully studied their tips.

"Interesting, that Atli himself bestowed the ancestral ring upon Rurik? Have I the right of it, Ketil?"

The great bearlike warrior grunted, brusquely nodding his head. Brienne thought he looked fit to smash something, anything, his color was so high.

Again, Rollo studied his tented fingers. "We have only begun to fortify our holdings. Should I commend Valsemé to your keeping, Hastein . . ."

"Condemn" would be more accurate! Brienne wailed within.

" . . . how do you envision the future of the barony? Of Normandy, for that matter? How wouldst you order the affairs of these lands?" the duke asked slowly, calmly flexing the joints of his long fingers.

With a sudden jolt, Brienne felt the snare slip into place, and she realized what the duke was about. Her heart picked up its pace as she attended Hastein's answer. Maddeningly, he related his thoughts in Norse.

"The land is what we have always craved, what we have spilt our blood for. The king's grant is but a beginning, a foothold, that we can expand into a Norse empire. Our course must first be to strengthen and solidify that which we hold. Then we can look to fresh conquests."

"In Francia?" Surprise lit Rollo's eyes.

"It can all be ours." Hastein licked his lips. "Charles is weak. 'Tis the individual lords who hold any real power. We can expand to become the mightiest force to be reckoned with upon the continent."

"And what of my sacred oath? Am I not to be a man of honor?"

Hastein's lip curled. " 'Twill be of little account to forswear yourself as duke to take title as King of Normandy."

Brienne saw Rollo's features darken with thought, but could glean naught from his shuttered expression. He put his question next to Rurik, and she was thankful when Rurik chose to repeat his answers in Frankish. Presumably, he did so for the benefit of the king's men and Lord Robert, officially the sovereign's envoy. There would be no misconstruing Rurik's stance or his loyalties when they reached the royal ears.

Rurik swept a glance over Brienne and then focused on his uncle. "My vision is not so filled with vainglorious ambitions. Normandy is prize enough. What glory can a man savor if he has not his honor? Lands abound apart from Francia to master. There be no need to break oath."

Rurik shifted his weight to partially face Hastein. " 'Twould be reprehensible to do so. An oath-breaker has no credence, his words no value. If one overlord can be so easily forsworn, then what is another, be he king . . . or duke?"

This drew a growl from Hastein and a raised eyebrow from Rollo.

"I do not presume to advise you on the affairs of Normandy, but of Valsemé there is much I would attend to. First, I would fortify by arms and by stone. We are unrivaled upon the seas, but on land we must learn from our Frankish brethren and mount our—"

"Stone, Rurik?" Rollo leaned forward on his elbows and clasped one balled hand in the other.

"Já." Rurik smiled lightly. "The quarries of Francia offer far better than the soft steatite of our homeland. We can raise more than cathedrals and monasteries." He let the duke ponder that thought as he continued. "Valsemé's soil is rich and fertile. But I wouldst see her flourish with more than crops."

"Defense works?" Rollo interrupted once again. " 'Tis a costly undertaking, be it of stone."

"Wealth need not depend on land alone. The barony is favorably located on the Toques, easily accessible to our trade routes. The expansion I propose is one of economy, of trade. Long have our people enjoyed and profited from the splendid offerings of the East. Miklagárd and the Caliphates are rich in silver, silks, and spices. Few of the commodities we Northmen take as commonplace reach the Frankish markets, and when they do, 'tis with no dependability or regularity. I would build Valsemé as a center of trade."

Seeing Rollo's favorable nod, Hastein's patience wore thin. "Rurik distracts us with pretty words and grand visions. But I have claim to these lands by right of blood. Let us convene the Assembly. Let the council decide."

A storm gathered on Rollo's brow, swift and thunderous. Veins stood out along his neck, and his color deepened as he slowly rose to his great height.

"I, Rollo, Duke of Normandy, do not call the Assembly. Not now or ever! Like it or not—and make no mistake in this"—he breathed hard and heavy like an angry bull—"Normandy is mine to rule and mine alone. I am its overlord, answerable to no one, least of all you, Hastein.

"My barons hold their lands in obeisance of me, *as my vassals*." Rollo emphasized each word distinctly. "Gruel Atli well understood that this fiefdom reverted to me at his death. He declared his preference when he conferred his arm ring. That I acknowledge, and give weight to it. But the choice remains mine."

Rollo's sharp, assessing eye prowled over the hall.

"If any have difficulty in this, I suggest you seek your future apart of Normandy, for I intend to keep faith with Charles."

When none stirred, he turned to Rurik. "Now wilt I accept oath from the new Baron de Valsemé."

"Nei!" The word escaped as a strangled cry from Hastein's throat, his face twisted with rage. He threw off his mantle and, with lightning swiftness, unleashed the battle-ax concealed at his side, wielding it aloft with both hands. Brienne screamed as the flaring blade burred through the air.

Rurik twisted away and dropped into a roll, barely escaping its deadly bite.

"Widow-Maker thirsts for your blood, *Barnakarl!*" Hastein rasped, sweeping the blade back and forth as Rurik rose to his feet.

Brienne lurched from her chair, nauseous with dread, but Brother Bernard restrained her. The heathen's eyes glittered like icy shards and his smile . . . his smile was cold as death.

Hastein swung once, twice, thrice at Rurik's midsection. Each time, Rurik leaped backward agilely, sucking in his stomach and landing with solid footing. A fourth sweep sliced through his leather jerkin. Hastein exulted, thinking he had drawn blood. He laughed low in his throat and, pausing, allowed the blade to sag. Without hesitation, Rurik sprang into the air and kicked out, catching Hastein squarely in the chest with both feet.

Hastein thudded to the floor, tumbling over in a backward somersault, and came to rest on the balls of his feet. Still crouching, he aimed a sweeping blow at Rurik's legs, a stroke purposed to divest his prey of limb.

But Rurik leaped above the humming blade and, as he found footing, delivered a stunning blow to the side of Hastein's neck. Hastein sprawled backward onto the rushes, and Rurik lunged on top of him, gripping the ax handle. The two rolled head over feet several times in quick succession, clutching the wood handle, and slammed against the wall.

Rurik gained the advantage and dragged Hastein up. Ramming him hard into the stone, he shoved the ax handle against Hastein's throat and choked the breath out of him. Hastein struggled to entangle Rurik's leg with his own and pull him off-balance, but he found himself solidly pinned.

Brienne's heart pounded wildly as Hastein's face purpled. She was exhilarated to see Rurik triumph yet horrified to watch the man she loved draw a life.

As Hastein's head lolled to one side, Rurik released the ax handle and Hastein crumpled onto the rushes. Several moments passed before he expelled a harsh groan, air assaulting his lungs.

Satisfied, Rurik hauled his half brother before the dais and threw him down before Rollo. "I give him to your mercy, Uncle." Rurik gasped for his own breath, sides heaving.

Rollo stepped from the platform to stand over Hastein, eyes fire bright.

"Curse the day Morrígú dropped you," he bit out. "From the cradle, your mother twisted you with her hatreds and blind jealousies. She poisoned you with the venom of her Druid heart. Your sire was a fool not to cast her from his longhouse. But he spared her a place and, methinks, this day was fated."

Rollo drew himself up, his features hard and fierce, and spat into the rushes. "I know you not," he thundered. "I spit you out. You are *ekkert* in my eyes, a nothing. From this day, you shall bear the name of *úrhrak,* outcast. You have till day's dawning to flee these borders. Dare you befoul my domain, or canker the soil of Normandy with your step, any may sever your worthless soul from its husk and claim it in my name." Rollo gave him his back. "Get thee from my sight."

Hastein shoved himself to his feet, his eyes flaying Rurik with sheer hatred, then stumbled from the hall.

"Any else who canst abide my dictates, or wishes to follow, do so now," Rollo growled.

Two of Valsemé's garrison slipped from the back of the chamber, but the duke's personal retainers held firm to a man.

The lines of Rollo's face eased as his anger abated. He smoothed his mustache and called for wine. Swiftly draining the cup, he relinquished it to a servant and faced Rurik.

"It pleasures me that you should hold title of these lands. I wouldst see them prosper under your hand. Now, if you be ready, I will receive your fealty and homage."

Rurik sent the battle-ax clattering over the floor and dropped to one knee before his uncle. Placing his hands within Rollo's in the age-old symbol of submission, he repeated the prescribed words, pledging himself by *bouche et de mains,* by mouth and by hands as the duke's commended man. This done, Rollo raised Rurik to his feet and bestowed the kiss of fealty full on the mouth, sealing their bond.

Next, a lance and a bowl containing a clod of earth was brought forth and presented to Rurik, symbolic of the service required of his overlord, to arms and to fief.

Rurik's hand hesitated over the small coffer of relics as he prepared to swear the oath of homage. Brother Bernard, who had moved from the dais and now held the reliquary, explained the king's condition that the men of Normandy accept the Christ and Holy Baptism. Since Rurik was *prímsigned*, the monk conceded that he could first receive instruction and the waters later. This agreed, Rurik placed his hand firmly on the box and swore himself to faithfulness, aid, and obedience.

Rollo clamped him firmly on the shoulder. "Arise, Rurik Atlison, Baron de Valsemé."

Cheers united the hall, leaving no doubt as to the soldier's acceptance of Rurik. Brienne swelled with pride, her smile brilliant and her eyes shining as she gazed on her golden warrior.

The smile dissolved as she spied Katla moving to stand at the fore of the crowd. The Norsewoman had withdrawn from the table on Ketil's heels when the duke first dispatched him in search of Rurik. Katla had evidently been lost in the throng of soldiers during Hastein's vicious attack, if indeed she had been present for it.

Brienne gave a small snort of disgust. Katla stood regally robed, having readied herself to officially assume her place as baronne. The mantle swathing her was edged with silk, and jewels sparkled at her ears and throat. The fiery mass of hair spilled gloriously about her shoulders, and Brienne thought she might have applied darkener to her eyes, for they appeared enormous and well defined.

Brienne's heart cramped. Katla was beautiful. And Rurik was snared in that beauty, by heart and by vow. She clenched the arms of her mother's high seat, knowing in brief moments she must surrender it to Katla.

"Is there aught you wish?" Rollo's hearty tones brought her from her thoughts as he gained the dais and settled himself in his great chair. "What be your first pronouncement as baron?" He smiled down at Rurik, taking up his huge goblet.

Rurik remained standing before the table, his eyes traveling to Brienne. Her heart skipped a beat as she girt herself for the inevitable and prepared to yield her place.

"If it pleases my lord, Lady Brienne journeyed forth from cloister to take vows with my father." Surprise touched Brienne's face. "This they so did, but as most here witnessed, Gruel Atli died before the marriage was complete."

Rollo's brow creased in puzzlement.

"Before it was consummated," Rurik supplied, bringing color to Brienne's cheeks. "I am assured that, according to Christian law, the marriage is not valid."

Brienne's pulse picked up its pace at a stunning speed. Did he give heed to her pleas after all?

"Before all, I release my claim as Lady Brienne's guardian and acknowledge the Church's rule in this," he declared firmly. "I recognize her as an unmarried maiden and ward of the king."

A mixture of gladness and despair grabbed at Brienne. 'Twas done! Rurik had granted her appeal, but in so doing he must now see her away, away to Levroux. Tears glistened at the corners of her eyes as she received his pronouncement.

"Lady Brienne has expressed her wish to return to her abbey. She is free to do so if she so desires."

Rurik's words were lead in her heart, and a lone tear trickled over her cheek. Was it not as she asked? Yet such misery, such heart-crushing pain it cost her.

"However"—Rurik captured her gaze with eyes more blue than gray—" 'twas the king's decree that Valsemé's heiress be restored to her holdings and marry its new lord baron." He smiled in earnest now. "As the Baron de Valsemé, I offer to take Brienne Beaumanoir's hand in marriage and fulfill the terms of that agreement."

Katla gasped audibly and Esternay wrenched himself upright in his seat.

Brienne sat riveted, perfectly stunned by Rurik's words. A tingling began in her toes and vibrated up through her legs, torso, and arms, sending her heart pounding and her head spinning. God's great splendor! Radiant Mother of God! For the briefest of moments her joy was boundless, her heart on wing.

But her soaring spirits quickly collided with reality and came hurtling back to earth. Her eyes shifted to Katla, and warnings of the *More Danico* passed through her mind in a quick rush.

Norsemen were accustomed to taking wives at will and as many as could be afforded. Certainly Rurik could afford the "many," but such was not lawful in Francia. Didst he not know this? Was he untutored in Frankish and Christian precepts, or had he not considered them? Still, it remained. He was espoused. Any other union was forbidden.

Obviously pleased with the turn of affairs, Rollo nodded favorably at Rurik's words. "How say you, my lady? Are you agreeable to my nephew's offer or wilt you still to Levroux?"

For a long aching moment her eyes clung to Rurik's, pleading for his understanding. A heaviness settled in her chest as she formed the words, and they could barely climb from her throat. Pressing her lashes together, she said in a raw whisper, "I will to Levroux."

She felt Rurik's hard stare boring into her but could not bear to meet his eyes.

Rollo sat back, clearly astonished. He looked to his nephew who stood coiled tightly, wounded by Brienne's words and glaring at her with whip-stung eyes. What objection could the lady possibly claim? Rurik was a fine stallion, skilled with sword, dauntless in battle, rich beyond imaginings, and so indecently handsome the maids fair swooned when he graced them with but a smile.

Rollo drummed his fingers on the arm of his chair, brooding a moment, then expelled a long breath in dismay. "As you wish, my lady, but indulge me. I wouldst have you favor me with a reason."

Brienne's head snapped up, appalled that he should have embraced Christianity for the full year past and still need ask.

"My lord duke, surely it has been explained to you that our Christian religion allows but one wife to husband, one husband to wife."

Rollo exchanged glances with Rurik, confusion etching his forehead. " 'Twould seem something doth escape me here."

"As myself," Rurik concurred. "Mayhaps my lady would clarify herself."

Brienne felt the pull of his eyes and met his burning gaze.
It tortured her heart. Must he have it so plainly? Very well,
then. She sighed in bewilderment.

"I cannot marry Rurik since he already has a wife. Mother
Church will not permit—"

"Wife!" The word burst from Rollo's lips and he near
tipped over his goblet. "What wife be that?"

Brienne wavered, suddenly unsure of herself. Rurik waited
expectantly, his hands braced on his hips. She took a small
swallow. "Why, Katla, my lord."

Rollo laughed richly, his voice resounding in the hall.
" 'Twill be a sad day for many a man the day Katla binds
herself to one pair of breeches."

Brienne flushed fully at the duke's earthy remark, then the
statement took hold and her eyes flew to Rurik.

"Rurik is not married?" she asked breathlessly.

"My nephew may be accused of other things, perchance,
but he has yet to tie the marital knot." Rollo grinned at her
stunned expression. "What say you now, my lady. Wilt you
accept Rurik as your lord husband?"

Brienne rose unsteadily, joy racing through her. She
descended the dais, her violet eyes anchored by those of
steel blue as she stepped before Rurik.

She lay her hand gently on his chest. "I beg pardon,
my lord."

"*Já eda nei,* my lady?" Rollo questioned impatiently.

"*Já,* my lord," Brienne replied with a smile as brilliant as
the sun, her heart overflowing. "I shall bind myself to the
Baron de Valsemé in marriage. May we both be worthy of
our titles and our people." She then added for Rurik's ears
alone, "May we be a most noble inspiration."

Joyous relief washed over Rurik and eased his soul.
He clasped Brienne's hands in his and drew her to
him. Caressing her with loving eyes, he bent to her
ear.

"Pleasure me in a small thing, *ástin mín.* Wear for me
your crimson and gold when next we meet at the church
doors, that I might behold you once again as when first we
met. For I swear, in that instant you laid siege to my heart
and plundered it fully. Naught has been aright since."

Brienne trembled under his tender admission, achingly repentant that she had caused him the least of pains from her own simplemindedness.

He tilted her chin and stroked his thumb along her fragile jaw. "Have you also a wish that is within my power to grant?"

Brienne's eyes sparkled with life. "This wedding, I would prefer to keep to good Frankish wine."

"Saucy wench!" Rurik grinned happily. His arms wound around her as he claimed his bride and kissed her deeply.

Shouts of approval reverberated throughout the hall.

Esternay gripped his goblet and sullenly downed its contents. Unnoticed, Katla stomped from the hall.

Chapter Twelve

❖ ❖ ❖ ❖ ❖ ❖ ❖ ❖ ❖ ❖ ❖ ❖

THE NEEDLE GLEAMED in the candle's soft light as Brienne
bent low over the fine Frisian cloth and burgeoned the breast
of a small silver falcon. The emblem grew beneath her nim-
ble fingers. With a final stab, she sharpened a tiny talon,
then snipped the thread.

" 'Tis done, Aleth." She smiled her pleasure, spreading
the garment to survey her handiwork.

Two full days had passed since Rurik departed the keep.
He did so, to her dismay, brief hours after their betrothal.
What he was about and whence he had gone, she could not
say. But it was clear he wished to gladden her with some
bridal offering and, at the same time, allow the soldiery to
continue the funeral feast and properly honor his father.

Normally, ten days would be set aside for such an occasion, seven for a wedding celebration. But, in truth, little
had been normal these scant days past. Brienne appreciated
Rurik's mindfulness to see Atli remembered fittingly while
not allowing the revelries to stretch without end from one
feast to the next. She sensed he wished Lord Robert gone.
Rollo, too, chafed to return to Rouen and to Poppa.

Whatever Rurik sought to procure, his eyes had sparkled
with such anticipation, and truly a whit of mischief, that she
could not argue his leave-taking. He vowed to join her upon
the church steps midmorn of this third day.

In his absence, she had scoured through both mind and
coffer, questing something suitable for Rurik's marriage gift.
Seizing on a costly robe of Frisian cloth, blue as a deep
summer night, she made it over into a thigh-length tunic

of the Frankish fashion. The wool was exceptionally fine and precisely woven. It had long been the gift of kings. Charlemagne himself had once favored the Persian monarch with cloaks of the prized fabric. This he did after receiving of the Caliph the most wondrous of animals, an elephant.

Brienne and Aleth had worked furiously, cutting and sewing the garment long into the first night of Rurik's absence. Her broidery box yielded a few small spools of precious silver thread, intended by the sisters to embellish vestments and altar cloths. These she claimed with a small amount of guilt, offering a *mea culpa* on the one hand and salving her prickly conscience on the other. Did she not bring her great Norse husband before the altar of God? And was he not a man of means? Surely the thread would be replaced.

She gave a last critical inspection to the row of shimmering falcons that bordered the tunic's hem. Precious objects, she had none to offer, nor coin to call her own. But what better than she present Valsemé's new lord with the symbol of authority and prowess borne by her father and her father's father—the Beaumanoir falcon. 'Twas not given lightly, and she hoped Rurik would claim it for his personal emblem to wear proudly, as had her sire.

Brienne blinked the soreness from her eyes and looked to the window where early-morning light blushed the skies.

"Does he come yet, Aleth?"

Aleth had been watching the stirrings below but shook her head. "I see naught of him. But faith, Brienne. He'll not leave you standing alone before the church."

Faith. How far had she traveled on faith? Brienne gave a small sigh and folded away the tunic. Perchance 'twas patience she needed the more, but she dared not entreat the Almighty, lest He send fresh trials by which to cultivate that virtue in her.

Seeing Brienne rub at her weary eyes, Aleth moved to her side. "Merciful Lord! Your betrothed mustn't find you like this on your marriage day. Let us freshen you and leave you rest atime."

Brienne conceded and accepted a cool compress dampened with clary water. Time winked past. Aleth was next rousing her from a light slumber and bidding her take nourishment.

Brienne complied, then she bathed from a deep earthenware basin kept warm before the fire. Together they combed the silky length of her hair and left it free to cascade over her shoulders and down her back.

Aleth had just finished lacing Brienne's gown when a soft rap sounded at the door. Lyting entered at her bidding, smiling warmly.

"Are you near ready, Lady Brienne?"

"He returns?" Her heart leaped madly.

"*Já.*" The dimples in his cheeks deepened and he swept his hand toward the door. "Wouldst you see for yourself?"

Minutes later, Brienne followed Lyting to the upper reaches of the keep, climbing high above the garret rooms by way of a narrow passage to the topmost chamber. It was a low-ceilinged room with a stout ladder leading to the roof. Brienne gave thanks that she left veil and mantle below as she plucked up her skirts and found footing on the crosspieces. Lyting, having preceded her, reached down and caught her beneath the arms, lifting her the last distance.

Wonder took Brienne as she turned slowly round in a full circle. The barony spread before her in every direction.

Lyting chuckled at her rapt expression. "You grew up here. Didst you not ever come atop the keep?"

"Never," Brienne tossed back blithely. "We lived in the manor house, not the keep." She could have added that her family resided here only in the dark times when Valsemé fell under attack, attack wrought most often by Northmen. But she did not wish to spoil the moment.

"Had I but known this splendor awaited me, I would have grown to maidenhood on this very spot. Others could have styled me the 'Lady of the Tower.' " She laughed gaily, pushing back long tendrils of hair as they stirred in the brisk wind and whispered over her face.

Lyting smiled down at her, then pointed to the silver ribbon of the Toques. There rode a great Norse longship with its red and white striped sail billowing in the breeze.

"Rurik comes."

Brienne's breath caught for joy. Yet the smallest of fears clutched at her Frankish heart as she watched the sleek, high-prowed vessel range over the waters. Ever before, their presence heralded naught but death and destruction. She took rein of herself. Today it bore life—her life and her love— back to her arms.

Did the villeins likewise tremble to see such a sight? she mused. Even here in Normandy? There was naught to distinguish one of the Norse "sea serpents" from any other save size. How could one tell if a longship offered peace or devastation?

Brienne's eyes narrowed. The men of the North were master shipwrights, their craft refined. She doubted they would soon alter the lines of their vessels. Still . . .

"Are the sails ever striped the red and the white?"

Lyting looked at her curiously. "Blue and green are favored as well. Of necessity, the looms produce the heavy woolen in strips. They are sewn together—"

"At what size is such a piece when finished?" she interrupted him excitedly.

"Measuring by *fot,* roughly twenty-three wide and thirty-six in length."

"Oh, Lyting, can you not see it? A sail of deepest blue emblazoned with a great falcon—a great silver falcon for my lord, Rurik." Brienne fairly sparkled, caught up in her imaginings.

Lyting's pale lashes brushed his cheekbones, then his lips eased into a sad, pensive smile. "You are happy, my lady?"

"Oui. Oh, *oui,"* she proclaimed most ardently.

Turning to him, she caught the grave tenderness in his eyes. He glanced away, toward the river. For a moment they did not speak. When he gazed on her again, the look was gone and the warmth of his smile returned.

"Then all is as it should be, my lady. I wish you every joy and happiness. Welcome once more into the heart of my family."

"Merci," Brienne whispered softly, and stretched up her hand to touch his cheek.

He pressed his eyes closed from the jolt of that contact, then blinked them open and turned to face the river. "Remember, my lady. If ever you have need, my sword stands ready to serve."

"Let us pray I never fall to such dire circumstance to warrant the need, but *merci* once again. I shall remember."

For atime they stood in silence watching the longship grow larger as it glided toward port. Brienne now saw that it was filled with people, and in their midst stood a tall and gilded man.

Brienne waited impatiently upon the church steps. She ached to greet Rurik at the water's edge but honored her promise to meet him here.

Lyting had given her over to Lord Robert's keeping before dispatching Sleipnir to his brother. Once again she was escorted with much merriment from bailey to church, but this time Rollo insisted on leading Candra the distance. Outranked, outmaneuvered, and outmatched, the Seigneur d'Esternay looked fit to snap off the head of any that crossed him. Now he scowled blackly in the direction of the river.

Singing, heavy with male voices yet spiced with lighter, feminine tones, announced Rurik's approach. Brienne anchored her gaze on the horizon. To the left of the steps, Aleth smiled widely, flushed and pretty as a bride herself. Young Waite and Patch held to her side and heel, awed by the grandness of the moment.

Then he appeared, astride the great black, his golden hair glinting in the sun, accompanied by dozens of men and women walking alongside him. Love and pride stirred in Brienne's breast. A cloak of sapphire-blue was pinned at his shoulder over clothes of pearl-gray. These skimmed torso and thigh to disappear into soft leather boots. His neck was collared with gold, his waist girt with a wide belt and jewel-hilted sword. He was a princely vision to her eyes, and that vision held her bound.

Then her gaze moved to his arms and she marveled to find a small sprite nestled there, clutching a fistful of wildflowers and riding with queenly dignity.

"Elsie!" Brienne cried out with joy. Tears stung her eyes as she recognized Bolsgar amidst the crowd, along with the child's mother and many faces familiar to her from Ivry.

Without thought or heed, her feet moved beneath her and she ran straight toward Rurik and the destrier, her arms outstretched.

A ripple of fear passed through Rurik as he saw the flurry of crimson and gold hurrying toward the great war horse. Sleipnir tensed beneath his thighs. Issuing a swift command, Rurik halted the mount and slipped to the ground, Elsie still in arm. Quickly, he closed the distance between himself and Brienne and caught her to him with his free arm. The couple's eagerness delighted the crowd.

"Oo-oo-oo." Elsie wriggled, trapped betwixt the lord and his lady. "You're squishing me," she protested.

"Sorry, sweetling," Rurik smiled then kissed Brienne soundly, making her laugh for joy.

Elsie fussed, shooing them apart with her little fingers. "My lord, you mustn't. Truly you mustn't," she scolded.

"I did but kiss my bride," he teased cheerfully. "Is there aught amiss in that?"

Elsie admonished him with her most stern and serious look. "You need marry m'lady before you get her with child."

Rurik chuckled deeply. "That I must." Giving the child over to her mother's care, he offered Brienne an arm and led her through the villeins and soldiers, back to the church steps and the waiting prelate.

Brienne could not keep her eyes from Rurik throughout the ceremony, nor he from she. They were like two children, stealing glimpses of one another. But when time came to profess their vows, Rurik looked on her fully, enclosing her hands warmly in his own. He treasured the love he found mirrored in her eyes as he repeated each word in strong clear tones. Brienne's voice was soft, touched with wonderment, as she gave hers.

No ill omen shadowed the ring this time as Rurik accepted it from his brother and slipped it onto her finger.

The crowd's approval rang in Brienne's ears as Rurik drew her into his embrace and covered her lips. Delicious sensations flamed through her and she leaned into him, wishing to taste more.

Rurik laughed deep in his chest. "Easy, *ástin mín*. There are still many hours before we can take our leave. I fear I shall be in discomfort enough just gazing on you throughout the day."

He smoothed a fingertip over her perplexed brow and wondered how much she knew of men. Did she not realize how easily she aroused him and how tormented would grow his condition left unrelieved all the day?

Sighing, he kissed the tip of her nose and turned her for presentation to the people. He then named Ivry as her dower land, taking Brienne fully by surprise. Rollo, upon banishing Hastein, had awarded him the fief. In turn, it pleased Rurik to bestow the holding on his bride, Ivry's fierce protectress.

The villeins of Ivry pressed forward past the soldiers to present themselves and their humble gifts, mostly offerings of food to augment the wedding table.

Elsie skipped up the steps to proffer her clutch of drooping flowers to Brienne. She slowed her pace on her descent, spying young Waite and the spotted dog. Sidling into her mother's skirts, Elsie pushed a finger into her mouth and eyed them curiously.

Brienne paid scant attention to the long mass that followed. Her thoughts were wholly consumed by her new husband who towered by her side. If there were regrets, it was only that Rurik could not partake of the Eucharist with her. She looked forward to the day when he would accept the Christian waters and renounce the pagan gods of the North.

When they left the church in a shower of grains, Rurik swept her atop Candra, then swiftly mounted Sleipnir. Side by side, on ebony and white, they led the merrymakers back to the keep.

Brienne found it a heady experience to have Rurik fully to herself. She laughed inwardly at that thought since the bailey literally overflowed with people. But until this day, they had been ever pushed apart, ever denied. Now Rurik was hers and she his and none could say them nay.

A delirious joy pulsed through her, ecstatic and boundless. She had gained her heart's desire. And as she reached toward the full measure of womanhood, she felt like a blossom unfurling beneath the warmth of the sun. Rurik was that warmth. He was her sun.

From the moment Rurik lifted Brienne from her horse and their bodies met, she found herself branded in a thousand ways. It was a gloriously primal feeling she savored as she slid down his hard length. Color swept over her cheeks and throat to blush her breasts where they swelled above the gown.

Rurik's touch caused flurries of excitement inside her, and in this he proved a merciless lord. As they lingered briefly among the garrison, receiving well-wishes and pleasantries, he kept her ever to his side, finding every excuse to touch her. If her hand was not resting upon his arm, he would place his own to the curve of her back or caress a tendril of her hair. Once, as he clasped her hand in his, he idly stroked the back with his thumb, rousing every nerve in her body to stand on tiptoe.

Even before they began their ascent up the long wooden staircase, she felt boneless. He matched his tread to hers, slipping his arm beneath her veil to embrace the side of her slim waist. Happily, she didn't care how long it took to reach the top. But when his fingers spanned over her ribs and his forefinger grazed the underside of her breast, she nearly leaped two steps for the sensations that jolted through her. It was going to be a very long day indeed.

As Brienne and Rurik entered the hall, they were greeted with the sight of the baronial high seats positioned side by side once more upon the dais. Rollo's great chair still held to the center, but Brienne's had been moved left of it, to sit right of Rurik's.

" 'Twould seem at long last we are to share a trencher," Brienne said with a laugh as they moved across the chamber. Then she added teasingly, "Will my lord baron prove as attentive as the great Duke of Normandy?"

Rurik lifted her fingers to his lips. "I intend to shower my lady with every consideration and courtesy till she begs me cease."

"Cease? Surely not."

"We shall see." He dropped a kiss to her shoulder as he seated her. "Later."

Brienne marveled that the food and drink still flowed aplenty. To her count, fewer courses were served, but the boards groaned with such abundance, none suffered complaint. True to his word, Rurik was ever attentive, selecting and slicing her meats, seeing that her goblet brimmed with sweet Frankish wine, and ensuring that bowls of sugared roses and almonds were always near to hand.

The harper's sweet chords and verses passing fair floated throughout the hall, while tumblers tipped on their hands and pitched backward somersaults. Jugglers amused with shiny brass rings and whirling brands of fire, but it was a small reed of a man that truly captivated the gathering. Lithe and supple, he twisted himself into grievous contortions almost too painful to observe.

Rurik preferred their wedding to be a festive yet subdued affair, since it directly followed, and somewhat eclipsed, his father's funeral celebration. No trials of strength were held, but the men were challenged to test their skills at spears and arrows.

Feeling no need to prove himself, Rurik declined from participating in the competitions. The last days were beginning to take their measure, and he wished to save himself for the coming nightfall and the sweet promise of his bride.

Rollo offered his great cup as prize for "spears," then quickly won it back. Drinking heartily of the goblet once more, he regretted aloud that he had not tested his nephew's skills. Atli ofttimes boasted of Rurik's proficiency with the weapon. If there be one thing the duke loved beyond a well-pitched battle and a good woman, 'twas a stout match.

Rurik would not be drawn. "Enjoy your cup a time longer, Uncle," he bantered. "We will to it another day."

Rollo toasted the promised meet with a long draught.

As the crowd moved to line the archer's range, Rurik bent to Brienne's ear. "My wager is for Lyting. His arm is strong, his aim accurate, and he can peg the eye of a snake from the greatest of distance. It has earned him the title Skarp-Øje, 'Sharp Eye.' "

"Lyting Sharp Eye?" Brienne grinned. "It has a music to it."

"At your service, my lady." Lyting suddenly appeared at her elbow, clasping his longbow that stretched nearly as tall as he. "Wilt you compete, *broðir*?"

"*Nei*. Have you not heard? I am better at spears," Rurik tossed back with a laugh.

"Better at spears?" Ketil choked from his position behind Rurik.

Rurik ignored the comment and looked back to his brother. "You must uphold our family honor today."

"Against our new 'kinsman'?" Lyting asked with a nod to where the Seigneur d'Esternay stood with his men, stringing his bow stave.

Rurik's eyes grayed and Brienne realized that he had not considered that Robert Coustance was now his brother-by-marriage through her. Either that or he chose to disregard it. She squeezed his hand, forcing a lightness to her words.

"At last Lord Robert allows his soldiers to join in the games. They have been sorely idle since their arrival. How think you they will fare? Bow and arrow are employed chiefly for hunting in Francia. I understand Northmen train with it for war as well."

She sensed she was on the verge of babbling. Esternay had glanced up from his labors and was now staring at her, his look hard. She stepped closer to Rurik.

"Of course, Sister Dalmatica—her brother is in Lord Geaune's service—claims the Roman crossbow gains favor amongst the troops since it does not require long training or great strength."

This drew a chuckle from Rurik. " 'Twould seem holy women have an uncommon interest in weaponry, and here I bethought they spent their time in prayer. *Nei, ástin mín,* do not look at me so." Rurik pressed a finger to her lips, smiling, before she could gainsay him. "If you wouldst know, hunting and warring demand different skills, but I am sure the king's men will show themselves well." He looked out over the Normans and Franks taking up their marks on the field. "Still, my silver is on Lyting."

"None for Normandy's duke?" she rejoined.

Rurik tilted a brow. "Wish you to wager coin, my lady wife?"

"Only if it be on you." She winked.

"Clever vixen, but you'll not lead me out. I wouldst spend myself more cheerfully on a different playground this day." His lips began to descend over hers, but a voice boomed from behind.

" 'Tis the sport here or afield?" Ketil called robustly. " 'Od's breath, have pity, Rurik. There be few enough women in Normandy. Leave the men their concentration long enough to pull their bowstrings." He chortled and trudged off to take up his place.

The contenders changed their mark after every shot, ever increasing the distance of the targets. These were stretched over bails of straw. As Rurik predicted, the Franks showed themselves well. After seven rounds, five remained, two Franks and three Normans. Lyting and Esternay numbered among them.

While the men refreshed themselves with ale and waited for targets to be relocated the additional distance, Rurik admired Lyting's bow made of yew wood. He was quickly caught up in conversation with his brother and uncle over the virtues of yew versus elm, which was heavier. From there, they agreed on the necessity of taking the long-grained wood from trunk rather than branch, which could own many knots, and that lightweight ash made the best arrows, fletched with goose for steadiest flight.

Brienne's thoughts wandered to Aleth who tarried nearby with Elsie, Waite, and his ever-present charge, Patch. She craved to speak with her friend, for she wished to release her from her duties within the keep. Mayhaps it served well at first for Aleth to pose as her personal maid, but she was an equal, a lady of blood and fine training. There were others who could attend as tirewomen. Aleth's abilities must not be wasted. She was a practiced and capable healer, fair adept in her skills. Together they would see to the needs of Valsemé and instruct others in the art.

Slipping from Rurik's side she went to greet her friend. Barely had they embraced than the knight Leveque approached.

"Best wishes for your marriage, my lady. We leave on the morrow for Paris and the king, then on to Roubaix. Might I carry a word from your lips for Lady Lisette?"

"Lisette." Brienne whispered her sister's name, then placed her hand on the knight's arm more urgently. "She does not know that I have returned to Valsemé, or that I have . . . that I have married a Norman." Faith! What untruths would Lisette be told? She withdrew her hand, remembering herself. "Lord Robert said she is grave ill with child. Is it true?"

A swift shadow passed over Leveque's features. "She grows stronger by the day." He swallowed the rest of what he would say. "Do not worry, my lady. I will watch over her as is within my power. She implores his lordship to send her to Chaudrey. Let us pray he concedes, for methinks she wouldst regain her health in those airs."

Brienne searched the young man's face, sifting his words, for they hinted at much yet revealed little. Did her mind play her a trick or did he bear her sister a special loyalty?

She puzzled at his offer to convey a message rather than assume she would send word through Lord Robert. Perchance he was simply courteous, or perchance he knew well his liege, who kept much from his wife.

"Do you place yourself at risk in this?" she asked quietly, her meaning in her eyes.

He smiled. "I think not, my lady."

Hope rose but prudence cautioned. "Then apprise Lady Lisette of all you have witnessed. Tell her that I am happy and that I long to see her but—" She cast about desperately for the right words. How could she explain that she must stay apart? That she dare not come to Roubaix for fear of the husband her sister so blindly honored?

As though her thoughts had conjured the man, Esternay appeared, nearly upon them. Brienne squared her shoulders and offered her hand to Leveque.

"Thank you for your wishes on my marriage and your many kindnesses throughout our journey. Thank you also for me Blanchard and Mortain. Mayhaps I will see you again—" She was about to add "at Chaudrey," but Esternay clipped through her words.

"Then you must visit us and soon, my dear." His lips twisted wryly. "Lisette would be joyed to see you, and I would assure myself that you fare well in Normandy.

But you need not commit yourself this moment. Consider the invitation ever open. Who can augur the future?" He dismissed his man with a sharp glance.

Brienne's eyes snapped violet fire and she crushed the gown beneath her fingers. He obscured his meaning for Leveque's and Aleth's benefit, but his intent remained clear to her. Such guile!

His mouth quirked at her cold, silent fury. "Ah, but do bring your husband if he cannot bide your absence. 'Tis no imposition. As I have told you, my dear, there are many rooms at Castle Roubaix. Think on it."

Brienne would have liked to scream her frustration and scratch the overconfident smile from his face. But as he retreated toward the field, a loathsome fear gripped her heart. She had refused to be partner to his schemes, yet he did not abandon them. Her rejection had little altered his course, only his level of pleasure. Her knees weakened beneath her. Robert Coustance would seek to kill Rurik—at some future time—once they had a son.

Rurik drew his gaze from the competition just as Lyting was stepping forward. He saw Brienne lay her hand on the arm of a Frankish retainer.

He recognized the man from his entertainment in the hall several days past. A small horn of jealousy pricked him, but he shook it away. Truly he was besotted to read more into that gesture than anything proper. Brienne's brow creased in earnest conversation while her woman, Aleth, listened avidly at her side. He looked back to see Lyting's arrow hit dead center.

Applauding the shot, he glanced once more at Brienne. His smile slackened. Brienne fairly bristled as Esternay joined her, giving some comment. For a moment her anger seemed to crackle about her like some live thing. There was a brief exchange, and Rurik started toward them but the knight took his leave. Brienne's fire suddenly abated. She paled, clearly stricken. Had it not been for Aleth taking her by the hands, he thought Brienne might have swooned.

Anger rode him dark and swift. Rurik stalked toward the field, passing Lyting as he went. He delayed long enough to relieve his brother of his longbow and a single arrow and advanced on Esternay, now taking up his mark.

Esternay glimpsed Rurik's grim figure moving across the green just as he released his arrow. The shot went awry, hitting the edge of the target, an embarrassing effort.

The knight took several paces back as Rurik strode glowing to the mark. But he could not resist a sneering comment. "So, the groom competes for his lady's attentions after all."

With lightning-swift speed, Rurik set the arrow, aimed, and released. The arrow whistled through the air and with a *thwack* split the shaft of Esternay's arrow in two.

Rurik turned steel-gray eyes on Robert Coustance. "As I said, I'm better at spears."

Giving the knight his back, he sought his bride and escorted her to the keep.

Brienne regained her good spirits under Rurik's mindful attentions. They partook of a light evening meal as day stretched toward its end.

A new sport rose in the hall as the men now tested their verbal dexterity with riddles and witty sayings. None could match the clever tongue of Brother Bernard, and for this he earned two silver dirhems.

Evyind composed a song to honor the bridal couple, afterwhich he was hailed, plied with wine, and cheerfully dispossessed of his instrument. Other would-be musicians plucked out their pieces with less craft, and when wit waned, quoted the salty wisdom of the old lays.

> Dally with girls in the dark—
> the day's eyes are many.
> Seek you some maid
> when from her bower she calls.
> Forget the stout cup—
> in white arms work your will.
> Bold men bare your blades!
> But beware, for 'tis found—
> drink steals more than one's wit.
> A wholehearted swain
> with dull sword cannot breech
> the portals of the fair-dight maid.

The crowd roared with delight and continued in their merriments.

Rurik observed that Brienne ate little, only a bit of broth and crust of bread. She appeared content though at times distracted.

"Have you tasted of the pomegranate?" Rurik snatched up a leathery-looking fruit from a neighboring tray and split it open with his knife. Brienne's eyes widened at the brilliant ruby flesh encasing multitudes of little seeds.

" 'Tis deliciously sweet." He stripped apart the membranes and carefully pared away the rind. "Well worth the effort." Lifting a juicy morsel to her lips, he added, " 'Tis fitting a bride eat of the pomegranate. 'Tis said it blesses her with many children."

Brienne's eyes fixed on his as she accepted the succulent offering from his fingers. A trace of juice lingered on her bottom lip and he brushed it away with his thumb.

" 'Tis pleasantly tart," she said with some difficulty. "Would you also eat of the pomegranate?"

"From your hands I will eat anything, *ástin mín*." He flashed her a smile.

She felt giddy under those steel blue eyes as he waited expectantly. The fruit was somewhat slippery to handle. She cupped one hand beneath the other so as not to lose the piece or drip its juice on his fine garments. He bent slightly forward to receive the delicacy, but in so doing, captured the tip of her finger, skimming it with his tongue before slowly releasing it from the warmth of his mouth.

"Parbleu!" Brienne jumped. She would have sprung clear to her feet had not Rurik placed a hand on her thigh, unseen beneath the table, and pressed her down. She whisked her glance about to see if any marked his play.

"I would have more," Rurik whispered huskily in her ear.

Her hand trembled slightly as she proffered the delicacy, experiencing a sweet joy at those words, but trepidation as well. This time he wrapped his fingers lightly about her wrist so she could not retrieve her hand. Taking the morsel, he then slowly sucked the juice from one finger, then the next. His

eyes locked on hers and he watched their color darken. Juice
had dribbled into her palm, and this, too, he sought, lingering
to draw a lazy circle there with the tip of his tongue.

A burst of sensation fired through Brienne. "Rurik!" she
gasped, squirming in her seat. "Have mercy."

"Do you beg me cease my attentions so soon?" He stroked
the inside of her wrist.

"I . . . I only . . ." Her mind was amuddle. Warmth tingled down over her breasts, stirring her stomach to knots
before it found the core of her womanhood. How swiftly and
instinctively she responded to his touch. It was as though she
had no rule of herself, and that afrighted her.

"Let us take our leave, *ástin mín*." His breath fell hot on
her neck and shoulder. "I grow weary of sharing you and
would seek our sweet nest."

Brienne's voice stuck somewhere in her throat as she read
the desire in his eyes. She swallowed. Of the intimacies
shared by men and women she knew little, only a most
basic knowledge and that sparing. She trusted Rurik would
be patient and use her kindly. But it was the force of her
own passion, sweeping her toward that unknown, that fed
her unease.

Rurik squeezed her hand as he signaled Aleth with his eyes
to gather the chosen maidservants and attend Brienne to their
chamber.

"I will try to convince the men to forgo the bedding ceremony and take my leave unimpeded. But should I fail and
you hear their approach, forget aught else and see you safe
beneath the coverings. They are as eager as I to glimpse your
tempting curves, *ástin mín*." Color warmed Brienne's cheeks
as Rurik pressed a final kiss to her fingers and released
them.

Raucous applause broke out as the bride rose and moved
from the dais. Much jesting accompanied her departure,
quickly giving way to earthier advisements and offers of
assistance to the groom.

Rurik bore this in good humor, joining his men in a toast
to his marriage, to his lady, to his lady's beauty, then to all
the dark-haired beauties of Francia and sun-bright maids of
the North. Drink flowed to the praise of full-bosomed maids

everywhere and small-breasted ones alike, to long-limbed wenches with firm round buttocks, to their silken thighs and hot tender loins. On went the rounds of toasts till they had drunk to every part a maid could own.

Hoping Brienne had time enough to complete her preparations, Rurik summoned a servant to fetch a flask from his private stock. This he shared at the high table. Esternay had absented himself long ago to the company of his retainers, but Rollo, Lyting, Brother Bernard, and Ketil, who now joined them, gathered round. They raised their cups this time to long life and children aplenty.

"I have seen fit to help you to those ends," the duke announced heartily. "My wedding gift awaits you in your chamber. Enjoy!" That said, he attended his cup but would not divulge the nature of the offering.

The conversation meandered and digressed, ever returning to Rurik's travels and exploits in the East.

" 'Tis said you shun the mail-shirt in battle, wearing neither metal nor bone sewn to your corslet. True?" Ketil tested the rumor he had heard long ago.

Rurik eyed the four steadily as he sipped the biting liquid, sensing where this would lead. "True." He took another sip, waiting.

"Well?" they asked in unison, their faces keen with interest.

Ketil's patience rubbed through first. "Well, man, do you defy death or have you a secret?"

Rurik suppressed his amusement, moving forward in his chair to rest his elbows on the table. "Reindeer hide," he pronounced confidentially.

"Reindeer hide?"

"Twelve layers. 'Twill turn a blow as well as any mail-shirt."

"I have heard of such but gave it no credence," Rollo said, twisting his mustache thoughtfully. "Twelve, you say?"

More discussion ensued until Rurik saw no other way to gain his leave than by promising to acquire like corslets for his uncle and old friend. Lyting declined his generous offer, preferring his own durable mail, and the churchman had no use for it.

"I will send to the North Lapps to have them made, but it could take a time to gather enough hides to cover the two of you. 'Twill require several herds, no doubt!"

This met with laughter, and Rurik thought them placated. Draining his cup, he gave over the remainder of the flask and called for another.

Rising to his feet, Rurik extricated himself with what he thought to be faultless and eloquent logic as he enjoined them to remain. After the tumultuous days surrounding his father's marriage, death, and funeral, he desired that his bride and he enjoy a more quiet and tempered occasion. "I see no need to hold to ceremony where the bedding is concerned."

"What?" Rollo came to his full height, slamming down his goblet. "No bedding ceremony? 'Twas a wedding I set my sail for, and a wedding I'll see well to its end. Men!" he bellowed, gesticulating to his table companions at the same time.

Before Rurik could protest, he was lifted clear off his feet and carted out of the hall.

Brienne shook her head at the monstrous bed filling the chamber. Immense and box-shaped, it stood before her as wide as it was long, and it was longer than any she had ere seen. The footposts were simply turned, plain, in truth, but the planklike headposts rose high above her, the heads of two unidentifiable beasts snarling down.

"It looks to be comfortable enough," Aleth soothed, seeing Brienne's trepidation, then spoiled the effort with a giggle. "At least when you're abed you need not look at them."

Voices clamoring in the passage stole away the retort poised on Brienne's tongue. All objection flew out the window, and with a gasp, she slipped from her robe and dove for the protection of the bed coverings.

A heartbeat later, the door burst open and the boisterous group entered, carrying Rurik feet first and half undressed. Brienne drew the sheet to her chin as their eyes strayed to the bed and they set him down before her. Amidst crude jests and offers of help, Rurik was divested of the rest of his clothes and heaved into the bed.

Aleth whisked the covers back as they did so, barely
allowing the men a glimpse of thigh. She blushed to the roots
of her hair for what she saw of Rurik and now hastily shooed
the jocular group from the room. Giving a last inspection to
the wine and fruit tray that graced the table, she followed the
servant women out and pulled the door closed.

Rurik released a long breath, grateful to be alone at last
with his bride, thankful for the quiet and their privacy. He
smiled down on Brienne, then his brow creased slightly. She
continued to clutch the linen to her chin, her lashes lowered.
Beneath the thin shield he could perceive that her shoulders,
nei her whole body, trembled.

Rurik raked a hand through his golden hair, then glanced
at the table. Wine would hearten her. Glad he'd had the
foresight to order a flask of the keep's best, he sprang from
the bed and padded across the chamber, perfectly at ease with
his natural state.

A sound escaped from the bed and he reeled round to
face Brienne, unaware of the image he created as he stood
illumined against the fire's flickering light, gloriously and
paganly naked. He caught the stark fear in her eyes as she
shrank back into the bed. For the most fleeting of moments
he imagined her reaction to be spawned by her fear of
Norsemen. The look was akin to the one with which she
had reviled him in the glade.

But as her shocked gaze remained fixated on his bold
display of maleness, he realized the cause of her distress.
He cursed himself for his thoughtlessness as he watched
Brienne color profusely and give a shudder that reached to
her toes. She was but a shy maiden faced with her first
mating, mayhaps more timid than most since she had been
shut away from men for so many years.

"Brienne . . . I did not think—" He faltered, wondering
whether to cover his arousal or quickly return to the bed or
both. *Nei*. He felt no shame, nor should she. Still, he did not
wish her to fear him.

Brienne instantly regretted her response, afraid she had
marred the moment. Worse, her actions may have prompted
Rurik to think *he* had marred it. And worse still, he might
think she found him lacking or repulsive in some wise. This,

of course, was impossible. He was truly magnificent, though she admitted her astonishment at the size of . . . but he was a big man, uncommonly tall. What did she expect?

Brienne composed herself. This was not the first time she had seen Rurik thusly, nor would it be the last. Granted, when they had discovered one another in the river, she hadn't *seen* all of him, but she had certainly *felt* all of him. She forced her mind to that interlude, recalling each rapturous sensation they had shared, and how those sensations had filled her dreams for so many nights since.

Brienne picked up her courage and rose from the relative security of the bed. 'Twas not Rurik she feared, only the act itself, the unknown. For a moment she clung to the sheet's slender protection, then, her heart beating high in her throat, she allowed it to slip from her fingers.

A wave of hot yearning pounded through Rurik as he gazed unreservedly on his wife's lustrous charms. She moved toward him with an unhurried tread, her full, rosy-tipped breasts swaying gently over an incredibly small waist and narrow hips. Pale thighs framed a dark triangle of curls and tapered downward to shapely calves and slim ankles.

Heat suffused his loins as Brienne presented herself to him and laid a cool hand upon his chest. He felt the tremor in that touch and was moved. How desperately he loved her.

Rurik laced his long fingers through the rich texture of her hair, tilting her face to his as he gently drew aside the mass of silken tendrils that veiled one shoulder. He wished every pore of her creamy flesh to be exposed to his view, and now he drank his fill of the heavenly vision before him, entrancing in the fireglow. Her temples pulsed beneath his fingertips and he searched her face, fierce desire hungering through him.

Brienne smiled up at him. Though her lips faintly trembled, love shone in her eyes. Rurik groaned deep in his spirit. At last the drought was at an end. There be no more waiting or denials. There be no need for restraint except where it might increase their mutual pleasure. Warm currents of understanding passed between them. This would not be a mere coupling of bodies, but a melding of hearts and binding of souls.

The moment seemed suspended on the brink of eternity as his mouth slowly descended over hers, caressing, tasting, tenderly exploring the sweetness of her lips. Brienne's hand fluttered over the steely planes of his chest, over his heart whose drubbing matched her own, then crept upward around his neck. Her lips parted under his, welcoming him, greeting him as her tongue met his, shyly at first then with wonderment and longing.

Rurik gathered her to him, one hand gliding over the fragile length of her spine. Her soft womanly contours yielded to his hardened muscle as he plundered the warm recesses of her mouth.

A delicate flame lit beneath Brienne's skin and swept like quickfire through her veins, blazing its way to the center of her being. She felt liquid and breathless. Flesh burned against flesh, and she ached with such need that she trembled at its force.

Rurik felt her limbs quake against him, his own alarmingly unstable as waves of long-suppressed emotion and elemental need crashed through him. Without interrupting the play of their lips, he bent to slip an arm behind her knees. Lifting her from her feet, he bore her to the bed and gently lay down with her.

Their kisses grew more urgent as their passions mounted. Their hands strayed, Brienne's chasing over Rurik's hard back, his trailing fire to a silken hip, hers venturing boldly over the smooth firmness of his buttocks, his singeing the satin length of her legs. She marveled at the feelings he aroused in her, but his torture had just begun.

Rurik's mouth left hers to sprinkle kisses over her brow, eyes, cheek, nose, and into her hair, stirring its clean scent. He traced a molten path over the smooth column of her neck and shoulder. Downward he continued, showering kisses over her breasts and beneath them, moving to the smooth flatness of her stomach, tasting her navel, the curve of waist and hip, skimming her thighs, the backs of her knees, then suddenly returned to press a burning kiss to the pulse point at the hollow of her neck.

On and on he inflicted his torment. He savored the delicious swell of her breasts, avoiding the pouting crests that ached for his attention, driving Brienne to madness.

When at last Rurik covered her nipple with the warmth of his mouth, she gasped and gripped him covetously. Exquisitely, he encircled the sweet bud, his tongue flicking over the swelling globe, then finally he tugged and sucked till she sobbed aloud.

A world of sensation awakened in Brienne, every nerve lay open and exposed, tingling and acute. Her consciousness ebbed as a fire storm of desire raged through her, converging between her thighs to leave her throbbing for some unknown release.

Attuned to her need, Rurik's hands strayed down over her abdomen, questing ever further and lower. Again and again he returned to tease and tantalize her thighs apart. She opened instinctively like the petals of a flower thirsting for the sun. When his fingers slipped inside to stroke her intimately, she was jolted, shocked by his boldness. But her mind could frame no protest as startling waves of pleasure washed through her. She prayed he'd never cease.

His hands continued to work their magic till Brienne moaned and writhed beneath him, nipping at his arm and shoulder in sweet delirium.

Nearing the limits of his own control, Rurik moved over her. He brushed back her hair and framed her face with his hands. "*Ástin mín,*" he whispered raggedly, "the first time . . . there will be pain. There is no help for it."

Brienne sought his lips, pulling him to her. "Love me, Rurik," she pleaded urgently. "Love me now!"

At that, he captured Brienne's mouth in a deep, ravenous kiss and settled himself between her thighs. Her legs twined about his and he entered her slowly, carefully. She was tight and so incredibly hot. He placed a steel grip on his control, wanting this first union to be perfect for her.

Pressing forward, he met with the dread barrier and paused in frustration, loath to hurt her. He debated whether to push with a gentle, steady pressure or break it with one rapid thrust.

But Brienne grew impatient. Eager to feel the full length of him, she tightened her legs around his and arched her hips forward. Pain sheared through her loins as she sheathed him completely.

Rurik hushed her cry, holding himself still as he lavished her with kisses and whispered endearments in her hair, her ear, though only he could understand them. The moment passed, and when she reassured him with a smile and caught at his lower lip, he began his seduction anew.

With skilled fingers and irresistible mouth, Rurik stirred the embers of her desire. Cautiously, he moved against her, guiding her hips with his hands till she matched his building rhythm.

Brienne's ardor flamed, sharp and bright. She panted breathlessly against his mouth as she hurtled toward the edge of some unknown precipice. Suddenly, she seemed to spiral free of all earthly bounds and explode into a starburst of light.

Just when Rurik feared he had exhausted the limits of his control, Brienne released a primitive moan and erupted against him. Her contractions triggered his own violent climax. Roaring his triumph, he joined her in a brilliant and shuddering release.

Together they rode their passions, blazing higher and higher, faster and faster, till at last they reached the heavens and touched the stars.

Chapter Thirteen

BRIENNE AWAKENED TO Rurik's warmth. Their long night of lovemaking had left her exhausted yet exhilarated. In the soft glow of early morn, she studied his features—the sweep of his golden brows, the darker lashes, the fine straight nose, the high cheekbones. The deep cleft in his chin beckoned her to place a finger there. Rurik's eyes opened immediately.

"Insatiable wench." His voice was deep with sleep. Enfolding her hand, he moved her finger to his lips. "You will scarce be able to walk if we continue in this madness."

Brienne traced her finger lovingly over the firm contours of his mouth, a dangerous mouth, she decided, as she glowed with intimate memories. "My body owns no complaint, my love. Truly, I am able enough to ride."

Rurik flashed her a smile in the dim light. It was the first time she had referred to him in that manner. "If my lady wishes to ride, then ride she will."

Rurik drew her atop him and settled her on his waiting manhood. Brienne's gasps turned to moans as he pulled her forward, poising her full breasts deliciously above his mouth. He sucked first one nipple then the other as he coaxed her hips into a steady rhythm.

An hour later they still lay entwined, Rurik now above, gently caressing her lips with his. Neither was aware of anything save the other until the chamber door swung open and the duke strode in, loudly commanding a half-dozen men to place their burdens before the hearth.

Mortified, Brienne slid beneath Rurik and tried to conceal herself. He covered her as best he could, yanking up the sheet while casting an impatient look over his shoulder to his uncle.

Hands planted on hips, Rollo's throat rippled with laughter. "Christ's toes! Do you mate her still? Give the doe her rest. She'll have naught of you this eve if she must ease herself on cushions. But, ho! Look here—another gift." He gestured toward an enormous oaken tub that was now being filled with heated water and a sprinkling of herbs.

" 'Twas sized for myself, but I imagine the two of you should fit comfortably enough. Poppa and I managed." He soughed at that thought, unconsciously smoothing a hand over his stomach, then adjusted his wide belt.

"Well, see that your bride soaks what you have abused so eagerly this night. *Njóta!* Enjoy! But don't be about it all day. The sheets need be hung so the king's man might view them and take his report to Charles."

Beneath Rurik, Brienne flushed three shades of scarlet.

Rollo stepped to the door and motioned out his men. "I, also, will take my leave. 'Tis constricting to be about the rompings of two so freshly wed. Take no offense that I go. There be thighs willing enough in the village, no doubt, but I find my loins ache for Poppa."

As abruptly as the duke had thundered in, he departed, leaving the couple to their privacy once more.

Rurik rested his forehead against Brienne's as she eased upward to the pillow. "Forgive me, *ástin mín,* I disremembered to bar the door. I shall have three more slats added if it pleases you." He brushed his lips over her burning cheeks and into her hair. "But I suspect 'twould delay the duke little if he truly wished to enter."

"Rurik, what of Poppa?" Brienne fretted. "She has just given birth. Would Rollo really force her to . . . ?"

Rurik lifted himself and kissed away the tiny line that creased her brow. "There are many ways to make love, Brienne. Poppa knows well how to care for her duke."

He chuckled at her perplexed look and rolled from the bed, Brienne still in arm. Crossing to the waiting tub, he stepped in with his prize and sank into its heated depths. The sensation was that of silk gliding over silk as her breasts pillowed against his chest and he settled her between his legs.

" 'Twould be inexcusable to neglect our liege's generosity, especially when it offers so many delights"—he nibbled the curve of her neck—"and possibilities."

The man was indefatigable, Brienne mused contentedly as he cupped her breast. She lifted a dripping finger and trailed it thoughtfully down the indentation in his chin. Droplets lingered there and she sought them with the warmth of her tongue.

"And these ways of love, wilt you show me well how to care for my baron?"

"Gladly, *ástin mín*." Rurik smiled, then released a pleasurable moan as Brienne's lips moved along his collarbone and tasted the smooth texture of his muscled shoulder. He shifted in discomfort. "But there is much time. My uncle spoke rightly. The doe needs her rest." At Brienne's pout, he laughed. "Besides, once again, I have neglected to latch the door."

Though their bath was unhurried, Brienne was loath to leave it and allow the world to intrude upon their happiness.

Rurik, too, was reluctant for their honeyed hours to end. He assisted his wife into her dress, keeping Aleth and the maidservants waiting outside the chamber. But he knew naught of tending women's hair, and when Brienne selected blue and green ribbons to weave through her long tresses, he relented and allowed the others in.

To Brienne's chagrin, the sheets were stripped and taken for display in the hall. She flushed as Rurik frowned after them. They were liberally sprinkled with blood.

Moving before her, he lifted her chin. "You are . . . all right, *ástin mín*?" he asked gently.

Brienne placed a reassuring hand on his and nodded.

In response, he dropped a kiss to her brow and drew her to sit on the bed. After stepping into the passageway, he voiced a command, then quickly returned with a sizable bundle.

"Ketil was instructed to keep near with your bride gift," he revealed as he placed the object across her lap.

Delighted as a child, Brienne pulled away the cloth and discovered an elegant silver casket detailed with scroll-

work and Christian images. Angular markings incised
the front, back, and sides in a continuous band. She
had seen such before. Her finger moved from the small
embossed figure of a saint to trace along the etch-
ings, then stilled. Katla's goblet of *nabid* bore similar
inscriptions.

" 'Twas purchased with honest coin, Brienne." Rurik
watched her hesitate over the decoration, then the runes.
Did she think the box to be pirated?

Brienne's heart twinged at his words and the fine edge
in his voice. She had not considered that the chest might
be booty, gained in a Norse raid. It pained her that Rurik
misread her. Uncertain how to respond without risking a
recounting of the episode with Katla, Brienne let the remark
pass and opened the coffer.

"Oh, Rurik!" she gasped in astonishment at the precious
girdle lying on folds of velvet.

It was wrought of fine gold links, each section set with
sapphires and pearllike shell. The sapphires alternated between
light oval stones and darker square ones set on their points.
These were flanked at the top and bottom of each link with
white iridescent disks.

"How splendid! Truly, I shall be the envy of every lady
in the realm, even the queen herself."

Setting aside the casket, she withdrew the belt and rose
to secure it in place. But the unfamiliar clasp thwarted her
efforts.

Rurik took it from her hands, but he had to laugh. A squir-
rel would be easier to harness, he thought, much amused.
Brienne scarce stood still an instant, dipping from side to
side to glimpse the finery, then bending over his fingers,
blocking his view.

He abandoned any attempt to explain the fastener and
simply enjoyed the sight of Brienne as she pleasured in
the gift and twirled full circle before him. Suddenly she
stopped, as she remembered something and hurried to her
coffer. A moment later she returned, smiling demurely.

"My present pales beside yours, I fear. But know, 'tis
given from the heart." She held forth the blue tunic that she
had carefully folded to display the Beaumanoir falcons.

Rurik accepted the garment, handling it with great care, and unfolded it. The warmest of smiles spread over his face and touched his eyes.

"Handsomer attire I do not own, Brienne. You fashioned it yourself?" He admired the border of gleaming birds. "Have I not seen you wear a like emblem?"

" 'Twas my father's and his father's. It has long been embraced by the barons of Valsemé. I had hoped . . . well, that you might—"

Warmth flowed through him. It stirred Rurik deeply that she would honor him in so personal and meaningful a way. "I shall wear it with pride, *ástin mín*."

"Then a favor, I pray," Brienne pressed, suddenly restive. " 'Tis more the season for linens than woolens, I realize, but could you wear the tunic till Lord Robert is away?" At Rurik's puzzled frown, she added more precisely, "I would leave no doubt that I accept my Norman husband."

"If it pleases you, *ástin mín*."

Rurik refrained from asking whether the gesture be intended for the Seigneur's benefit or the king's. Something had transpired between Brienne and Robert Coustance. Something that upset her thoroughly. Rurik hoped in time she would confide in him. For now, he would not press.

A short while later he questioned that wisdom as he stood with Brienne in the crowded bailey, accepting the Seigneur d'Esternay's leave. She had been taut as a bowstring since they had first entered the hall and the knight approached them.

Rurik had watched the fire bank in Esternay's eyes as he stared at the tunic, then challenged Brienne with a glaring look. She had simmered with defiance and boldly returned the hard gaze but said nothing. Now, as Esternay sat mounted at the head of his retinue, extending the hospitality of Roubaix, Rurik felt Brienne's fingers digging into his forearm. It was not until he uttered some vague, noncommittal response that her grip eased.

Rurik fast became vexed with himself for not drawing the details from Brienne. He disliked seeing her so troubled. Of course, if that revelation had truly outraged him, he might have decided to have the man's lungs for his supper—a poor way for a new baron to begin relations with his sovereign, dining on the emissary!

Brienne avoided Lord Robert's eyes, which were glowing like heated coals in their sockets. Instead, she scanned the familiar faces among the Frankish soldiery, silently bidding her farewells. Leveque she acknowledged with the faintest of nods, then her gaze drifted over the ducal retainers and Valsemé's garrison, who were congesting the courtyard in no particular order.

As the Seigneur d'Esternay turned his roan and commanded his men from the bailey, Brienne expelled a long sigh of relief. But as the last of the Frankish contingent clattered across the bridge, she felt strangely bereft, for they were her kindred.

A small, unreasonable thread of fear penetrated her consciousness and coiled round the back of her brain. Her eyes traveled slowly to the sea of pale and fiery heads—Norsemen all—in her father's keep.

In their first weeks of marriage, Rurik and Brienne rarely found time to themselves except in the deep hours of the night. They were ever attended or sought out, having to make countless decisions, to direct and advise. Neither was wholly prepared for such obligations. The absence of the privacy each had once enjoyed grated on them sorely.

True, cloistered life was communal, not private in the literal sense of the word, but 'twas ordered and predictable. Brienne had always been able to find quiet moments to renew herself throughout the day, be they in prayer and reflection or amidst her chores and duties. Even while gathering fruit in the orchards with twenty other souls, she could find a degree of solitude, for she was not constantly approached with the needs of others.

Rurik, on the other hand, had known extraordinary freedom since leaving the emperor's service. Generously gifted for foiling a palace plot and saving the imperial neck, he traveled widely, increasing his wealth, bound to no land or man. For the years past, he had come and gone as pleased him, answerable to himself alone. Nor were any dependent upon him. Now he was both lord and vassal, ruling over fief and serf, in command of his own troops, all the while pledged to serve Normandy's duke and defend the Frankish domains against his countrymen.

Now, too, he had a wife to provide for, care for, and cherish. Wife! The thought still tugged a smile from his lips. He had had little intention of taking on that particular responsibility when the royal schemes brought Brienne into his life and into his arms. Rurik had believed he would never love again. Now he wondered if he had ever loved at all. Brienne was his heartmate. Were he free to do so, he would sweep her away to a secret trysting place and not return for the waning of many moons.

But the ceaseless demands of the barony left him no time for even the smallest of indulgences. Garrison, keep, land, and villeins pressed him on every side. Admist all the concerns, the monk proved intent on lessoning him in a god he felt every compunction to reject. He had nearly embraced the Christian god once, for Helena's sake. But where was that god when she lay dying? When her pain was without end? Where was his power to save? Rurik's disenchantment with the old gods did not impel him to accept another in their place. If the Christ was divine, Rurik doubted he took interest in the pleas of a Norseman. It bothered him no more than his father to give lip service to this deity if required. What truly disturbed him was the gnawing void his uncertainty left within.

Bolsgar proved invaluable in the running of the estate. Having managed the *demeine* under Richard Beaumanoir, he was fully knowledgeable of its many-sided operation. Rurik restored him at once to his former position as steward.

Initially, they spent a hefty portion of each day immersed in the details of the barony. Bolsgar apprised him of the Frankish system of tenure and explained its rents and liabilities. The spring plantings had begun under Atli but, for the lack of hands and time, only a portion of the fields allotted were tilled and seeded. Rurik ordered that the grain stores be counted throughout his holdings along with the stock: oxen, pigs, goats, and sheep. The month of June, *Brachmanoth*, was upon them and the fallow land must be broken. The hemp, linen, and flax necessary to make cloth still needed to be sown, and soon enough it would be time to plant the autumn crops, wheat and rye.

Like his father, Rurik worried over how it was all to be accomplished. Much to the consternation of the Frankish nobility, Normans, regardless of rank, willingly set aside sword for plow to work the fields. They sprang from the land. Their love of the soil ran as richly in their veins as did their lust for warring. But what concerned him most was that Charles could task Rollo, and thus himself, for arms at any time. Valsemé's villeins were a pitiable number to rely upon.

Brienne involved herself more in the domestic provisioning of the keep. She overstepped Bolsgar's duties, she knew, for it was a steward's charge to see that the smoking and salting of meats and preparation of dairy items all met prescribed standards of cleanliness.

Both she and Bolsgar were surprised to discover that the manor lacked a cheesemaker. Katla had previously supervised its production. The Norse were fond of a variety of cheeses and particular in its making. None had seen Katla since the night Rurik swore his oath and bid for Brienne's hand in marriage.

At the end of the third week, Rurik sat at table well pleased with his progress. Additional fields had been cultivated, the manor house was under construction once more, and early each day, he trained his men with Varangian discipline in the exercise yard.

He lingered over dinner this night, tired but content, Brienne at his side. Lyting, Ketil, and he were discussing the breeding of horses for size when Brienne drew his eye. She sat quietly, absently pushing chunks of meat around in her stew with the edge of her spoon while she studied one of his soldiers in the hall. The man smeared butter on a thin board of dry fish, then consumed it with gust. Rurik laughed silently as Brienne wrinkled her nose and downed a mouthful of wine, as though washing the imagined taste from her mouth.

He squeezed her hand beneath the table. " 'Tis not so vile as it looks, especially when chased with good, stout beer." His eyes crinkled at her grimace. "*Nei?* Then perhaps with the mulberry wine our steward has promised. Think you it will need age long or can you bide the wait?"

"I can bide the wait till pigs swim and horses fly," she declared outrageously, then bubbled with laughter as his brows shot up.

Recovering his wit, his mouth spread into a devilishly irresistible grin. "Mayhaps you will acquire a taste for it once you're increasing. 'Tis said a woman with child craves the strangest of foods."

"If 'tis so, mayhaps I should keep you from my bed," Brienne teased, cuffing his arm. But Rurik entrapped the offending hand.

"Would you suffer naught for me, my vixen?" He feigned to be wounded. "Could you cast me aside with such ease?"

"Nay, love," she answered softly now. " 'Tis one wait I cannot abide."

Rurik smiled and pressed her fingers to his lips. "Would that I could snatch you away for a month of honeyed nights, the *hýnætur*. 'Tis custom, when possible, that a groom secludes himself with his bride and together they indulge in blissful idleness."

Brienne tilted her head, the corners of her mouth turning upward. "And in what way is it 'honeyed'?"

A gleam of pure mischief entered his eyes. "Because each day the happy couple shares a cup of mead." As she made a disagreeable face, he quickly amended, "But for you, I shall bring a cask of the finest Frankish wine."

"A cask? Really, Rurik." She laughed and admonished all at once. "Shall I remember naught of this *hýnætur*?" Her lightheartedness suddenly faded a degree. "I would love to hide away. Our private time has been sore lean, and if you would know, I have ever found this keep a cold and cheerless place, even as a child."

"The manor house will soon be finished. The men began laying the floors this day." He brushed his thumb along the curve of her jaw.

Brienne's eyes darkened at his touch, her senses kindling. "There be one place to secret ourselves in this tower," she voiced a bit breathlessly. "Will you come when I send and see that none mark your progress?"

Rurik felt the blood surge through his veins as he read her desire, his curiosity high.

Shortly after Brienne took her leave, he charged his brother and Ketil to address any need that might arise and guard that no one disrupt him in the hours to come. He then quit the hall at Aleth's bidding and followed her to the top of the keep.

It was a slow, tiring climb for the girl, Rurik noted, but she did so without complaint. When they reached the uppermost step, she ushered him into a low-ceilinged chamber where a pallet lay spread and candles glowed softly. He stood for a moment, uncomprehending.

Color blossomed in Aleth's cheeks and she gestured to the ladder. "Your lady waits above, my lord. I will keep watch here."

Rurik thanked her with a swift smile and mounted the rungs, thoroughly intrigued. As he emerged from the small opening, his breath caught in his throat. Brienne awaited him, a vision in white, her dark hair loosened and stirring about her, the long tendrils caught on the wind.

Brienne stepped past the thick mattress, claimed from one of the garret rooms, and crossed to Rurik. Displaying more nerve than she in truth possessed, she allowed the robe to slip from her shoulders and sit poised provocatively over the tips of her breasts.

Rurik's mouth went dry when Brienne drew his hand to the heat of her bosom and the gown fell away.

Blinding passion roared through him. Rurik took no time to take her down to the mattress or rid himself of his clothes. One moment they were standing apart and the next flesh was searing flesh. Their mouths clung and devoured, ravished and plundered. Tongues parried and chased with impatient urgency. Their first coupling was fierce, primitive, as though long starved for one another. Together they exploded in a shattering climax. Only afterward did they fear their shouts might bring the whole garrison, believing the worst. None came. Rurik and Brienne made love again, slowly this time, tenderly exploring one another, savoring each new discovery.

Rurik found his wife's back to be deliciously and erotically sensitive. Brienne's hands wandered over her lover's golden skin, wishing to know his secrets yet timid. When he guided her apprehensive fingers to his ready shaft, she sucked in her breath. He waited as she cautiously touched him, then gently showed her how to stroke and caress. She pleasured him then as he did her. When they could bear it no more, she pressed him home.

As dawn crimsoned the skies, they stood together, Brienne leaning back against Rurik. He encircled her with his arms, slipping one hand within her robe to caress her breast. Enormously satisfied, they stood in silence and looked over the verdant landscape.

A short time later they returned to their chamber. Rurik bid her rest awhile, then disappeared. He returned in good cheer and, finding her asleep, swatted her backside.

"What a lazy wife I've wed!"

Brienne slowly opened one eye but came full awake as she spied her coffer being carried from the room. Rurik loomed above her, maddeningly pleased with himself.

"Get thee awake—we are off within the hour. Perhaps 'twill not be a true *hýnætur,* but we shall journey these lands we now rule and make ourselves known to our people." He stole a kiss from her lips. "Ah, my heart, I wouldst always have you look on me as you did last night. We both needs be away."

Elated, Brienne flung her arms about Rurik's neck and pulled him atop her.

The days to follow were among the happiest Brienne had known. Side by side, they wended their way throughout their domain, heading a modest escort of soldiers and wagons.

It fascinated her to watch Rurik administer the barony's affairs "from the hoof," as she termed it. By his direction, one third of the garrison traveled with them while another remained at the keep under Lyting's command. Ketil ranged between the two points with the remaining number, rotating the troops with each visitation. In addition, he updated Rurik on the manor's progress, apprised him of new arrivals, and carried missives back to Lyting.

The soldiers welcomed the diversity. Rurik ensured they were challenged whatever be their task, whether at manor or in the field. Those who imagined their service of escort to lord and lady would be an idle affair quickly learnt otherwise. Each morn Rurik tested the skill of ten men. None ever bested him, though it became each man's ardent wish to do so. Wagers were made, and a quantity of silver crisscrossed hands. But as the weeks passed and the baron remained undefeated, it turned into a matter of pride. None truly wished to see his liege routed, try though he might. The soldiers' boasts swelled as did their respect for Atli's son. The man was impressive with sword, magnificent with spears.

To Brienne's delight, Brother Bernard and Bolsgar also accompanied the retinue. Aside from Rurik, there were few with whom she could converse, and the two ever afforded her diversion with their varied and dubious tales.

Entertainments aside, Brienne realized that they traveled apurpose. The monk brought the sacraments to the outlying districts, and the steward, quill and parchment to make his accountings.

But Bolsgar served his lord in another, equally important role—that of assessor. After patiently detailing the Frankish provisions for justice, he was rewarded when Rurik agreed to reestablish the local court of law, or *mallus*. The new baron vowed to convene the assembly each month and whenever visiting the distant vills as now. While it was the lord's role to preside over the hearing, it was the assessor's function to "find the law" and make advisements.

This Bolsgar did, bearing the weight of his office with great solemnity. But where he expected Rurik to adhere to the Norse codes and anticipated resistance or a clash of values, none arose. Norman though this lord might be, Bolsgar recognized in Rurik a man of equity and insight. As they traveled from village to village, Bolsgar's admiration increased a hundredfold. He ruminated over that admission, for it cost him. Yet he knew of not one Frank better suited to take up the standard of Richard Beaumanoir and serve Valsemé's needs.

For Brienne, the days blended leisurely one into another as they journeyed beneath azure skies through the gently rolling hillside. Life settled into a rhythm of sorts. In the cool of early morn, Rurik practiced his men and, after dipping in the river, returned to their gabled tent. Brienne awaited with a light fare to break their fast, but it went forgotten more often than not.

The camp was dismantled quickly, owing to the Norse love of collapsible implements and furnishings. On the days they approached no vill, the retinue selected a new site early and indulged in a hunt.

By Rurik's orders, the baronial tent was erected at a distance, near a private sector of the river whenever possible. Here, he and Brienne lingered throughout velvet nights, two lovers exploring the beauty and mystery of one another. They cherished with lips, tasted with tongues, memorized textures and contours with covetous fingers, and relished each intimacy, each new joining.

Had Brienne known how close Rurik set his guard, she would have been thoroughly abashed. He did not tell her. Instead, he saved her embarrassment by covering her rapturous cries with his mouth. It eased her little, however, when his own shouts near brought down the tent.

On those days they prepared to enter a village, the baron and baronne dressed with care. Rurik invariably favored his wedding gift and Brienne selected from one of several fine gowns. Together they presented an imposing image as they headed the retinue, her dark beauty contrasting with his gilded looks, the shimmering white palfrey striding beside the glossy black stallion.

As became their custom, Rurik and Brienne dismounted in the village center, usually a clearing of some size boasting a well. While the animals were watered and their portable chairs assembled, they accepted offerings of ale and cider from the villeins. Then, assuming their seats, Bolsgar took up his stance, made several pronouncements, and convened the *mallus*. He urged those bearing grievance to set them before their lord baron and his baronne.

Many hours were thus spent in the warmth of the midday sun, attending all manner of complaint. Most arose from misunderstandings and obstacles of language, but they were easily resolved.

The vills were peopled in part by Frankish villeins, predominantly women, children, and elderly serfs. Rarely did freemen number amongst them.

Increasingly, Northmen swelled the sparse populations of the villages. Ships arrived regularly to Normandy bringing farmers, smiths, and adventurers. This dealt Rurik a double-edged challenge. While he needed and welcomed their skills, many resisted the Frankish order of nobility and land tenure, insisting they be freeholders.

Others balked at the strictures of the treaty of St.-Clair-sur-Epte that the duke upheld. Most accepted the new religion, if only superficially, but some opposed blooding their swords on their kinsmen to safeguard a weak throne. Those who would not comply typically found their way to their kinsmen on the Loire.

Once the assembly ended, Rurik met with the village officials previously appointed by his father. Brienne asked of ailments, and Bolsgar made his tallies. Brother Bernard conferred penance, baptism, and on one occasion marriage to a couple whose babe was near due. Their visit concluded with a mass of thanksgiving and the escort departed.

As the weeks stretched into the fullness of summer, the retinue made its return. Brienne thought on those times as idyllic, magical. She folded the memories into her heart. It was not until the escort was within an easy day's ride of the keep that the long shadow of doubt cast itself across her happiness.

Their circuitous route brought them to the small holding of Luc. The last *mallus* no sooner convened than a leathery little man with raisin eyes, a Frank, stalked forward and jabbed his thumb toward two much larger Normans hulking on the fringes of the crowd.

His first spewings were unintelligible. When Bolsgar calmed the man with an upraised palm and bid him begin anew, it became evident that the villein's annoyance stemmed from more than a simple misunderstanding of tongues.

" 'Tis a scourge, an affront to God!" he blustered, undaunted before his lord. "Befouled the land, they did, with their heathenous rites." He leveled an accusing finger at the two who exchanged amused glances.

"They forced me to till the soil toward the sun—three furrows—then crumbled in good oat cakes and tossed ale over beast and plow, invoking . . . nay, I shall not repeat that name." He pinched his lips tight, nostrils flaring.

"Frey." The taller Norman ambled forth, barely suppressing a chuckle. "Guntram, here, worries for naught. Our fields are twice blessed."

Laughter sprinkled the edges of the gathering where the Northmen clustered.

The Frank spun around. "Cursed! 'Tis cursed! The Almighty will set His face against us." He turned anxiously to Rurik, but expecting little sympathy from a Norse baron, he dropped to his knee before Brienne.

"My lady, the animals stand besmeared with dirt and the plows wreathed with flowers. Allow me to right this, for God will surely smite us."

Brienne beseeched Rurik with her eyes as Brother Bernard stepped forward and bent to his ear. Rurik masked his expression, but a muscle leaped in the hard set of his jaw.

She felt his irritation and thought it peculiar. Did he object that the old man had made his entreaty to her, or was it something the churchman whispered? Surely he did not approve the rite. But then she remembered the many times she sat with her husband and the good brother during instruction, remembered how Rurik argued the monk round and round on every point and tenet of the faith, how he questioned each teaching and how rarely they made progress. She found herself as frustrated as Brother Bernard at those times. Rurik's reluctance seemed as thick and impenetrable as the stone walls of Valsemé's keep.

Rurik *was* annoyed. Annoyed to be confronted with a matter of religion so soon, while he himself was unsure where to place faith. Provoked that by his oath he must champion a god with whom he had yet to come to terms.

He well understood his kinsmen's uncertainties and their desire to ensure the harvest. Just how many clung to the old gods and how many embraced the new he couldst not say. Perchance few resisted as he, but when he took up a cause 'twas with his whole being. For the present, as baron, he deemed it more urgent that his men adhere to the new structures of authority. The rest would follow with time.

But how greatly should a man's cloth be altered in one fitting when the changes cut into fabric woven from youth?

Fabric whose warp and weft twined a man's soul, whose dye ran deep.

The crowd began to shift restlessly when at last Rurik nodded to the cleric. "Take your waters and sprinkle the fields if that be your wish." He turned to the hunched Frank. "There be no reason the animals must stand unwashed. See it done and give over the garlands to their makers. They might do with them as they will."

Brienne recognized his words to be but an appeasement. It disturbed her that he did not denounce the pagan act outright. For a moment she wondered if he truly intended to accept the one true God, or if, like his father, Rurik's faith would skim shallow depths.

Brienne still tumbled those troublesome thoughts about when a young woman broke through the assemblage, clutching a bundle to her bosom. Hurriedly, she threw herself down at Brienne's feet and none too soon, for she was dogged by a strapping man who grabbed a fistful of veil and hair and dragged her upward. But the woman caught at Brienne's gown, found an ankle beneath the folds, and gripped tight, nearly unseating the baronne from her chair.

Rurik, six soldiers, and Bolsgar bolted to give aid. They quickly overpowered the man, fettering him with a tangle of arms, and brought him to his knees. Brienne felt herself lifted and secured against her husband's powerful chest, while the sobbing woman was drawn from her hem.

Swift words passed between Rurik and the man who named himself as Herjolf. Impatient for a translation, Brienne steadied her footing and eased from Rurik's grasp. Dipping down, she raised the woman to her feet only to find her to be no woman at all but a girl, perhaps of fourteen.

Tears streaked paths over the girl's smudged cheeks. "Have mercy, my lady," she cried miserably, clutching the bundle high against her throat. "Do not let him kill my baby!"

"Certainly not!" Brienne exclaimed roundly, and skewered the man, Herjolf, with amethyst spears.

As if to emphasize the surety of her words, she encompassed the girl with one arm and laid a hand protectively over the small lump of cloth. The bulge shifted and snuffled beneath her touch. Had the circumstance been otherwise, she would have smiled.

Brother Bernard wisely chose the moment to intervene. "In the Northern world, 'tis the father's right to accept or reject his newborn," he explained carefully for Brienne's benefit, noting that Rurik once again cloaked any show of feeling. "After a birthing, the child is laid before its sire. If hale and whole the father will take the babe upon his knee. But if weak or deformed, he will spurn it. Such an innocent would be exposed . . . or drowned," he added, emphasizing the callousness of the practice, and was rewarded by shocked gasps among the villeins and a buzzing of voices.

Bile climbed Brienne's throat and she squeezed her eyes shut. When she opened them, her gaze locked with Rurik's. Silently she pleaded for a denial, pleaded that at least he would safeguard this tiny being. But his thoughts were closed to her. Icy slivers of dread shunted through her.

"Take courage, my lady. There be minds and hearts to win to God and a life to be spared this day," Brother Bernard murmured, then he turned to the girl. "Might I hold the child?"

She gripped the wriggling bundle to her breast. The monk stepped closer, an understanding smile warming his face as his plump hands closed over the infant. "You do wish the babe baptized, of course." It was more a statement than question.

The girl twisted her hands and bit into a knuckle as the monk laid open the cloth. " 'Tis a girl child," she said quickly, fresh tears welling as the precious face appeared.

The infant blinked at the light, then crossed her eyes at the stranger hovering above her. The rosebud mouth instantly puckered then opened wide to let loose a lusty squall. She pumped her tiny feet and thrashed the air with small rigid arms—one whole, one withered.

"My lady, mayhaps you wish to examine the child and see that she is sound. She appears to be scarce—what—a couple of days old?" He chatted easily, as though nothing were amiss, and deposited the infant in Brienne's arms. Again he spoke in undertones. "When done, see you present her to Lord Rurik."

Brienne stole a glance at her husband and was encouraged that his expression had softened. She cooed soothingly to the child as she inspected its soft little nose and mouth, its miniature ears and bright blue eyes. Drawing away the swaddle, she flexed the small limbs, checked the drying navel cord, and, turning the babe over her arm, assured its spine was straight. This done, she instructed the girl to unfasten her mantle, fold it, and set it on the ground before the baron. After settling the child onto the cushion of cloth, Brienne rose before Rurik and clasped her hands to hide their faint tremble.

"My lord husband, the babe suffers no ailment that I can detect. She is as fit and healthy as any." A pain weighted her heart, but she continued. "The arm will be no more trouble to her than . . . than Aleth's leg is to her."

Just then, Herjolf crossed his arms staunchly over his chest, averting his face from the child, and uttered something tersely in Norse. When Rurik did not immediately respond, the misery of doubt engulfed Brienne. For a long, painful moment she could not bear to look at him. Then a tortuous thought struck at her core: someday, her own children could be at such risk.

Rurik felt his heat rise and his gut clench when Brienne cast her eyes from him. He had never agreed with the practice of exposure. The realization that she believed him capable of such an act lanced through him and left him raw. Not all were hardhearted like Herjolf.

When Bolsgar started to speak, Rurik stayed him with a sharp hand. He had no need to "find the law"—Frankish, Norse, or otherwise. Some values were basic to life. His code was written upon his heart.

Rurik shifted his gaze over his men. They watched him, as did the villeins, each looking to him to uphold their own notion of equity, each ready to judge him if he did not. It was sobering to wield such power, to so totally affect a man's rule, his faith . . . his family.

Looking upon the infant, he watched her tiny arms club the air and smiled inwardly. Truly he was the "Children's Man." If his soldiers deemed it a weakness, well, he cared not a lick as long as they served him well.

"Many a man born whole has forfeited a limb to battle and still lived a useful life." Rurik passed a critical eye over the Norsemen that lined the crowd, then marked with great satisfaction that Herjolf himself lacked a portion of one finger. "A *demeine* has many needs, requires many talents. I have need of each and every soul who wouldst help Valsemé prosper."

Rurik lifted the naked baby to his knee, accepting her as her own father would not. He nudged her little hand, the one twisted, not whole, till she curled the frail fingers about his own.

"This child will have a place in my hall. Bring her to my wife at such time as she is weaned. Until then, see she is well cared for. I will send my man to attest it is so."

He paused for a moment, absorbed Herjolf's ruddy shade and downcast eyes, then looked to the mother.

"Has she a name?"

"Catherine, my lord." The girl wiped her wet cheek. "I call her 'Rina.' "

"Rina." He teased the babe's chin with the tip of his trapped finger. Rina opened her mouth, birdlike, and eagerly sought nourishment. Chuckling, Rurik handed her back to her mother.

"If there be aught you need, or complaint you suffer"—he cast a warning look at the father—"send to me."

Not for the first time, Brienne was ashamed of her quick assumptions, her lack of trust. Above any she had ever known, Rurik was a fair and just man.

Many hours lumbered by before they gained privacy in their tent. When they had undressed and laid down, she clung to him, hot tears of regret spilling from her eyes over his bare chest.

"Forgive me, my love. That I should have believed you able to . . . that you might allow . . . Oh, 'twas wrong and undeserved and—"

Rurik covered her mouth as he felt a sting in the back of his throat. He held her tight, blocking out the day's disagreeable memories. Rolling her beneath him, he continued to hush her with strong kisses and gave himself to teaching her more of the ways of love.

Brienne opened herself to him, denied him nothing, followed his lead. With her lips and body she adored him. It was a healing, a renewal. And as they joined and scaled the sensual heights, she was determined never to doubt Rurik again.

Elsie loved feasts. She had decided that on her lord's wedding day. She also decided that he set the finest table in the land, quite possibly finer than the king's. There had been food aplenty that day, more than she had seen in the full sum of her years, being six. Celebrations were a rarity in Ivry and none so grand.

Now Lord Rurik ordered another feast—her second such—and this promised to surpass even the first. Her lord and lady had been in high cheer since the manor house had been completed, and declared a holiday so all might be rewarded for their labors.

This, of course, meant that Waite's mother would prepare the warm crumbly cakes the lord preferred. And indeed she had. They sat cooling on the kitchen's long worktable, dozens of them, neatly aligned like little ducklings marching in a row. Well, ducklings were not nearly so neat, and better for her if these were not also. Then one—or two—would not soon be missed.

Elsie cast a covert glance to where Waite squatted outside the door, then eased up to the table and slipped a loaf into her skirtfolds. As she reached for a second, the first dropped out and broke on the floor. Patch scampered from Waite's hold, tail wagging as he scurried in and gulped the chunks down.

"Here now! What's this? Out with you!" Waite's mother hastened across the room and shook her skirts at the mongrel. "And the two of you—do you think to idle about while the rest of us toil? Here." She snatched up a small wooden bucket and thrust it toward the children. "We'll be needing berries for the sauces and tarts. See that you bring this back—*filled*, if you please—and don't be to it all day."

Elsie took the container and Waite trapped his furry charge. They left quickly, missing the motherly smile and wag of head that followed them.

Suddenly the little girl stopped short, causing Waite to stumble into her. "Look!" she cried.

Waite followed the length of her pointing finger and sighted Lord Rurik and Lady Brienne riding side by side, leading the hunt from the bailey.

"Soon I will move into the manor house," Elsie announced importantly.

"Says who?" Waite squinched his brows together, vaguely annoyed with her airs.

"I am to care for the lord's babies when they come. And since they will sleep in his outer chamber, then so must I."

"Humph." Waite thought of his lady's fine, slender shape and his mother's, round as a melon with his new baby brother. It *had* to be a brother, he thought, eyeing Elsie. "And what makes you think they'll beget their babies so soon?"

Elsie sniffed. "Mama says that any man who looks at a woman as our lord looks at his lady will keep her full of wee ones. Mama says."

"Humph."

Brienne caught sight of the two waifs and bedraggled pup and sent them a wave and sunny smile. Over the bridge she clattered after Rurik and urged Candra forward, abreast of Sleipnir.

She had warned Rurik that she was no huntswoman, but he had insisted she ride out nonetheless, wishing to keep her near. If Normans shared one trait in common with the Franks, 'twas their passion for hunting. And her Norman was no exception.

But 'twas a glorious day, even for one who did not appreciate the sport in and of itself. Glorious because all was right with her world. Because Valsemé flourished. And because her days were replete with love.

At times a vagrant fear fluttered about her heart. It whispered that such happiness was fleeting, that it could not long endure, that it would soon be spoilt or stolen away. But she believed in Rurik's love, and whenever he looked at her, her fears dispersed like so much chaff before the wind.

In recent weeks villeins had begun to arrive at the keep, having heard of Rurik's justice and that he dealt with men fairly. This was greeted with great joy on both sides, for harvest would shortly be upon them.

Norsemen, too, continued to find their way to her husband's service. Among his requirements, Rurik insisted his men gain the basics of Frankish, hoping to alleviate future difficulties and misunderstandings.

Brienne, in turn, took it upon herself to learn an assortment of phrases in Norse. This proved highly useful during the week past when the household goods were moved from the great tower to the manor house.

The manor house. Brienne was supremely happy. Not only was it complete, but it was furnished handsomely as well. Rurik provided new counterpanes, pillows, and bedclothes. Exotic tapestries, brocaded cushions, ivory carvings, and brass decorated their new bedchamber—and, of course, Rollo's great bed.

Brienne scanned the marbled, brilliant blue skies and breathed the ripe, heavy fragrance suffusing the meadows. Elegant blossoms—yellows, pinks, and creams—gossiped in the sun while bees darted crazily about, trying to catch snips of their tittle.

'Twas a day made for sport. Brienne skimmed the edge of the forest as they approached, this sector familiar to her from her youth. She smiled secretly. Made for sport *and* diversion. Mayhaps she would share the secret of the underwood.

Brienne waited precisely three boar and five deer. The traps had been emptied of rabbit, quail, and curlew. Pheasants and herons were taken as well.

As the party emerged from the cool depths of the wood into the warmth of the noonday sun, Brienne drew open the drape of her head scarf and fanned her throat.

"The boar was well won, my love, but you have yet to win the doe."

Rurik cocked his head, a half smile playing on his lips. "There be the two stags. Do they count for naught? Or has my wife discovered an overpowering lust for the hunt?"

"Lust for a surety," Brienne replied, laughing. "Come, my lord, the sport is not yet done."

Rurik had no moment to puzzle her words, for Brienne leaned into Candra and turned her across the open field. He galloped after her, amazed when she pulled the veil from her head and loosed her hair on the wind. He urged Sleipnir forward, closing the distance, then eased back on the reins so as not to overtake her entirely.

Brienne was a glorious sight, one with the horse. Her dark hair flowed in the breeze, lifting and falling with the rhythm of the hooves. She smiled back at him, exhilarated, eyes sparkling and cheeks flushed. Her mantle billowed wide, exposing the soft pitch of her breast, small waist, and trim derrière. Rurik felt his heart pulse, felt the power beneath him, and pressed the stallion to close alongside this vision of beauty.

But Brienne veered away, heading toward a wooded copse. She freed her cloak and sent it floating behind her as she disappeared into the trees.

Rurik slowed as he entered to follow the hidden path scored with fresh hoofprints. It was a dense grove, the trees rather dwarfed, crowded and spindly. The wood ended abruptly and Rurik found himself squinting against the crystalline shimmer of a small lake.

Movement and laughter drew his eyes right. Brienne had already dismounted and was in the process of discarding her tunic and leggings. Rurik swung down from his saddle and tossed the reins over a bush. Before he could accomplish another step, Brienne bounced to her feet and dropped her shift to the ground.

"Hurry!" she called, running naked into the water and diving into the clear shallows.

Rurik was momentarily transfixed by her shapely form, pearllike and leggy, gliding beneath the surface. Then his fingers came alive, hauling the vest from his frame and stripping away boots and pants. His clothes joined Brienne's in a pile and he plunged in after her, then angled into a shallow dive.

Brienne heard the splash behind her and stroked for the center of the lake. Standing shoulder high in the refreshing water, she turned. Rurik was nowhere to be seen. She glanced along the shoreline then over the light fretting on the water. She frowned, perplexed.

Just as she formed his name, two hands clasped her waist and lips closed over her breast. Rurik's bright head broke through the surface, as he hoisted her upward into the air, his mouth still possessing the lush mound and taut nipple. In a single, swift motion he brought her down again, sheathing his aching desire in her heated depths.

Brienne exulted with throaty, triumphant approval. She twined her legs around his waist and buried her hands in his hair, tingling with excitement. She felt all-powerful and totally vulnerable. This was Rurik, gloriously male, his passions unleashed, his hunger unrestrained.

He molded her hips to his, kneading the soft curve of her buttocks with fevered haste as he began to forge against her. With lip and tongue, he scorched a path over her cool, glistening skin, gathered droplets from her throat, shoulder, and bosom, and drank from the valley between. He then feasted on the breast that had gone unattended, savoring its beaded peak as fresh fires erupted through him.

Brienne felt Rurik shudder beneath her hands, felt the muscles bunch in his shoulders as he braced his stance and gripped her tightly. He surged against her with stunning force. For a moment, it seemed he would drive up to the very core of her soul.

On and on he quaked, exploding within her, groaning with a pleasure akin to pain, till at last he had emptied himself.

Heart pounding, certain he had raised the temperature of the entire lake, Rurik sank back into the water. He grinned wickedly, drawing Brienne half atop himself, and drifted.

"You should know better than to tease a man armed, *ástin mín*."

He gave her no chance to reply, rolling to caress her mouth pleasurably with his own, his hands wandering to intimate ground. And of complaints she had none. Not then—nor later—nor later still.

Rurik and Brienne visited the lake again the next evening and the two after that. A week later, when they plotted to steal away once more, they were forestalled by sullen skies.

By midafternoon, an unnatural darkness shrouded the land as surly clouds invaded from the west. Winds kicked high, bringing the fresh, heavy scent of damp earth, and thunder belched its approach. Hastily, animals were herded to shelters or penned, tools and implements stored, dwellings secured, and children accounted for.

The first huge drops of rain presaged a roaring downpour. Roads turned to mire while lashing winds whipped at trees and clawed the thatching from cottages.

The storm railed long into the evening, losing little of its choler. Jarring bolts of lightning and thunderous peals split the skies and rain sheeted against the manor house.

But within the great hall its menace went largely unnoticed, if not ignored. Fires crackled in each of three hearths, warding off the day's uncommon chill. Torches blazed brightly along the walls and the harper played above the dull rumblings.

Brienne smiled from the dais, pleased to be in her father's spacious hall. This night recalled others from childhood. Her gaze drifted to the heavy timbers arching overhead, and she watched as a small, high-set window flashed with momentary brightness. Then she drew her eyes downward to peruse the Byzantine carpets and decorative shields cheering the walls. Richard's hall but Rurik's, too. It bore his seal in many ways, she mused, her smile deepening, such as the small bathing chamber he added off their bedchamber.

"Does aught gladden you?" Rurik leaned to her ear.

"There is much here that gladdens me." She squeezed his hand beneath the table.

Looking out again into the busy hall, Brienne nodded toward Aleth and Ketil. The last remnants of supper were being cleared away and the tables dismantled. The two remained at their trestle, Ketil shooing away the servant who sought to take it down, and Aleth adeptly setting out a gaming board with little bone pegs.

"Think you I should worry over yon maiden?" Violet eyes teased steel blue.

Rurik rubbed his jaw and grinned. "Didst they share a trencher again this night? Mayhaps I should set them a guardian, but more for Ketil's behalf. 'Twould appear your lady tames that bullish creature, and I can ill afford to lose his warrior prowess to more gentle refinements. He'd be of little use unmanned."

"Methinks Aleth would agree."

Laughter broke out somewhere in the hall, eclipsing Rurik's response. But his lips brushed the curve of her neck and his hand moved along her thigh, telling her he was of a mind to retire.

As he drained his goblet and prepared to rise, the sturdy planked door of the manor house burst open. His man, Eirik, entered grim-faced and dripping into the far end of the hall to announce an arrival. Behind him, a figure was poised at the portal, concealed within a heavy hooded cloak.

A sudden streak of lightning illuminated the night skies without, outlining the specter against the howling torrent. The form moved slowly into the room and crossed the rush-strewn floor. With no hint of identity, it came to stand before the dais but remained at a distance. Hands gloved to the elbows appeared from beneath the cloak and pushed back the rain-soaked hood. Bright red hair tumbled out, molten in the glow of torchlight.

Rurik brought the goblet from his lips and set it firmly on the table. Brienne's heart slammed against her ribs. A single word escaped her: "Katla."

Katla smiled malevolently, glorying in the attention she now commanded. She allowed her gaze to stray over the faces for a measured moment.

"Am I to receive no welcome?" She tugged at her gloved fingers and removed their covering. Her eyes swept to Rurik and gave him an extended, appreciative look. "Do you not bid me welcome, my lord? Or am I so soon forgotten?"

"*Gott kvöld*, Katla," he said tonelessly.

"You seem surprised to see me." She tapped the gloves to her chin. "But, *já*, I didst leave rather hurriedly and without word. Dare I hope my absence distressed you?" She shrugged when he did not reply, her green eyes taking in Brienne. "But of course not. You have been occupied with your new *duties* to the barony." The implication hung clear. This wife was but a duty, a millstone Rurik must bear.

Rurik's jaw hardened. "How is it you travel about on such a night, Katla?"

She stepped closer to the dais, her eyes glinting with needlepoints of firelight.

"'Twas imperative that I return to Valsemé, and to you, my lord baron. It seems whilst I was apart—soothing my wounded pride—I found myself in possession of something that is yours. Being of good conscience, I have returned."

"I know naught of mine that is missing."

"Missing? *Nei*, Rurik, I pilfered no chests. But there be this—" She unclasped the jeweled brooch at her throat.

As the cloak fell away, Brienne gasped audibly. The hall was stunned to silence, not a breath heard drawn.

Slowly, Rurik rose to his feet. His hard, silvered gaze lowered to the swell of her abdomen.

Laughter floated from Katla's throat and rose to mingle with the sound of the storm raging without.

Chapter Fourteen

❖ ❖ ❖ ❖ ❖ ❖ ❖ ❖ ❖ ❖ ❖

"YOU ARE A fool to let her stay and more the fool to believe the child can be yours. God's teeth! Katla lifts her skirts to near every pair of breeches she encounters."

"You overstep yourself, *broðir*," Rurik grated, moving from the shadows of the small chamber set off the main hall and into the flicker of torchlight.

"Do I? How think you she gained passage from Danmark? Her coffers were filled long before your arrival, no doubt each piece well earned."

Rurik advanced on Lyting, but the younger man stepped back and flung a hand to the air.

"Forsooth, the babe could easily be any man's, even our father's or brother's. I cannot believe you gave place to that *hóra*."

"What are you saying?" Rurik demanded, brought up short by his words.

"Only that Katla spreads herself for more than what a man's trousers or purse can yield. 'Tis power she craves. Position."

Lyting fixed Rurik with a sharp, layered look. "When our father gained the barony, she followed him from Rouen and applied herself eagerly to his bed. Atli recognized her game but did not deny himself her pleasures. He shared her equally with Hastein before passing her to the others."

"Including you?" Rurik snapped, his ire peaked.

Lyting gave a harsh laugh. "I wasn't interested and for once Katla didn't offer. She realized she would gain no place of permanence with Atli and set her sights on the son

he boasted of so often in the hall, the son who obviously
would inherit."

Lyting pushed a hand through his pale hair, feeling the
keen bite of Rurik's eyes. "I would have cautioned you, but
I thought her wiles plain enough. Women are in short supply
and Katla unquestionably fair. Why should you withhold
yourself from what most others enjoyed?"

Rurik braced his elbow against the wall and dragged a
hand over his face. "I didst not know the full of it, but I
suspected her snare." He smiled faintly. "I thought to put
her aside but had no pressing reason. None till first I met
Brienne."

"Then do so now. See Katla away. She'll not long be
satisfied to sit in your wife's shadow."

"Would that in good conscience I could, but if her reckon-
ing be correct, the babe is very likely mine. I cannot ignore
that. The circumstance of birth is no fault of the child. I
wouldst give it a place in my hall."

Lyting expelled a long, exasperated breath, planting his
hands low on his hips. Did Rurik honestly think Katla's bed
ever grew cold? That she was capable of fidelity even during
that first brief month after his arrival to Valsemé? When
Rurik departed to meet the bridal escort, Katla kept herself
well amused. There had been sufficient boasting amongst the
garrison.

" 'Tis a high-minded gesture, Rurik, and I fault you not
for that. But be wary of repeating our father's mistakes.
Think on it. Wouldst you see Katla set this child against
those Brienne will bear you, even as Morrígú set Hastein
against us?"

Rurik's eyes hardened. "Katla can be sent away once the
child is born."

"Do not underestimate Katla, broðir, whatever else you
do. I tell you, she is like an adder coiled up. Give her no
corner from whence to strike."

Rurik gazed upon Brienne's sleeping form, dimly outlined in
the depths of the great bed. One of the window's thick, inner
shutters stood ajar, admitting a faint stroke of light and crisp,
rain-scented air. The storm had subsided to a dull, steady

patter. On the table, a flame fluttered in a stub of candle before it hissed at a random breeze and went out.

Folding his clothes over a chair, Rurik slipped between the sheets and carefully drew Brienne into his arms. As he rested his head atop hers, he felt her stir and her hand drift to his chest. For the moment, he wished only to hold her and blot out the day's tumultuous close. He thought of making love to her, long and tender and sweet, of assuring her naught could obtrude upon their happiness and all that they shared. He would not allow it.

Brienne lifted her head from his shoulder, and he felt her eyes upon him in the dark. Neither spoke. Gently he stroked her arm, knowing she waited on his word, on what decision he had made. Brienne had tactfully withdrawn from the hall soon after Katla's arrival. Well it was, too, for the woman proved in high fettle, as fitful and erratic as the storm without.

Painful though the subject might be to his wife, Rurik was determined that Katla not become a wedge betwixt them. He decided on directness and honesty, hoping she would not wall up her heart.

"Katla occupies one of the upper chambers." He waited to feel her stiffen. She did not. "There is every possibility the babe is mine." Her hand seemed weightless where it rested, but again, no response. "Lyting would have it that there is greater probability 'tis another's. Until I can be more certain—and mayhaps I might never be—I purpose to keep the child under my hand, leastways till it attains the age of fosterage."

Brienne digested his words and took a careful breath.

"And Katla?"

"What of Katla?"

"Wilt you also keep her here?"

Rurik knew she spoke of the time after the child's birthing. He shifted her solidly against him.

"*Ástin mín,* you are my heart. I think only of the child. 'Twas conceived ere we met. Could you look on me with respect if I turned out the woman who carries my babe, or provided naught for its well-being? I know not what your Frankish customs decree. I know only what is right, here."

He pressed her hand to the place over his heart.

Brienne knew she must trust Rurik, though it disturbed her that he did not answer directly. She laid her head against his chest and listened to the drumming within.

Silent, they held each other in the dark cavern of their chamber. At last Rurik's breathing became even, and Brienne floated into a restive sleep.

The skies brightened about her and she found herself once more upon the road to Valsemé. Brother Bernard rode his shabby little palfrey alongside.

"What are the Norsemen like?" she heard herself ask. "I would know how they treat their women."

"Do not worry overlong on it," the monk comforted. "In general, they are good to their families, though I would warn you of one thing: the *More Danico*."

Ketil's hand disappeared into his blazing thicket of hair as he scratched beneath his chin. "This be the one, my lady. Your ring should bear the key."

Brienne and Aleth, more than a little winded, joined Ketil before the small storage shed. Despite his efforts to slow his pace, the man possessed a fearsome stride.

" 'Twould be wound with a bit of red thread," he advised, watching Brienne sort through the bulky collection that hung at her waist. "On Rurik's coming, I aided him with his ship's cargo. The household goods from Limfjord are in this building. He marked the keys that secure his mother's belongings with the wool."

"Be you sure he will not object?" Brienne felt ill at ease disturbing Ranneveig's possessions in Rurik's absence. For the second time in a fortnight, he was to Rouen. 'Twas Lyting who told her of their mother's loom, this after a lengthy discussion of sails and the task of weaving one.

How desperately she needed to immerse herself in some project, one that could win her mind from Katla. A sail seemed the perfect choice and one that would surely please. Still, she felt troubled at violating the outbuilding. What if Rurik preserved it as a sanctum to his mother?

"My lady," Ketil began, smiling down in a most warm and patient manner, as though instructing a small child, "whatever keys a husband sees fit to place upon his wife's ring, it follows that he gives her sanction to use what lies beneath their locks."

Brienne regarded the cumbrous assortment beneath her fingertips, nodded with a smile, and plucked out a large spade-shaped key tagged with red.

Sunlight plundered the depths of the room, slashing a brilliant swath through the darkness and raking the far wall. Predictably, the interior proved oppressive and hot. Its stale, earthy odors weighted the air and twitched the nose.

Brienne surveyed the room's contents, which were neatly stored and claimed but half the space. Iron-bound chests sat to one side, and riveted cauldrons occupied two corners. Their collapsible stands with clawed feet lay banked against one wall, and with them, long-shafted iron oil lamps.

She moved to ponder several yew-wood containers, round with matching lids that locked through their tops, then delighted in a small boxy chair, obviously a child's, its woven rush seat lacking its cushion.

Ketil sifted a collection of boards, some plain, others richly carved. He drew out two matching planks, each with sizable holes bored down their length and a hooklike brace affixed to the rounded end.

"These be the uprights, my lady." Ketil glanced about the room, leaned them temporarily against the doorframe, and cleared away the cluster of wood containers and the little chair.

"Our Norse looms are simple affairs," he explained, bracing the uprights against the wall to show her. "Easy to assemble and dismantle. Very portable."

He stabilized the boards with a third plank fastened between them across the bottom, then positioned a slender, loglike beam horizontally over the top braces.

"We shall need the pegs for the heddle rods and the weights as well. The chests should hold them."

Brienne picked through the keys till she found six nested side by side, wrapped with the telling thread.

The day could not have been more delightful, she decided as she opened one chest after another. 'Twas the best of diversions, and diversions were precisely what she required whilst Rurik was away and Katla ever near, vexing in so countless and guileful ways.

But this distraction was better than most. She smiled as she lifted a long-handled frying iron with a revolving disk and set it spinning.

Aleth exclaimed over the treasures she found in the chest she searched: carved whistles, bone skates, and the prize of all prizes, a small cushion woven with diminutive green figures and horses. It perfectly fit the chair.

Brienne tried to imagine Rurik perched on it as a child, then envisioned Lyting. Amusingly, the illusions squirmed and fidgeted just as boys were wont to do, unused to stillness and impatient to be gone. Brienne wondered if Ranneveig had similar difficulty with the two, if that was why the pillow was unworn and in such good repair.

Ketil located the forked sticks he sought, inserted them in opposing holes in the uprights, then stretched across a slim rod, lodging each end firmly in a prong.

"The loom needs be braced," he explained, readjusting the contrivance against the wall and testing its sturdiness. "The heddle rod can be raised or lowered to any position, wherever there be the holes. I still need cap the beam with a turning stick so you might roll your cloth as it lengthens. The warp weights still need be found as well."

"You know much of looms," Brienne teased, then wondered if she had embarrassed him. He was, after all, a rugged and seasoned warrior.

"That I do, and you can lay it to my grandmother." His bewhiskered mouth split into a wide grin. "Many a bitter night did I sit at her knee as she wove her linens and woolens. I had a great fondness for her sword paddle, and she would allow me to beat up the weft. You can be sure I gave her a tight weave!"

He surprised the women with a sparkling wink, then squatted beside an open chest and rummaged through its contents. Brienne slanted a mirthful glance to Aleth and shook her head to think of Ketil as a barefaced lad.

One chest drew Brienne's attention more than any other. Footed, it was heavily reinforced with iron bands and ornamented with a profusion of tinned nailheads.

" 'Tis Rurik's sea chest, my lady," Ketil tossed over his shoulder, noting her interest. "Aboard ship 'tis used as a rowing bench while it carries the farer's goods."

"Think you it could hold the weights?"

Ketil shrugged, but Brienne thought amusement lurked beneath all the fiery hair.

" 'Twould do no harm to see, my lady." He turned back to his chore.

Brienne smoothed her fingers over the chest's coarse grain, roughened by years of exposure to rain, wind, and sea. She imagined Rurik sitting on its hard top, putting his strength to the oars, his powerful arms rhythmically swelling then slackening as he plowed the whale's acre.

She slipped the key into its lock, twisted, then, almost reverently, lifted the chest's lid.

Atop lay a red woolen blanket. Brienne blinked. Its dark shade possessed the same bluish quality as did the threads upon her keys. Had Ranneveig woven the covering for her son? Had he sheltered himself in its folds on many a storm-tossed night, benumbed with cold?

Brienne drew out the cloth and rubbed its prickly texture against her cheek. A man must love the sea to endure its hardships, she thought as she breathed the scent of oak and brine entrapped within its weave.

Rising to her feet, Brienne dragged the remainder of the blanket from its resting place, but in so doing, sent something tumbling from its folds back into the chest.

She followed the object with her eyes, then her gut clenched. She fell back a pace and grasped the fabric to her breast.

Memories of Katla and her graven cup assailed Brienne as she looked down on dozens upon dozens of wood flats, all bearing like markings to the vile goblet of *nabid*.

Ketil rose to his height, mystified by her behavior. "Does aught afright you, Lady Brienne?"

He peered into the chest, scanned the numerous rune slats that filled it, and wondered if some small, furred creature had managed to make a home in its depths. He rifled the pieces, but chancing on none, his puzzlement grew. Aleth had moved to Brienne's side and she, too, seemed disquieted.

"What be they? Charms? Curses?" Brienne's voice broke in a hoarse whisper.

"Curses?" Ketil echoed, baffled.

She took a hard swallow. "Be they Rurik's? Didst he carve them?"

"Carve them he did, as any merchant would carve the markers for his goods. But charms? *Nei*, my lady. 'Tis but a cipher—runes. Their purpose is no different than . . . than your Roman script."

Brienne edged toward the chest. "Markers? To what purpose?"

"They bear many uses, my lady. They might give an owner's name, record a transaction, label a bundle sold. . . ." He was unsure of what reply she sought.

Gingerly, Brienne lifted one of the slats and touched a finger to a twiglike character.

"Runes." The word came more as a statement than question. "A script, not a charm?"

"That one carries your husband's name. Each rune is a sound, though a clever man can combine several sounds into one form."

Brienne traced the angular inscription, each line being a straight or sloping stroke.

Ketil rumpled the underside of his beard. "Legend says that Odin handed down the runes to man, but a secret charm? *Nei*. If one employed them to that purpose, certainly a Norseman would believe they carried great power. But would not the same words, written in your Roman letters, seem equally enchanted?"

Brienne considered this as Ketil's shoulders lifted and fell in a careless shrug.

"We Norsemen have a fondness for inscribing anything we might put our knives or chisels to. Have you not noticed our swords and drinking horns, even our needle and comb cases?" Brienne thought of the silver casket that held her bride gift.

"I myself favor incising metal and stone. 'Tis a more practiced art than the graving of wood." He squinted to a far corner, weighed a thought, then drew his gaze back to Brienne.

"You best be aware, Rurik is partial to putting runes to the finery he acquires. In truth, 'tis I who does the inscribing. Rurik prefers working with wood and thinks I have the lighter hand." He threw out an amused laugh at that, then cleared his throat. "Be not distressed should he gift you with jewelry bearing the marks. 'Twould be but your name or mayhaps"— his eyes shifted away—"an endearment."

Ketil had obviously revealed more than he wished and now dragged on his beard, looking for all the world that he had spoiled some surprise.

Brienne comforted him with a smile. "*Merci* for setting me aright. I am sure I shall be greatly surprised should Rurik gift me, whether it bears the runes or not. But I shall remember."

Brienne and Aleth set to opening the yew-wood containers that held Ranneveig's weaving tools—spindles and distaff, iron combs, shears of three sizes, skein winders, and more. Ketil located the loom weights—small soapstone wheels— and explained how they were to be used to hold the warp threads straight.

The day's venture more than pleased Brienne. Yet through the course of the hours, her thoughts strayed again and again to Rurik's sea chest, to the runes, and to Katla.

"*Drink the* nabid," Katla's image tormented. "*This keep will not hold the two of us, nor do I share Rurik!*" Her haunting laughter clogged Brienne's mind and constricted her heart.

While Rurik answered the duke's most recent summons, Ketil and Lyting cleared one of the less-used outbuildings and transferred the loom and weaving goods.

The maidservants took keen interest in the undertaking, cheerfully offering of their hands, time, and advisements for the creation of the baron's great falcon sail.

Quantities of hemp were steeped with woad leaves that yielded the deepest of blues. From daybreak to nightfall, the shed fairly hummed with activity as the *canevas* took shape beneath countless agile fingers.

But when Brienne arrived each day, shortly after the midmorning meal, the women waited to test her mood.

Increasingly, she grew pensive and grave and desired to work alone.

'Twas rumored amongst the maidservants that the Norse-woman's presence plagued the baronne as much as her husband's absence. Ofttimes did they witness the sharp-tongued Katla baiting their kind lady. Someone should apprise the baron but certainly not a servant.

When Rurik returned, he teased Brienne considerably over the secrets of her weaving shed, but Brienne extracted his promise to keep from the building and this he honored.

With two solid strips of the sail complete and a third under way, Brienne grew eager to draft the pattern for the falcon. If all progressed well, she could present it at Christmastide.

How greatly she wished to gift him! He had gladdened her immeasurably this sennight past by removing Katla from the manor house to a cottage in the village. Brienne agreed that Katla could continue to oversee several of the kitchen functions—supervising the making of *skyr*, cheese, and Norse-style beer. 'Twas Katla's idleness that Brienne feared more than her participation.

For the most part, Brienne managed to avoid the Norsewoman altogether. It relieved her enormously to no longer suffer Katla's antagonism in the hall. Brienne's happiness lasted all of ten days. Lasted till one luckless encounter when Katla intimated that Rurik ensconced her in the village so he might visit her there.

Brienne refused to believe Katla's viperish tongue, but her words continued to flicker through Brienne's every conscious thought nonetheless. It pained her all the more that the previous night Rurik fell asleep when she wished to make love. She hated the suspicions Katla spawned. Hated herself for wondering if he was already sated.

Brienne stared at the deep blue cloth, cumbered with heavy thoughts. The others she had sent away long ago. Now she sat, weaving sword in hand, motionless before the loom.

Why could she not purge Katla's venom from her mind? There had been more intimations—significant looks and insinuating smiles. Lies! All lies! She trusted Rurik but

Katla not at all. Still the poison seeped into the crevices of her soul.

A movement brought her eyes to the door where Elsie clutched a bouquet of cheerful wildflowers—sky-blue succory, bright yellow tansy, and purplish tufts of wild marjoram. Quietly, she padded across the floor and lay the blossoms on Brienne's lap.

"Oh, m'lady. Be not sad. M'lord loves you so."

Tears stung at Brienne's eyes. She blinked away the moisture and smiled into the child's sweet, round face.

"Didst he tell you so, Elsie?"

"He need not, m'lady. M'lord's heart shines in his eyes. Mama says."

"Ah, mama."

Elsie squinched her straight little brows together. "Must I nursemaid *her* babe, m'lady? 'Tis not m'lord's."

"Oh?" Brienne's face mirrored her surprise.

Elsie wagged her head with the greatest of certainty. "My lord wouldst do no such thing. He loves *you*, m'lady," she said with a child's innocent logic.

Brienne's heart dipped, knowing that Rurik *had* done "such things" before they were married. The babe could full well be his. But she said naught. Elsie adored her handsome lord.

"Mama says Katla is evil, that she's bewitched m'lord. Oh, m'lady, must I care for her babe? M'lord will give you many babes, and soon, I think."

Brienne drew Elsie into her arms and hugged her warmly. "And does mama say this, too?"

Elsie nodded.

"Mama knows much, I think."

"You will speak to m'lord?"

"I will speak to him."

"And I need not tend Katla?"

"You may tend me, little one." Brienne glanced over the loom. " 'Tis time you learnt of weaving. Think you might like to beat the weft?"

Elsie brightened at the sight of the sword paddle.

Waite and Elsie giggled as they plopped dark, sweet berries

into their mouths and scavenged the brambles for more.
Brienne and Aleth laughed with them. Few of the berries
gathered this day made it into their pails. Those that did
were crushed to juice long ago in the bottoms. The berries
were a rare find this late in the season, and these had been
hidden deep in the forest.

Having eaten her fill, Brienne wandered near at hand,
seeking whatever prizes the woodland might yield. She need
find a birch tree and take of its bark and leaves. One of the
young maidservants suffered a skin disorder.

Patch reappeared, yapping and exuberant, then scurried
back into the brush. Waite bounded after the pup, upsetting
the pail and causing Elsie to scold. Brienne chuckled softly
as she bent to survey a shrub.

Inexplicably, the hair at the nape of her neck began to rise.
Uncertain of the cause, Brienne drew a feathery leaf through
her fingers, listening, listening. At length she sighed and
massaged her brow. She didst not sleep so well of late.
'Twas fatigue, no more.

Brienne moved further into the forest until she spied
several birch trees with their smooth white bark and
graceful boughs spreading downward. Just as she touched
her fingertips to a leaf, a distinct rustling sounded off to
her left. Brienne stilled. It came again, this time from
ahead. Then all fell to silence. A deep, foreboding silence.

Brienne turned slowly round, ears strained for the slightest
of sounds. None came. Not the twitter or cawing of birds,
the chirp of insects, or any of the other skittering noises that
belonged to a forest.

Catching up her skirts, Brienne hastened from the place,
hastened back toward Aleth and the children. Twigs snapped
beneath her feet—so loud, it seemed—shouting her passage.
She feared to look back for what she might find. Onward she
hurried, her pace quickening.

Aleth and Elsie were squatting happily side by side, sorting their paltry sum of berries, when Brienne came upon
them.

"Aleth, get Elsie from this place, and quickly, too. Did
Waite yet return?"

When Aleth shook her head, Brienne urged her to be gone, then rushed in the direction where Waite had disappeared earlier.

Branches scratched her hands and tore at her hair as she pushed impatiently through the greenery. Silence still swallowed the wood. Unable to bear it longer, she called out his name. Suddenly there came a rustling, then a voice—Waite's voice—and blessedly, Patch's yapping.

Waite appeared moments later, plunging through the growth.

"M'lady! Come, m'lady." He pulled anxiously on her hand, dragging her deeper into the forest.

Brienne protested but the boy did not listen, tugging her firmly along. He led her to a small clearing. In its center rested a large flat stone covered with blood.

Brienne's stomach lurched. "We must be away from this place, Waite. 'Tis fraught with things most dire."

Brienne did not go again to the forest, but on Rurik's return she apprised him of the incident. To her knowledge, he investigated the sight but, oddly, did little more.

Immersed in thought, she strode across the bailey toward the weaving shed. As she passed the kitchen buildings, a movement drew her eye in time to see Katla step—or did she stumble?—into Rurik's arms. He raised one hand to her hip, pressing part of his palm and the length of his thumb against her swollen abdomen. The other he slipped around her back and waist.

Heat blistered Brienne's cheeks as Rurik continued to embrace Katla thusly. Unable to bear more, she withdrew and sought seclusion in the weaving shed.

Hollowly, Brienne sat before the loom. The falcon stared back at her with its piercing blue eye, the head near complete.

'Twould be a wondrous sight when finished, stretched to the sun above the high-prowed ship, heralding the lord baron's approach. She should be cheered. But inside, her heart was crumbling.

Desperately, desperately she longed to give Rurik a child.

Tears rose and spilled. Gripping a fistful of warp thread, she wept against the upright.

Her courses had come again today.

Rurik headed toward the practice field in a disagreeable temper. Katla continued to beset him. Last week she would have fallen and injured the babe had he not caught her up. Today she employed other brazen tactics.

He tired of her ploys, and tired of the smirking looks he received from his men. Most were amused by his dilemma, especially the new arrivals. But a good sum of his father's garrison disapproved of Katla's presence. As vigorously as they would defend a man's right to keep whatever woman he pleased, their sympathies lay with Brienne. She had found a place in their hearts.

Brienne. His brows drew together. A sadness shadowed her of late. Her courses came and went, troubling her afresh. But despite his attentions, she remained despondent.

Rurik rubbed his neck. The duke demanded of his time, the harvest preoccupied the barony, and Bolsgar once more reported that stock was missing. From the signs in the forest, he suspected that some had been offered as sacrifices. This concerned him more as a sign of unrest and contempt for his authority than as an abandonment of the new religion. He would bide his time, keeping open-eyed vigilance.

Rurik greeted his men as he arrived at the field and experienced a familiar stab of guilt. The recent constraints on his time prevented him from practicing and conditioning with his men as was his habit. Today he craved to discharge his frustrations in a spirited match. He stripped away his tunic and unsheathed his sword.

First he took on Gunnar and Hoth, two of his most capable swordsmen. Then Lyting came forth to try his steel.

"Your arm is swift and hard today, *broðir*." Lyting spurred him on. "Who is it you fight?"

"Do you wish to idle here the day, prattling like a *kjerringa,* an old woman, or shall we be to it?"

Rurik delivered strong, sweeping strokes that Lyting returned blow for blow but not without effort. When at last their arms tired and their bodies glistened with sweat, they ended the sport and slaked their thirst with a horn of ale.

Nearby, two men postured, unfamiliar to Rurik. Their eyes slid to him from time to time, one's voice louder than the other's. He caught the last of their exchange—*"Barnakarl."*

Rurik downed another mouthful of the beverage, then confronted the two. "Is there aught that disturbs you?"

"Nei, my lord." The older man, lean and bearded, straightened. " 'Twas a most proficient match."

"For a *Barnakarl?"* Rurik challenged but did not wait on an answer. "You have lately arrived to Valsemé?"

"Já, my lord."

"I do not recall testing your skills."

The man slid his companion a wary glance as the baron gestured to one of his soldiers.

"Nei, my lord. We presented ourselves to your man, Ketil, in your absence. We wish to serve Valsemé's illustrious lord."

"Pretty words, but you need be able . . . and stout-hearted."

Rurik ungirt his belt and passed both sword and scabbard to Lyting. Hoth, shouldering a half-dozen spears, joined them. Rurik selected two.

"How are you called?" He examined the keenness of a spearhead as Lyting and Hoth retreated from the field.

"Óttar, my lord, and this be Rig." The man motioned to his friend, aware that the other soldiers had ceased their activities and gathered to watch.

"Well, Óttar, Rig, you look capable enough." Rurik hefted a spear to each. "Take up your stance there and there, before the straw bales."

When the two had positioned themselves, Rurik stood facing them, legs braced.

"Aim your spears for me," he ordered.

"My lord? *Nei,* lord," Óttar objected.

"Be you soft-spined? Mark me as though an enemy, and cast your weapons with intent to kill. And men, once the spears be released, do not move if you savor your life."

Óttar and Rig traded uneasy looks. Hoisting their weapons, they steadied the shafts and sighted the baron's chest.

Grunting through gritted teeth, they heaved the spears, each with a mighty thrust and deadly accuracy.

But Rurik dodged to one side then the other, catching the spears backhanded in midair, and returned them without pause, swinging his arms full circle. The next moment found Óttar and Rig anchored to the straw. One spear secured Óttar's wrist by his sleeve, while the other moored Rig by the side of his hair, exposing a ringed ear.

"I thought I saw a glint of gold," Rurik said, smiling with satisfaction as he took up his jerkin. "My curiosity overcame me, Rig. 'Tis good you can take orders. And, Óttar, next time, do not move your hand. You near lost it."

Óttar paled considerably at the thought of a "next time," and Rig continued to gape at Valsemé's lord, thunderstruck.

Leaving the two skewered to the bales, Rurik strode from the field to the applause of the crowd and made his way through the press of cheering onlookers. He headed for the keep.

Gaining the great wooden staircase that spanned the motte, Rurik climbed its long flight. Once inside, he continued his ascent up the steps of stone. Higher and higher he climbed until he reached the topmost chamber in the tower. He needed this. Needed the exertion. Needed to be alone.

Surprisingly, the small trapdoor to the roof lay open, the ladder braced in place. The sight that greeted him as he emerged atop the keep swelled his heart. Brienne stood looking out over the barony, her veil and mantle astir with the breeze.

"Ástin mín?" He did not wish to startle her.

She turned to face him, her eyes red and swollen, her cheeks wet.

Pain cut through Rurik and he moved to take her in his arms. "What distresses you, my heart?"

Brienne attempted to twist away but he would not have it. She gripped him then, with aching need, and buried her face against his chest.

"Rurik, I fail you. Forgive me. I have prayed and prayed, but I . . . I cannot . . ."

Concern seized him and he held her back so he could look

into her eyes. "Brienne, what is it you say?"

"I think I am barren." Her voice broke miserably.

Unable to meet his eyes, she looked away. Tears gathered on her lashes. Her throat felt raw.

"If 'tis so, I can provide you no heir, Rurik." The tears trickled downward. "You may need seek another."

"*Nei!*" he denied harshly. "I will beget my sons—and daughters—of you, my wife. None other."

"But your heir, Rurik. If I be barren—"

"None other," he declared adamantly. "*Ástin mín,* have patience. We have been wedded scarce four months. There is much time for children and I can bear the wait, however long."

"But if—"

He pressed a finger to her lips and brushed the wetness from her cheeks. "One of my aunts did not bear her first babe till the sixth year of her marriage. Then she and my uncle begat so many, their hall could scarce contain them!"

A small smile flickered over Brienne's lips. "Be that true or didst you weave the tale to cheer me?"

"*Ástin mín,* you wound me sorely." A note of amusement colored his protest. "Ask Lyting of our notable aunt if you doubt me."

"I shall." Brienne smiled broadly now. "Has she a name?"

"Borghild." He nuzzled her ear. "Shall we name our first maid-child after her?"

"I think not." Brienne felt a ripple of warmth follow a homeward path and settle betwixt her thighs.

"*Ástin mín.*" His breath fell warmly on her ear. He began spreading kisses along her jaw and neck. "We speak much of begetting babes but 'twill require more than mere words to accomplish the feat."

Brienne leaned back in his embrace to survey the stone beneath their feet, then kissed the base of his throat. " 'Tis a hard bed we must bide. The mattresses have all been removed to the manor house."

Her hand slipped inside his jerkin. His moved to encompass her breast and tease the soft nipple erect.

"There be this lake I know of. . . ." Rurik captured her lips then groaned as she moved against him.

*   *   *

Katla paused in the shadows, watching Rurik's and Brienne's passage from a distance. Their hair was wet, hers a sodden tangle, dripping past her waist. They clasped hands and laughed—laughed!—as they strolled toward the bailey.

Katla clenched the knife at her side.

"Enjoy your time of him, bitch. Enjoy sitting beside him, enthroned upon your high seat. They both shall be mine. Soon, soon," she vowed on the wind.

Chapter Fifteen

BRIENNE STRETCHED slowly, like a drowsy cat. Drawing a long, contented breath, she reached out to Rurik but met with cool air.

One eyelid dragged open, and she scanned the empty space beside her, then looked at the sunlight spilling past half-opened shutters and into the chamber. Brienne moaned to have overslept, then smiled for all the reasons she had.

She stretched once again, extending her arms wide and sweeping them overhead. Her fingers brushed against cold metal. Inclining her head, she rolled to one hip. On Rurik's pillow rested a beautifully wrought silver brooch.

Brienne rose, smiling as she took up the piece and envisioning Rurik placing it there whilst she slept. Obviously, he was as well pleased with their night of lovemaking as she.

As Brienne delighted in the fine detailing of the brooch, the underside rasped at her fingers. Hesitantly, she inverted it in her palm. Runic characters etched the back in a single, crowded band, several of the scorings rough and unfiled.

She gazed on it for a prolonged moment, mindfully recalling Ketil's words. Her name, perchance? An endearment?

Curiosity surged in her. Brienne slipped from the bed and hastened to dress.

Rurik entered the hall with brisk, purposeful strides, accompanied by Lyting, Ketil, and Brother Bernard.

Servants bustled to assemble the tables for the midmorning meal and set out basins of water. Avoiding the paths of activity, the foursome proceeded to a side hearth where a small fire crackled.

Rurik cast a swift glance about for Brienne but found that Aleth directed the hall in her absence. She had noted his entrance and summoned a servant to fill his goblet, but Rurik motioned the woman away. He had no taste for wine this morn. Indeed, he had little appetite at all.

"What manner of *blót* do you think it to be?" Rurik spoke Norse, not wishing to concern any who might hear.

Lyting shook his head. " 'Tis difficult to know. We found pigs, hens, and sheep, three of each kind sacrificed. But deeper in the wood we discovered a *vé*."

Rurik's eyes cut to Ketil. "You are sure?"

"*Já*." Ketil nodded forcefully. "A triangular area be marked out upon the ground and lined with upright stones. 'Twas used for ritual."

Rurik stroked his thumb along his jaw and chin, considering what significance might lie in that.

" 'Tis not uncommon for men to falter from time to time when they embrace a new faith, my son," Brother Bernard interjected. "But 'tis needful we redouble our efforts of conversion and instruction, lest they endanger their immortal souls."

Rurik shot him a look of impatience. "If I seem short-spoken, take no offense, but their souls be your concern. My care is more immediate."

The monk began to object, but Rurik pressed the point. "The sacrifices may indicate unrest and discontent amongst my soldiers. Not all accept the duke's unbounded authority despite their oaths. Some wax jealous of his power. Others, I suspect, are like-minded with Hastein and wouldst carve Normandy free from Francia's side as a country to its own. Regardless, I must see my men honor their oaths—not only to me but to duke and king alike—lest we divide against ourselves within our own borders."

"And what of God?" the monk blustered. "The very oaths of which you speak bind the men to Christ as well as liege. They have taken the waters."

"Then do what you must, churchman, as shall I."

Brother Bernard gave Rurik a ponderous look. "Do not

discount the import of faith to a man's disposition. Sword and faith—the two are intertwined. And have you forgotten your own vows? A soldier looks to the example his lord sets. If your concern be oaths sworn and honored, then 'twould strengthen your position to take Holy Baptism and rightly honor your own. 'Tis time, think you not, my son?"

Rurik turned and gazed into the fire. "There still be matters I need reconcile. I have told you as much."

Lyting shifted his stance, displeased with the response, for he held the Faith more dear than did most of his kindred. "You cannot delay indefinitely, *broðir*."

"Nor shall I. You have my word on it. But for now we must determine whether these sacrifices be offerings simply to worship the gods, or if someone leads the men to other purposes." He ran his hand through his hair. "We need find something more specific than the *vé*, something of substance that could point to an individual."

"Have you a thought as to what that might be?" Ketil asked gruffly, tugging on his beard.

Rurik shook his head, studying the flames. The sound of his name drew his attention back to the body of the hall. His spirits lifted to see Brienne cross its width.

Brienne smiled as Rurik took up her hand and pressed it with a kiss. "My lord," she greeted, eyes sparkling, then nodded to the others. "Good morrow."

"My lady seems surpassingly happy." Lyting tipped his silvery-blond head in what might pass for a bow.

"If it be so, 'tis the fault of my husband. See how he spoils me." Brienne held forth the handsome silver brooch. "Of course, 'tis fair maddening that he secrets messages beneath its shell and leaves me to ponder the cipher."

Rurik grinned and took the brooch from her hand. "Be you sure you wish it divulged before these ears?"

As Brienne made to reply, he reversed the piece and glanced down at the markings. His brows pulled slowly together.

"Ketil? Have you been clever again or do my skills fail me?"

Ketil relieved Rurik of the brooch, chuckling that the inscription should baffle his lord. True, he favored com-

pressing several words into a single character, but Rurik
knew the device.

"Your duties as baron have sapped your wit, 'tis all," he
quipped, chuckling once more. But his smile stilled as he
looked on the markings, then faded altogether.

"Flesh and blood! These runes have been altered. Look—
here, here—and here again! Fresh lines have been added and
hastily, 'twould seem. See, the incisings be left coarse and
unpolished. My own I smoothed so as not to tear at my lady's
fingers."

The disquieting words caused a shiver along Brienne's
spine. She looked restively from one man to the next.

Rurik's expression darkened. "Can you construe its meaning?"

Ketil puzzled over the characters. His lips moved with
each word, then abruptly he stopped. His eyes wrenched to
Rurik.

" 'Tis a *rati!*"

Rurik snatched the brooch and glared at it. A chill, winter-
cold, rippled through him. Without hesitation, he flung the
ornament into the fire.

Aghast, Brienne started forward but Rurik gripped her by
the arms and held her firm to his chest.

"Let it burn, Brienne. It bears a curse."

" 'Tis a 'baying man' we deal with." Ketil downed the contents of his cup.

Rurik leaned forward on his elbows, one hand fisted into
the other, and watched as the servants cleared away the
remains of the meal.

"What makes you so certain?"

"One rune in particular, *ōðila*, was refigured to the like-
ness of a head wearing the horned helmet of a high priest.
Such a man would have knowledge of the runes . . . and
curses."

Lyting rose at his place. "Let us act swiftly to find him,
then, or there shall be sacrifices aplenty and discontent skulk-
ing at our door."

Rurik motioned his brother to reseat himself. "Not overfast,
broðir. We must move with care."

"You mean to let it bide?" Lyting asked, rankled by his brother's caution.

"*Nei*. I am as eager as you to reach the heart of this matter, but we know not who is part to it, and who can be trusted."

Rurik eased back in his chair, waited as a manservant refilled their goblets and removed the salt cellars, then came forward once again.

"Sound out five you deem the most reliable, and set watches by night, deep in the wood. Likewise, double the guard over the stock. The offenders will seek to thieve again."

"There still be several goats and an ox unaccounted for. Perchance they are confined hereabouts," Brother Bernard ventured, having followed the discussion silently till now.

"*Satt*. True. Ketil, take a complement of men of your choosing. Patrol the reaches if you must. 'Twill be expected that I shall seek what is mine, and I have delayed overlong as it is. Your ride should breed no undue attention."

Rurik looked to where Brienne spoke with a maidservant. He must warn her to keep from the forest. *Nei*, he must forbid it outright. Brienne had a will of her own when her medicants fell in short supply.

Brienne felt Rurik's eyes upon her. As she lifted her gaze to couple with his, horns sounded at the bailey gate without, two short blasts that announced a sole rider.

Rurik rose at once to quit the hall, sparing her a brief glance and a shade of a smile as he stepped from the dais. With a second thought, he stopped and waited with open palm for her to join him. She did so at once.

There was a tenseness in his grip, a leashed energy that belied his calm as they passed out of the hall, Lyting, Ketil, and Brother Bernard following behind. What unwelcome news did he wait on? she wondered. Rurik rarely commented on his affairs with the duke.

Brienne questioned whether she should have prepared a goblet to welcome their visitor, as was her duty. But the highborn traveled with escort, not alone. 'Twas likely a messenger, no more. He would seek his respite in the kitchens once he had delivered his missive. But what missive might that be?

She looked anxiously to the rider dismounting in the court-yard. Rollo's envoys came and went most often by water, the journey a short distance by river and ocean. But this man arrived by courser, a distinctive mount with one stockinged leg. 'Twas familiar, as was he. No Norseman here, but Frank. He was of an age with herself, smooth-faced and lean, having yet to grow into his strength. Her journey from Levroux did not lay so far in memory that she should forget him. And in remembering, she knew whom the courier served.

A shiver of apprehension ran through her. Her discomfort grew. *What mischief now, Lord Robert?* she asked silently as the man gave his greetings from Castle Roubaix.

Rurik closeted himself with Lyting, Ketil, and the messenger. When they emerged, it was with solemn countenance, yet they seemed afire with purpose. The scent of battle filled the air and bestirred the soldiers to action.

Brienne received the news with noble forbearance. Franconian troops had brazenly looted and burned the king's great hall at Creil and must be dealt with sharply and swiftly. Esternay called upon Rurik to join him at arms, summoned him, in truth, by the tie that bound their houses—the blood bond of marriage. He had boldly made known his request to Charles. To refuse meant dishonor to Valsemé's lord and insult to the king.

As all was set to readiness for the morrow's departure, Brienne cloaked her distress and slipped for a time to the weaving shed. There, she worked out the warp and weft of her thoughts—dark thoughts that kept crowding back—and grappled with her fears. Would Lord Robert seek to harm her husband? Should she caution Rurik of the deceit that knight harbored?

The great falcon, half complete, stared down, reproving her, it seemed, for the secrets she kept hidden. But there be necessity for caution and prudence, she contended, beating up the weft solidly as he gave her deaf ear and continued to glare.

At length, she exhausted her argument. Her fingers cramped and her head ached. Surely no treachery would be dealt before she was with child. For the first time, she could be thankful she was not.

Nightfall drew its veil over the land. The keep blazed with torchlight as final preparations were completed.

Rurik returned to the manor house, crossing the bailey after his last check with the gate's watchman.

A soft hiss from a darkened outbuilding brought him from his thoughts. Katla stepped from the shadows and beckoned him to join her.

Rurik wondered briefly if she was unwell. She stood with hands clasped beneath her swollen stomach, a line of worry marring her face. But she did not waver as one ill, he noted as he softly crossed to where she stood. She held tall and firm yet coiled with an urgency.

"There is danger," she warned, her intense green eyes catching splinters of torchlight.

"Danger?" His lips slid into an uncertain half smile. "When is there not in battle? I have never known fear in you, Katla."

"Nor do you now, only disgust, disgust for Frankish treachery."

Rurik's mien hardened, pleasing her. She tossed her fiery hair, pleased again when his eyes followed it, knowing how the torches lit it with gold.

"Mayhaps I *should* fear. You are blind where your wife is concerned. She plots your death even as she warms your bed."

Rurik grabbed her by the arms, nearly jerking her off her feet. "Make yourself plain if you seek to malign my lady," he snarled.

"Ask your wife what evil she and her kinsman dream on. I overheard them in her chamber—*já*, Rurik, he visited her in her chamber, the night before she wed Gruel Atli. Together they plotted death to Valsemé's lord."

He glared at her with a face of thunder, his fingers biting into her flesh. A smile spread through her. He cared for the bitch. And because he cared he would fall the harder and the bitch the longer from her pedestal of grace. She, Katla, would be waiting to ease his pain and salve the gashes in his heart. Then wouldst he turn to her and her child, no more to trust or seek his comforts in Frankish arms.

"Poor Rurik, caught up in the spider's craft. Your lady has spun her silken threads tight about you, but beware. Her bite brings death. 'Twas to be achieved upon the battlefield and appear an accident."

"Why? To what purpose?" he stormed angrily, half believing, half not.

"They seek to regain control of the barony through the heir, the next Baron de Valsemé."

"I have filled her with no child as yet. If what you say be true, he will not strike." Rurik warred against Katla's charge, fought to believe in Brienne's innocence.

"Do not rest assured. The Seigneur d'Esternay desires to accomplish the deed himself so the heir will, in truth, be his."

Outrage whipped through Rurik, pain flaying his face.

Katla's eyes glinted. Her words dripped fresh venom into his heart. "Did he not invite you both to Castle Roubaix? There would be many rooms in such a place . . . many dark corners."

She tilted her chin up, a trace of a smile touching her mouth, eyes glittering beneath half-closed lids.

" . . . *like an adder coiled up* . . ." Lyting's words echoed through Rurik's thoughts. He withdrew a pace and eyed Katla warily.

"I didst not know you were attendant to Lord Robert's parting, for 'twas then that he extended the courtesy of Roubaix."

"I have heard the tale," she assured him. "There are those who speak easily enough. I am also to understand that your lady wife did not object."

Rurik recalled how Brienne's nails dug into his arm, how agitated she became. And there was the time on the archery field when he thought she would swoon. Was there truth in what Katla said? Was this what upset Brienne so? It eased him a portion, for it avouched her resistance to Esternay's designs. And surely the scheme be his for it reeked of his foul stench.

"You best not lie in this, Katla," Rurik said through clenched teeth.

"You have but to ask your wife," she replied easily, confidently. "She conceals her hatreds well, but be mindful. 'Twas Norse blades that slew her father and brother. She seeks vengeance for the House of Beaumanoir."

Katla tossed her head. "The Seigneur d'Esternay is more simply obsessed with greed and power."

" . . . 'Tis power she craves. Position."

Rurik measured her a long, searching moment. "I need wonder if he stands alone in that."

Her eyes blazed. "Believe what you like," Katla spat, filled with sudden fury. "You are warned."

Rurik watched as she turned back into the shadows and disappeared.

He tarried a while longer, tumbling Katla's words over and about, searching their many angles. Katla would make Brienne appear the worse to advance her own goals. Did love blind him? He thought not, but if he was wrong, he would not be the first to be brought low by a woman's trickery. A maid's heart is made on the whirling wheel, does not the poet say? But, *nei*. Unfair. 'Twas a bitter poet who set the verse, once spurned in his own pursuit of a lady.

Until this encounter he trusted Brienne with his life. His instincts told him to continue in that trust, at least a time longer. He would wait upon her to share what had transpired betwixt herself and Esternay. But he would not wait forever.

With that he headed for the manor house.

When Rurik entered their chamber, he found Brienne awake beneath the coverlets of the great bed. Her pale countenance drew his concern.

"Does aught distress you, *ástin mín*?" He eased his weight onto the mattress edge, discarding his tunic.

"I wouldst have you come back safe to me." She clasped his hand and pressed it to her cheek. He felt the warmth of a tear.

"Should I not, my love?" He lifted her face and looked at her searchingly.

Brienne's throat caught as his eyes held hers. He waited, somehow expectant. Again she ached to speak her thoughts. Again she dreaded to do so.

For all her love and trust of him, Rurik bore the heart of a Norseman. 'Twas a harsh race with harsh ways. She feared what retribution a Norseman might exact for treachery such as Lord Robert's—even if only conceived, and ill conceived at that. And—dear God!—would he think her part to it? She thought not. But should Rurik issue challenge to Lord Robert and either be . . . nay, she could not live with their blood upon her conscience.

Was she a coward? she wondered, then minded that Charles vehemently opposed his barons warring upon one another. Scandal all the greater should the houses be bound by blood, as were theirs. Danger *and* dishonor lay upon that path. Coward, mayhaps, but she would bide her time. She carried no child. Esternay wouldst make no move.

"The warrings of men have cost me dearly," she said at last. "Forgive a woman's weakness that I should fear the clash of arms."

She half rose from the bed to slip her arms about Rurik's neck. In so doing, the covers tumbled downward, exposing her soft, pink-tipped breasts. Flesh pressed against flesh.

"Take heed. I am a most selfish wife," she whispered against his lips. "When I be aged and gray and tottering about our hall, I wish to do so at your side and have you still to comfort me in the night."

Brienne drew Rurik down with her into the pillows. The worries and uncertainties that hovered betwixt them lingered on the moment's edge, then silently took their flight.

At dawn, the troops stood armed and mounted in the bailey. Brienne accompanied Rurik from the hall as he charged Lyting to secure the keep in his absence. There was something about holding the stock from the forest, but it made little sense to her and Rurik ended his instructions in Norse.

Katla waited in the courtyard with a loaf of fruited bread. With this she gifted Rurik and bid him safe return. Though she said no more, something passed between their eyes.

Brienne felt challenged in some manner. Wanting none of it, she diverted her gaze to the baggage wain. Torn, wracked through by the dark possibilities that threatened the days to come, she bore no patience for the Norsewoman's games.

Sleipnir snorted and stamped, keen to the high energy

that livened the yard as the groom brought him forth. Rurik
stepped quickly to calm the stallion, bantering in deep, soothing tones while he stroked the horse's neck.

Brienne looked on with admiration as Rurik gentled the
mighty steed. Dear God, how she loved him. A rush of
panic swarmed through her. She must tell him, forewarn
him of Lord Robert's duplicity. But if the tale should so
distract him that in the midst of battle . . . Nay, best wait.
He need concentrate at present lest it cost him his life. She
would let it bide until his return when the clash of steel had
ceased. Merciful God, he *must* return.

As Brienne struggled with her thoughts, Patch barreled
into the courtyard out of nowhere. Full of himself, he scurried along the file of horses, darted amongst several of the
foot soldiers, then went yapping after a new curiosity—Ketil,
fitted in shaggy fur boots.

Ketil plucked the pup up by the scruff of its neck and
laughed heartily. With a flash of inspiration, Brienne hastened to retrieve the mongrel. Taking the squirming ball of
mismatched fur, she spoke in low clear tones so none but
Ketil could hear and so he could not mistake.

"By the oath that binds you—by the friendship that ties
you there—watch my lord's back, I pray. Watch his back."

"My lady?" Ketil's brows shot up, but she was already
moving away.

Rurik made a final check of the straps. Turning to Brienne,
he gave her a swift, hard kiss, then vaulted into the saddle.

Brienne watched as he set his helmet in place and accepted
shield and lance. She had never seen him thus, equipped for
war. His armor was a mix of Norse and Byzantine garb—
thick leather corslets, one upon another, tall, square-toed
boots, vambraces and greaves splinted over forearm and
leg. The conical helmet—so painfully familiar—concealed
his features behind protective eye and nose guards. Yet she
would know his mouth and line of his jaw at once, she told
herself, and the steel-blue eyes that grazed her now from iron
sockets.

With a shout, Rurik wheeled the great black and led
his men thundering over the bridge, out and through the
village.

Brienne grabbed up her skirts and ran for the keep. She scaled the wooden steps, then the stone. Pain seared her lungs, but she hurried on till at last she reached the topmost chamber. Scrambling up the ladder, she pushed open the roof hatch, climbed through, and rushed to the crenellated wall.

Across the valley, the dark line of soldiers advanced, spears bristling above their heads, shields swung to their backs. She strained to pick out Rurik's blue mantle where he rode before his men, then smiled when she thought to glimpse it.

There she remained, hands grown cold upon the stone, watching with mind's eye long after the dust resettled, long after Rurik had passed with his men into the distance and beyond the horizon.

Chapter Sixteen

❖ ❖ ❖ ❖ ❖ ❖ ❖ ❖ ❖ ❖ ❖ ❖

THE SCRATCHING CAME again, a soft clawing upon the door. Brienne lay quiet in the dark and breathed a thin shred of air. Patch growled from the foot of the great bed where Aleth's pallet was spread.

"Aleth," Brienne called in a soft, urgent whisper.

"*Oui*. I hear it. 'Tis as before. Shall I light a tinder?"

The scraping ceased.

Silence oppressed the chamber for one long, unbearable moment.

Then the grating began anew.

"I'll see to it." Brienne slipped from the bed, the floor chilling her feet. She flamed a candle and prompted Aleth to calm Patch.

As she eased toward the door, she prayed Rurik would soon return. The unsettling nocturnal occurrences had begun short of his leave-taking, nigh on to a month ago.

At first she thought it some ill dream that awoke her, spawned by her fears and longings for her husband. Then one night, from the depths of sleep, she felt a foreboding presence. When she fought through to a groggy consciousness, she discovered herself alone. Yet a vague scent lingered about the bed.

After that, Aleth moved her pallet from the antechamber and Patch was invited to join them. Brienne spoke to none of the incident save her friend. Lyting seemed overburdened of late with some matter concerning the barony, and Brother Bernard was away to Rouen. How mad would she appear to complain of—what?—ethereal visitations tormenting her rest? 'Twould seem she be unsound.

She was relieved when several weeks passed without event. Then the dull grating began, three nights past . . . and now once more.

Brienne paused and listened. Didst the guards in the passageway sleep? she fumed. How could any go unnoticed or gain the room without? Her hand trembled and the flame capered.

Flesh or shadow? What be you? she raged silently, temper eclipsing nerve. As her fingertips brushed the door's handle, she took a deep breath.

Patch suddenly nipped at Aleth and scrambled free. Barking raucously, he darted across the floor and scrabbled at the door.

The scratching stopped. Something clunked on the other side followed by a faint shuffle, then silence.

Brienne swung open the door and thrust her candle into the outer room, punctuating the darkness.

Cool air played over her. The chamber stood empty. Yet an indefinable scent lingered about the portal.

"Brienne?" Aleth drew behind her, dragging an iron poker from the hearth.

"There be naught." Brienne strove to collect herself, her bravura flown.

As she turned back to the bedchamber, the candle's narrow light arched across the door.

Brienne's blood ceased its flow as her eyes fastened to the oaken panels—to the runes carved fresh upon the wood.

Rurik wiped the sweat from his brow with his sleeve and settled back in his saddle. Tucking his helmet beneath his arm, his eyes roamed over the soldiery for the hundredth time, then he peered into the distance.

He disliked the situation. Sharply mistrusted it.

The attack on Creil had proved in part a display of Franconian force, a warning, and in part retaliation.

Barely a year past, when the East Frankish king, Louis the Child, died, Charles succeeded in regaining Lorraine on the eastern frontier, lost to him a decade earlier. The people of Lorraine readily accepted Carolingian Charles when the unpopular Duke of Franconia, Conrad, was elevated to the East Frankish throne. Conrad, for his part, vowed reprisal.

Creil's destruction was an insolent slap, dealt to Charles's heartland. But 'twas more than the assault that weighed on Rurik. How were the Franconians able to penetrate Francia's borders so deep and remain unmarked? How, lest they received aid from interests within?

As the combined forces of Normans and West Franks pushed the raiders back to the frontier, an unshakable impression beset Rurik. It seemed the Franconians baited them, drawing them ever toward Burgundy's borders to some appointed hour.

Burgundy. A burr lay in that. Before he could work through the thought, Ketil drew alongside.

"A dragon must lie near," Ketil rumbled, pulling off his helmet. "It reeks a foul breath hereabouts."

"I smell it as well. 'Od's blood, 'twould seem we march into that great worm's jaw." Rurik shifted his gaze left to the ranks of Neustrians. They had joined Esternay's banner scarce a fortnight ago. "Ofttimes I wonder whom I distrust the more, Conrad's forces or our own. What know you of our comrades there?"

"Only that I'd prefer meeting them head-on to having them at my back." Ketil squinted over at them. "You didst know that the late Marquess of Neustria wore the crown before Charles. *Nei*? The magnates rejected Charles due to his youth and offered the throne to Odo. But later, some of the more powerful lords revolted and crowned Charles whilst Odo fought in the Acquitaine. Francia was not reconciled under one crown till Odo's death."

"And the present marquess?"

"Brother to Odo—Robert. He pledges loyalty to Charles easily enough."

Ketil nodded to where a dark, thickset man rode, conversing with Esternay. "He has sent us his son, Hugh. Already does that one gain honors in battle. But what might interest you the more is the marquess's son-by-marriage, Raoul, Duke of Burgundy."

"Burgundy," Rurik muttered. "Therein lies the burr."

"Or the 'worm.'" Ketil smiled grimly.

"That, too, my friend. That too."

The bray of trumpet brought their eyes to the distance. Dust clouded the horizon.

"The Franconians have turned," Ketil observed.

"*Já*, with Burgundy to their backs and Neustria at our sides."

"Think you Esternay is part to this?"

Rurik shook his head, unknowing. "As I understand it, he won his land and spurs of Charles, and claims title as king's champion."

"Mayhaps beneath the title he is a man of shifting loyalties." Ketil pulled on his helmet.

"Mayhaps." Rurik resettled his own. "Tell the men to give heed. Our Norse archers will precede the slingers and pikemen for the first attack. Let them fold back into the shield wall. We be strong there. But our cavalry is thin. We must rectify that in the future. For now, Esternay's troops will gird our lines where they be wanting. Let us hope he does not forswear the sovereign now."

Ketil began to move off, but Rurik stayed him with a last thought. " 'Tis against my grain, and yours, I know, but our footmen will be sore disadvantaged once the cavalry breaks through the shield wall, and our greater portion lies there. If needs be, bring down the horse to gain the man. The face of our enemy is unbeknownst this day. We may yet find him on all sides."

A distant horn sounded as the Franconians made their advance, sunlight glancing off their spears. The Seigneur d'Esternay's standard-bearer returned the challenge, trumpeting defiance. Staunchly, the two armies progressed across the open field, quickening their tread.

As the Norse bowmen hurried to group themselves ahead of the ranks, Rurik silently rebuked himself. 'Twas he who suggested the tactic. Franks seldom utilized archers in battle. But so caught up was he in his own strategies that he did not question the enthusiasm his plans met, nor the ease with which he persuaded the Franks to employ the measure, especially Hugh. Now he fathomed why.

With the Norman strength concentrated in the bowmen and footmen at the fore—Neustrians holding to the left and Lord

Robert's to the right and behind, "fortifying" the cavalry—
his men were caught in a pincer. Maddened, Rurik spurred
Sleipnir forward to give charge to his archers. He addressed
them in Norse.

"If there be steel in your veins, prove so now. Wait long
as you dare and mark the horsemen. Range your arrows high.
On first strike, surprise is yours. On second, their shields
will be raised. But these will not cover them wholly. There
still be legs and, with luck, a sword arm unprotected or a
shoulder to disable. Then ready your axes when your work
be done and draw back to me. Much havoc shall be wrought
this day."

The men took up his cry as Rurik wheeled back into the
ranks.

As the two armies converged on one another, the archers held firm to their positions, steel-nerved and exposed
before the enemy. Then, at the last possible moment, they
released a shower of arrows, followed by a second and
a third.

Many a knight fell under the barrage, the shafts finding
home in chest and neck. Others more fortunate bore the wood
in thigh and arm. The luckiest, in their shield.

The slingers had barely shied a volley of stone when a
roar went up and the Franconians surged forward.

Steel rang out on steel. Lances clashed and shields shiv-
ered beneath ax. Blades ran crimson as the armies locked in
battle.

The foot soldiers tightened their ranks, laboring hard with
short sword and hatchet—cut and thrust, parry and turn.
Shields slammed rim to rim, steel clanged, one stroke meeting another. A man shrieked as an ax sliced off his arm.
Another cried out as a spear skewered his side.

Rurik gripped his broadsword, knees pressed tightly against
Sleipnir, reins and shield in the other hand as he prepared to
join the thick of action. He watched the spot where the shield
wall had begun to waver.

The Franconians pushed forward and the Neustrian line
appeared to collapse. The enemy poured into the gap, effec-
tively severing the Neustrians from the main body of the
army and widening the fissure to create a second front.

Predictably, the Franconians turned their efforts inward against the Normans.

"Rot you, Hugh!" Rurik's blood boiled as his sword sang out.

Esternay's men were conveniently buffered by his own. More Frankish cravenness! Rurik cursed them all as the shock of sword met shield. He rained blow after blow down on the Franconian that beset him, then with a quick thrust and stab, sent the man toppling to the ground.

Rurik quickly found his metal hard tested and was grateful that Hoth fought to his back. He briefly glimpsed Ketil as the fiery giant thrust his spear through an enemy shield, then dragged the soldier from his saddle.

Another East Frank drove from the left, but Rurik felled him with two strokes. When he looked up, Esternay was battling his way toward him, dark with rage.

"Sod them!" the knight swore as he delivered a hacking blow and planted his blade in a Franconian neck. "Damn the Neustrians to hell!"

Heartened, Rurik raised his steel and met each new attack. Rivulets of sweat poured from beneath his helmet as he slashed and hewed through the torrent of battle. A gurgling cry from behind told him that Hoth had been taken down. He swore fiercely, pivoted Sleipnir, and swiftly avenged the young man.

Esternay joined him just as a knot of men descended. Their interest was fixed on Rurik, but the knight drew off one after another.

Rurik felt it strange to be abetted by Esternay but could not think on it as he twisted to turn a blade with his shield. No blade did he meet but a club spiked with metal. The blow fell hard, shattering the wood upon his arm.

Esternay looked to Rurik as he took the sundering blow. Yet another Franconian closed in on Valsemé's lord, whose back was now unguarded. Esternay marked the man. Bringing up his sword, he slashed through the air. But at the last instant, he angled his stroke wide of the mark.

Pain splintered through Brienne's left arm, causing her to drop the bucket of apples.

"My lady!" Elsie's mother quickly captured the rolling vessel and runaway fruit. "My lady, you needn't be about this labor. 'Tis servants' duty."

Brienne only half listened to Galwinth's scolding as she massaged her arm and looked across the bailey to the east. A shiver ran through her. For a moment she stood unmoving, then a shadow fell over her. She gazed up into Lyting's crystal-blue eyes.

"Be you still intent on stocking the keep yourself?" He smiled, but worry lined his brow as it had since early morn when first he learned of the runes. "I fear we shall next lose you under a sack of oats or barrel of wine," he continued in a light vein.

Brienne shook off the dire feeling that enfolded her and answered his jest. "Wouldst you prefer I worked at the sail and anchored you to my weaving shed all the day? Really, Lyting, you mustn't feel you need guard me every minute. This morning's incident—"

"More than an incident, Brienne. 'Twas another *rati* that was carved upon your door, directed at you as the Baronne de Valsemé. I cannot give you the precise rendering, but someone appears ill content to bide under Frankish law even *with* a Norman lord. You may be at risk."

Confusion clouded her mien. "But why? I have naught to do with how men govern their affairs."

"Yet you are the baronne, the symbol of Frankish nobility, of your father before you, and of the king. In truth, the curse may be aimed equally at Rurik. It can be argued that the runes were put to the *baron's* bedchamber and cast against *his* wife. We know not wholly with what we deal."

Brienne found no ready response. She looked toward the keep.

"There be comfort in work, or, at least, distraction. Michaelmas will soon be upon us when the accountings must be taken. The tower was fairly stripped when we moved to the manor house. 'Tis good that we take stock of the siege provisions and provide some simple furnishings. A secure keep is one prepared—for whatever emergency."

She gave Lyting a meaningful look.

"Very well, let us make an accounting, but leave the apples, and the heavier work, to the servants. We shall raise their choler if we usurp their duties," he bantered as they crossed the courtyard and began the climb up the long wooden staircase. "Think you Bolsgar shall be maddened that we tend to his cipherings?"

"Mayhaps," Brienne replied with a smile. "Best we bid him join us with his writing implements."

As Brienne approached the top of the steps, she rubbed the dull ache in her arm and gazed once more with uncertainty toward the east.

The hours passed swiftly as Brienne immersed herself in the details of the keep. Aleth joined her along with a number of maidservants. Together they saw the stale rushes cleared from the hall, the chambers aired, and the burnt torches replaced with fresh ones.

Brienne wished to partake in more of the work herself, but Aleth and Galwinth reproved her every effort. A lady's place was to supervise, they admonished time and again. Brienne saw latent promise in Aleth as castellan, and Galwinth should have been born to title for her stout tongue and ability to dictate. They paid her little heed when she made comment, and only kept her from further soiling her hands.

At least Lyting eased his watch when she was well companioned. He aided Bolsgar in the depths of the keep, tallying the stores of foodstuffs, drink, and fuel.

Wearied by a long day of more idleness than toil, Brienne left the women stuffing pallets with fresh straw and moved into the passageway. A single torch blazed upon the wall, illumining a narrow stretch of corridor and leaving the rest in darkness.

Brienne made her way in the dimness to an adjoining room. Just as she prepared to enter, a crisp current of air rushed over her and parried with the torch's flame. Hesitantly, she stretched out her hand and felt the cool flow against her palm. It emanated from the far end of the passage where all lay cloaked in impenetrable shadow.

Removing an unlit torch from its bracket, she kindled it with the other's fire. Cautiously, she progressed down the corridor, tracking the breeze till she came to a stone wall.

To the right, as she anticipated, a stairway joined it, leading upward into the highest part of the tower.

Brienne lifted her skirts, torch held aloft, and began to climb. The draft was strongest here, fresh and sweet-scented. She followed it, ever upward, till she attained the uppermost reach of the keep and entered the familiar low-ceilinged chamber.

The room's chill slid over her as she stepped further inside, its inky dark scattering before the torchlight to crouch in corners and shift along walls. Her eye drew to where the day's grayed light spilled through the open portal overhead. A ladder stood braced in place, rising to the tower roof.

As a fresh gust of air curled over her, Brienne shook away her unease and moved to close the small door. Apparently, someone had been there apart from herself. She shut the thought from her mind along with the possibilities. The trapdoor above opened outward, challenging her nerve. She would need climb the ladder to get hold of it.

Brienne gripped a rung and canted her head, listening for a long moment. All was silence. Plucking up her courage along with her gown, she mounted the crosspieces one by one, carefully placing each foot, mindful of the cloth about her ankles and the torch above her head.

Dusk veiled the barony as Brienne emerged atop the keep. She swept the fire before her full circle, quickly searching out the shadows, then sighed her relief. She was alone.

Briefly, she allowed her eye to travel over the darkened contours of Valsemé, amazed that the day should have slipped so rapidly toward eve, unnoticed by herself and those within. As she bent toward the door, something gleamed in the fire's light an arm's reach away.

Brienne stretched to take up the item, her fingers meeting the coolness of metal. It proved to be a slim copper box, round and hinged. Turning it over, she worked the square catch with her thumb and pressed the top open.

Brienne cried out, dropping the case as though burned. Several minutes leaped past before she could recover her breath. When the object of her distress remained unmoving, she stooped to retrieve it with the greatest of caution. Hesitantly, she examined the receptacle. What appeared to be a snake coiled within proved to be only one's skin, perfectly preserved.

Hastily, she closed the lid and secured it. Despite her best effort, she could not master the tremor that began in her hand then quaked along her arm to find the pit of her stomach.

The torch sputtered in the breeze, hissing and smoking. Brienne threw it to the stone, maddened and unnerved. Its rush was ill prepared, the tallow already spent. In the dimming light, she descended the ladder and felt her way from the room and down the stairs. When at last she reentered the passage with its single, flaming torch, she heard the women's muted laughter and chatter in the chamber beyond.

Lyting was foremost in her thoughts. She must find him at once and show him the talisman. No need to distress the others. Brienne moved silently down the corridor, listening, watching, then slipped unseen past the chamber door.

On she rushed, hurrying down another flight of steps and into the great hall. Several torches crackled about the walls, mottling the chamber with patches of light. But the greater portion remained swamped in darkness. Impatient to reach Lyting, Brienne quickened her pace, glancing neither right nor left as she crossed the chamber, her purpose of more import than prudence.

As she passed through the portal, a shadow unfolded behind her.

Aleth threw a swift questing glance into the last of the garret rooms. "Brienne?"

To her mind, Brienne had been gone far too long. She returned to the passageway and quickly limped down its length.

Brienne slowed her step on the stone staircase that spiraled to the depths of the keep. Many a torch was missing from its bracket. Only a few blazed in place.

She had ordered the old ones replaced earlier, and such negligence was inexcusable. The steps opened clear to the bottom, a considerable drop even to the first level where the entryway expanded. Clutching the copper box more tightly, she vowed to deal with the servants later and continued her descent.

The sparse light distended her shadow, spilling it down over the stairs before her to clash with the curve of the wall. Brienne paused as she caught the faint echo of male voices, Lyting's and Bolsgar's. Relieved, she began to take another step when she felt the air stir and heard a soft scuffing from behind.

"My God . . . Brienne!" Aleth's scream broke from above as she shrieked a warning.

In the same instant, a shadow rippled over the steps past Brienne. Hands came down hard upon her shoulders, thrusting her toward the open edge of the stairway. She jerked violently away, twisting back to the wall. But her foot met with air and she toppled forward, dragging her attacker off-balance and over the side.

As Brienne plunged full length down the stone, Katla's piercing cry rang in her ears followed by a sickening thud.

Pain exploded through Brienne's head, then all fell to darkness.

Chapter Seventeen

❖ ❖ ❖ ❖ ❖ ❖ ❖ ❖ ❖ ❖ ❖ ❖

THE KEEP ROSE staunch and somber against the evening sky—a welcome sight to Rurik's eyes. Sounding out his call, he pressed his men the last distance. His thoughts quickened to Brienne.

A blare of horns accompanied the baron's return, repeated along the watch points as Valsemé's soldiers drove across the terrain, through the village, and on into the bailey. Grooms, servants, and garrison hastened to greet them. Impatient for Brienne, Rurik quickly scanned the faces, then looked to the steps of the manor house. There, Lyting stood alone, his countenance solemn.

A knot twisted in Rurik's stomach. He detected a guardedness amongst the castle folk. He dismounted slowly, favoring his left leg. Fresh pain fired through his thigh. He set his jaw and willed the discomfort from his face. The gash he bore had been seared but 'twould require little to split it anew.

Striving to hold the limp from his gait, he mounted the stairs. Rurik locked eyes with Lyting, acknowledged him with a curt nod, then entered the manor without word. Surely Brienne awaited him within.

Scarce inside the great hall, he halted, stone-still. Aleth came forth with sober countenance, bearing his goblet.

Rurik rounded on Lyting, dark thoughts riding him. His throat so constricted he could not find voice but demanded explanation through his stormy gaze.

Lyting exchanged glances with Aleth then took a step toward Rurik, proffering a hand. "*Broðir* . . . Brienne, she . . ."

All color left Rurik's face. Without thought, he seized Lyting by the arm. "Where is my lady?" he growled.

"I am here." Brienne's voice fell softly across the chamber.

The three turned as one to see Brienne move with measured pace into the hall. Her hair fell unbound and her robes flowed about her as though she had just risen from bed.

Rurik crossed the space, ignoring the complaint of his leg. Anxiously, he embraced her, drawing her tight against his chest, against the sharp sudden fear that lanced him there, more keen than any blade. Rumbling endearments in a rush of Norse, he buried both his face and hands deep in her hair.

Brienne dragged in her breath under his touch and sought to pull away. Surprised, Rurik drew back and looked down upon her strained features. Alarm lurched through him. Bruises spread into her hairline and blotched her neck. He followed their path and gently eased the gown from her shoulder, uncovering more discolorations.

"By the gods, Brienne, what has befallen you?"

She stilled his lips with her fingers. "Come, love. There is much to tell and your journey has been long. You need to freshen and—"

"*Nei*, I will have it now," he insisted, then cast a steely gaze at Lyting.

Lyting relieved Aleth of the goblet and bore it to Rurik. "Best fortify yourself, *broðir*. 'Tis a disagreeable tale."

Ketil joined the others as they moved to the dais, and Galwinth was called over. Lyting carefully recounted Katla's attack, how she had secreted herself in the keep and attacked Brienne on the open stairs only to be foiled by Aleth and plunge over the side herself.

Brienne's fall had been broken by the curving wall, but still she had tumbled a considerable length down the stone and was struck unconscious.

Katla had been less fortunate. Though she had miraculously survived without breakage of bone, she had fallen full upon her abdomen and lost the child. Galwinth had attended her while Aleth ministered to Brienne.

"Screech she did, and claw at me too," Galwinth charged, round-eyed. "That and more, my lord. When the babe was birthed dead, she cursed your lady, Aleth as well, and vowed revenge."

Wringing her skirt in her hand, the maidservant hesitated, then looked Rurik full in the eye.

"You need know. The babe was not yours, my lord. Katla hid her months well, but her time was far advanced. The babe proved small yet well formed, its hair black, black as a crow's wing."

Rurik's brows rose at her words. Then warm release flowed through him, release from a burden of conscience that had weighed sore heavily upon him these many months. Resting back in the baronial chair, he massaged his temples and forehead.

"Where be Katla now? I need deal with her."

Lyting met him with steady eye. "I cast her out in your name, *broðir*. She is gone. I took her to Valsemé's borders myself."

Rurik held Lyting's gaze for a long moment. The silence became strained.

"*Gott*, good," he breathed at last. "You have done well."

Turning to Brienne, he brought her hand to his lips. "Forgive me, *ástin mín*. I put you at risk by allowing her to remain. Should she have—"

Brienne stroked his cheek. "God's arm is mightier than Katla's, my love. 'Twould seem the Almighty has His own plans for us. She could not thwart His will to keep us as one."

"Nor could the Seigneur d'Esternay." Ketil cleared his throat, drawing every eye to him. "I did as you bade, my lady, and looked to your husband's back, but it cost the Seigneur d'Esternay his sword arm."

Brienne took a sharp breath, shocked that the knight had indeed striven to kill Rurik. Then the last of Ketil's words hit her full force and she paled.

"Rurik was occupied with two Franconians. When Esternay aimed a blow at his back, I righted the matter." Ketil shrugged lightly and downed a mouthful of ale. "I dispatched the affronting limb to the king," he added matter-of-factly. "Charles needs know what treachery is wrought behind his throne."

Brienne squeezed her eyes shut at the image that conjured. Her revulsion quickly passed. 'Twas fitting retribution, and she found quittance in the measure. Dishonor was a far more bitter punishment than death, though death be justly deserved.

"*Merci*, Ketil. You are true friend to us both."

That Brienne had enlisted Ketil to mind Esternay's movements both surprised and pleased Rurik. Now he listened as she related the knight's scheme to regain Valsemé and gave voice to her fears of cumbering him with such deceit whilst he faced the perils of battle. His heart gladdened. Brienne was never part to the knight's perfidy as Katla had charged.

Inevitably, the conversation turned to the clash with the Franconians.

"Esternay's was not the only treachery dealt us," Rurik pronounced, signaling for more wine. "Neustria and Burgundy hold hands with Conrad. They aided the Franconian attack on Creil and then betrayed us whilst making it appear that they joined the king's banner." Rurik smiled crookedly as he stretched out his leg. "They have no qualms about spilling our Norman blood."

"Rurik, you are wounded!" Brienne gasped as she spied fresh blood seeping through his pant leg. "And here you sit gossiping away the hour like an old woman—"

"A *kjerringa*," Lyting supplied, eyes twinkling with a hint of mischief.

"A *kjerringa*, then," Brienne amended. "My medicants are in our bedchamber. Let us see you there so I might tend you and see you to rest."

Rurik flashed her a grin. " 'Tis why I returned so swiftly, though not to rest."

"Rurik!" Brienne colored, sweeping a glance to the others as smiles broke over their faces.

Rurik chuckled, then rose to accompany her from the hall. He rested his hand at the small of her back and commented broadly that he required no assistance.

When they entered their chamber moments later, he booted the door closed before servants could follow though it cost him a measure of pain. His hand dropped to explore the roundness of her backside.

"Rurik, your leg needs tending," Brienne insisted, turning toward him.

Her eyes widened at where this brought his hand. As she opened her mouth to protest, he pressed his palm intimately against her and began caressing her with gentle, rhythmic strokes.

" 'Tis my lust that plagues me the more," he said huskily and claimed her lips, intent on having his way.

The flesh required various ministrations, Brienne thought hazily under his intoxicating assault. She felt her gown part and knew better than to argue with her Norseman.

The last weeks before Michaelmas came and went without incident. The harvest was gathered and the hedges opened to allow the cattle to graze upon the stubble of the fields. In that time, Brienne's bruises faded and Rurik's leg healed under her care. She suspected it remained tender, but he made no complaint.

Brother Bernard arrived back from Rouen but prepared for a quick return to the duke's court and to St. Wandrille's nearby on the Seine, where his cousin had recently been installed as abbot.

During his brief stay, Brienne sought his private counsel to discuss a deepening concern. Since their marriage, Rurik had made small progress in his Christian instruction. Truth to tell, she admitted sadly, he seemed averse to taking the waters of Holy Baptism.

The monk shared her frustration. He promised to confront Rurik on the issue upon his return and press him to honor the baronial vows. Meanwhile, he urged Brienne, should she have need, to send to St. Wandrille's. If he be not there, his cousin would see her message delivered with all speed and discretion.

Early morn, late in the third week, Rurik and Brienne sat quietly at table breaking their fast. A brooding look weighted Rurik's eyes as it had for several days past. Brienne reflected on this as she broke a crust of bread, restraining her impulse to ply him with questions.

The glint of metal caught her eye as he slipped a small round case from his jerkin and turned it thoughtfully in his

hand. Brienne recognized the talisman at once. It did little
for her appetite.

Just then, Bolsgar entered the hall with apparent urgency.
Before he reached the dais, Lyting appeared at the portal,
followed by Ketil. They, too, hastened with purpose before
Rurik.

"My lord, two more oxen were taken during the night,"
Bolsgar spilled out before Rurik could stay him. "That brings
the number to nine. Nine oxen, nine pigs, nine goats, mayhaps as many cocks—males all. By the Mass, where will it
end, my lord?"

Rurik's eyes went to Lyting and Ketil. Something passed
betwixt them. Brienne felt a ripple of alarm.

Clearly, Rurik kept affairs from her. The stock and what
more? she wondered. And what significance lay in the number nine, or in the copper talisman, for that matter?

She studied his profile as he pressed Bolsgar for the names
of the watchmen responsible for the oxen. Then her gaze
drifted to Lyting who listened impatiently. Shadows deepened his eyes, and a pale stubble covered his jaw and chin.
He looked to have gone for nights without sleep. Indeed,
she had missed his presence in the hall these two days
last.

Rurik rose abruptly, interrupting the conversation to adjourn
to less communal quarters. Before he departed, he charged
Brienne firmly to keep from the forest.

Rurik, Lyting, and Ketil rode out within the hour, each
with a small company of soldiers, each driving in different
directions. Rurik left without remark other than to say that
so many animals could not long be kept secreted.

Brienne's nerves knotted up, memories of runes and snake-
skin, of scratchings in the night and watchers in the wood
haunting her. She decided to exhaust her time and ragged
energies in the weaving shed whilst she awaited Rurik's
return. It had been closed up since her fall, the great falcon
left near complete.

As Brienne headed across the courtyard, the young maidservant she had sent to air the shed came back in a rush,
exclaiming that the hut's door had been broken open.

Brienne ran the distance to find the entry yawning wide. Cautiously, she stepped inside, then her hands flew to her mouth. She stood in stunned silence.

The sail hung in shreds on the loom, the Beaumanoir falcon slashed to ribbons.

Brienne withdrew to her chamber and for a time took to her bed.

Aleth sought to becalm her, offering light refreshment, goblets of perry, and gentle conversation. It was not until Waite and Patch appeared below her window, full of antics, that Brienne's mood lifted. Long after they moved off, she remained looking over the grounds, mulling through her thoughts.

'Twas as Lyting said: the offenses committed thus far were affronts as much against Valsemé's baron as his baronne. To the malcontents—whoever, wherever they be—she represented the age-old order of nobility. Thus was she recipient of their misdeeds—the curses upon her brooch and chamber door, and now the destruction of the great sail. But their message was unmistakable: they would not be fettered with the yoke of Frankish law.

She recognized that if Rurik concealed things from her, he did so with reason—no doubt so as not to distress her. The thought warmed her. She trusted Rurik. Trusted him to set the barony's troubles aright. Trusted him to expose the dissenters and deal them a swift, stern justice.

She offered a hope-filled prayer that the greater portion of his men held faithful. Though the original garrison that once served under Gruel Atli, now Rurik, appeared outwardly content, reports reached her on occasion of quarrels amongst the new arrivals. Evidently, some expected Normandy to replicate the North in all its practices.

But this was Francia. Its soil, by any name—Normandy or otherwise—was flesh of the Frankish kingdom. Above all, this was Valsemé, holding of her forebears and of her children to come. She would neither shrink in the face of discord nor shirk duty or calling. *Certes*, she would put on her best and greet her husband cheerfully before all. Let the dissenters mark it well. A Beaumanoir does not cower before adversity.

Fresh energy flowed through Brienne as she moved to her coffer and chose a fine azure gown. She coupled it with a snowy underdress, then bid Aleth bring her bride gift, the golden girdle set with sapphires and iridescent shell.

As she finished robing herself, Waite appeared briefly below her window in search of Patch. Apparently, the furry scoundrel stole off with a tart from the cookhouse, rousted by a severe tongue-lashing and several well-aimed objects. Brienne laughed in earnest. Most likely, the pup was enjoying his booty somewhere under a bush.

The day grew late, and still Rurik and the others had yet to return or send word. Brienne delayed the evening meal, then paced the chamber, her nerves raveling once more.

Aleth soothed her, sitting her down and combing out her long tresses. As she wove them with ribbons, Brienne closed her eyes and allowed her thoughts to drift back over the day.

The morning's events played through her mind—the abrupt arrival of the men in the hall, Bolsgar's and Rurik's exchange, Lyting's exhausted appearance, and Ketil—what tidings didst he bear? Rurik had halted the converse before Ketil could give them voice. Now, Bolsgar's words came back to harry:

"Nine oxen, nine pigs, nine goats, mayhaps as many cocks—males all."

Brienne's brow furrowed. So many animals, but no mention of hounds. Still . . .

She bit her lip as Aleth finished dressing her hair. No need to burden her friend. The last ribbon secure, Brienne admired the creation in a small hand mirror, then she bid Aleth to see the hall readied for supper.

Minutes later, Brienne descended the steps of the manor house and crossed the courtyard in search of Waite and Patch.

After a hurried check round the manor and keep proved fruitless, Brienne progressed to the smithy and stables. When this yielded naught, she pressed on to the various outbuildings, asking those she encountered whether they had seen the lad or pup. Only one recalled the earlier ruckus about the cookhouse. None remembered seeing either since.

As a tide of apprehension welled inside her, Brienne returned to the manor house to check the cellar, a prime place for a boy to tuck himself away with an ostracized pet. Disappointment twined with growing unease. They were not to be found.

Her footsteps carried her fleetly to the kitchens. Too fleetly, she reproved herself. But though she strove to conceal her worry, she could scarce slow her pace.

Of purpose, Brienne delayed this visit till last, knowing the rascally pup would be least welcome here. She would need speak with Waite's mother and fretted on distressing her prematurely, for the woman was heavy with child.

Brienne's presence caused an immediate stir. The servants assumed she came to order the supper served up, or worse, to give complaint or both. To their dismay, she issued no directives whatever. The meal remained held.

Just inside the door, Brienne found Elsie ladling out mustard sauces into bowls. She chided herself for not seeking the girl out straightaway, for the children ever ran together.

"Elsie, I have need of young Waite. Know you where he tarries?"

Her brows puckered. "Down to the village, methinks. Your Patch got away." She wore a mixture of embarrassment and guilt. Brienne wondered what role the sprite played in the earlier incident.

"Can you show me where he might be? Have you children a favored place—somewhere the pup might hide?"

Elsie slowly placed the spoon on the table, obviously reluctant to reveal such a secret.

"Come, Elsie,'twill soon be dark," Brienne prodded more urgently. "We must find them."

At that, Elsie nodded and doffed her apron. Taking her lady by the hand, she led her out of the cookhouse and toward the bailey gate.

As they approached the bridge, Brienne realized that her most immediate challenge lay in convincing the guard to allow them to pass without escort. Rurik most likely had left word that she need be companioned outside the walls, but who could she trust? What was to distinguish a loyal soldier from a dissenter? She would feel safer simply moving amongst the villeins in the village.

Predictably, the guard gave argument, but Brienne cited her own authority in her husband's absence and pointed out that she would be clearly visible from his perch as she and the child were but headed for the church. Not quite an untruth, she thought, and hoped the misstatement earned her no penance in purgatory.

The dour-faced guard relented at last but Brienne felt his keen gaze burning into her back as she crossed over the great ditch and hastened down the road.

"Elsie, to where do we pass?"

"Why, to the church as you said, m'lady." She smiled up and gave an impish wink. Brienne thought she glimpsed herself in that small jest, but years younger. "There be a copse nigh, across the field, behind the building."

Brienne and Elsie slipped around the side of the church that faced away from the guard, hoping it would appear from his view that they actually entered the building. The wood lay a greater distance away than gave Brienne ease, but she hurried as Elsie tugged her along.

As they arrived at a grove of scrubby trees, they shouted out to Waite and Patch. No answer came. Brienne's disquiet returned as they made a thorough search and gained naught but brambles and stickers.

"Where else, Elsie?" Anxiety threaded Brienne's words as she crouched down and caught the girl by the shoulders. "The light fails. Quickly, child, where else might they be?"

Elsie felt her lady's urgency and pointed across the field to the edge of the forest. Pulling from Brienne's grip, she dashed off. "In the glade . . . amongst the berry bushes, m'lady," she called back.

"Elsie! You were told to stay away from there! Elsie!"

Brienne hurried after the child, but the field was fair uneven and its stubble grasped at her dress. She was near upon the wood before she reached the girl and could apprehend her.

" 'Tis not far, m'lady. Please, let me show you. They will be there. You will see," Elsie assured her, wriggling within her grasp.

Before Brienne could decide whether to send back to
the keep for assistance or brave the wood herself, a figure
emerged from the shadow of the forest. She quickly thrust
Elsie behind her as the form drew near and took the shape
of a wizened woman, bent with years.

"Baronne," the crone hailed, quickening her hobbled step.
"Praise the saints that I've found you." She stopped and
cocked her head, seeing the lady shrink back. "Do you not
remember me? I be Gilles the Forrester's wife, from the *cot*
in the glen."

Brienne did not recall her, but she watched as the woman
extended a gnarled finger toward the wood.

"My husband waits there now, my lady. Found a small dog
sore injured. Some devil took a blade to its leg. But the pup's
a scrappy piece. 'Twill allow none near. My Gilles vows it
be yours, my lady."

"What of the boy?" Brienne asked, her heart pounding.

"Boy?" The woman crooked her head, shifting her yel-
lowed eyes behind wrinkled lids. "Ah, I thought to hear a
voice a time ago. Think you he could be hurt as well?" Her
gaze held a curious glint.

Brienne turned to Elsie. "Run to Lady Aleth—quickly!
She will know what to do. Hurry now! We must have help."

Elsie raced off as rapid as the hares. Brienne minded her
retreat for a minute, then turned. Holding rein on her fears
she followed the old woman into the forest.

Dusk wrapped its dim cloak about the wood and obscured
the paths, but the crone picked her way with certainty.
They traveled deeper and deeper into the timber. Lofty trees
loomed dark and silent all about. Too silent, Brienne realized
uncomfortably, fighting back the claws of the underbrush.

"Mayhaps we should turn back and await the others."

"Just ahead, just ahead." The woman pressed on.

The trail narrowed. From somewhere above came the sudden cry of a hawk. To Brienne's horror, when she looked up
she spied several dark shapes circling, wings outstretched, as
they marked some carrion.

"Where be the dog?" Brienne demanded fiercely.

"A mite further, 'tis all."

"You lie. Let us go back."

Brienne turned, but the hag seized her roughly by the arm and shoved her ahead. Brienne struggled, but the woman possessed uncommon strength and propelled her on till they burst into a clearing moments later.

Black bolts of fear ripped through Brienne. From every tree in the glade hung the gutted carcasses of animals: oxen, goats, pigs, sheep, fowl—and some dogs she recognized—their blood still soaking the earth.

A piercing scream rang in Brienne's ear, then she recognized it as her own. The old woman gripped her tight and forced her to look upon the signs of ritual—a triangle stamped out with upright rocks and the crimsoned altar stone.

Brienne's thoughts flew to Waite. Her strength and will surged. She kicked back, catching the woman sharply in the shin. The crone loosened her hold enough for Brienne to tear free and clout her alongside the head, sending the creature to the ground.

Shrill laughter filled the glade and rippled over Brienne. She turned to see Katla step forth from the cover of the wood.

The Norsewoman wore a blue cloak strapped over her bosom and set with stones down to the hem. Strings of amber crowded her neck, and upon her head she wore a wide black hood, cuffed to expose its white catskin lining. In her hand she gripped a staff capped with a gleaming brass knob and set with precious jewels.

Katla continued to laugh as she came forward, but when Brienne's gaze fell to the limp in her gait, the laughter changed to a snarl.

"Highborn bitch! Didst you think to have what is mine? Didst you think yourself a match to *me*, Katla of the Valsgärde?" Her eyes flashed with hatred.

Brienne began to fall back before the Norsewoman's advance, but the old woman shuffled to her feet and grabbed her once more.

Katla's lips curled back in a harsh semblance of a smile. "Better for you to have drunk the *nabid*. Look about you." She gestured to the trees. " 'Tis the ninth year. The year of Festival. Nine of every creature must be sacrificed. But, lo! The rite is incomplete." She leveled a burning gaze at Brienne. "It lacks a human offering."

A deathly chill found the core of Brienne's bones. Pain centered in her breast. "I thought the victims were to be male," she gamed for time. If no persons had yet been killed, then Waite was safe, but she doubted 'twould be for long.

"*Satt.* True." Katla tossed her head, the hood slipping back. "But given that this is Francia and that you Frankish sows have so bewitched our men that they forget their own bright maids of the North"—the look in her eyes held more hatred than Brienne thought possible—"mayhaps the gods won't object because you are a woman. One Frankish whore for nine Frankish bastards," she spat.

"Hold her firm," Katla commanded the hag as she reached for the skin pouch at her hip.

"The coin. You promised coin," the old woman whined.

"When we are done."

"You said naught of killing. The girdle, then. I will have the lady's girdle for my service."

Katla narrowed her eyes over the woman, slid a glance to Brienne's jeweled belt, and smiled archly.

"Very well," she replied all too compliantly. "When we are done, I shall give you fit reward."

She dipped her fingers into the pouch and drew out a wicked-looking spine.

"The Sleep Thorn." The words hissed through Katla's teeth as she held it before her. At the sight of it, Brienne tried to jerk free of the crone.

"Hold her, I say!" Katla snapped.

She cut her eyes from the woman to Brienne, then her lips spread into a malicious smile. "You need rest atime while we prepare you. But do not fret." She stepped to Brienne's side and took hold of her arm. "You will not miss the ceremony."

With a quick thrust, Katla stabbed the thorn deep into Brienne's flesh.

Pain coursed through Brienne's arm to join with the panic that flooded her. Terrified, she twisted round and sank her teeth into the crone's hand. The woman shrieked and released her hold, giving Brienne the moment she needed to shove her to the ground.

Brienne whirled and backhanded Katla across jaw and cheek. The Norsewoman reeled, screeching as she fell back upon the triangle of jagged stones.

Brienne ran, heart and lungs bursting. Ran without looking back, fear providing her with an explosion of energy.

Branch and bramble tore at her. The underbrush blurred. But just as quickly as her vigor flared, it deserted her. Her limbs grew heavy as she fled through the forest, the thorn taking its effect.

Brienne snatched at her arm, wincing as she tried to wrest the spine free. But her fingers slipped on her blood and she could not grasp it firmly. On she stumbled in a sluggish haze, battling back the tangles of growth that rose to block her passage. Without warning, a root trammeled her foot and sent her pitching forward.

For the briefest of moments, Brienne found herself in flight. Then pain sheared through her as she crashed to the ground and plunged down a long incline, toppling head over heels, stone and twig tearing at her, till at last she slammed to a halt in a thicket at the bottom of the ravine.

Brienne lay motionless, wanting to cry out in despair and for the desperation of her plight. If her body was broken, she could not say. There was no pain now, only a numbness that spread through her limbs.

She strained her ear to the rim of wood above and, through trembling lips, prayed that the mantle of darkness and brush would conceal her.

Brienne's thoughts began to slip and her fears dimmed. As the effects of the drug-dipped thorn overtook her, she faintly heard Aleth's voice calling in the forest.

Chapter Eighteen
❖ ❖ ❖ ❖ ❖ ❖ ❖ ❖ ❖ ❖ ❖

BRIENNE MOANED AS she stirred to a groggy consciousness. The dank, rich odors of the earth—bark, leaf, and soil—filled her lungs. Something teased at her cheek. A frond, she thought vaguely, and lifted a hand to brush it away. Fire shot through her arm at the slight movement. Every inch of her felt bruised.

Dragging open her eyes, she met with blackness. High above, a parcel of sky hinted of deepest blue, illumined by the moon's brilliance and seeded with stars. All was silence.

Waite. Aleth. Patch . . . poor Patch. Her thoughts skittered. Was he among the animals slain?

Cold dread writhed through her. She must get to the keep. Find help. Rurik. She needed Rurik.

Brienne pushed herself up, enduring fresh spasms of pain. Her limbs seemed consumed with unnatural fatigue, leaden. She worked them, each movement costing her as a portion of strength returned.

With shaky arms and unsteady legs, she began the steep climb, gripping vines and saplings to drag herself upward. Her feet sank, slipping on the soft layers of earth and leaf.

At times, she stopped to catch her breath, once taking up a branch for use as a cane only to have its decaying wood crumble in her hands. Tears stung her eyes, and she wondered if the Almighty intended her to rot here as well.

Scraped and soiled, with her hair pulled from its braids,

Brienne clawed to the top of the ravine. She lay panting a
moment, then pulled herself to her feet and stopped to lean
against a tree.

Which way to go? She was unsure of her bearings, but
knew that the forest stretched indefinitely in several directions. Her only choice was to return the way she had come,
keeping well away from the glade and hoping to emerge
somewhere near the church.

Brienne swiped the dirt from her cheek and pushed away
from the tree. Time might be crucial for Aleth and Waite, if
it was not already too late.

God all powerful, all merciful, she implored. *Help me
reach Rurik.*

Locating an animal trail, she hastened along its narrow
confines. Branches whipped against her and stung. Her arm
throbbed. Remembering the thorn there, she felt for it, seized
hold, and with gritty determination, drew it out.

On she rushed as fast as she dared and could manage. At
times, she feared the path swung full circle, but with few
alternatives, she continued to follow its track.

When she thought she had retraced the distance she had
fled earlier, Brienne left the trail, praying to avoid the dread
grove. She made her way through the unbridled wood, instinct
guiding her direction.

In a short time, she connected to another trail, one she
hoped would lead her from the forest. Her confidence rose
and she hurried now, less cautious of the crackling of twigs
underfoot, or the sporadic gasps she uttered when assaulted
by briars and brambles.

Abruptly, she wrenched to a halt, then abandoned the
path altogether and sought shelter. Light radiated through
the foliage ahead. Her pulse surged. Mayhaps her instincts
were not so rightly directed. She distinguished voices, male
voices, but Frankish or Norman she could not say.

Brienne crept closer. She recognized that these could well
be the men who perpetrated the lurid, heathen sacrifice, but
she hoped against hope that they were Rurik's faithful soldiers, sent in search of her.

Relying on the shroud of darkness, she advanced near-
er than she knew to be wise. Inch by inch, guarded and

watchful, she progressed toward the light, crawling the last distance to a clump of bushes.

Voices rumbled. Norsemen for a surety and many. Fire crackled against the night. Brienne could nearly feel its warmth. A distinctive odor pervaded the air, but it was not the burnt fragrance of hardwood. More of incense— an indefinable musky scent. A scent she recalled now with alarming clarity. A scent that once lingered about her bed and chamber door.

Hands trembling, she reached out and parted the bushes. Instantly, her eyes encountered the bloodied carcasses still slung from the trees. She sucked in a sharp breath, appalled to discover that she had returned to the site of the sacrifice.

In the clearing before her stood a circle of Northmen, shields in hand, waiting, it seemed, their attention directed to the right of her. She strained forward to mark their interest, then choked back her astonishment at the sight of the Nordic high priest.

He sat imposingly upon a low stool, wearing a great horned helmet. Elaborate nose and cheek guards masked his features. Skins were draped about his shoulders. In his gloved hand he gripped a staff—Katla's staff—with its brass and jeweled crownpiece. Brienne cast a glance about. Katla was nowhere visible.

Suddenly, the Northmen began beating their bucklers in a steady drum. Several men came forth to stand before the priest. Brienne saw now that a large crucifix lay on the ground at his feet. Her eyes rounded wide. It looked to be the very altar cross from Valsemé's church!

The beat of the shields increased. The first of the men strode forward. He solemnly exchanged words with the priest and then, to Brienne's stunned surprise, spat full upon the crucifix and ground it beneath his heel. The second man followed, repeating each action, then kicked dirt over the the cross in parting.

Horrified, Brienne turned away, unable to watch. But moments later the beating ceased. She dragged her gaze back to the grove as the space cleared before her. The men who had desecrated the cross were retreating into the wood opposite her. A dozen more Northmen quit the glade and followed them out, the ceremony at an end.

Brienne huddled in the cover of the shrubs. But in the next moment, her breath congealed as the high priest rose to his feet and turned directly toward her. He threw off his mantle of skins and began to remove his ceremonial helmet. Something gleamed at his chest, catching the firelight. Her eyes fell on the round talisman suspended there just as golden hair spilled from beneath the helmet.

Rurik! She swallowed a strangled moan.

Brienne's heart thundered in her ribs. Swaying with shock, she bit into the back of her hand to stifle a cry of disbelief. Thoughts would not connect as her world careened and crashed on its end.

"Away. I must be away," she whispered to herself with fevered haste, blood pounding.

Brienne scrambled from the bush and stumbled through the darkness. Barely had she begun her flight but she toppled over an unseen obstacle and sprawled atop it. She pressed back frantically, realizing the mass possessed head and limb.

Anguish rent the fiber of her soul as she felt the thin rail of a leg.

"Aleth! Dear God!" she keened.

Tears burned their passage from the depths of her being, scalding her eyes as they tumbled over her cheeks. Shattered, Brienne cradled her friend's head in her lap, then felt the slickness of blood.

Voices sounded from behind, followed by the heavy fall of footsteps and the crunching of sticks.

"I shall avenge you, Aleth," Brienne vowed with a hushed sob, her breast aching.

Gently, she eased the lifeless form to the ground, then stole into the underbrush and fled.

Great agonies of doubt swept through Brienne, ravaging the landscape of her heart and leaving it a barren desert. For a time, she sat doubled over with great racking sobs, then emptied her stomach on the forest floor.

Vile, soulless barbarians! Her father's words harangued her from the grave. *Everything contemptible and base. Northmen be the Devil's excretion. The scourge of God's creation.*

Brienne crawled to a nearby tree.

Deception. All was deception. Her thoughts were in rubble. A pagan kingdom. The Norse intended to establish a pagan kingdom on Frankish soil. They never purposed to meld with her people or uphold their oaths.

She closed her swollen eyes and leaned her head against the tree.

Rurik had returned to his pagan ways. Nay, she corrected. Never did he forsake them. Why did she not foresee this sorry end, knowing he argued his Christian instruction with the monk, knowing he resisted the waters of Holy Baptism?

And what of the others? What of oaths sworn? Such mockery.

Pain stabbed through her head. She could barely press out another tormenting thought. She knew only what her eyes had shown her. Knew only that Aleth was dead.

Brienne pushed herself upward. She must get from this place. The king need be warned. Desperation quickened her thoughts.

St. Wandrille's. She heartened, remembering the monk's words. Though the abbey lay near to Rouen, his cousin, the abbot, could aid her and get word to Brother Bernard. She would take sanctuary if necessary.

Sanctuary. A wave of desolation washed over her. Mayhaps she never should have left it, those many months ago.

As the skies lightened, Brienne emerged from the forest. She gave thanks at the sight of a small holding across the glen. At her approach, she noted that one dwelling sat apart from the others, and quickly headed there.

A short, squarish woman, head kerchiefed with a white cloth and thick ankles visible beneath her hem, stood in the wood-yard scattering grain to the hens.

She looked up as something teased the edge of her vision, then dropped the contents of her apron in a heap at her feet at the sight that greeted her. Stunned, the woman stepped back, oblivious of the flapping of wings and pecking of beaks.

Her eyes grew huge, straining in their sockets, as she stared at the Baronne de Valsemé, white-faced with exhaustion, her fine dress soiled and tattered, her hair snarled and loose to her waist.

The woman hurried to assist the lady, thinking she looked ready to swoon. With as much haste as could be allowed, she guided the baronne inside the mean hut and sat her down. Bringing water and cloths, the woman proceeded to cleanse the baronne's face, neck, and hands, observant of the many scratches she bore.

"Ease yourself, my lady. I shall fetch my husband from the fields," the woman said in a rush, setting out a thick slab of bread and bowl of hot broth.

"Nay!" Brienne seized the woman by the arm, her look haunted. Like as not, the man was Norse. She struggled a moment, then took hold of herself. "Nay," she repeated more gently, releasing the startled woman.

Brienne raked a shaky hand through her hair. She had no wish to afright the woman. Even if the man proved Frank, should she rave charges against the Northmen, it would serve only to spawn terror amongst the villeins. Above all she must reach St. Wandrille's. Salvation lay with the king.

"I need only rest atime. My horse didst but throw me," she fabricated. "I shall require another."

"A horse?" the woman gasped, abashed, for she owned no beast that would befit a lady. "Let me send to your lord husband, baronne. You look to have wandered the forest this night."

"You know me?" Brienne's eyes cut to the woman, unease flooding through her.

"Of course, my lady. I didst see you in the neighboring vill this summer whilst you and Lord Rurik convened the *mallus* there. Such a splendid lord. Surely he searches for you even now." To her surprise, tears trickled over the baronne's cheeks, and she looked away.

The woman sank to her knees and took the baronne's hands in her own. "My lady, you are ill. Sleep awhile. I shall send for—"

"Nay!" Brienne's grip tightened on the woman's fingers. "Tell no one I have been here. Do you understand? I command you."

Brienne's agitation mounted. Her thoughts scattered. She

could not conceal her presence for long. 'Twas too dangerous to stay. Too dangerous for all. Once it be known what she witnessed . . . Her eyes riveted on the woman.

"If there be a nag or mule or anything with four legs that I might ride, I pray you bring it," she ordered with urgency. "Then lead me to a track that will bear me north. I must reach St. Wandrille's." Brienne wished to recall those last words as soon as they were out, reproaching herself for having revealed the whole of her destination.

"As you will, my lady," the woman replied cautiously, as though she thought Brienne to be unsound. "Our only mount is a bit of a scrag, but it should bear you, methinks. There be a road the merchants use to haul their goods, neglected as any, but it leads to Rouen."

The woman rose and packed scraps of food in a pouch. She then searched through a crude chest and returned with a cowbell and a homespun cloak owning a deep hood.

" 'Tis unsafe to travel about unescorted. If I cannot 'suade you, then leastwise shroud yourself in this, and if any approach, ring the bell as do the lepers. Even should they glimpse the fine cloth of your gown, no doubt they will grant you wide berth for fear of contagion."

Brienne thanked the woman, touched by her concern and impressed with her cleverness. She waited as the woman brought the mare to the side of the hut, then followed her across the pasture till, at last, they came to a weed-choked road.

"The track ends at the river Seine. When travelers tarry here, they ofttimes complain of the bargemen there. You will need offer them payment, my lady. Best give them the scrag."

Brienne nodded as she fastened the cloak and adjusted its folds, regretful that her visitation should leave the woman that much more impoverished. Her hand brushed the jeweled girdle. Gazing down on it, a profound sadness wrapped itself around her heart. Rurik. Her life. Her love. Love treasured. Love betrayed.

Does not love transcend all? Aleth once asked.

Mayhaps not all, dear Aleth. Not all. Slowly she unclasped the belt and pressed it into the woman's hand.

"My lady, nay—"

Brienne refused the woman's efforts to return the girdle..

"You have aided Valsemé and Francia this day more than you know. Take the belt and pray for me." Tears clogged her eyes and throat. "And pray for my lord baron," she whispered.

Joyless, Brienne led the nag down the derelict road and out of sight.

The woman stood astounded, belt in hand, as Valsemé's baronne passed from her view. Dropping her gaze, her eyes rounded as she more fully examined the piece. She clutched it tight and ran back across the meadow, beyond the hut, and out to the fields where her husband labored, turning the fallow.

Thrusting the gem-studded belt at his chest, she poured forth the incredible story.

"She be not right of mind," the woman contended excitedly. "Fell from her horse, she said. On her head, I'll wager. I couldst not hold her here. She took that seedy animal and handed me this!"

The man doffed his soft cap as he took the girdle, then whistled low over its precious gold links and costly stones. His eye ranged to his wife then back to the wealth that lay in his hands.

Little did he understand of the ways of nobles and great lords. He did understand that since coming to Valsemé his stomach had been full and he had been dealt with fairly. The baron was a just man. Rightly, he should apprise the lord that his lady wandered ill about the domain.

He hefted the belt in his hand.

But he also understood the value of the girdle. It could afford him many comforts in Paris. Indeed, a new life.

Chapter Nineteen
❖ ❖ ❖ ❖ ❖ ❖ ❖ ❖ ❖ ❖ ❖ ❖

BRIENNE FELT HER ribs jar apart as the scrawny beast bore her along the rutted pathway. She would favor walking didst her feet and legs not pain her so. Even now their muscles threatened to cramp.

When she could bear it no longer, Brienne slid from the animal's back and led it from the road into a shallow cover of wood. Earlier, when a lone rider overtook her by surprise, she realized the need to conceal herself at every turn.

A faint smile crossed her face, remembering the man's expression as he took in her garb. She did no more than burrow into its coarse folds and clang the bell twice. 'Twas enough to send the man wide and speed him down the track, cursing each gouge and furrow that delayed him.

Brienne settled herself with a chunk of rude bread that she found in the pouch, unsure whether she possessed the energy to chew it. Bone weary, her head nodded as she sat resting.

With a jerk, she snapped back awake, the dull rumble of hooves reaching her ears. They sounded from the direction she had just traveled. Brienne scrambled to her feet and pulled the nag deeper into the timber. Anxious the mare would call out to the others, she foraged in the pouch for the fruit she remembered there, then gripped the reins tight.

Erelong, a small force of soldiers tramped past. She spied them imperfectly through the lace of leaf and branch, but their shouts marked them as Norse. Brienne shuddered as she plied the beast with bits of an apple and clutched the harness. Though the road might lay in neglected disrepair, 'twas by no means forgotten or untrod. Plainly, it served the ducal court at Rouen. She would need exercise all the more caution for that. At last the troop moved on, unsuspecting of her presence.

The hours crawled past, and Brienne and her sorry mare pressed north. The road stretched mercilessly before her, yet she progressed without incident. For that she gave thanks.

Toward dusk, the nag caught the scent of water. Brienne allowed the horse its head and soon found herself at a breach in the forest where a creek tumbled over a rocky course.

Wearied and worn beyond measure, she refreshed herself with the tingling waters and drank long of it, as did the mare. She then climbed the gentle slope, drawing her mount a fair distance into the sheltering brush. After she secured the nag and heaped leaves into a small pallet, Brienne curled up within her mantle, utterly benumbed, and fell into a dreamless sleep.

The smell of roasted meat tickled Brienne's nose. She lay very still as she eased her eyes open in the pitch-darkness and listened to the low murmur of men's voices. Quietly, she pressed herself to her feet and edged down the incline. A campfire flickered past the brink of wood. She stole closer, secreting herself behind the expanse of an oak.

In the clearing, she observed two robed figures. One moved to crouch on a spit of sand by the water's edge and fill a skin. The other sat enveloped in cloak and cowl, facing the fire with his back to her.

Brienne felt warmth pour through her. They looked to be monks—or pilgrims, perchance. She began to step from her cover but hesitated as a third man came into view and stood before the one seated. He was uncommonly tall and she thought to see a flash of metal at his hip. A moment later he pushed the hood from his head.

Brienne flattened herself against the tree, her heart vaulting to her throat. The man's face was a mass of scars, his skull baldpated, one ear sheared off.

"Brigands!" Brienne breathed.

Swallowing her fear, she withdrew into the swamp of darkness and hurried from the place.

*   *   *

The great Seine posed a far more dangerous challenge than passage of its broad, winding depths and ever shifting currents. The crossing point was dominated by three fierce-miened bargemen, Norsemen all.

Brienne regarded them from a distance, her every nerve aquiver. She realized at once that she could not shield herself with the cloak and bell, for she would never win transport. 'Twas more than likely they would drive her from the place under a barrage of stones and the threat of sword.

With tense fingers, she folded away the sorry disguise, then tried to smooth the tattered folds of her once fine gown that marked her nobility. Mayhaps if they understood her relation to their duke, they would deal her no harm. Her husband was, after all, Rollo's blood kindred as well as his baron. She fully intended to exploit every advantage that offered.

Mustering her last ounce of courage, Brienne proceeded toward the quay, dredging her sparse Nordic vocabulary for the words she required.

The Northmen watched her approach through wary eyes. One started forward, a slow grin spreading over his face as he surveyed her contours. But a second stepped in his path and halted him with an outstretched arm. A hint of recognition tinged the second man's eyes.

Brienne steeled herself and continued under the weight of his scrutiny. At her approach, he greeted her in broken Frankish, his grasp of the language as limited as her own of Norse. The man listened without comment while she framed her tale. Again came the look of recognition.

A dark presentiment stretched through Brienne as she recalled the troop of soldiers that passed her along the road. Conceivably, they searched for her. If so, they would have alerted the rivermen. Brienne blanched. These men might intend to hold her there.

A sense of urgency gave her strength. 'Twas imperative she reach St. Wandrille's and claim sanctuary. Emboldened with need, Brienne decided to deal with the men straight on. She made no pretense that she traveled to Rouen but made it plain she sought passage to St. Wandrille's.

Surprisingly, the man did not oppose her transit or argue her destination. He refused, however, to accept the nag in payment. When his gaze went to the gold on her finger, Brienne's temper flared. Despite all that had gone before, deep in her heart she could not relinquish her marriage ring. 'Twas odious he should seek it.

Brienne clenched her fingers into her palm and reproached the man. He stepped back, blinking in the face of her onslaught. Through gestures and broken sentences, he declared that he would transport her without charge. He simply did not want the nag.

Brienne calmed herself, a trifle embarrassed. She vowed ample recompense in Rurik's and Rollo's names if he would deliver her to the shores near St. Wandrille's. Double if he could scratch out a map that would take her directly to the abbey steps.

The man agreed, obviously envisioning rich reward from duke and baron alike. Brienne did not fret over her deception. No doubt he would head straightaway to Rouen to barter his knowledge for coin. But, in fairness, she insisted on leaving the nag. The Norseman little realized the beast's value, or the great price at which she had made its purchase.

The passage downriver lasted well over an hour. At Brienne's insistence, the bargeman set ashore a safe distance from the abbey's normal avenues of traffic. Once they disembarked, he traced a map in the damp soil, detailing a short route through the woods. It would bring her to the Fontenelle Valley where the monastery lay.

Brienne committed the directions to memory, undoubting of its accuracy. Norsemen, after all, knew well the road to St. Wandrille's. They had devastated it ofttimes enough.

Late in the afternoon, Brienne emerged from the forest path to discover herself in the little vale of Fontenelle. She near cried for joy. At its heart rose the centuries-old monastery, staunch and sound. Relief renewed her energies as she hurried across the clearing.

Blessed St. Wandrille's! Who had not heard of it? She quickened her pace. Famed throughout the ages as a center of learning, its library was renowned. Home to the saints—

Einhard and Ansegise amongst them, laboring long for the emperor, Charlemagne.

As she advanced across the open field, she imaged St. Wandrille himself as he first toiled there, freeing the land of root and stump, easing her flight this day to his abbey door.

But her cheer dampened as she approached the ancient enclosure walls. Something chafed at her, an odd, unsettling feeling. She paused to peruse the empty terrain that surrounded the monastery. There was no life there. All lay stark and forsaken, vacant of human, beast, or vine. Where wondrous vineyards once flourished, the fields now lay untended. A few blackened stakes survived, rising like grave markers over the ruined tillage, mourning the Northmen's destruction.

'Twas said the holy monks returned to St. Wandrille's and restored it. Yet as Brienne stepped through a side entrance in the thick wall, she wondered whether they secluded themselves within or had abandoned it afresh. She evidenced no sign of man. Was there none to aid her in her plight?

As Brienne passed out of the portal, she came to a standstill, realizing 'twas no portal at all. Slowly, she turned back and saw that a portion of wall had been demolished. Again, she turned. Rubble was everywhere, segments of stone great and small lay scattered over the grass.

She proceeded down a path amongst the smaller service buildings, all roofless shells, many half standing. The wooden structures had been torched long ago, though their foundations remained. As she verged on the cloister she found much of it despoiled. One arm of the colonnaded portico upheld naught but the cloudless sky. The grand abbey church, to which it led, stood charred over much of its side. Whether 'twas further defiled, she could not immediately judge.

Brienne wished to weep over the wreckage. The fragments of St. Wandrille's illustrious past lay at her feet. Her anger deepened and flamed her loathing and revulsion.

Norsemen! 'Twas a race that thrived upon death and destruction. Couldst they do naught else but blood their swords? How many of Wandrille's gentle sons didst they run upon their blades? How much holy blood was spilt and now hallowed these grounds?

Brienne burned with bitterness and fury. The heathens wouldst gut all of Francia if allowed, slaughtering and pillaging and wasting the domain. Long past had they robbed her of everything she held most dear . . . and now, once more. Her gaze dropped to the rust-colored stains marring her skirt where she had cradled sweet Aleth, lifeless in her arms.

They must be stopped! At all costs, their steel must be met and turned lest all of Francia lie in ruination.

A movement at the edge of a nearby building caught Brienne's eye and pulled her from the haze of her choler. A dark-robed figure stepped out upon the path. Immediately, another man followed, taller by a head and wearing the red mantle of a Norseman.

"Dear God, nay!" Brienne started back. "Do not deliver me to their hands again."

She clutched up her gown and ran toward the abbey church as though the demòns of hell were at her heels. Voices called after her, but she drove herself all the harder, desperate to reach sanctuary.

As Brienne gained the first step, her foot skidded on debris that littered the stone and she sprawled forward. White-hot pain seared her arm as it was scraped raw.

Prostrate upon the stairs, she looked to her goal. The heavy square tower frowned down on her and the remaining climb seemed an eternity. But shouts fell near, giving her no moment to dwell upon the distance. The two men drew fast upon her, and now she spied more red mantles.

Brienne thrust herself to her feet, heart pounding as she hoisted her skirts and scaled the course. Her side cramped and her lungs ached, but she forced herself up the last of the steps to the top. Without a backward glance, she rushed for the portal, her objective near gained.

One of the substantial double doors stood open. Confidence welled inside her. The arms of the Lord waited to enfold her. She wouldst not be left beating upon the door, barred at His gate.

As Brienne approached the portal, a figure emerged from the shadowy interior. His large pectoral cross and heavy, unkempt brows marked him at once as Brother Bernard's cousin, the abbot. Elated, Brienne hastened forward. But in the next instant she halted as a second, more imposing figure materialized from the depths of the church, a man powerfully built and golden of hair.

Shocked, Brienne staggered back as her eyes locked with his steel-blue gaze. "Rurik!" she choked out.

Two others issued from the interior of the church—Lyting and Ketil. Those who trailed her now closed behind.

Brienne started to shake violently as Rurik advanced, relief breaking over his features. But she threw up her arms to ward off his embrace, violet eyes flashing as one possessed.

"Pagan cur! Keep your hands from me!"

Rurik went to rock, but Brienne railed on without notice as she frantically entreated the abbot.

"Grant me refuge, father! Do not let him take me! He commits offense against God and king. I saw him. I saw them all . . . performing heathenous rituals in the forest!" She splayed her hands as though she visioned the scene. "Animals . . . strung from the trees all round . . . and the cross . . . desecrated beneath their heels and spat upon."

Brienne leveled an accusing finger at Rurik, though her voice grew anguished. "And he, my lord husband, hast betrayed us more grievous than any other. *He* is their great high priest!"

Stunned, Rurik took a step toward Brienne, but she shrank back, wild-eyed.

"Nay, touch me not! I know what I speak. My eyes didst not deceive. Norsemen are faithless to the fealty they pledge. They heap sacrilege upon their oaths. 'Tis clear they mean to vanquish all of Francia and perpetuate their heinous rites.

"God have mercy upon our souls." Her voice was strained as tears congested her eyes and throat. "The Northmen's hands are drenched with the noble blood of Francia . . . the blood of her sons . . . the blood of my father, my brother . . . and Aleth."

"Aleth?" Ketil burst from his silence. "Naught has befallen Aleth. She is safe at Valsemé."

"Nay, she lies dead," Brienne cried. "I held her in my arms. Her blood marks my gown."

Ketil shook his head with solemn assurance. "Not Aleth, my lady. She led us to the wood in search of you and later bid us Godspeed upon the manor steps when we departed Valsemé. Though"—he hesitated, tossing a glance to Rurik—"we didst find another in the forest. A crone, in the underbrush."

Brienne grew statue still as she compassed his words. The hag. Katla had promised her "fit reward." For a moment, Brienne relived the nightmarish events—her panicked flight, her fall atop the lifeless form shrouded in darkness. 'Twas the thin leg that gave her to believe 'twas Aleth. Yet she misjudged. Aleth lived. What, then, of the other? She witnessed it plainly . . . didst she not?

A terrible silence fell.

Rurik speared Brienne with eyes of steel. Her words cleaved him. In that raw chasm she laid open, his anger gathered like a mounting storm. It rose, building in intensity till it broke through him, sweeping every thought and emotion into the maelstrom of his fury.

"Two days," he began in a low, tightly leashed voice. "Two long, excruciating, torture-ridden days didst I search for you, turning the countryside over and tearing it apart. I am fully acquainted with the grim details of our Nordic sacrifices. My dread for your fate was unspeakable."

Rurik freed the pouch at his waist, his face stony. "Fortunately, there are those Franks who favor living under Norman rule and honor their vows of service. One such villein brought me this."

Brienne watched aghast as Rurik drew her precious gold and sapphire girdle from the bag.

"I clung to the man's words and prayed—*já*, I prayed—to whoever in the heavens wouldst listen. Lyting and Ketil set out with their parties by land, whilst I sailed for St. Wandrille's. You will recall, *my wife*"—he hurled the words as though they were hollow—"water is much faster than land. Ardently, I hoped to find you here in advance of me, safe. If not, I was prepared to uproot every tree betwixt the abbey and the Seine. But it seems my cares were misplaced."

He shoved the belt back into the leather pouch and cast it at Brienne's feet. His features remained sharp and unyielding.

"Your eyes didst not deceive you. I 'played' the great high priest. But didst your trust in me go no further than your sight?" His voice was filled with bitterness and disappointment.

"Dissenters bided in our ranks—as well you have known—men who wouldst forswear my rule and the duke's aiike. They eluded me these weeks past, convening in secret to devise their plans and appease the gods. 'Twas they who raided the stock and carried out the sacrifice in the grove. When you disappeared, I feared they had seized you as an offering to Odin, that I wouldst next find you—"

He did not finish his words, but Brienne saw the pain that lanced his eyes and perceived the anguish he had suffered for her sake.

"I was determined to find you and to root out the malcontents in the doing, once and for all. You might denounce my tactics as ruthless and uncommendable," he stormed on, "but I promise you, they were effective.

"In our search we discovered a store of priestly robes and articles of ritual. I put them on. Every soldier who holds oath of me was summoned to the Grove of Sacrifice. There didst I portray the high priest, declaring my intent to renounce my oaths and return to the old ways. Of those who wouldst join me, I demanded they desecrate the cross."

Brienne's eyes grew huge and her lips parted to speak, but Rurik slashed his hand through the air.

"Didst you think any wouldst refuse to kiss the cross? *Nei*. They wouldst all have embraced it. But even if a man reveres many gods, he will not defile an object he considers sacred.

"Loyalty can be measured in many ways, Brienne." He held her with an unwavering gaze. "Those who honor their fealty to the realm and adhere to their baptismal promises refused to violate Christ's cross. But those who despoiled it were seized at once and questioned till I was satisfied."

Rurik paused and wiped his brow. A muscle leaped along his jaw, warning Brienne that his anger was unabated.

"Wouldst it disappoint you to know that the dissenters proved to be a small group, leaderless save the one who led them in ritual? No priest but a priest*ess*, daughter of a 'baying man' and knowledgeable of the runes. Need I give voice to her name?"

"Katla," Brienne whispered, heavy with remorse. She had dealt Rurik a fierce wrong.

"*Já*, Katla," he growled. "Katla of the Valsgärde. Few knew her origins. She is revealed, though she has slipped from our grasp."

"What of Waite and Patch?" Brienne asked softly.

Rurik's eyes burned into her, as though she held him responsible for their plight. "Found, cowering in the forest. They witnessed much, but they are now safe in Aleth's care."

A gulf of misery washed over Brienne. She took a small step toward Rurik and lifted a shaky hand. But he allowed her no quarter, his furor pitching to full gale.

"Throughout these many months I have striven to be a fair and just lord to *all* the people of the barony, Frank and Norman alike. But no matter how hard I—or my men— strive, you are ever willing to believe the worst of us simply because we are Norse. You preach a loving and forgiving God, Brienne, yet you cling to your hatreds and refuse to open your mind or your heart to my people.

"I require more of a wife." His anger towered about him. "I require her faith and trust of me, despite all. Return to your abbey!" he thundered. "Live out your days there, since you wilt never be able to accept marriage to a man of the North."

Rurik strode to the edge of the steps, then hesitated and turned back to Lyting.

"Since you are so ever ready to serve 'my lady,' you can conduct her to Levroux. Take my longship. 'Twill deliver her there that much quicker. I find I have need to ride out my anger."

Rurik descended the steps, snapping out orders that the horses be brought forth. Ketil and the other soldiers followed.

Brienne remained wrapped in her grief atop the church steps, flanked by Lyting and the abbot. Her eyes darkened with pain as she watched Rurik throw himself up into the saddle. The truth of his words struck deep into her soul.

How wrong she had been. How greatly she had failed him. She held little faith she could ever set it aright.

As moisture collected in Brienne's eyes, Rurik pivoted his horse and signaled his men to ride. In a moment so brief yet so wrenchingly long, he passed through the great arched gate of the ancient enclosure wall and out of her life.

Tears flooded Brienne's eyes till she could no longer see, her chest an aching void where her heart once beat.

"Do you aid me, then?" Katla leveled her gaze over the crackling flames.

The hooded figure returned a glassy stare. "How do you know that she be near or yet unfound?"

"I *know* because Rurik's men continue to scour the country in search of her. I *know*," she said with burgeoning impatience, "because they concentrate their efforts in this region. We must move quickly if we are to capture her. I *want* her taken."

Katla whisked a glance at his two companions standing on opposite sides of the campfire—one disfigured with scars, the other unimpressive—then returned her gaze to the hooded figure.

"I should think you would enjoy the sport." Her lips drew into a sardonic smile. "All of you. Pleasure yourself on the bitch till you tire of her, then sell her as a slave at Hedeby. Whether she goes to the Northern kingdoms or the courts of the East 'tis of no matter, as long as she never returns."

"You surprise me, Katla. I would think you to prefer that I slit her throat." The man smirked as he drew on his cup, taking a mouthful of ale.

"And have her bear but a moment's pain? *Nei!* Brienne Beaumanoir must suffer a lifetime. Let the men use her prim thighs to their contentment, and the women work her till she's haggard and bent and too loathsome to look upon."

"Careful, Katla. Hatreds devour more keenly than lusts, and I know your appetites to be many."

"Do you lecture *me* whilst your own bitterness feeds upon your gut?" Katla tossed her chin defiantly, her delicate nostrils flaring. "I want the bitch gone from these shores. Forever!"

"So you might supplant her as baronne?"

"That and more. I wilt have Rurik."

The man tossed out the remaining drink from his cup but kept all emotion from his face. Katla gloated, knowing she had touched a nerve. Yet he was dangerous when in such humor. She did not wholly trust him.

"Very well," he rasped. "Brienne Beaumanoir will satisfy my purposes." He weighted the words with double intent as he drew his dagger and thumbed its sharp edge.

Triumph spread through Katla's breast. But when she looked back, her smile slackened. The man's eyes had crystallized to icy shards as he sat lost in his thoughts, his look as cold as death.

Chapter Twenty

✖ ✖ ✖ ✖ ✖ ✖ ✖ ✖ ✖ ✖ ✖ ✖

BRIENNE KNELT UNSEEING, unfeeling upon the cold slabs of stone that floored the abbey church. A winter of despair blanketed her heart. Spirit seemed severed from substance.

"My lady. Lady Brienne. Come. You must take nourishment." Lyting enfolded her icy hands within the heat of his own and lifted her to her feet. She met his concern with tear-swollen eyes.

"Oh, Lyting, do you hate me too?"

"Nei." He shook his head with the most tender of smiles. "Nor does anyone else. Least of all Rurik."

Huge droplets rolled over her cheeks. "He must," she denied, her throat aching raw. "The things I said, they were so cruel, so horrid. I wouldst blot them out if words could be recalled. But they cannot, and ever shall they burn in Rurik's heart. He shall never forgive me. Never."

"Cease, my lady. You torture yourself to no avail. 'Twas not Brienne Beaumanoir who spoke, but a distraught young woman who had suffered the outrages of another's madness and survived. You *survived*," he emphasized, "despite untold peril and pain and shock of loss—no less real for being imagined. Within himself, Rurik realizes you were not of right mind. Once he overcomes his anger, he will not only forgive you each word, but lament his own. Then shall he return."

"If only that be true," Brienne said through her tears, "I'd wait a lifetime for him."

Lyting smiled, his crystal blue eyes shining softly. "You won't need to. Rurik will repent his harshness soon enough."

303

Not wholly believing, Brienne's head sank forward, but
Lyting tipped her chin up with a finger.

"Has heart loved that has not grieved? That has not borne
its trials, and shouldered wrongs, or harbored regret? 'Tis
written, in fire gold is tested, and silver, seven-dross refined."
He wiped a lingering tear from her cheek. "Have faith in your
husband, Brienne. He shall come for you."

Brienne touched his cheek. "Lyting. So full of wisdom
and compassion. I have erred in much."

"Enough." Lyting drew away her hand. "Brother Bernard
has arrived from Rouen. He and Abbot Godfrey await us in
the refectory. Come. You need strengthen yourself. Tomorrow is already in God's care."

The thick soup and fragrant monastery bread, drawn fresh
from the oven, brought warmth back into Brienne's bones.
She sat listening to Brother Bernard's chronicles of Norman
court life, with Abbot Godfrey seated to her left at the head
of the table and Lyting to her right.

At one point, Brother Bernard rose at his place across
from her, impassioned as he detailed the duke's many under-
takings. It seemed that Rollo made it a point of honor to
repair the devastation wrought by himself and his marauding
kinsmen over the past century. The banks of the Seine were
currently being reinforced with quays, the riverbed narrowed
and deepened. Marshlands were designated to be built up
and downstream islands linked to the mainland. At Rouen,
the duke planned to endow a magnificent cathedral. This
enthused both churchmen, and they fell to discussion of it
and then to the restorations begun at St. Wandrille's.

Brother Bernard's recountings heaped coals upon Brienne's
conscience. Rurik had been right. Beneath her carefully
maintained exterior as baronne, she held herself apart of
the Normans, preferring to grip tight to old hatreds, ever
willing to believe the worst should doubt arise, and equally
minded to ignore the qualities that recommended them.

Brother Bernard wouldst not approve, she thought dully,
avoiding his gaze. 'Twas his life's mission to "win the
hearts and the minds" of the Norsemen to Christ. They
were "all God's children," he impressed upon her distant
months ago, "the same flesh and blood." She imagined he

would have much to lesson her on the capacities of Christian forgiveness.

Brienne paused, her cup at her lips, as Brother Bernard pushed his bowl to one side and set his goblet before him.

"My child," he began, his gaze a solemn sea of green, "Lyting and Abbot Godfrey have apprised me of all that befell you at Valsemé and here at St. Wandrille's. Let us praise God in His mercy that you are safe, as are the others who await you at the keep."

Brienne's heart contracted. "I afear they wait to no avail. Rurik sends me back to Levroux. He sets me from his side."

"And for how long?" The monk smiled, shaking his head as though he believed her visit there would indeed prove brief. "Meanwhile, Rurik has favored you with the use of his longship. Methinks the rivers wilt provide the safer transport," he added mysteriously.

Brother Bernard's wayward brows drew together. "I have other news you must bear. Rumors abound that Hastein has returned to Normandy."

Brienne lost what color she possessed, and Lyting stilled.

" 'Tis said he travels with two companions. One is Kalman the Hebridean."

"Kalman One-Ear?" Lyting frowned.

Brother Bernard nodded. "The same. They travel in disguise, changing often, I expect. But Kalman is a distinguishable creature with his scarred face and shining pate."

The earthen goblet slipped from Brienne's fingers and crashed to the floor.

"God forbear! I encountered them on my journey here, south of the Seine. They were dressed in churchmen's robes. I came upon their campfire."

"Sweet Virgin, Brienne! Didst they harm you?" Alarm tore at Lyting's eyes.

"Nay, I was well hidden in the forest. One sat with his back to me, hooded. But the two others were visible enough. When I saw the scarred man I thought them to be brigands and fled." She turned anxiously to Brother Bernard. "But why does Hastein risk returning to Normandy when he is marked for death?"

" 'Twas ventured at court that he would seek Rollo's pardon. But thus far he has dispatched no messengers nor issued any appeal." The monk rubbed his bristly chin. "Hastein is a simple man, governed by simple passions. If he deems himself wronged, naught will change his mind."

" 'Tis true." Lyting leaned forward. "Hastein is one to fixate upon his grievances. He wouldst return for but one thing. Revenge."

Brienne bolted to her feet, legs quaking. "Then he seeks Rurik!" she cried. "And because of me, Rurik rides south to Valsemé and into his snare."

She rounded on Lyting, violet eyes desperately pleading. "I love Rurik above life itself, though sorely have I failed him. Help me set it aright. I beseech you. Ever have you pledged to aid me. Then do so now, Lyting. *Now!* We must warn him, lest it be too late."

Lyting rose at once. Looking down into her tortured face, he knew she would not be left behind. He turned to Abbot Godfrey who had sat in silence throughout the entire discourse.

"We shall need mounts. Rurik left with my own. Can you arrange for two?"

The abbot's heavy brows slashed straight upward, and he shuffled to his gaunt height, which left him shy of his cousin by two inches.

"We have no better than Bernard's nag, but we can get you to nearby Caudebec by wagon. Swifter horses can be had there."

"So be it." Lyting slipped his sword partway from the scabbard, examined it, then thrust it back. "Let us be away."

Rurik watched the firelight splinter red and gold into his wine. He swirled the liquid round the cup and lifted it to his lips.

"Females!" Ketil huffed as he stretched his legs toward the campfire. "They're a thorny lot, with enough tongue in their heads to beshrew a man."

He rolled an eye toward Rurik to garner the effect of his words. "Well, if God had to bestow that member upon them, leastwise there be the convents to shut them in. No man need be fettered with a fitful wife. There's nectar aplenty to gather from the other fair blossoms of Francia."

Ketil replenished his drink and waited, but Rurik continued to sit without comment. "Of course, some value a woman with mettle. Not Valkyrie fierce, mind you, but with spirit and courage. And should she possess great beauty as well . . ." He let the thought trail away. "Some wouldst overlook much for such a prize."

"And some wouldst keep their tongues in their head if they mean to keep it!" Rurik snapped sourly.

Ketil shrugged and drew on his wine, the corners of his mouth spreading upward beneath his whiskers.

One soldier headed from the line of horses and approached the fire. But at Rurik's surly look, the man hesitated and diverted his gaze to Ketil. Bewildered, he gestured to the horses, still saddled and awaiting the baron's orders. Ketil raised and dropped his brows. He could offer no encouragement that they wouldst soon press on or pitch camp. Rurik remained as restive and bearish as he had throughout the day.

After leaving the abbey, Rurik drove the men hard to the river, but once there, he changed his mind and set west for Lillebonne. Halfway to their destination, he reversed himself again and turned east for Rouen. An hour outside the city walls, he ordered a respite. Darkness fell. Fires were built. And now the moon filled the sky like an amber plate. And Rurik sat bedeviled, his cup yet brimming with its first fill of wine.

Ketil expelled a wearied breath. Young bucks! Pride fighting with heart. Why not shut his wife up in his own tower until he couldst decide his mind, rather than some distant monastery? 'Twas only a matter of time before he'd be taking the door from its hinges to have her. Meanwhile, they couldst all rest easier at Valsemé. And for himself, there wouldst be the added pleasure of Aleth's company.

Rurik stared into the gamboling flames, his face fixed in solid lines. Anger had blunted his senses long ago. Why, then, this throbbing ache in his heart?

Had he traveled the world to its ends, won fame upon his sword, amassed riches, and ruled men to be unmanned by

the tongue of one woman? And then exist half whole for the
want of her?

He dropped his gaze to glower into his cup. As though
some deep-seated desire conjured her, Brienne's image took
form upon the wavering surface. Rurik clenched both jaw
and cup. But try though he might, he could not hold on to
his anger. Deep inside, the truth gnawed at him. He was a
fool to let her go.

Even whilst she raged, he knew 'twas anguish and exhaustion that spoke. But he had allowed her words to bite. Anger
answered anger. He released the fears he had borne for two
days, and heaved back the pain she inflicted. Fool again.
Naught had been the same since he had spurned her upon
the steps of St. Wandrille's and stormed from her side. Nor
would it be, so long as they were apart.

Blood began to pound through his veins as will forged
action. Whatever grievances Brienne held against his people,
she wouldst have to come to terms with them. Above all, she
was his wife. *His!* If he had to keep her under lock forever,
he meant to have her back!

Rurik suddenly thrust himself to his feet, startling Ketil as
he tossed down his cup and hastened toward the horses. The
soldiers stirred to motion, alert that their lord was about to
alter their course once more this day. One rushed to untether
the baron's steed and bring it forward.

Wordless, Rurik leaped into the saddle without touching
the stirrups, seized upon the reins, and rode off at full gallop.
The others scrambled to mount, but by the time they were
horsed, he had far outdistanced them.

Rurik leaned into the gray and rode with the wind. Lyting's
courser was smaller than Sleipnir but swifter. He should
reach St. Wandrille's easily before night's breaking, before
his brother set out with Brienne for Levroux.

He took heart. Brienne might not accept him as a Norseman,
but she ever loved him as a man. Their passions had been spent
in every corner of the barony. So wouldst they be again, till
"Frank" and "Norse" no longer mattered, till heart and flesh
melded to one.

Rurik spurred the horse on. It lengthened its stride, churning the earth beneath them. Against the fiery moon, he

thundered the gilded road, outpacing the others and leaving
them to trail far behind.

Brienne clung to rein and saddle as she raced alongside
Lyting over the moon-washed road.

The Caudebec steeds were strong and stouthearted, but the
ill-kept roads beleaguered their efforts. Fear and impatience
abraded every nerve. If only she could sprout wings to fly!

The boathouse at the quay came into view, illumined
by the soft spill of moonlight. Lyting shouted out for the
bargeman as they pulled their mounts to a hasty halt. The
warming fires lay cold by the river's edge. No one appeared.
Lyting flung himself down and disappeared into the hulk of
the building. He emerged a moment later, dark-faced and
somber.

"The man's throat has been slit," he said tautly, throwing
a brisk glance about before hurling himself into the saddle. "We must not linger here. Another crossing point lies
downriver."

They wheeled their horses from the boathouse but had
gone no farther than a league when the shadowy forms of
two riders descended from a cover of brush and blocked their
passage.

Lyting's sword flashed from its scabbard. "Behind me, my
lady!" he commanded Brienne.

Laughter, dark and rasping, grated against the night.
Hastein's eyes gleamed in the black depths of his cowl.

"*Broðir*. 'Tis a surprise to find you here and in possession of what I seek. Does all Normandy lust after this
woman?" His companion shared in another spate of laughter.

Lyting uttered something akin to a growl, deep in his
throat, but did not answer. He steadied his blade, ready.

"But, come! I have little quarrel with you, Lyting. We
can share her, can we not?"

"Rot in hell, Hastein," Lyting snarled.

A smile spread, hard and narrow, over Hastein's face,
curving upward to colorless eyes. A serpent's smile, Brienne
thought with panic as she struggled to control her horse.

Hastein pushed back his hood. "I cautioned you long
ago never to cross me, little brother. But of course Rurik

was ever there to interfere, shielding you till you grew into your strength. How much of a man are you now?" Hastein taunted, eyes glinting. "Come. Let us test your steel and see who takes the woman."

Hastein's sword arced from his side as he heeled his horse forward. The beasts collided. Steel rang out on steel. The second man joined them, heaving his blade, and together with Hastein, the two hammered down on Lyting.

Stroke upon stroke, Lyting met their blows. But he was hard tested, for even saddled, Hastein was like a eel, swaying and dipping, drawing Lyting's sword so as to open him to the other's strike.

Brienne groped for her small eating dagger, then remembered she had none. She was helpless to aid Lyting in the least of ways.

Hands suddenly seized her about waist and hip. Brienne cried out in terror as she looked down into the Hebridean's grizzled face. But before he could dislodge her, the horse reared, startled by the attack. Kalman stumbled back. As the beast's hooves returned to earth, he lunged once more.

Brienne whipped the reins across Kalman's seamed face. He flinched not at all but grinned the wider and dragged her from the horse. Throwing her to the ground, he sat astride her and bound her hands. For a heart-stopping moment he reached for the fabric covering her breast and she thought he meant to tear it away. But Hastein's curse drew his attention to the fray. He muttered something indistinguishable to her on foul breath, then drew a blade from his belt and fixed it between his teeth. Still grinning through the bank of scars, he rose and swung up on her horse.

Brienne struggled to gain her feet, but as she won her knees, she was shoved down again. Nails dug deep into her arms. Roughly, the hands jerked her upright and forced her to sit back on her legs. A cold blade pressed against the bare flesh of her throat. Bracelets clinked, followed by Katla's contented laughter.

Brienne looked on with horror, unable to move or call out. Lyting's pale head, shining in the moonlight, marked him all too well amongst the other dark forms. Blades angled and glanced, parried and thrust. Lyting turned blow after blow

with hardly a breath to strike his own. Hastein's companion
surged forward, raising his sword a fraction too long. Lyting
caught him straight on, slicing deep to the bone then up and
out. The man screamed, his arm falling useless to his side,
but he clung to his saddle with the other.

The measure cost Lyting, opening him to Hastein's blade.
He pitched low, barely missing the slash of steel, but its tip
caught his cheek and laid it open. As he came up again to
deflect the next blow, Kalman advanced from behind and
to the right. About his shiny head he swung three chains
suspended from a rod and weighted at their ends with iron
claws. The broadswords clanged as they met and locked.
But as they scraped free, the chains lashed around Lyting's
wrist, entrapping his sword arm. With a mighty yank, the
Hebridean hauled Lyting from his horse and hurtled him to
the ground.

Lyting rolled with the fall and sprang immediately to his
feet. Miraculously, his sword lay several paces away. He
dove for it but came up amidst a tangle of hooves as Hastein
and the others crowded their beasts round him.

Metal flashed and sang out. Brienne's pulse throbbed
against the knife's blade as she lost sight of Lyting. She
needed no great training of warfare to know he was sorrow-
fully disadvantaged afoot beneath sword and hoof.

Then Kalman's broad movement drew her eyes. In one
long motion that branded itself in heart's memory even as
it was wrought, the Hebridean grasped the dagger from his
teeth, arced it high overhead, and plunged it into Lyting's
back.

"Lyting!" Brienne shrieked from the depths of her agony.
She struggled in Katla's hold, pressing against the blade
till she felt its sting and the warm trickle of blood on her
throat.

Lyting pitched forward upon the ground. Still they slashed
at him. Brienne sobbed, cursing them. Cursing her helpless-
ness. When at last they ceased, he lay motionless. Even in
the dim light, she could see that his beautiful snow-pale hair
was bathed in blood.

Hastein dismounted to stand spraddle-legged over his brother. " 'Twas your bane that Ranneveig's blood flowed through

you," he panted. "And a greater curse that you so strongly resemble her firstborn—the one I truly seek."

He bent and wrested the knife from Lyting's back. Wiping it on his thigh, he then hefted it to Kalman.

Hastein's glassy eyes drew to Brienne.

"Bring her," he snapped. "We ride for Fécamp. There my longship lies moored. We'll sail for the Faroes and wait the next turn."

In the clash, Lyting's horse had bolted for the wood. But with Brienne's mount, the troop possessed three. Hastein took Brienne up before him, while Katla climbed behind the wounded man. Kalman rode alone.

"I shall enjoy pleasuring myself on you, my sweet." Hastein caressed Brienne's breasts before taking up the reins. "But I'm willing to wait until Rurik can join us and witness our first coupling."

His dark laughter spiraled behind them as he kicked into the horse's flanks and led the mean band east.

Brienne dared a final glance back. Lyting's still form lay sprawled in the dust. But for the briefest of moments, her eyes played her a trick. She thought that silvered head didst lift itself then bow again to the earth. She blinked away fresh tears. She was wrong, she knew. The form lay as it had, death still, wrapped in a soft mantle of moonglow.

Chapter Twenty-one
❖ ❖ ❖ ❖ ❖ ❖ ❖ ❖ ❖ ❖ ❖ ❖ ❖

RURIK BORE DOWN hard upon the steed, setting a brutal pace. Impatience rode his concern. For a countless time this night, he swore an oath for want of Sleipnir.

He had exhausted the limits of his brother's gray on his rapid return to the abbey. Then, learning of Lyting's and Brienne's departure, he was compelled to secure fresh mounts for himself and his men at Caudebec.

He chafed at the time lost but was rewarded when the stable grooms remembered the couple from the previous hour. Rurik estimated that he could yet overtake them if the horse served well. Still, he wouldst have the black and hold every advantage now that Hastein was back.

Rurik concentrated his thoughts to the crossing downroad and urged the mount on.

The small troop rounded a narrow neck of road, its edges collared with growth. As the course straightened, they beheld a horse impeding their passage. It tarried, steadfast and vigilant, over a bulk in the center of the road.

A shaft of foreboding lanced Rurik. The shape took the form of a man sprawled facedown on the ground. As he closed on the figure, he spied the pale luster of hair.

Rurik hard-reined his mount to a skidding halt and flung himself to the ground.

"Lyting! *Nei!*" he denied on tortured breath as he dropped to his knees.

He reached out, then hesitated to touch his brother. Blood soaked Lyting's back. His clothes lay slashed to ribbons.

Rurik shed his mantle, cursing the craven whoreson who

had wreaked this butchery. He placed the cloak aside Lyting then eased him upon it with infinite care. Beneath Rurik's hand, blood flowed warm. The movement brought a faint, anguished groan.

"*Broðir*," Rurik gasped, astonished that Lyting yet lived. He bellowed for torches and whatever might serve as wrappings.

Without waiting, he looked to the seepage of blood on Lyting's back, its source a vicious gash. With the pressure of his fingers, he staunched the issue.

Ketil hastened to him with a kindled brand while Gyrr and Eirik stripped away their tunics. Another, Gunnar, unfastened his leggings, which he wore in the Frankish fashion, wound with bands of cloth.

Anxiously, Rurik listened for the strength of Lyting's heartbeat. It fell dim but steady. Someone handed him a flask of wine and he set it to his brother's lips. Lyting managed a portion, but most spilled over his chin and down his neck. Rurik swore at himself and blotted the mess, cleansing away blood in the effort.

"*Broðir*, who did this to you?"

Lyting stirred. His lids parted over pain-clogged eyes. When he managed to mouth an answer, it came so faint, Rurik had to bend his ear to catch the words.

"Ha . . . stein."

Rurik started to straighten, but Lyting closed his fingers on the fabric of Rurik's tunic with a feeble grip.

"Bri . . . enne." Each word purchased new suffering. "To Fécamp . . . Rides . . . to Fécamp. . . . Longship . . . Tis you . . . he wants."

Lyting shuddered then as though a chill stabbed through him. Indeed, his hands were like ice, his face ghostly. Rurik worked swiftly, binding his wounds in silent fury. Ketil aided as well, cutting away the bloodied tunic and lifting Lyting when necessary. The slightest movement brought much pain, and Lyting quickly lost consciousness.

" 'Tis better for him," Ketil reassured Rurik.

They finished their hasty ministrations after relieving several more men of their tunics and wrapping Lyting in no less

than five mantles. Rurik rose to his feet without ceremony
and enjoined his men.

"Fashion a litter that will bear my brother to St. Wandrille's
with the least discomfort or jolting. Carry the pallet yourselves
if you must, but don't kill him in the transport!" He pushed his
hair back from his face, worry set upon his brow.

"Give him over to Brother Bernard's charge. One amongst
the churchmen must be able to tend his wounds. My longship
yet lies near the abbey. When Lyting can withstand the
voyage, sail with him to Valsemé and place him in Lady
Aleth's care."

Rurik turned his thoughts eastward. His face hardened in
implacable lines. He cast a glance to Ketil then back into
the dark.

"Choose the two swiftest steeds. Unburden them of packs
and unneeded trappings. Keep our provisions spare. We ride
for Fécamp."

Ketil nodded in brusque agreement and began to stride past
Rurik, but Rurik's hand shot out and trapped his arm. Their
eyes locked. Even in moonlight, Rurik's shone as though of
highly polished steel.

"One thing more, Ketil. Hastein is mine."

At gray dawn, Brienne and her captors galloped across the
vast chalk plains of the Caux toward the cliffs of Étretat.
The raw salt breeze stung her face. Benumbed, she took no
more notice than she did of the occasional clumps of trees
that relieved the monotonous plateau. Only the sea drew her
interest. It stretched bleak and unwelcoming, churning in its
bowels.

"Are we to ride another day without respite?" Katla shrilled.
"I am chilled stiff to the bone and wolfish with hunger. Have
a care, Hastein. We stop, or I'll warm myself as I roast your
liver and feast on it as well!"

Hastein laughed at her threat, then ran his gaze along the
jagged coastline where the cliffs dropped dramatically to
the sea. Little of the shore was visible from their elevation.
The tide swelled high and angry, blunting its temper against
rock and sand.

"There—we'll halt by the wood." He pointed to an outcrop

of trees sprouting in monkish solitude from the yellow marl.
"Be quick with your fires. We'll not bide here long. Fécamp
lies another hour north."

Hastein led the party toward the break of timber, drawing
Brienne's mount along by its reins. She clung to the saddle's high front, her hands bound before her, and strove to
maintain her perch. Strove to purge the latest horrors from
memory—so much blood spent in one day's passing.

After the bitter attack in which Lyting was slain, they had
ridden at a heated gait along the Seine to Lillebonne. There,
they turned north and east to press seaward. At a merciless
pace, they traveled through hillside and valley till one mount
misstepped and fell lame.

Hastein's anger overtook him, and he slew the beast in a
most pitiable way. Later, 'twas his own man who delayed
him, white-faced and faint for loss of blood. Lyting's blade
had hewn deep and wide. With so much constant jarring,
the wound was impossible to keep staunched and bound. In
the end, Hastein dealt the man the same fate as the horse,
though swifter.

New mounts were acquired as they renewed their flight,
four in all. Their owner was sharply displeased with the
transaction, which left him with two hard-spent animals and
at a loss for the others. Now he, too, was unable to argue the
matter. Brienne closed her lids against the gruesome details.
God's mercy, the hours ran red before her eyes.

Hands trapped her waist and her eyes flew open as Hastein
caught her down from the saddle. Brienne tried to twist from
his hold, but he grasped her the tighter and dragged her to
where Katla massed a small pile of kindling. He dropped
her there, then strode restlessly toward the edge of the cliff
and onto one of the needlelike projections that overhung
the sea.

Kalman tethered the horses then came to squat before the
smoldering twigs. Displacing Katla, he coaxed them to an
unsteady blaze and ordered Brienne to feed it with sticks.
The flames battled for life against the damp wind, but their
warmth felt good against her hands. Katla set cups of wine
to heat by the fire and withdrew a round of *flatbrauo* from
her pack.

Hastein soon rejoined them, taking the offered bread and wine from Katla's hands as he settled himself beside Brienne. She cringed at his nearness and would not look on him. When he proffered the drink at her lips, she jerked her head aside, repulsed by the thought of sharing his cup. Bemused, one half of his mouth stretched into a leering smirk.

" 'Tis an arduous crossing to my island. You will need nourishment, my sweet." She continued to avert her face. "If not for me, then for Rurik. You do not wish to look haggard when he comes in search of you."

"Rurik? What are you saying?" Katla bit out tersely, pausing as she reached for her wine.

Hastein drew a knee up and tore away a portion of bread with his back teeth. His eyes gleamed with satisfaction as he chewed the piece.

"Rurik knows I have his precious wife, or will soon enough. I have left a wide, unmistakable path, and comment in enough ears at Lillebonne to direct him to me. Didst you think I paused there for naught? No matter. Rurik knows of my stronghold in the Faroes, though he's never breached its shores." Hastein withdrew his dagger and watched the sky's light reflect along its smooth length of steel. "When he comes, my men and I shall be waiting with our welcome."

Katla so paled that her skin appeared translucent. Veins stood out clearly along her temples. Then her eyes grew fierce and emerald hard.

"Naught was said of this! 'Tis Brienne I wish to be rid of, none other."

"Foolish bitch! Do you think your petty jealousies mean aught to me? Rurik is the one I crave. Only his blood shall quench my blade."

Hastein shoved himself to his feet, paced away, then turned back.

"Long have I waited for this day," he growled on rasping breath. "*I*, Atli's firstborn, shall have my due. And Ranneveig's dropping shall have his."

Hastein plunged the knife back into its scabbard as though he stabbed someone there. He cut a glance over Katla.

"Do not dream long on winning him to your arms and gaining title as the next baronne. Look not in my direction either," he added with a mocking smile. "I heartily doubt Rollo wilt offer the barony to me. But then, I shall have all that I desire—Rurik's head, spitted above my gate."

An anguished cry escaped Brienne, and she dropped her face to her bound hands, unable to bear more.

"Do I distress you, my lady?" Hastein moved to stand above her. "But be consoled, Rurik dies for love of you."

He leaned over and sank his hand into her hair, fisting it at the nape and forcing her to look up at him.

"Because of you, my beauty, will he hunt me, bedeviled to gain you back. Because of you will he forgo caution and prudence and be all the more vulnerable. His passion for you is his weakness. He'll come willingly into my snare. And I'll be waiting," he hissed. "Waiting to cut him down."

Heart filled with loathing, Brienne spat full in Hastein's face. She half hoped he'd be done with her then, but he only yanked her head back the harder. She winced, certain the hair would pull from its roots.

"Such spirit!" he rumbled with perverse amusement as pain marred her brow. "I shall enjoy mating you, my sweet. But I'd advise that you not provoke me. There are many ways to kill a man. 'Twill go worse for Rurik if you anger me."

He ravaged her lips, crushing one breast beneath his callused hand. Just as abruptly, he released her, and she fell back hard upon the ground. Straightening, he gazed down on her and uttered something akin to a laugh. Then he stalked away to the cliff's edge and looked out over the sea, wrapped in his dark thoughts.

Sullen, Katla rose, then gripped Brienne by one arm and forced her to her feet.

"Where do you take her?" Kalman demanded.

"Where eyes cannot pry. I need relieve myself, idiot, and no doubt so must she. If I must be shackled with her, then she must come now. I'll not trouble myself again."

Katla pushed Brienne ahead of her to the cluster of trees where the horses stood tethered. Proceeding to the opposite side, she thrust Brienne to her knees amidst the sparse cover of brush and bared a small dagger from her waist. Brienne gasped, but the Norsewoman threw a hand across her mouth and held it firm.

"Listen, bitch, and listen well. Rurik is a dead man—a dead man, do you hear?—as long as Hastein holds you."

Katla cast a quick glance through the thin shield of wood, espied the men, then turned back. She lowered her hand and set the blade to Brienne's bindings.

"Hastein spoke truly. Rurik will risk himself for want of you, without care to his own well-being. Do you know aught of the Faroes? They are difficult to gain, the waters turbulent, the shores rocky. Hastein's island is among the most dangerous, ringed with 'Fenrir's Teeth,' some say. There be few places to win the shore. *All*, Hastein knows like his hand in the dark.

"But should Rurik land safely, greater peril awaits. Hastein's men number strong in his lair—an army of miscreants—outcasts the lot. Even if Rurik arrives with a force to outmatch them, think on how easily Hastein might bait his trap. All he need do is bring you forth with a knife at your throat, and Rurik will lay down his arms."

Green eyes bore into those of violet. "Do not misjudge Hastein. Amongst my own kindred, he is considered a treacherous man. He is also considered quite mad."

The leather strips fell away. Brienne rubbed her chafed wrists, mind and heart racing.

Katla's words must hold truth, she reasoned. Naught else would impel the Norsewoman to free her bonds or hazard Hastein's reprisal. That Katla was full aware of Rurik's abilities and still deemed him in such peril alarmed Brienne. And that she herself, by Hastein's possession of her, endangered Rurik tore at her insides.

As Brienne crouched next to Katla, she did not deceive herself. 'Twas not *she* the Norsewoman aided. Only Rurik and Katla's own ends. Brienne knew that Katla would as soon see her dead. Mayhaps that was yet her design. Once they eluded the men, there would be naught to forestall the Norsewoman from slaying her and awarding the deed to Hastein. Brienne gripped hold of her apprehensions: 'twas far better to flee unbound and alone with Katla than to remain trussed and in the clutches of all three.

"Do not slow me, bitch," Katla warned as she seized Brienne by the arm and began to rise.

Brienne felt the knife prick at her ribs, proof that Katla yet considered her a captive. She bit down on her resolve and refused to give way to fear.

"Untie the two mounts on the left whilst I slit the girth straps beneath the others," Katla ordered, shoving Brienne forward as she released her. "Time is narrow. Be quick about it."

Together, they threaded among the trees toward the horses. As Brienne slipped from cover, she spoke gently to the animals so as not to afright them. The reins pulled free with a tug.

But Katla took no such precautions. She pushed hurriedly between the other two mounts and grabbed for the strap of one where it ran beneath the belly. Her sawing upon the girth unnerved the beast. It stepped sideways and snorted. Still, Katla persisted. The horse shied again, bumping haunches with the steed beside it and jostling Katla's hand as she severed the leather. The horse screamed as the blade glanced awry and skimmed along its stomach.

Kalman's head jerked round at the disturbance. He lurched to his feet with a shout. Hastein, in turn, wrenched himself from his thoughts. Seeing the women's attempts to escape, he pivoted from the cliff's edge and threw himself into a full-hearted run.

Brienne read the fury in Hastein's eyes as he hurtled across the plain and closed the distance with Kalman. She forgot to breathe in that moment, so savage was his look. Then all swirled with commotion.

The horses capered. One tore its reins from her hands, burning a trail across her palms. She clung to the other as it pulled against the restraint. Frantically, Brienne moved to its side, pitching the reins over the beast's head, and jammed her foot into the stirrup. The horse skewed, drawing her along on one foot. Hastein's nearby roar scoured her spine.

Desperate, Brienne soothed the animal with a rush of words, reset her foot, and sprang up enough to grab the saddle, front and back, and haul herself upward. Needing no urging, the jittery horse took to the hoof before she settled herself, and left Hastein to spit the dust.

Infuriated, he lunged for the untethered mount and, with devil's luck, trapped it by the dangling reins. Heaving himself into the saddle, he kicked to a gallop and drove after Brienne along the edge of the cliff.

Katla, meanwhile, had released the one horse whose straps she had failed to cut, climbed astride, and struck back for the road by which they had come.

Kalman marked her as he lumbered for the last steed. Aware of her handiwork, he grasped the saddle with a meaty fist, jerked it from the animal's back, and hurled it to the ground. Fixing his dagger in his teeth with a growl, he slung himself onto the horse and rode bareback after Katla.

Hooves exploded across the vast plateau. Hastein moved like a squall above the sea, outstripping the wind as he raged after Brienne. Kalman shattered the plain, whipping his horse to a lather, and crashed down upon Katla. As the distance between them diminished, he reached to his hip and freed the menace of chains.

Rod in hand, he swung the deadly linkage over his head, high above the thunder of hooves. Closing alongside her, he leaned out and, with a snap of his wrist, snared Katla about the neck. Katla shrieked as the barbed ends sank into her flesh. Kalman tightened his hold, slipped the blade from his teeth, and thrust it between her ribs.

Katla stiffened, eyes huge disks of green. With a stout yank of rod and chain, Kalman toppled her from the horse and left her discarded in a mangled heap—so much refuse.

Skirting the edge of the cliff, Brienne raced barely apace of Hastein. He pressed her ever toward the rim where rifts fissured the plain and slowed her escape. But the steed plunged ahead, full of heart, bounding over the chinks and ruptures.

Hastein continued to crowd her, forcing Brienne to ride near the precipice. To her horror, the crevices began to widen. Many ran their course toward the lip of the plateau, carving deep hollows and gorges that opened over the sea.

Intrepidly, her horse breached the first narrow cleft, then the second. But the next gaped like a yawning maw. The animal swerved, and Brienne fought to rein it tight and turn it full circle. Breathless, she strove to break away from the precipice but promptly found her path obstructed by Hastein.

More adept with horseflesh than she, he blocked her passage with ease. Maneuvering the beast from side to side, he forced her retreat and trapped her against the edge of the cliff.

"There is no escape, Brienne." He fixed her with colorless eyes. Eyes of crystal and ice. "Come. I shall deal you no harm. Only pleasure. I have many plans for you."

"Like those you devise for Rurik?" she retorted boldly. But fear twined its tentacles about her heart.

Hastein prodded his horse forward but stayed it when Brienne continued to back her own mount toward the edge of the promontory without heed.

"What choice have you, my sweet-breasted dove? Look behind you. To the side of you. 'Tis a sheer drop all round. Come now. I am more man than Rurik to see to your needs. I grow impatient. You cannot elude me. Our journey awaits."

Brienne halted the mount abruptly, discovering she stood on a projection of cliff that jutted armlike over the sea. The waters heaved below, swollen and contentious. Only a narrow sash of shoreline lay visible along the coast. But this, too, seemed about to be consumed as waves buffeted it and thieved its sands.

Brienne marked her bearings. She was hemmed in on three sides by sky and sea. Ahead, Hastein barred her way with smug assurance, ready to seize her. Bitterly, she realized that she was trapped, bereft of hope or aid.

Katla's warnings and Hastein's callous boasts returned full force to haunt and torment her. Echoing in mind's ear, each word inflicted fresh torture.

Rurik is a dead man as long as Hastein holds you. He will risk himself . . . without caution or prudence. His passion for you is his weakness. Because of you . . . he'll come willingly into my snare. He's a dead man . . . a dead man . . . a dead man. . . .

Brienne's heart twisted with anguish. A torrent of despair flooded her. For all the world, she wished she could enfold Rurik within the depths of her love and protect him. She tasted the salt of a tear. He must not die for her. Even the thought was too fierce to bear.

Brienne looked on Hastein, and terror for Rurik flamed

stark and pure within her. She had been helpless to save Lyting from his treachery, but 'twas yet in her power to alter Rurik's fate. If there be destinies given and destinies to be met, then this day wouldst she take up hers.

"Rurik," she whispered as she visioned him once more and embraced him in her heart. "Now and for all time, my love. . . ." Tears spilled over her cheeks.

Her eyes drew to Hastein once more, and a fury overtook her, unrivaled by anything she had known before.

"Curse you, Hastein!" she blazed. "If there be hells in which to burn, may you roast an eternity in their bowels!"

Hastein had watched the play of emotions and frustration on her face. Now he laughed with confidence. She was his.

"May the Lord God Almighty curse you till the end of your days!" she reviled. "May you find no rest till Rurik sheathes his blade in your black heart!"

Hastein's smile wavered, the words settling ill. Then the smile seeped back. The chit's only recourse was to relent, yet, cornered, she ranted like a lioness, fierce and bare-clawed. This one wouldst not bore him for many years hence.

Brienne's horse stepped restlessly on the narrow width of land, drawing upon the tension that charged the air. She tightened the reins as a tempest of emotions gathered about her. Brienne's dark hair rose on the breeze, and her eyes flashed with a violet storm.

"Rurik will avenge me, Hastein! He will hunt you with a bloodlust. There be no rock beneath which you can slither. No crack in which you can hide. He wilt have you, Hastein. Upon his sword, wilt he have you. My soul thirsts for the justice of that day!"

Face grim with resolve, Brienne lashed her steed and bolted straight toward Hastein. His smile spread as he watched her approach. His throat began to vibrate with a grating, self-assured laughter.

But just before she verged on him, Brienne wheeled the horse unexpectedly and rammed her heels into its flanks. Whipping and lashing it the harder, she charged full tilt toward the brink of the cliff.

Rocks scattered in her flight and plummeted over the edge.

The peninsula itself appeared to quake at her passage. On she roared without restraint and won her goal.

As the horse's hooves lifted from the ground, Brienne cried out upon the wind, "Rurik, I will wait for you. . . ." The horse and rider arched high and wide against the sky. "I wait for you . . . until the end of time."

Hastein leaped from his mount as Brienne and her horse plunged from the airy heights and into the icy sea below. Running breakneck toward the precipice, he threw himself down at its rim and scudded to a halt on knee, thigh, and hip.

The waters swashed wide and heavy where they swallowed their prey, then rushed to cover their greed.

The blood fled Hastein's face. He scrabbled back from the edge of cliff, stunned by Brienne's sacrifice. Her ominous words clung to him as his mind raced with disordered thoughts. Sighting Kalman, he leaped to his feet.

"To Fécamp! To Fécamp!" he shouted.

Regaining his horse, he threw himself up and gouged in his heels. There was yet time to reach the Faroes. In his lair, he wouldst cast his plans anew and await Rurik. Then wouldst they have their day and see it to an end.

Chapter Twenty-two
❉ ❉ ❉ ❉ ❉ ❉ ❉ ❉ ❉ ❉ ❉

THE CHILL WIND whipped at Rurik's face as he drove his steed unsparingly toward the cliffs of Étretat. The tracks he shadowed were fresh, laid within the hour.

"There! Ahead!" Ketil shouted, wide of his left and slightly behind him. Together they closed on a snarl of blue mantle and glimpse of red hair.

Ketil bound to the earth first, dropping his reins, and quickened toward the shape. Rurik dismounted more slowly. Dark presentiments wreathed his gut. Katla.

Lyting had not mentioned that she rode with Hastein. Yet it surprised him little. Dirt clinging to dirt.

He had followed Hastein's trail of blood and found both horse and a man dead along the road. A short distance later, the prints revealed the passage of four horses, not two. He could imagine at what price Hastein made their purchase. But he had not guessed who rode the extra mount.

Rurik came to stand over Katla, wondering if she had outplayed herself with Hastein and how she had earned his wrath. The thought bit into him. Was it that she had tried to harm Brienne?

Ketil shifted Katla from her side. Her head rolled back, exposing the torn flesh of her throat. Then to Rurik's and Ketil's amazement, her chest heaved and she coughed—a thick, gurgling sound. Ketil raised her slightly. This brought on a fit of coughing and a spill of blood from her mouth.

"Easy, Ketil." Rurik lowered to one knee while he bridled his emotions. By the gods, she best not die before she could give him some answers!

Katla labored to breathe. Her eyes drew open. They fastened on Rurik, glazed with pain, the pupils dilated till her eyes were no longer green but wholly black. Her lips lifted in a dim smile. She strove to raise her hand and touch Rurik's cheek but could not manage it. Her hand fell against his, then her lids squeezed shut with pain.

"She's been knifed in the side," Ketil told Rurik. " 'Twould seem the steel missed her heart but pierced her lung. From the sound of her breathing, she'll not linger long."

Rurik realized the truth of that statement as he removed Katla's hand and placed it over her waist. The fingers were cool, bluish beneath the nails. Her face lay colorless within the blaze of hair, marble against fire.

"Katla." Rurik spoke in strong tones, hoping she could hear him. "What has passed?"

"For . . . you," she murmured vaguely, trying to reach out to him again.

A rush of apprehension and distrust surged through Rurik. "Brienne. Has Hastein taken Brienne north?"

Katla's brow furrowed, then smoothed.

"You . . . truly . . . love her?"

"Thor's teeth, Katla! Where be my wife?"

"Dead."

The word jolted Rurik physically as it sliced to his core.

"What mean you?" he lashed out fierce-hearted.

But Katla's eyes had begun to dim, her senses leaving.

"Katla!" he roared, and gripped her by the arms. "Where is Brienne?"

Katla stirred. "Cliff . . . drove horse . . . over cliff."

"*Nei!* You lie!" he raged, anger engulfing him that she would do so even at death's door.

"You . . . save . . . you."

Rurik did not know if she spoke now of Brienne or herself. Her words became increasingly difficult to follow. Her eyes stared as though sightless.

"Hastein . . . Faroes . . . trap—" Pain seized her. "Brienne . . . bait."

"What of Brienne?" he demanded. Her utterances crushed like a millstone upon his heart.

"Escaped." Katla labored for breath. "Hastein trapped . . .

against sea. . . . Knew . . . you dead man . . . whilst he
held her. . . . Drove horse . . . over cliff. . . . Save you.
. . . Dead."

"*Nei!*" Rurik ground out harshly. He wouldst not have it
so!

He blocked his mind to Katla's tale as though simple
denials would alter events. Brienne could not have sacrificed
herself for him. He would not allow it. *Nei!* He would break
the cast of fate, if he must, and reshape it to his own will. But
he need not. Katla lied. Ever she lied. Certainly she spoke
falsehoods this time as well.

Rurik started to question Katla once more, but another
strained spell of coughing seized her, bringing more blood.
Her eyes rolled back as she whispered with her final breath,
"All . . . for you."

Rurik released Katla as she sank into death. He watched
Ketil ease her lifeless body to the earth and close her eyes.

Abruptly, Rurik rose as the dread words centered in him.
He fell back a pace and clenched his hands. Pivoting, he
broke toward the cliff, spanning the distance with rapid
strides. He fast discovered the trail of two horses and heeled
after them along the precipice to a jutting tongue of rock.

A scuffle of tracks lay across the access. Hastein! Rurik
boiled. Hastein had entrapped Brienne here. He rushed on
and marked where Brienne's horse had churned the thin
soil as it turned. Heart thudding and thighs burning, he
ran alongside the prints to the very end of the peninsula.
They disappeared at the ledge, into the very air.

Rurik dropped to both knees. The sullen sea stretched
before him, vast and empty. Of horse or rider, there was
evidence of none. Nor within its icy hold or upon the lone
strip of sand to a near distance below. The sea had consumed
the offering without a trace.

Overcome, Rurik's head and shoulders sagged forward.
Brienne. Gone. Ripped from his life. He had been so close
to her rescue. Yet he had failed her. He visioned Brienne,
all courage and beauty, driving her horse into the sea. For
him. 'Twas unendurable.

For a time, Rurik remained unmoving, still as the barren
cliffs. Then he began to shake as anguish forged with anger,

grief with hate. A violent shock of emotions erupted from the pit of his being and exploded full force.

Heart bursting and full of fury, Rurik thrust himself to his feet, clenching the neck of his tunic. He rent the fabric from his chest as he unleashed a full-throated cry, a cry that tore from his soul to rise up and rage against the heavens. Again, and again he cried out. His bellows convulsed across the sea to traverse the horizon, filled with bitterness and wrath and infinite pain.

Rurik swung from the cliff's edge, eyes fever bright, his veins living currents of fire.

The bloodlust was upon him.

Hastein shifted impatiently in his saddle as he watched Kalman readying the longship on the beach below. He looked back over the sea, then stared at the jagged rocks that footed the sheer drop of cliff. Anxious to be away, he turned the horse from the ridge to join Kalman.

Hastein halted at the sudden sight of Rurik mounted before him, hard-eyed and bare-chested, sword gleaming in his hand. Hastein's lips slid into a smile. Eyes aglow, he drew the long blade at his hip.

"At last! To the death!"

"To the death!" Rurik rejoined.

Both kicked their mounts and drove them forward, meeting with a bright clash of steel. The horses reeled, then turned. Earth and air shuddered with the shock of sword and drum of hooves. Blade sang upon blade, sparking and clanging above a swirl of dust.

Rurik's rage and Hastein's contempt arced back and forth. Beast pushed against beast. Neck to neck, they drove the steeds along the cliff. The ledge crumbled as hooves pounded its rim. Just when it seemed the shelf would give way, the two seething warriors locked steel and clattered back down the ridge.

Their great broadswords continued to hammer and hew without pause. Rurik gave Hastein no quarter, raining down blow after blow till he smashed Hastein's blade from his hand. In a heartbeat, Hastein released his battle-ax from his belt and sliced it through the air.

Rurik canted, but the flaring edge skimmed his chest, leaving a slash of red. He flinched not at all, as though the bite went unfelt. Hastein whirled the ax again, but Rurik smote it clean through, sundering the wood handle and sending the axhead spinning out over the cliff.

With a half growl, half laugh, Hastein snatched the dagger from his belt and lunged from his saddle, taking Rurik from his stirrups. Both hit the ground with a jolt and rolled apart. Rurik's sword slipped from his hold.

Hastein sprang to his feet in advance of Rurik and hard-booted him in the jaw and neck. But as Rurik slammed onto his back, he twined his feet in Hastein's legs and yanked him to the dirt. Flinging himself upward, he vaulted atop Hastein. Together they rolled over several times till they tossed beneath the restless horses.

Hastein flailed the sharp-honed knife, but Rurik seized his wrist and stayed its point. The animals skittered at the upheaval, narrowly missing Rurik's head but one catching Hastein in the thigh with a hoof. He grunted in pain. Again the men rolled, breaking apart as they came free of the horses.

Instantly, they regained their feet. Hastein swept the steel before him, scoring the space. Rurik closed in, stalking Hastein round in a circle, hands spread wide, his dagger still sheathed at his waist.

Hastein laughed with panting breaths, baring his teeth with his smile. The expanse between them diminished. Hastein leaped forward. But quicker than eye could follow, Rurik snared Hastein's arm, then dropped and rose to seize him where groin met thigh. Heaving Hastein up and over his head, Rurik hurled him through the air.

Hastein collided with the earth, scudding for several feet. A groan burst from his lips, and he let go his hold on the knife. As Rurik came at him, he twisted to retrieve it, only to find Rurik's sword lying near to hand. Hastein strained for the hilt and grabbed hold of it. Swinging it upward, he aimed to lay open Rurik's midsection. But Rurik foresaw the move. He kicked out strong and solid, contacting with hand and hilt, and sent the blade soaring toward the edge of the cliff.

Gripped in the white heat of anger, Rurik dragged Hastein

to his feet and shattered his jaw with a powerful blow.
Hastein lurched and fell to his knees. But again, Rurik
wrenched him upright and plowed his fist into his cheekbone
and struck him across his nose.

Hastein plunged to the ground. Dragging himself up on
knees and palms, he spit blood and teeth. Rurik closed in
again.

Quickly, Hastein coiled himself into a half crouch and
locked hands. As Rurik bent for him, Hastein burst straight
up, smashing Rurik's chin heavenward, then slogged him in
the throat.

Rurik reeled backward and dropped to one knee. His
vision blurred momentarily, and he beheld two images of
Hastein moving for the sword. Rurik shoved himself to
his feet and bounded after him. He lunged for Hastein and
together they thudded to the ground.

Struggling over the blade, they captured it between them.
Over and over they rolled till they hovered at the cliff's edge.
Rocks spewed over the ledge and gnashed at their backs.
Still, they wrestled for the steel.

Muscle locked against muscle. The sharp, double-edged
blade shuddered betwixt them, nicking and grazing them till
the steel was mottled with crimson.

They pitched again, Rurik rising atop Hastein. But Hastein
snaked out a hand and trapped a fist-sized rock then smashed
it against Rurik's temple and brow. Rurik sprawled backward, stunned by the blow.

Lurching to his feet, Hastein caught up the sword in one
hand and stood spread-legged on the brink of the cliff. He
gasped for air as he looked down on Rurik. The dog barely
stirred. He grinned and reversed his grip on the weapon.
Hastein's dark laughter filled the air as he grasped the hilt
with both hands, blade down, and pointed it at Rurik's chest.
Eyes glittering, he raised his arms above his head to plunge
the sword home.

Rurik watched through slitted eyes and rolled at the
last moment. Coming up on one knee, he snatched the dagger
from his belt and hurled it with every ounce of strength that
remained. The knife burred through the air and lodged in
Hastein's breast.

Hastein froze in his stance, arms upraised, eyes wide with shock. The sword dropped from his hands, and he took a few unsteady steps backward. The ledge of the cliff began to crumble. Before Rurik could rise, the earth gave way beneath Hastein's feet and he plummeted from sight.

Hastein's strangled cry reverberated against the wall of stone as he fell, and then it ceased abruptly. Only the chink and clack of loose rocks could be heard. Then all was silence.

Rurik dragged himself to the very edge of the cliff and lay gasping for breath. Below, Hastein's contorted body was spilled over the rocks. His vacant eyes stared up as the sea pounded against the shore. Not even the cry of a lone gull mourned him.

" 'Tis done," Rurik murmured. He drew himself up and crouched at the edge of the precipice as time passed unmarked.

Ketil huffed loudly as he trudged up the steep incline from the shore, bearing Kalman's chains. Rurik questioned the piece with a lift of his brow.

"The Hebridean sought to use this toy on me. But when he whirled it above his gleaming pate to deliver his attack, well . . ." Ketil shrugged. "A man needs protect himself and the invitation was clear."

Rurik rose slowly to his feet, his every muscle a dragging weight. Even his blood pulsed sluggishly through him.

"There be one last thing we must do." Rurik met Ketil's eyes briefly, then returned his gaze to the sea.

Ketil nodded in solemn agreement, with no love for the task.

"Bring Hastein's longboat. I will drag the stone."

Heavy-hearted, Rurik returned to the cliffs of Étretat. Together with Ketil, he labored long and without word to raise a great stone, a *hautasteinn*, in honor and remembrance of Brienne.

Hastein's longship yielded several chests, one containing sufficient tools to carve the *kenning*. Hollowly, Rurik gave over the chisel and hammer to Ketil, then drew together his thoughts.

His heart compressed as though some unseen fist squeezed

it. Clearing his throat, he fastened his moist gaze on the distant horizon.

"Set your finest hand to the stone, my friend. Grave the runes thusly: 'Rurik raised this stone in memory of his beloved wife, Brienne, Baronne de Valsemé. Be it known that she gave her life that he might live. For hers—' " A rush of hot tears congested his throat and stung the back of his eyes. He finished in a roughened whisper: " 'Hers was a valiant heart.' "

Unable to speak further, Rurik moved away, leaving Ketil to his efforts, and strode to the empty peninsula. There, he retraced the path Brienne had ridden to the sea, then sat upon the lip of the cliff, looking out over the expanse, over the watery depths that held her.

His every sense was deadened. For a time he simply watched the seabirds swoop and dive for fish, then watched their landings and departures from the nearby skirt of shore below. The bank was deeper now that the tides had receded. The skies themselves seemed to have brightened at Hastein's death. But not so his heart. No light shined within that empty chamber. Brienne was his light— his sun, his moon, his stars. Her brilliance had been stolen from him, extinguished forevermore. All was an aching, fathomless void. Rurik drew a quavering breath and gave in to his grief.

The sky, sea, and sand shimmered through his tears. He made no effort to staunch the flow. A dark speck intruded at the corner of his vision and made a slow path through the liquid haze. He swiped at it, clearing the droplets away. The speck remained. He blinked several times, then squinted as his eyes focused more clearly on the shoreline below. The blot sharpened into a tattered figure of a man plodding toward the sea.

Rurik bounded to his feet. Mayhaps the man knew aught of Brienne! Mayhaps he had witnessed her fearsome dive to the waters below! Heart outpacing his strides, he sprinted back the length of the promontory and chased along the cliff's cragged rim. Farther down the coast, where the longship was moored, Ketil had managed to climb the rock to the top of the plateau using the many hollows and valleys that ruptured Étretat's face. Surely there be those here that would serve him as well.

Remembering the ropes with which he had dragged the stone, he ran back to where Ketil busied himself with the inscription. Grabbing a cordage of hemp from the ground, he wheeled on his friend and motioned excitedly to his hip.

"The chains, Ketil! The chains!"

Astonished by Rurik's outburst, Ketil rose but did as bade and freed the Hebridean's flail from his side.

Rope and iron firmly in hand, Rurik raced to the ledge and descended into a gorge. He followed the rugged grooves to their end, then made his way across the cliff's furrowed face to a deep ravine that cleaved the rock halfway down its scabrous height.

Rurik hastened on but slipped on a vein of rubble and slid partially down the incline. Undaunted, he secured his footage and continued his descent to the base of the chasm.

Swiftly, he tied the hemp through the heavy ring of the flail. Then he wedged the clawed chains and rod in a cleft in the rock and tested for fastness. Gripping it firmly, he climbed down the crannied wall to the rope's end. With a shove, he swung out from the rock and dropped the short distance that remained.

Rurik rose and quickly scanned the shore. The man was gone. But a second glance caught the shabby figure as it disappeared into the face of the cliff. Rurik fixed his eyes on the point and hurried across the strand. The shifting grains beneath his feet slowed his pace. Heart pounding, he drove the harder as he saw the breach in the rock.

Without easing his steps, Rurik burst through the opening and entered the cramped hollow of a cave. He locked eyes with the startled man, who scuttled back crablike into the shallow recess. As Rurik started forward, his gaze fell to the rude floor. His breath caught in his chest. Brienne lay motionless before a small fire, swathed in a coarse mantle.

Incredulous, Rurik sank to his knees beside her. For a moment he only stared, consuming the sight of his love. He trailed his gaze over her still form and waxen features, then brushed the back of his fingers along her cool cheek.

Heart rending anew, he bent and kissed her tenderly upon the lips.

Rurik willed that life should flow from him to Brienne through that kiss, and that she should awake to him. But she lay unresponsive. He began to withdraw, then felt the faint warmth of her breath. Hope surged. He lifted his gaze to the ragged man who yet retreated against the rock.

"She lives." Rurik voiced the obvious, needing to hear it said.

Apprehensively, the man came away from the wall of the cave. "*Certes,* my son. *Certes.*"

Rurik took a hard look at him and realized for the first time that he was one of the reclusive wanderers of whom he had heard tales—a hermit and a holy man. From his shredded robes and fearful manner, Rurik guessed him to be one of the many monks who had fled in the wake of his Norse brethren and took to the open roads. This one did not appear Frankish, though he apparently understood the tongue and spoke it.

"You have saved my wife," Rurik said with genuine gratitude. "Ever shall you be welcome in my hall."

The hermit edged closer, showing relief at the words, yet he remained wary. "I didst but pull her from the waters, my son. There was no help for the horse, though I could scarce have aided it had it lived. The beast broke the fall for your lady and spared her. But—" He hesitated, plainly concerned how his next words would be met. "Your lady has yet to wake. Methinks she rests in the 'endless sleep.' Lest she awaken within the next days, she cannot long endure."

Rurik nodded, his chest thickening with a knot. He knew well of the deep, unnatural "sleep" from which few awoke. He had witnessed such, a lifetime ago, in Byzantium.

Feeling powerless and fearing death was near, Rurik took a long, raw swallow that reached from his heart to his soul. If Brienne was to die, she must not die here. Not in this cold, miserable cave, half frozen by the sea. *Nei.* He wouldst take her back to her beloved Valsemé. There wouldst he wrap her in the finest furs and brocades. There wouldst he keep vigil over her.

As night fell, Rurik and Ketil lashed torches around the sides of the captured longship and laid Brienne gently inside on a bed of blankets. They covered her with a mantle lined with marten, found, as were the woolens, within the sea chests. The holy man declined joining them, but stood upon the shore and prayed as the fiery ship began its homeward voyage.

Though they raised the great square sail to speed their journey, Rurik set his muscle to the oars, in need of the physical exertion. The high-prowed ship plowed the waves of Normandy's coast, ablaze against the pitch-dark night. Small fires sprouted along the shoreline at their passage. Rurik recognized them as signs of honor and reverence. Only the celebrated and the highborn would be carried upon a funeral barge. Such must they appear. For a breath of time, he did not feel so alone.

As he plied his strength to the oars, Rurik watched the golden glow of torchlight play over Brienne's serene features. How exquisite she was. The delicate arch of brow and tilt of nose, the high, fine bone of her cheek and fragile jaw, the soft lines of her lips—all he stored to heart's memory.

Never wouldst he forget the days of their love. *Nei*. Never wouldst he forget the fires of their passion. Even in the winters of tomorrow wouldst he remember Brienne as he first saw her, arrayed in crimson and gold. Remember the joy of making love with her, the sweet tastes and silken caresses, the feel of her flesh pressed against his, and his burning inside hers. Remember the blaze of ecstasy as they melded together and became one.

Nei, he wouldst not forget. He wouldst hold her, heartfast, and love her for all time. He wouldst bear her back to the barony, to the soil from whence she sprang. And when the time of her passage came, he wouldst lay her to rest in Valsemé's sweet earth. Then wouldst he watch over their lands for the remainder of his days. And, when his own time found its end, he wouldst join her in that sleep and take up his place beside her.

The fiery vessel sliced through the dark waters. Curving wide, it entered the river Toques and passed into the night.

Chapter Twenty-three
❂ ❂ ❂ ❂ ❂ ❂ ❂ ❂ ❂ ❂ ❂ ❂ ❂

THE PULL AT Rurik's sleeve brought his attention from the chamber window. He glanced down to find Elsie tendering up a clutch of catkins and fragile pink campion. She looked up at him with huge, doleful eyes that swallowed her face. Her bottom lip quivered. Rurik lifted her in his arms and hugged her close. Slipping his strong fingers into the mass of curls, he drew her head down to rest on his shoulder and turned back to the window. They waited, comforting each other in silence, as the women finished their ministrations to Brienne.

Below, villeins and soldiers alike gathered in the courtyard to pray. At any time, day or night, dozens upon dozens collected, dinting the earth with bent knee, heads bowed over folded hands. Others shuffled gravely about their duties, their supplications moving over their lips.

One could not pass through the great hall or corridors without having to step about the kneeling forms. At the door of the lord's chamber, they crowded thickest. Ofttimes Rurik would order them away, for the air grew so oppressive he thought he wouldst suffocate. But never didst he remove young Waite. The boy crouched even now at the portal, Patch steadfast beside him.

Early morn of the second day, Rurik's longship arrived from St. Wandrille's bearing Lyting, his men, and Brother Bernard. During one of Lyting's short spans of wakefulness, he learned of Brienne and insisted that he be carried to her chamber so he might pray in her presence.

Rurik had objected at first, fearing for his brother to be

moved yet again. Lyting was exceedingly weak, his condition precarious at best. But Lyting fretted so much, writhing in his sleep as he relived each horror, that Rurik decided to give in to his wishes before his brother ripped his many stitches. Lyting calmed once he was settled on a pallet in the bedchamber and could hold Brienne in his view. Rurik deemed it best in the end. Aleth was better able to tend both her wards in one room, and Lyting slept most of the time.

The soft whispers behind him alerted Rurik that the women had completed the change of linens. To his surprise, Ketil had entered with a fresh gathering of herbs for Aleth. They spoke quietly, together with Elsie's mother, Galwinth, their gazes all centering on Brienne.

Rurik set Elsie down and bid her to cheer Lyting with the flowers, for he looked to have awakened. Then he crossed to the others and asked of Brienne. When Aleth would not meet his eyes, he tensed. She moved away to the bed and lifted Brienne's hand in hers.

"My lord, Brienne has lingered thus for a sum of three days."

"That I well know, Aleth." A muscle worked along his jaw, and he steeled himself. "What more?"

"We cannot hope that she will last beyond a fourth. Yet there be a small hope, but with it, great caution."

Rurik came to stand on the opposite side of the bed and looked down on both women. "Speak, Aleth, lest you intend that I go mad with the waiting."

Aleth pressed her friend's hand to her cheek, then replaced it at Brienne's waist. She met Rurik's troubled eyes as levelly as she could manage.

"Her signs be encouraging in that her skin is dry, not moist or cold. Her breathing is clear, and her lungs free of fluid. When last you stepped from the chamber, I didst test her response." Aleth shifted her gaze aside. "It required that I prod her—"

"Prod her?"

"Jab her, my lord. Jab her with my pin." Rurik's color began to rise and Aleth added quickly, "But lord, both hand and foot didst move when tried."

Rurik bolted round the bed and caught her up by the shoulders. "What do you tell me, Aleth, that she will wake?"

"Lord, lord," Aleth pleaded, more for him to becalm himself than loose her from his hold. "There be but one day's passing left to her, and she stirs not at all. But even should she wake, she may not possess her right mind."

Rurik released her at once and fell back several paces. "What say you? That she wilt be simpleminded? A child evermore?" He stabbed her with his eyes, but there was no solace that she could offer.

Aleth's head bent with the weight of her misery. "The coming hours will take her from us or give her back, but whole or unsound, I cannot say."

Rurik backed to the door, her words crashing through him. He looked to Brienne, then Ketil and Galwinth and Aleth once more. Aleth sank to the floor, burying her face in her hands.

Unable to bear more, Rurik left the chamber and pressed his way through the crowded antechamber before any could clear a path for him. He hastened on through the hall, maneuvering about more bodies, and quickened out the portal and down the steps.

On seeing the baron's hasty departure from the manor house, one of the maidservants in the courtyard began to wail and beat her breast, believing the baronne dead. Rurik was forced to stop and reassure all that their lady yet lived. Wrapped in his grief, he hurried on to the stables and saddled Sleipnir, then clattered from the bailey on the huge black.

Without thought to direction, he rode his mount hard. In a short time he found himself at the secluded lake where, not so long past, he and Brienne had cherished one another most passionately. Rurik tied Sleipnir to a sapling, then pushed through the brush and headed to the lake.

Beneath the clear, brilliant sky the waters sparkled, jewellike, as though diamonds had been scattered over its surface. Rurik lost himself in a void without time whilst he stood on the bank, staring at the play of light, and struggled with the conflicts within him. This interminable waiting ground upon his soul.

At the rustle of branches he turned to see Brother Bernard approach, then he cast his glance back to the lake. The monk came to stand beside him but kept his peace. Without word, they watched the light spangle the water's surface. Unexpectedly, Rurik drew a bracing lungful of air and broke the silence.

"I wouldst pray, good brother, if I knew in whom to trust my appeals, and whether the All-Being wouldst even listen."

"But you *have* prayed all this while, my son. Mayhaps without words, but better. You have prayed with your heart."

Rurik bent his head, swallowed the roughness in his throat, then fixed his gaze on the slashes of fire that splintered the lake.

"She dies, and I am helpless to aid her."

"Do not look with your eyes, my son, but with faith in your heart. God has the power to heal, regardless the circumstance. It requires naught but His will."

"And was it His will that Helena should die as she did?" Rurik's grief ruptured and he was scarce able to contain all the emotions that collided within him. He gave a harsh, shaky laugh.

"Once was I prepared to take the waters of Holy Baptism, for Helena's sake. But before my eyes, she fell ill. Her flesh wasted, and each day became an agony, so great was her pain." Rurik's eyes clouded with the memory. "I prayed, brother, and I prayed. God's answer was that she slipped into the 'unending sleep' and died before the dawn could shed its light."

His tear-glazed eyes drew to the churchman. "And now I look upon Brienne, trapped in that same sleep, and you ask for my belief? Faith?" he questioned bitterly. "What know I of faith?"

Brother Bernard's brows drew downward as he pressed his lips together and mulled over Rurik's words. "And yet 'twas faith that brought Brienne to Valsemé when she agreed to wedlock with your father."

Rurik wrenched his eyes to the churchman and bored him with a hard look. He remembered the tale, but held his tongue as the monk continued.

"Truly, 'tis said, faith is a gift. But, Rurik, too often we hold tight to the reins of our lives as though we, in truth,

determined their course or could alter their direction one *fot*.
In the end we but get in the way and block the workings of
the Almighty."

Brother Bernard shrugged. "The will of God, who can
fathom it? But faith, my son? Faith oft begins with a grain
of trust. Let go of the reins. They bind you, my son. Step
from the pathway. Be open to God's will."

As Rurik continued to stare out over the water, a small
window of light opened in the darkness of his heart. He was
flooded with a profound sense of relief as, deep within, he
released his hold and passed the reins to Another. Stepping
into the lake, he felt, in some wise, that he touched Brienne
through their waters. His heart found peace.

"Set His Seal upon me, brother. My shield is at God's
feet."

Brother Bernard smiled. Joining Rurik in the lake, he bent
to scoop the crystal liquid in cupped hands.

It seemed that she was surfacing, swirling upward toward
the light. Voices murmured about her, hushed whisperings.
There was Elsie . . . and Aleth . . . and . . . Rurik! Rurik,
so very near. Brienne surged toward his voice and broke
through to consciousness.

She squinted, blinking several times as her eyes adjusted
to the room's brightness. Aleth turned from the fire just then
and started forward, an earthen goblet in one hand and a
bedraggled plant in the other. She looked up, of a sudden,
and their eyes met.

Aleth squealed, dropping the cup to smash on the floor
and startle every occupant in the room. It seemed they all
drew their breath as one and held it, anxious and expectant
of something. Brienne sensed they waited for her to speak,
though she could not imagine why. She was too tired to
reason it. Her throat was as parched as sun-baked sand, and
her body ached as though bruised all over.

Brienne glanced about for Rurik, but her head throbbed
and her vision blurred with the slightest of movements.
Someone stirred at her side. The mattress sank and joyously
Rurik came into view as he eased himself down on its edge.
He, too, looked on her intently, waiting.

Brienne dragged her gaze back to Aleth, worried some-what, for she still stood rooted solidly in place, eyes enor-mous, strangling the poor plant in her hand. A faint smile flirted across Brienne's lips.

"'Tis a weed," she croaked out in a hoarse whisper.

Aleth's hands flew to her mouth, and tears spilled from her eyes. "Nay, mugwort." Her voice was strained. "'Tis a powerful medicant, you know."

Brienne and Aleth shared a smile, their thoughts attuned, and chorused, "Sister will know the truth of it."

Brienne turned her head, though it pained her to do so. Her smile widened as she gazed lovingly on Rurik.

"Do not dispense of your weed too quickly, Aleth. I may yet have a use for it."

Aleth shook her head, smiling softly. "Nay, dear friend. Of this I be sure. Your great Norman has no need of such potions, not where you be concerned."

Rurik's warm hand closed over Brienne's where it rested at her waist. He had not entirely followed the women's banter, but the play of wit assured him that Brienne was unimpaired and whole of mind.

As he leaned toward her, firelight glinted off the small gold cross at his neck. Brienne smiled at the sight of it. As she lifted her free hand to touch it, Rurik captured her fingers and pressed them to his lips. Then he bent, embracing her as he buried his face in the midnight tresses at her shoulder.

"*Ástin mín*, I thought you lost to me."

Brienne touched her hand to his golden mane, her heart overflowing. "And I, you. Surely Heaven smiles upon us, my love, for you are with me still."

Rurik raised himself to gaze down on her, steel-blue caressing violet. "Always, *ástin mín*. Till time has ceased its passage and the stars burn out."

As love enveloped them with its fervent glow, they folded their words to silence. Rurik gathered Brienne tenderly in his arms and covered her lips with his. Their hearts were one.

Epilogue

❖ ❖ ❖ ❖ ❖ ❖ ❖ ❖ ❖ ❖ ❖ ❖

A SHOWER OF grain and jubilant cheers greeted Aleth and Ketil as they emerged from the portals of Valsemé's church.

Brienne and Rurik followed, and they, too, were caught in the downpour. They laughed happily, remembering their own wedding. Brienne shielded her eyes against the spatter and turned to the shelter of Rurik's chest. His arms enclosed her at once.

"Easy, *ástin mín*." Rurik cautioned her of the steps. "I wouldst not have you fall upon our babe."

Brienne grinned up at him and smoothed her hand over the considerable swell of her abdomen. "Then 'tis well you should aid me. 'Twas your doing that rendered me thus, like a great, oversize pear."

"I heard no complaints." Rurik bent and kissed her beneath the ear, sending warm shivers down her neck and on to her toes.

"Wilt you two keep the rest of us trapped here the day?" Lyting chided from behind. "There be feasting to attend. And *other* matters." He winked, in high spirits, his crystal-blue eyes sparkling.

As Lyting quickened past, Brienne's smile saddened a little. Lyting wouldst always bear the scar upon his cheek wrought by Hastein's sword. Truth to tell, he bore a multitude of scars because of her. But Aleth's able hands and the finest of her own poultices had seen most healed to smooth, faint tracings. Yet could she ever look on him without remembering what he had endured?

Rurik gave her shoulder a gentle squeeze, as though he

342

read her thoughts. "Lyting is whole and hale," he reassured her, nodding after his brother who now sprinted toward the bridal couple.

Swooping up Aleth, Lyting twirled her about and kissed her full on the lips before setting her down again.

" 'Tis a day to be generous," Lyting teased Ketil. "You wilt have fair Aleth to yourself evermore."

"Bah! Find your own maid," Ketil growled, but a grin split his blaze of whiskers.

"Not overloud, friend. The good brother intends that I remain celibate all my days and wed Holy Mother Church." He nodded back to where Brother Bernard stood upon the steps aside Bolsgar.

"Then you'd best hurry, lad, before he snares you to that purpose," Ketil returned good-naturedly. "But this one be taken." With that, Ketil lifted Aleth atop the palfrey and began to lead her toward the keep.

Brienne and Rurik laughed. Just then a gaggle of children bustled merrily past, Elsie at the last, trailing spring violets. They watched as the sprite suddenly broke away, spying Waite, and lured him to the shadow of the building. Not to be forgotten, Patch scurried behind, tail beating furiously.

Brienne and Rurik exchanged amused glances as Elsie produced several little cakes from the folds of her dress and offered one to Waite. But it slipped from her fingers, and the spry little pup pounced on it and devoured it in a blink.

Brienne and Rurik broke out in full-hearted laughter. They turned to see the children's mothers standing side by side, wagging their heads.

"I best learn them *both* of the kitchens and soon, or the tables will be bare at supper," Waite's mother, Ealdryth, remarked as she gently bounced the babe at her hip.

Brienne could not keep her eyes from the sweet little nursling, nor could Rurik. They stepped closer, but the mite instantly shied away, thrusting tiny fingers in her mouth and burrowing her head against her mother's bosom.

Ealdryth chuckled at her daughter, Waite's new sister. "Be not dismayed, my lady. Babes are ever partial to their mothers. Soon enough you shall have both your arms amply full."